FOREST OF WHISPERS

WHISTLER IN THE WOODS

FOREST OF WHISPERS

WHISTLER IN THE WOODS

HOLLY KNIGHTLEY

For my Grams

CONTENTS

CHAPTER ONE
Midnight Show

Pleasant Mills, New Jersey: Present Day

Ivy Teller climbed into bed pulling the worn comforter up to her chin. It had been a long time since she'd made the steep climb to the small attic bedroom of her grandmother's old house and longer yet since she'd slept there. Things were just how she remembered them. Her grandmother hadn't done a thing with the room since she was a little girl. The room still had the same ugly cream wallpaper featuring brown flowers haphazardly printed on a thick glossy finish. The wallpaper shined as if someone had sprayed down the walls with a value-size can of hairspray.

Ivy's nose burned with remembrance as she sniffed in the long-acquainted smells of mothballs and dryer sheets. Oh, how she didn't miss the smells of her grandmother's house or the feel of the attic bed she was now planted on. It creaked and groaned every time she moved a muscle. It answered her tossing and turning with a voice of its own. The bed wasn't happy she was on it, and Ivy wasn't sure yet if she was happy to be there either. But it looked like neither of them had a say in the matter. Ivy was there to stay the summer—and maybe longer.

If the moaning bed wasn't enough, Grams, as Ivy called her grandmother, kept the four-poster, twin-size bed centered in the middle of the room facing the attic window. Every time a car went by, she saw the glow from the headlights tap dance across the vintage wallpaper. As a child, the unusual marriage of the dancing lights and songs from the roaring car engines had frightened her. The familiar unease slowly crept back in, as if being in the attic magically transformed her into a scared little girl again. She turned up her favorite defense: rock 'n' roll. Here, in her cocoon of love ballads and amazing guitar riffs, she felt safe. Music had become not only Ivy's favorite pastime, but her go-to when she was feeling vulnerable. Music calmed her, soothed her teenage soul, helped her connect to someone else feeling the same way she was. And as of late, she was feeling a lot. She wished she could turn it off as easily as a bad song.

There Ivy was, rocking and rolling in her attic bedroom filled with childhood memories of yesteryear when she noticed something atypical dance over the flowered wallpaper. A bright red light filtered in through the small attic window, casting her room in a crimson glow. She got out of bed and pulled back the shear curtains. She expected to see a police car or an ambulance, but the red light was coming from across the street from the equally small attic window of the neighbor's house.

There was something about this red light—the way it spilled into the night, over the street, and into her room, that made her feel disoriented. It was like she was stuck in an alien's tractor beam and couldn't look away.

"What the heck?"

Her pulse surged as she dug her nails into the windowsill, her fingernails flexing under the burden. She had to turn away. She closed her eyes, jerking her head back toward her bed. Breathing a little easier, her eyelids lifted hoping the strange red light was gone. But it wasn't, everything was painted in red, as if the room and everything in it absorbed the light becoming saturated with color. She glanced at the oversized digital alarm clock her grandmother placed in her room, it was midnight. The glowing red numbers flashed in the monochromatic room, hardly readable in the redness.

"The witching hour," she whispered to herself, the corners of her lips gradually dipping into a frown. "Knock it off Ivy Teller. Don't go scaring yourself. You have to sleep all the way up here, all by yourself, for the next couple of months—or maybe forever."

In an attempt to steady her nerves, she exhaled slowly through parted lips. It eased some of the tension in her shoulders but there was no silencing her heartbeat that thudded away to an ever-soaring tempo. "Get a grip, Ives, it's probably some jerk-kid trying to contact aliens through a homemade laser beam." She scoffed. "That's sure to get Mommy and Daddy's attention, along with Homeland Security."

Ivy was lying to herself again. She was good at that—lying. Another defense mechanism, another layer of her self-made armor. She'd noticed the house across the street that morning. She hadn't recalled seeing it when she last visited her grandmother and it had taken her by surprise, if a house *could* surprise you.

The Uber driver had driven down streets of lovely homes with manicured lawns and white picket fences. She'd watched kids play merrily in the front yard while their parents worked in their veggie gardens. Pleasant Mills was a nice place to live. It was a small river community nestled in the Pine Barrens where over a million acres of New Jersey forests are protected from development, making the Pine Barrens ideal for those seeking a quiet life.

The picturesque cadence continued as they pulled onto her grandmother's street, then her driveway. Grams had welcomed her with a big hug, and over her shoulder Ivy took in the three-story Gothic Revival home across the street.

The house looked hungry for attention, but its cold demeanor was far from welcoming. The house was guarded by a mature weeping willow tree that stood to the right of the property. Its long melancholy branches swept the ground like a mourning blanket. The forest butting up to the house rivaled the tenebrous willow. Yes, Pleasant Mills looked like a nice place to live as long as your eyes didn't settle on the woods. Protected or not, the forest around the town was different from other pockets of protected land you came across in the Garden State. The town seemed to have a living fence that started at the forest, enforced by tall, closely rooted pines that wrapped the small river community in a shadow.

The shadow seemed to mass over the house across the street as if a permanent storm cloud loomed over it. The large, arched-topped antique shutters were drawn shut, concealing all the windows, apart from the small attic window that poked out of the roof. The house was clad in old cedar shakes that were so weathered they looked black in the daylight. Ivy was sure the siding would crumple under her touch. The house was old, decaying in plain sight, in an otherwise charming neighborhood. The front door was painted bright red. It stood out against the charred shakes like a gaping mouth. It was the same shade of red that made Ivy think of blood, and death, and vampires, and everything bad. She hated that color. Give her maroon, give her cranberry, she would even take pink, but never give her red.

Ivy heard something—something strange. She pulled out her earbuds to make sure the noise she heard wasn't from the amped-up bass playing. Sure enough, there was a low continuous hum coming from the house across the street. *Lub dub . . . lub dub . . . lub dub.*

She couldn't force herself to turn around. —She wouldn't turn around. The tractor beam would have to suck her out the window, before she would look again.

She blinked and just like that the red was gone. As abruptly as the midnight show started, it ended, and with it the red light and that peculiar sound that had resonated in her eardrums, making the little hairs in her ear canal tingle.

Ivy glanced at her alarm clock again. It was now 12:01 a.m. "Talk about *weird* New Jersey," she muttered, a nervous titter escaping. Of course, her grandmother had to live in a state with that moniker.

She returned to her bed, this time pulling her covers up to her eyes. It was true, she was still that same little girl, frightened of her grandmother's attic. Her dark brown eyes, the size of saucers, unavoidably glanced up as the piercing headlights of a passing car highlighted the cobwebs that hung from the rafters like a dreamcatcher from Hell. The wispy webs dangled down shrouding her in a living nightmare. She put her ear buds back in and cranked up the tunes. It was going to be a sleepless night for Ivy Teller.

CHAPTER TWO
Chorus of the Frogs

A loud knock on the attic door stirred Ivy from sleep. "Get up Ivy, or you're gonna be late!" her grandmother yelled.

"Urgh," Ivy groaned as she placed her blanket snugly over her head. "Go away, Grams!"

"Now Ivy!" Mary Teller barked. Her pounding assault on the door, rocked her loose dentures in her mouth. After a barrage of knocks, that would've flattened any door that wasn't solid wood, Mary pressed her good ear to the door in anticipation of the old attic bed letting out a Saturday morning sigh of its own. She smiled, hearing the bed groan. "Good, she's up," Mary said to herself, tucking her flyaways behind her ears. Her grays always seemed to have a mind of their own, and the upwind motion of walking up three flights of stairs was enough to send her silvery sparklers flying about like fireworks on the Fourth of July.

After Mary tended to her hair, she carefully started her descent downstairs. "Getting too old for this," she said, holding on tightly to the dark-stained handrail for some much-needed support. The trip down from the attic always proved more difficult for Mary Teller. She had stubborn feet like her stubborn mind. She had to stop on every stair tread to make sure both feet were firmly planted on it before taking her next step. As she waited for her feet to cooperate, she listened for the stairs to release a frog-like hiccup. Once the croaking of the staircase ceased, she would take another calculated step down. Mary continued her slow descent down the narrow staircase, all along listening to the choir of the frogs, her heavy breathing providing backup vocals to the singing staircase all the way to the kitchen.

The Teller kitchen looked more like a demo on scrapbooking than a functional kitchen. Mary had a handwritten label on everything—drawers and appliances alike. Mary's way of keeping her cluttered kitchen organized and her mind straight.

She reached into her vintage breadbox, conveniently labeled 'breadbox', and pulled out two pieces of Jewish rye with seeds and popped them in the toaster. She leaned on the butcher-block counter, taking the weight off her feet as she waited for her toast to get crispy and her tardy granddaughter to make an appearance.

Mary wanted to get her granddaughter on the right track, and if that meant waking up early to climb three flights of steps with a bad knee, then she was going to do it.

Ivy left a bad situation to what Mary was hoping was a better situation—living with her. Ivy already hated everyone and herself. She was just another jaded, misunderstood teenager lost in the fishbowl of adolescent misery. Mary could relate. Though it had been decades since she'd shaken off her pubescent woes, trading in her Girl Scout badges for a handicap sticker, she was still just as misunderstood. She was Pleasant Mills's very own Grinch.

But with Mary's age came wisdom. She knew deep down inside that what she and Ivy were really mad at was themselves. Mary hoped that Ivy being around a like mind would help her. She wasn't exactly sure what two bitter women, mad at the world, could do if they put their minds together, but she was feeling optimistic that it would help Ivy cope to know that she didn't have to go at it all alone—misery loves company after all.

Mary also had a sixth sense about those sorts of things—the sorts of things that came with feelings. Ivy coming to stay with her would be good for the both of them, if they could survive each other. Mary knew as long as Ivy heeded the large alarm clock in her room, they would survive and have one heck of a summer.

However, Mary's optimism about Ivy's survival dissipated with every bite of her well-done toast topped with apricot jelly. She was now sitting at her kitchen table tapping her fingers on the plastic tablecloth, waiting for her granddaughter. She looked down at her watch as she chewed. Ivy was cutting it close, and patience was a virtue Mary was thin on. Ivy had used up just about the last drop of Mary's patience with her hike to the attic that morning.

Mary had signed her granddaughter up for a little community service to thaw Ivy's icy heart. She was to meet the local youth group every Saturday morning to help the community. To Ivy's dismay, Mary had signed her up for trash pickup, nursing home visits, and much more. Mary was less concerned with helping the community and more concerned with helping her granddaughter. She thought this could be an outlet for Ivy to open up a little. She had been hearing good things about the young pastor that ran the group.

Mary had given up on God and all things holy when her husband had died before his time, but she thought it wasn't too late for Ivy. She hoped Pastor Uriah Leeds could help polish her granddaughter's rough edges.

Ivy came down the stairs with loud heavy stomps as she dragged her feet. Mary's chorus of frogs were now loud, bloated bullfrogs croaking with vengeance. Reaching the kitchen, Ivy gave her grandmother a cold stare, proving how icy she was.

Ivy wasn't going to get out of youth group by picking a fight with her grandmother. Mary was too clever for that. Mary popped in her last bite of toast and slurped down the last drop of her coffee. Without saying a word, she took Ivy's hand and led her out the front door.

The air was hot and humid. They got no reprieve from the muggy weather when they climbed into Mary's old, white station wagon; the air conditioning hadn't worked right since the nineties. Ivy rolled down her window as Mary backed out of the driveway and made her way to Pleasant Mills Church.

Mary idled outside of church letting her fossil fuels fill the air of the Pine Barrens as she waited for her very stubborn, like-minded granddaughter to get out of the car. "Go now," Mary said to Ivy who sat motionless in the passenger seat staring at her feet.

Mary could see a group of kids already hanging out in front of the church. "Go!" She handed Ivy a water bottle she had tucked away in her purse and gave her a firm push. Ivy opened the car door to get out. She was stuck to the leather seat like her body was made up of teeny tiny suction cups. She felt like a kraken sprung out of the ocean as she pulled herself away from the hot car interior, leaving a puddle of sweat in her wake. Ivy looked back at her grandmother with the angry eyes of something worse than a mythological sea creature—an angry teenager. "Bye Grams . . . thanks for dropping me off at Hell."

CHAPTER THREE
The Extraordinary Pastor Uriah Leeds

Ivy's little stunt made her grandmother late for her dentist appointment. Mary's not so cooperative foot hit the gas with a mighty stomp. She literally put the pedal to the metal, causing the accelerator to hit the floor with a loud pop. Her past-their-warranty and past-their-life tires kicked up a cloud of dust as she peeled out of the dirt parking lot.

Talk about making an entrance, Ivy thought to herself as her eyes darted to the group of teenagers nearby. She coughed; she couldn't help it. The dry sand in the air from her grandmother's *little stunt* found its way into her mouth, sticking to the inside of her cheeks. Ivy took a sip from her water bottle. She could still feel the gritty sand stuck in the pits and grooves of her teeth as she sloshed the water around in her mouth and spit the sandy water into the dirt like a camel. She took another sip of water to clear her throat.

Ivy swore she could feel the weight of the other teenagers' stares as they looked her over—passing judgment on the new girl with manners that were a far cry from ladylike or even polite. Spitting like that was a mistake. The embarrassment colored her cheeks the red she hated so much.

If looking like a plump Jersey tomato wasn't bad enough, she felt underdressed. She didn't know there was such a thing as being underdressed to pick up trash, but apparently in Pleasant Mills that was a very real thing, and Ivy was finding out about it the hard way.

The youth group kids were all dressed like it was the first day of school. They had sharp new footwear, freshly groomed hair, and accessories galore—and the girls had makeup on like they were going to a school dance.

PLEASANT MILLS CHURCH

"This is some lucky trash," Ivy muttered, passing her own judgment on the Saturday morning faithful.

Ivy had decided to sleep in until the last second possible, ignoring her very large, obnoxious alarm clock and skipping a shower. She had her long, dark hair tied back in a ponytail and had on a loose-fitting tie dye T-shirt with jeans. She'd made sure to put on a comfortable pair of sneakers. "The *appropriate* footwear for picking up trash on the side of Pleasant Mills Road," she told herself.

As Ivy got closer to her peers, they turned their heads and acted like she didn't exist. She wasn't sure if it was better to be stared at like she had two heads or to be ignored. So, she stood quietly a couple feet away from the congregated teenagers and let them talk amongst themselves. She didn't want to come off needy or too excited to be there. Even though everyone there seemed thrilled to pick up trash on a hot Saturday morning. "These kids must be high on God to be up this early on a Saturday and be happy about it," Ivy mumbled, knowing that for any normal teenager Saturday mornings are sacred. For Ivy Teller, sleep was the only scripture she believed in.

Ivy was just about ready to bail on Saturday morning youth group and walk home when she laid eyes on Pastor Uriah Leeds. He came out of the double doors of Pleasant Mills Church like an angel taking flight. She swore she could see a halo hovering above him. It was just the intense June sun overhead, but it gave him the look of godliness all the same. A sign Grams was right; she should come to youth group. She'd found something else to worship. *Sleep is for the wicked,* she thought, taking in the beauty that was the young pastor. *I'm at the altar of Uriah Leeds . . . man, pastor . . . maybe angel.*

Pastor Uriah Leeds was of average height, but that was the only thing average about him. He was extraordinary. A pure feast for the eyes and the teenage soul. He had large, light-blue eyes that would make the heavens jealous if they'd allow themselves one sin. His celestial globes gleamed against his dark-brown hair and light, flawless skin. His face was divine, as if Michelangelo, himself, hand-carved it, making sure each detail was just right. Everything was perfect. The perfect nose. The perfect smile. The perfect square chin. And to go along with his divine perfection, a heavenly voice.

"You must be Ivy Teller," Pastor Leeds said, walking over to Ivy to shake her hand. "Your grandmother has told me all about you. I'm glad you were able to join us this morning."

"No more than me, Pastor Leeds," she said, smiling. She couldn't help herself; her lips had a mind of their own and they beamed. She no longer minded being dragged out of her bed on a Saturday morning and picking up trash seemed like a noble pursuit. *Go green!* She cheered in her mind.

Pastor Leeds excitedly made the introductions. "We've got Sammy Lopez, Mike Handover and his sister Tammy, and Elsa Tilton with us this morning."

"Hi," Ivy said. She was trying to play it nice in front of Pastor Leeds, but she could care less about the upstanding youth of Pleasant Mills; her mind was on white doves and wedding bells. The youth group kids said hello with a small, not-so-enthusiastic wave.

Pastor Leeds started off the Saturday morning meeting by reading a short Bible verse. Ivy found herself smiling again. When he laughed, she laughed, her giggling incessant. She didn't know what she was giggling about, or if she should even giggle, but the high-pitched yelps escaped her lips all the same as she tried to smother her joy.

Ivy zoned out as Pastor Leeds gave a briefing on what the mission for this hot summer morning was. She wasn't hearing his voice, just watching his lips move up and down, taking in the sweet sounds his tongue made as it hit the roof of his mouth. His words were music to her ears. She wasn't ready to trade her rock 'n' roll in for gospel just yet, but she was well on her way to joining the hallelujah chorus.

"Are you alright, Ivy?" Pastor Leeds asked when he noticed Ivy's saliva dripping out of the corners of her mouth. Ivy looked comatose as she reveled in her rapturous daydream featuring her new favorite pastor. Her high hopes for a spring wedding spawned a lot of drool. She was leaking like she was a Saint Bernard with a gland problem.

Pastor Leeds put his hand on Ivy's shoulder to make sure she was indeed alright and wasn't suffering from heat stroke. "Ivy?" he asked, concerned.

Ivy snapped out of her reverie at the pastor's soft touch, wiping her droll with the back of her hand. "Oh . . . what . . . yeah . . . let's go clean up the environment!" she said, dazed and confused, and very much in love.

"I like your enthusiasm," Pastor Leeds said with a dreamy smile.

I like you, Ivy said back with her inner mind. She was hearing those church bells again. And just like Pavlov's dogs, the sound of the bells made her drool.

CHAPTER FOUR
Pleasant Mills Road

Ivy walked along Pleasant Mills Road spearing trash, surprised by the amount of rubbish tossed on the side of the street and how many people drank Dunkin Donuts coffee and thought a Styrofoam cup was somehow magically biodegradable.

Ivy wasn't surprised, however, that Pastor Leeds looked just as good from a distance as he did up close. From her vantage point across the street, she could take in his whole person. She had woken up wishing it was not so hot, but now she was grateful for the heat. Pastor Leeds's T-shirt was getting weighed down by his perspiration and clung to his biceps. Her heart fluttered every time he speared a piece of litter into his trash bag. She felt like her body temperature was easily a hundred degrees Celsius and rising with every bead of sweat that dripped from Pastor Leeds.

Ivy now knew why everyone was dressed so impeccably for trash pickup. Elsa and Tammy were the founding members of the Uriah Leeds Fan Club; they were stuck to Pastor Leeds like gum on the sidewalk, and the boys were dressed up in an effort to compete with the pastor's good looks.

Ivy was a little jealous at first that Elsa and Tammy had teamed up with Pastor Leeds to clean the opposite side of the street, leaving her stuck with Sammy and Mike, but figured she got a better look at him from across the way. Ivy smiled to herself as Elsa's mascara dripped down her face, giving her raccoon eyes. Elsa the raccoon seemed a fitting mascot for youth group, and Ivy knew she'd giggle about it every Saturday morning from here on out. A few low-grade cackles were at Tammy's expense. Her red, curly hair frizzed under the humidity, making her look like Ronald McDonald thanks to her heavy makeup.

Besides, Ivy reasoned her drool would be less noticeable from the other side of the street. However, her drool never did reach garden-hose status. Her pastor-watching was constantly being disrupted by Sammy, who insisted on walking next to her as they picked up trash. Her salivations of lust were further hindered by his continuous questions.

"So, you're new in town?" Sammy asked, picking up the stray water bottle Ivy had walked past in her daze.

"Yeah, something like that," she answered, distracted—her eyes and thoughts still on Pastor Leeds.

"What grade you going into?"

"Junior."

"Me too. Maybe we'll have some of the same classes."

Ivy let out a loud sigh, frustrated Sammy brought up school in the middle of summer vacation. She'd just gotten over picking up trash on a Saturday morning and now Sammy wanted to throw another thing she wasn't happy about her way—school.

"Maybe," Ivy said, not caring one way or another if she ever saw Sammy Lopez or the rest of the fine teenagers of the Pleasant Mills Youth Group again.

"So, you're Old Lady Mary's granddaughter?"

"You have a name for my grandmother?" Ivy asked, shocked that Sammy would be so blunt. She wasn't shocked, surprised, or even dazzled that her grandmother had the distinguished honor of being given a nickname by the town. Old Lady Mary seemed like it fit the bill to her.

Sammy laughed out of embarrassment, his dark hair tousled by the sudden jerking of his head. He had a bad habit of saying what was on his mind without thinking. He didn't want to give Ivy a bad first impression, but he was pretty sure he'd just put his foot in his mouth. "Yeah, sorry . . . not smooth."

"*Not smooth* in the slightest. But yeah, I'm Old Lady Mary's granddaughter."

"You have brothers or sisters?" Sammy asked, trying to recoup from his earlier blunder. "I have two little sisters."

"I do," Ivy answered plainly.

"Where are they?" Sammy asked, trying to keep the conversation going, his blue eyes intently focused on her as if they weren't walking with Mike.

"With my mom."

"Why are *you* with your grandmother?"

Ivy stopped walking and stood still for a moment while she thought. The how and why of coming to stay with her grandmother was a little foggy. She thought it was possible she did have heat stroke. She couldn't give Sammy a straight answer even if she wanted to. So, she went with a tease. "Secret," Ivy said in a hushed voice.

Sammy smiled, his grin shifting to one side where little dimples highlighted the corners of his handsome face. "Got it," he said. "I'm asking too many questions."

Ivy nodded, spearing another empty Styrofoam cup.

"Last one, I promise." Sammy said, his grin widening. He couldn't help himself. "Are you coming to the lock-in tonight at the church?"

Ivy's head cocked to the side. "Lock-in?"

"Yeah, it's a church event to kick off the summer. We do it every year. It's lots of fun. We lock ourselves in the church and stay up all night until service the next morning."

"Oh," she said. "Um . . . I don't think so."

"You should think about it. It's gonna be fun. I'll be there."

"Right Mike?" he said, elbowing his best friend. "Tell her it's going to be fun."

"Loads," he said flatly, pushing back a red curl that stuck to his forehead. "So much fun, you should come."

Ivy thought about it. Fun was not much of a selling point. But a church event meant Pastor Leeds would be there. She glanced across the street again. *Hmm . . . maybe I'll go.*

CHAPTER FIVE

Car Ride from an Angel in Training

The afternoon went by quickly. Team Go-Green, as Ivy now referred to them, did their part to clean up the town and circled back to the church, where one by one the youth group kids got picked up. Ivy was now alone with Pastor Leeds as she waited for her grandmother.

Ivy was happy to finally have her chance to talk to the angel in training one-on-one. While picking up trash, she'd daydreamed about all the things she would say to Pastor Leeds when she had the chance, but now that she did, she found herself suddenly speechless. She awkwardly squeezed her empty water bottle as she looked out over the headstones of the church cemetery.

The headstones of the small cemetery were plentiful and came right up to the dirt driveway, giving Pleasant Mills Church its own unique border that the *Addams Family* would have been proud of. Ivy read the names off the weathered tombstones to herself as she searched for the perfect words to say to Pastor Leeds.

She squeezed her water bottle tighter. The sound of the plastic bottle crushing under her fingers only added to her anxiousness, but having something to squeeze helped to ease her anxiety. She was trapped in a cycle of self-peddling pandemonium, spinning her own wheels.

When she had read through the names she could decipher on the timeworn headstones, and still had nothing to say, she really panicked. Ivy had already called her grandmother five times and had texted her at least a dozen. She sent devil emoji after devil emoji to illicit a response from Grams, but still she heard nothing back.

Ivy had apologized to Pastor Leeds a dozen times for the inconvenience. The only words her mouth were able to form were 'I'm sorry.' And she said those words over and over, clinging to her empty water bottle.

Uriah, to ease Ivy's blushing cheeks, made it seem like her grandmother being late was no big deal. He was kind like that, intuitive. A real people person and a good listener. Despite the extraordinary Pastor Leeds assuring Ivy that her delayed grandmother wasn't holding up his Saturday plans, Ivy's face continued to redden until it blended in with the red swirls on her homemade T-shirt.

"Ivy, I live across the street from your grandmother. If you want, I can drive you home? That is, as long as you have a key, and it's okay with your grandmother."

Ivy called her grandmother one more time. "Grams, where are you?!" she asked in a hushed whisper.

"Sorry, stuck at the dentist. You're done already?"

"Yes. Pastor Leeds said he can drop me off."

"Great, do that," Grams said, hanging up the phone with a loud click.

Her lobster skin told the tale of her embarrassment. "I'll take the ride," she said, looking down at the sandy driveway of the parking lot.

Ivy got into Pastor Leeds's compact black Nissan. She put her seat belt on and glanced over at him, the air conditioning just as heavenly as he was. They were so close now; her heart beat loudly in her chest. Ivy smiled to herself, glancing out the window. She was glad Grams was stuck at her appointment.

PLEASANT MILLS CEMETERY:
JESSE RICHARDS MONUMENT

"How do you like historical Pleasant Mills so far?" Pastor Leeds asked, pulling out of the church parking lot and heading to Ivy's house.

"Good. I like the history here."

"Yeah, it's great! We've got the Richards family buried right here on the church grounds."

"I saw that," Ivy said with a smile. Jesse Richards's grave was hard to miss. He was buried under a monument right next to the church. His grave marker was a play on a mausoleum, but on a much smaller scale, still it stood out amongst the small headstones of the cemetery. Its shape reminded Ivy of a pyramid. She thought it looked like someone could slide off the top of the stone monument and be face-to-face with Jesse Richards, or what was left of him. It was the perfect spot to get a human skull if the mood suddenly struck someone to reenact the famous scene from *Hamlet*.

"Nice to see someone so young into history," Pastor Leeds said with an angelic smile. His smile was a bright line of perfect teeth, his lips being well-formed and not too big or small—perfect.

Ivy blushed; she wasn't that into history. Maybe the history of rock 'n' roll. She had no clue who Jesse Richards was, just that he had one heck of a tombstone.

"I love it all! Uriah said, not seeming to notice Ivy's blush. "It's so nice to have the pioneers of Batsto Village right at our doorstep. You know Pleasant Mills wouldn't be what it is today without Batsto Village."

His eyes glanced at her before going back on the road. Ivy knew Batsto Village was part of the state park next to her house. It was a cluster of small houses and buildings from the 1700-1800s. There was a visitor center and a mansion you could tour for a small fee. But that was all she knew.

"That's where it all started, and it was the Richards family who made Batsto what it is."

She nodded, making notes in her head. *Richards family put Batsto Village on the map. Batsto Village put Pleasant Mills on the map. That seems easy enough to remember.*

Uriah was brimming with excitement, his fingers tapping on the steering wheel as if to an invisible beat. "The Richards family made a booming business out of mining for bog ore and making cannonballs for the Revolutionary War. George Washington ordered firebacks from our little town for Mount Vernon. To think, a piece of Pleasant Mills is in his home. The idea that one of our founding fathers may have walked the same path we did today as we picked up trash is thrilling."

He was talking a mile a minute now; Ivy was surprised he didn't have to stop to breathe. "Makes you feel like you can really touch the history. It's all right here at our fingertips to enjoy. And then there's the church; it's an amazing piece of history all on its own. The past and the present all in one place. The Pleasant Mills Church we see today is the church built in 1808 by the Richards family. It still has the original pine siding and has remained white with green doors and green shutters for generations." Coming to a stop, Uriah glanced at Ivy, his eyes lingering on her. "Here's an interesting fact for you, the church was actually built on top of the foundation of a much older church. It's fun to imagine the Batsto villagers taking the walk from town to my church every Sunday for worship. This land has been God's land for a very long time. I'm honored to be a part of this town's history."

It was Uriah's face that blushed now when he noticed Ivy's unblinking eyes.

He made the turn onto Ivy's street, his pink glow highlighting the high cut of his cheek bones. "Sorry . . . I can get a little intense. I just love it here."

Pastor Leeds pulled into her driveway.

"We're lucky to have someone so intense," Ivy said, unbuckling and getting out of the car. She liked history, because he liked history. If he loved it here, so would she. "Thanks for the ride, Pastor Leeds. Sorry again for the inconvenience."

"No inconvenience." Her heart fluttered when he echoed her sentiment. "I'm glad we got to talk one-on-one."

Ivy smiled, her heart jumping a beat. She was glad too. More than that, she was ecstatic. She could've squealed, but she didn't. She would act as normal as possible. She had to play this cool, if he was to ever like her.

"Oh wait!" Uriah called to Ivy just as she was about to close the car door. "I almost forgot to tell you," he said, exuding the same excitability he had on the car ride. "If you're into the folklore surrounding the town, make sure you come to the lock-in tonight at the church. We're starting at eight. I'll be talking about the town's history and local hauntings." He chuckled, it sounded like music to her ears. "I know I'm more qualified to lead Bible study, but I've been reading up on everything Pleasant Mills and am excited to share what I've learned."

"Sounds great, Pastor Leeds. The little bit I got on the car ride was great—beyond great." She wished she could've come up with something more profound to say, but that was it. Everything was great.

He gave her a big smile, his eyes twinkling, and she knew that was what Heaven must be like. "I can expect to see you tonight at church then?"

"I'll be there," Ivy said, her cheeks blushing again. She hoped he didn't notice.

"Great! See you tonight and thanks again for all your hard work today."

"It's a date," Ivy muttered to herself as she quickly made her way inside. She ran to the living room. Moving aside the flowered curtains, she peaked out the bay window desperate to see which house belonged to Pastor Leeds. She watched him back out of her grandmother's driveway to only pull into the driveway belonging to the old boarded-up Gothic house across the street.

"Wow, he wasn't lying when he said 'across the street'. Hmm . . . I wonder what Pastor Leeds was doing in his attic last night."

CHAPTER SIX
The Lock-in

Ivy walked through the double doors of Pleasant Mills Church to see people scattered throughout the small sanctuary. She was surprised by how small the church was once she stepped over the threshold. It seemed so much larger to her from the outside, but as she walked down the aisle, she felt like the walls were closing in on her.

Ivy spotted Sammy right away. He seemed to be the center of attention. He was with Mike, Tammy, and Elsa, and a teenage girl and boy she didn't recognize. Taking a deep breath, she walked over to them. *Play nice with the natives, Ives. You're only doing this because you want to see Pastor Leeds.*

"Hey, Ivy," Sammy said.

Ivy gave a wave.

"This is Megan," Sammy volunteered, pointing to the girl with dark-brown hair who Ivy didn't recognize. "And her cousin Zachary."

"Call me Zac," he said to Ivy with a big grin.

"Hi, Zac," Ivy said trying to be nice.

Mike laughed. "Yeah, poor kid has Zachary Disease."

"Zachary Disease?" Ivy asked.

"Yeah, the poor kid's face looks Zachary like his ass."

Megan laughed. "That never gets old."

"Not funny," Zac pouted.

In an attempt to be personable, "So Megan, are you part of the youth group too?"

"Nope, just here for the weekend and figured I'd tag along with Zac." Megan leaned in and whispered in Ivy's ear, "I'm here to see Sammy."

Ivy smiled awkwardly. "Uh . . . yeah . . . he's something."

Zac shared his cousin's brown hair and eyes and was younger than the rest of them. Ivy could tell by the way Zac mimicked every little thing Sammy did, he was trying hard to fit in. Sammy laughed, he laughed. Sammy put his hands in his pockets, Zac put his hands in his pockets. Ivy understood where Zac was coming from; she just wished that watching him wasn't so painful. One Sammy Lopez was enough for her.

Sammy walked away from the group when two teenage boys came through the church doors.

"Who are they?" Ivy asked, curious on how Sammy knew them.

"Louie Grindhouse and Tyrone Jones," Zac replied.

Ivy watched as Sammy talked to one of the guys. He was tall with a nice build.

"Easy, Ivy," Tammy warned snapping her bubble gum. "The guy Sammy is talking to now is Louie. He's only thirteen. He's just big."

"He's a hotshot football player," Mike declared as if insulted Ivy couldn't tell just by looking at him.

"Louie and Tyrone are gonna be freshman like me," Zac said. "The Jersey Devils will win the whole season with Louie as the quarterback!

"You play football too?" Ivy asked Zac.

"No, I just—"

Megan cut him off with a laugh. "Zac, play football? He's too small. He's just a cheerleader."

Zac nudged his cousin hard. "I'm not a cheerleader. I go to all the games because I have team spirit." He pointed at himself. Sure enough, Zac had on a Jersey Devils Football hoodie featuring a devil wearing a football helmet.

Megan pushed on his chest hard. "Nice stain, dweeb."

Ivy couldn't help but smile at the large red stain on the front of Zac's sweatshirt. It looked like he spilled fruit punch all over himself like he was some grade-schooler. But she did feel bad for Zac when his cheeks turned as red as the stain on his sweatshirt.

Ivy tried to take attention away from Zac before his cheeks exploded. "That's cool. Sammy play?" Ivy asked.

"Nah, his mom won't let him," Mike said. "Afraid her baby will get hurt."

"It's too bad!" Zac exclaimed. "I bet Sammy would be a great running back. He does track."

Mike chuckled. "Zac, never misses a track meet either."

"You're sounding like a cheerleader," Ivy whispered to Zac.

He blushed again. "Mike never misses one either. He's Sammy's shadow."

Mike shrugged it off. Ivy had picked that up. While Sammy had interrogated her as they picked up trash, Mike had been quiet, just following Sammy around like he *was* his shadow.

"Sammy's tight with Louie because he used to date his sister," Tammy volunteered.

"Oh," Ivy said, pretending not to be interested, but she was. She instantly didn't like Sammy when she met him. She found him obnoxious and annoying, but there was something about him that made her want to know a little more. She was sure it was his smile. She would give him that, he had a nice smile and nice hair, and maybe a nice face if he ever stopped talking.

"Yeah, Trudy Grindhouse," Zac said, his eyes widening as if the name Trudy Grindhouse was supposed to mean something to her.

Ivy's face twisted in confusion.

"A knockout!" Zac told her with a fawning sigh. "Trudy's so much older than him. Sammy's my hero."

Ivy mumbled, "I'm sensing that."

"Sammy dated a girl who's in college!" Zac shouted as if he didn't think Ivy understood how cool it was.

Megan shoved her cousin. "Trudy's only three years older. She *starts* college this year. When they dated last summer, she wasn't in college, so it doesn't count."

"Someone sounds jealous, cuz," Zac teased. Megan elbowed Zac this time. "Easy, Megan, you know Sammy likes Elsa. So stop acting so desperate," he said with a chuckle.

Ivy couldn't help but notice the big smile that flashed on Elsa's face when Zac said Sammy liked her. Ivy guessed Elsa knew it and was playing hard to get. Ivy had noticed that Sammy continuously glanced at Elsa while they'd picked up trash earlier that day. They had even bumped into each other a couple of times because they were both distracted by what was across the street.

Ivy didn't know what Trudy looked like, but Elsa looked like Barbie, and was pretty sure she would be considered a knockout by Zac and most guys. She was tall and thin with a great figure. And to top off the perfect bod, she was a natural blonde. Yeah, she was a knockout.

"Is Trudy coming tonight?" Ivy asked, interested in how Elsa fared against Sammy's ex-girlfriend.

"Not likely," Zac said. "She already moved into her dorm room."

"Are Louie and Tyrone church regulars?"

"Louie comes when he can," Tammy said. "In the summer with practice he's usually not here, but we'll see more of him when the football season is over. Tyrone only comes if Louie comes. They're best friends."

Elsa whispered to Ivy, "Tyrone is Tammy's, so don't get any ideas."

"Got it," Ivy whispered back.

Sammy walked over with Louie and Tyrone. Louie shook Ivy's hand hello. Ivy felt a little nervous shaking his hand. Louie may have only been thirteen, but he was mature, and the handshake proved it. She only got stares from the others. This boy had manners; her grandmother would approve. If Ivy had to guess she would've said he was her age or maybe older. Still, he was cute with blue eyes and polite, and reasoned that he would be worth going to a few Jersey Devils games for.

Tammy threw her arms around Tyrone like she was an accessory. *Talk about overbearing,* Ivy thought to herself as Tammy hung from his neck.

"So, what exactly do we do at a shut-in?" Ivy asked awkwardly. She put her hands in her sweatshirt pockets and looked down at the ground.

"Lock-in," Tammy corrected, kissing Tyrone's cheek.

Elsa pushed her blonde hair off her shoulders. "Give our parents a date night."

"Don't listen to them," Sammy said. "Tonight is gonna be a lot of fun. There're different stations we can do."

Elsa rolled her eyes. "Yeah Sammy, we can sing with the decrepit Mrs. Ball, learn to crochet with the Henry sisters, do Bible study with your father, or get a history lesson from Pastor Leeds."

Tyrone laughed. "Your dad is doing Bible study this year?" he asked, looking at Sammy in disbelief. "I've got to hear that!"

"That's funny because?" Ivy asked Zac.

"Um . . . Mr. Lopez is known to get a little serious."

"Pastor Leeds needed a volunteer," Sammy mumbled.

"There's also a video game station, but the nerds are all over that," Tammy snickered.

"I like video games," Tyrone said. "I'm not a nerd."

Tammy giggled. "Of course not, honey."

"The point is," Sammy said, trying to get everyone excited, "to stay up all night having fun and end it all with church in the morning."

"Sounds like *a lot* of fun," Ivy sarcastically commented as she looked around underwhelmed.

"So what if the activities are a little lame, we still get to be out of the house all night. And don't forget the church butts up to a creepy old cemetery. We can play chicken. Who knows, maybe we'll run into a real ghost," Sammy said as a mischievous smile bloomed across his face. He went to a church window and peered out at the masses of headstones.

"We're not allowed outside," Elsa hissed.

Sammy's smile twisted into a sneer. "Says who?"

"Says Pastor Uriah Leeds."

"I bet she's scared," Zac teased.

Mike laughed, "I think you're right for once."

"Am not," Elsa stated sternly, crossing her arms over her chest.

Ivy glanced out the window. She had to admit the Pleasant Mills

Cemetery was creepy during the day, but at night, as the flood light showered a yellow glow over the tombstones, the hallowed grounds possessed a supernatural quality. There was something about the way the light seemed to illuminate the ground, while keeping the headstones and the names written on them in shadows. It looked like the ideal place to film a Hollywood zombie flick.

Ivy's eyes were glued to the tombstones as she tried to recall some of the names she'd read off of them earlier that day, when Sammy grabbed her shoulders attempting to scare her. She turned around, giving him a scathing look that would have had Old Lady Mary shaking in her boots. "Nice try; I don't scare easy."

"I know Ivy, you're a tough cookie."

She really disliked Sammy. She decided his smile wasn't that nice.

"More like ate the cookie," Mike said under his breath.

Ivy pretended not to hear him, turning back to the window to hide the flush that traveled up her neck in blotches. She disliked Sammy Lopez and hated Mike Handover. Hated all of them. She had noticed she was the heaviest girl there, but that didn't mean she ate cookies all day long.

"I'm not scared of some stupid old cemetery," Zac said, trying to sound cool.

Louie laughed at Zac's seriousness, pushing back his dark hair. It was a good-natured laugh. Ivy couldn't clump him into the hate that bubbled in her stomach.

"Prove it then," Megan said to her cousin. "Go outside."

Zac chuckled nervously, "What?!"

"Or are you chicken, Zac?" Tyrone asked with a laugh. His laugh was not like Louie's, there was a challenge in it.

"You heard me," Megan said. "Go outside and we'll watch you from the window."

"Well . . ." Zac said hesitantly.

Sammy chimed in. "What's wrong Zac, you scared?"

"Of course not."

"Tell you what, it was my idea to play chicken, so I'll go first," Sammy volunteered. He clearly wanted all eyes on him. Ivy had never met a bigger narcissist than Sammy Lopez.

Sammy snuck out the back door and made his way to the side of the church that faced the graveyard. They waited for Sammy by the window.

"He's such a liar," Elsa snickered. "He didn't go out there."

Suddenly, Sammy hit the church window, and Elsa screamed. His face looked distorted, darkened by shadows before his smile beamed into the church like its own light. Ivy was startled even though she knew it was coming, but she had to laugh at Elsa who turned crimson. And so did everyone else.

When Sammy made his way back into the church, he was laughing hard. "Elsa, you should've seen your face," Sammy chuckled, trying to wrap his arms around her in some sort of weird apology hug.

"Better hope it doesn't stay like that," Mike mumbled under his breath.

Ivy felt a little better, it looked like Mike was a jerk to anyone who wasn't Sammy.

Elsa pushed Sammy away from her. "Not funny." He went in again, this time, hugging her from behind. She let him, which made him very happy, his smile one of pure joy. Elsa, on the other hand, still looked irritated. Her lips were pursed in a flat line, her jaw locked.

"Pastor Leeds is ready for the next group, let's go," Tammy said.

Sammy groaned, loosening his grip. "Fine."

Ivy's pulse skipped. Pastor Leeds was the reason she was there and there was nothing she'd rather be doing than hearing his sweet voice.

Ivy and the rest of the group made their way over to Pastor Leeds. There were a few chairs set up around him and blankets on the floor for extra seating. Ivy went for the blanket, getting as close to him as she possibly could.

"I'm going to start with a scary story," Pastor Leeds said. She could tell, even though he spoke in front of people all the time, he was nervous. In between his words he'd nibble on his bottom lip. She knew he really wanted to make tonight fun. She wished she could tell him the night already surpassed her expectations. He had on dress slacks and a dress shirt. He rolled the sleeves of his shirt up, giving way to a path of sight the let her see the veins visible under his lean arms, making her imagination run wild.

"Oh no Elsa," Sammy whispered to her in a teasing voice where she sat next to Tammy on the blanket. It looked like Ivy, Tammy, and Elsa all wanted the best seat in the house.

Elsa didn't validate Sammy with a response; nevertheless, the cold shoulder didn't deter him. Sammy continued to grin that sideways smirk of his.

"This is the story of the Leeds Devil, better known in these parts as the Jersey Devil," Pastor Leeds said with a large smile.

Sammy mirrored him, beaming and leaning over to Zac to whisper in his ear: "This is great, we can use whatever Pastor Leeds says in his story to scare the girls later."

Ivy rolled her eyes. He may have been good at track and field, but he wasn't very good at whispering.

Pastor Leeds spoke in an exaggerated tone meant to scare them, not that he sounded scary. He was too handsome and too kindhearted to ever be considered frightening, but Ivy appreciated the effort, and she was sure at the minimum so did Elsa and Tammy. "Long ago on a dark, dark night . . . here, in the place we call home, the wind howled like hell-hounds. Beasties and demons filled the moon-lit sky. In graveyards, spirits woke from their eternal slumber, stepping out from their sacred beds to haunt the land, for tonight, there was magic in the air. It hovered above the ground like a blanket of fog, creeping into the Pine Barrens and making its way deep into the forest until it reached the home of Deborah Smith Leeds.

"You see, Deborah was to deliver her thirteenth child on this hellish night. A baby she didn't want, but a baby the Devil sought. A baby the Devil took great interest in. He waited for hours outside her home, peering in through the window, watching and waiting as Deborah endured a grueling labor.

"Deborah gave in. She had to. She could bear it no longer. The pain, the suffering, the thought of having another mouth to feed, was too much for her and in that moment, she gave the Devil her thirteenth child."

Uriah raised his voice, nothing menacing, but it was a nice touch. "'Let it be a devil!' Deborah shouted into the night just as the grandfather clock struck midnight. The ominous chime echoed in the Leeds home, welcoming the arrival of a baby boy.

"The Midwife slowly approached Deborah with the baby, kneeling by her bedside so she could look upon her newborn son. It is true, the baby was her son, but no longer could you call him a baby. The Devil had wasted no time collecting what was his. The baby was now a creature of the night, a demon with wings. From his back sprung wings like a bat and his hands and feet became cloven hooves. He grew twisted horns that protruded from his head like an ox.

"At the sight of the Leeds Devil, Deborah let out a bloodcurdling scream that shook the house and filled the sky. The villagers locked their doors and windows and cowered in fear at the sound of Deborah's screams over the approaching storm. The demonic beast slaughtered his own parents and shot up the chimney, taking flight over the Pine Barrens, where he haunts our town to this day."

Uriah put his hand to his ear. "Listen. Listen closely. Locals say on a night like tonight, you can hear the song of the Jersey Devil as he stalks these very woods looking for his next victim."

Sammy grabbed Elsa's shoulders, much as he had grabbed Ivy's earlier, but unlike Ivy, Elsa screamed. It must've sounded close to Deborah Smith Leeds's bloodcurdling scream upon seeing her baby transformed into a devil. Ivy was forced to cover her ears.

Sammy, along with everyone else, laughed. Even Pastor Leeds let out a burst of laughter. "Elsa, you're such a scaredy cat."

"And you're a jerk," she said, getting up and stomping away. Sammy chased after her, no doubt looking to give her another apology hug.

When no one was looking, Zac made his way outside. He had a great idea that was sure to frighten everyone. He was going to go outside and whistle a song by the window, so they thought the Jersey Devil was coming to get them.

"If Sammy's not scared, I'm not scared," Zac told himself as he creeped around the side of the church, making his way to the graveyard. "Sammy is going to think I'm so cool when I scare Elsa." Zac was a few feet away from the window when the floodlight overhead flickered, forcing his eyes upward. "Better hurry this up before I scare myself," Zac muttered. He put his fingers in his mouth and let out a short, quick whistle. "Shoot, I'm not very good at this."

He was going to make another attempt at a whistle when from

behind him, he heard the sound of his short, quick whistle returned to him from the graveyard. He froze, his feet planted in the ground. He didn't want to turn around, he wanted to run back into the church. But he didn't. He knew it was one of the guys. If he ran now, they would be laughing at him the rest of the summer.

Zac gasped when the whistling turned into a low-pitched harmony. The sound seemed more than a sound. It gave the impression it weaved around the headstones on an invisible current.

Trembling, his legs like spaghetti, he turned to face the graveyard. "Sammy . . . is that you?" Zac asked in a soft voice.

The graveyard fell silent as the tune moved through the dead, sinking into the dark depths of the Pine Barrens, into the tall, rooted pines that kept everyone locked in town.

Zac turned back around, peering through the church window. He could see Sammy and the rest of his friends. He heard the whistled tune again. And again, it came from behind him, but this time the whistle was louder, much louder, as if the whistler was walking his way. Zac's heart pounded in his chest; his breathing labored. Whoever was in the graveyard was not one of his friends. As he turned around to face the whistler, the floodlight went out, leaving Zac in complete darkness. He instinctively reached for his phone in his pocket and turned its flashlight on. It shined on the ground, illuminating a pair of men's dress shoes. He swallowed hard, slowly raising his phone to see the man's face.

"Boo."

Zac fell to the ground, shocked. "Mr. Lopez . . . I'm sorry. I know we're not supposed to leave the church. Really, I'm sorry. Please don't tell my mom," Zac begged in a panic.

"Don't worry Zachary, I'm not going to tell your mom anything about tonight."

Zac sighed in relief. "Thank you."

"Tell me Zachary Lewis, are you scared?"

"No Mr. Lopez, I'm not scared," Zac lied, picking himself up off the ground.

"Good boy, Zachary. Now tell me the truth, do you really want to scare your friends?"

"Uh, yeah."

A smile spread across his face, twisting his lips. "Good, because you're in for a real treat. I'm going to do more than just scare you and your friends."

Megan walked around the small church looking for her cousin. Not finding him, she circled back to her friends.

"What's wrong?" Sammy asked, noticing Megan's flushed face.

"Zac—that idiot. He's not answering his phone and I can't find him anywhere."

Sammy waved his hand dismissively. "He has to be around here somewhere."

"What if he went outside?"

Sammy shrugged. "Even if he did, he'll come back in. I wouldn't worry about it. He'll turn up."

Megan looked out the window, scanning the cemetery. "I don't know," she said, her eyes webbing over in red. "I'm worried. I'm telling Pastor Leeds. I don't care how much trouble he gets in."

Jeffrey Lopez pulled his son aside. He, along with the other adult chaperones, were beyond concerned when they couldn't find Zac inside or outside the church. "Cut the crap, Sammy," Jeffrey said, furious with his son. "I know you went outside to scare everyone."

Sammy looked down, avoiding his father's dark eyes.

"Did Zac go outside after you?"

"No Dad, he was with us for story hour with Pastor Leeds."

"Then what?"

"Then, I don't know. I scared Elsa and we went to Mrs. Ball's station."

"Was Zac with you?"

"I'm not sure. I was trying to make it up to Elsa for scaring her."

"Sammy, this is serious, Zac is missing," Jeffrey said, his face hardening, not that Sammy would know, he kept his head bowed and his eyes on his feet.

"I told Zac we could scare the girls with Pastor Leeds's story about the Jersey Devil. I don't know . . . maybe he did go outside."

"Shit, Sammy."

Jeffrey went outside with Uriah to look for Zac again while Mrs. Ball and the three Henry sisters stayed inside the church with the kids. Together, Jeffrey and Uriah walked over to the floodlight where Sammy had been earlier that night.

"Find anything?" Sammy asked.

"Sammy, I told you to stay inside. When will you learn to listen?!" Jeffrey said exasperated.

"I know, but I can help."

Jeffrey exhaled through his nose. "Alright fine, you're already out here, just stay by my side."

"There!" Sammy yelled, pointing to the ground. He saw a phone lighting up in the tall grass. Sammy picked it up. "It's Megan calling. This is Zac's phone."

"Zac, this isn't funny anymore," Jeffrey shouted. "If you're hiding, come out."

"You're not in trouble Zac, just please come back inside," Uriah added.

"You got me. Got all of us!" Sammy yelled, his voice hitching.

"I'm getting very worried," Uriah said to Jeffrey. "It's not like a kid to part with their phone."

"Agreed. I'm calling Zac's mom and Devan," Jeffrey said. "Something's not feeling right. Come on Sammy, Uriah; let's get back inside."

Police Chief Devan Rainier showed up at the church within a couple of minutes with Detective Pearl Steele. They were just down the road when

Devan got the call from Jeffrey.

"It's too early to officially call Zac a missing person. No point in unnecessarily upsetting his mother and scaring the town folk," Devan said to Uriah and Jeffrey when they were alone. "But when a kid is involved, I'm not taking any chances. I called in some back up; we're going to walk the woods." Devan addressed Pastor Leeds, pushing back his salt and pepper hair, "I think it's time to send the kids home."

CHAPTER SEVEN
All Shook Up

Ivy hopped into the passenger seat of her grandmother's station wagon. "What's all the commotion about?" Mary asked, pointing to the cop cars.

Ivy glanced back at Devan as he talked to youth group kids' parents. His dark eyes looked almost black against his fair skin. "A boy named Zac disappeared."

Mary raised her eyebrows skeptically. "Disappeared? Like, poof, magic?"

Ivy rolled her eyes. "Magic isn't real, Grams. I think he was trying to scare everyone and musta got lost in the woods or something like that."

"Hmm," Mary mumbled, putting the station wagon in reverse. "I wouldn't want to be lost in these woods. No place for a kid. The Pines are haunted, you know?" Mary turned her head, taking her eyes off the road to give Ivy a stern look. "I don't want you going into the woods alone."

"Give me a break, Grams. It's just a bunch of ugly old pine trees that happen to sit on some protected land. There's no magic, no hauntings. Just old pine trees and stupid boys."

Grams laughed. "*Old pine trees and stupid boys—*sounds like the name of one of those bands you listen to."

Ivy crossed her arms over her chest. "Grams, you just don't understand music. The names have to sound cool like: Smashing Pumpkins, Placebo, Dramalove, Red Hot Chili Peppers, and my favorite band in the whole wide world, The Killers."

"Yeah, Ives, sounds really cool," Mary said sarcastically. "Cool if you're into wasting perfectly good food when there're starving children in this world." Ivy rolled her eyes as Grams went on. "Or if you're a hypochondriac, a drama queen, fond of indigestion, or are a member of Ted Bundy's family. In my day we had the King."

"I know Grams," Ivy huffed. "Elvis Presley, The King of Rock and Roll."

"That's right, kiddo." Mary turned into the driveway. "Sorry about tonight. Sorry you got all shook up," Mary said in her best Elvis voice.

"I didn't. I'm not scared," Ivy lied through her teeth.

"Uh huh," Grams said, looking over her fidgeting granddaughter as she struggled to unbuckle her seatbelt.

"Uh huh uh," Ivy said in her Elvis voice, trying to convince her grandmother she was fine.

Grams laughed. "You still got it! But all Elvis aside, you can stay with me tonight if you want. If that old attic is too spooky for you, I've got plenty of room."

"For Heaven's sake Grams, I'm sixteen, not six! I'm not scared of the attic anymore. And I don't sleep with a teddy bear and monsters aren't hiding under my bed."

"Okay, fine. Just saying, I'm here for you if you need me. Got that deviated septum fixed; I purr like a baby now."

"Uh Grams, babies don't purr, cats do. Babies coo. And I think the saying goes sleep like a baby."

Mary threw her hands up in the air incredulously. "Poppycock! Never knew a baby that slept. Part of the joys of motherhood, you learn to function on no sleep." Grams rubbed her eyes. "But those days are long gone, and I need my beauty rest." She got out of the car and stretched.

Ivy noticed her grandmother was still in her nightgown. "Thanks for picking me up."

"All in a day's work of being the best grandmother." It was true, she had a coffee mug that said just that.

They walked to the front door together. Once they were inside, Mary locked the door and the dead bolt.

Ivy gave her grandmother a quick hug. "You're the best Grams, but don't let that go to your head."

"Off to bed with you now," Mary said, shooing her granddaughter toward the attic. "Remember, if you get scared, I'm just downstairs."

"Grams! Again, I'm not scared, but thank you. Good night."

"Good night."

Ivy made her way to the attic. She hated that her grandmother was right, she was shook up. Zac going MIA mid lock-in really bothered her. Zac didn't exactly strike her as the brave type. She couldn't imagine what it would be like to be lost in the woods at night. Whether they were haunted or not, Grams was right again, they were no place for a kid. She hoped Zac would hear the police sirens and find his way back to the church.

Ivy went to her window when she heard Pastor Leeds pull in across the street. She watched him unlock his door and slip inside. She glanced at her alarm clock. It was almost midnight. Ivy had this funny feeling in the pit of her stomach. She couldn't quite put her finger on it, but it was a gnawing consciousness, similar to intuition. Somehow, she knew the bright red light would appear again at midnight. She pulled her desk chair to the window and waited.

Sure enough, at the stroke of midnight, a red light spilled out from Pastor Leeds's attic window. She stared on, mesmerized by the light and the humming rumble. There was still something about the light that innately frightened her, made her stomach twist into a pretzel, but staring it down as she was, made her feel like she was in control of her fear. After tonight, she felt like she needed to be in control of it more than ever.

Ivy snapped out of it when the midnight show ended abruptly at 12:01 a.m. like it had the night before. Having enough for one night, she crawled into bed before she was abducted by aliens. As if her comforter could protect her from extraterrestrials, old pine trees, and stupid boys, she placed it over her head.

CHAPTER EIGHT
House of the Believers

Mary and Ivy squeezed into a pew just in time. All three rows of pews at Pleasant Mills Church were full, but that didn't stop more people from piling in and standing behind the last pew. Ivy was pretty sure they were beyond maximum capacity and were breaking every fire code in the book, all while in God's house. She reasoned it was okay because the law came here to worship too. She spotted the two police officers from last night when they walked in.

Mary pinched her nose, "Urgh, Devan Rainier, you can smell him coming a mile away." Ivy's nose twitched from Chief Rainier's strong aftershave, causing her to turn. He now stood behind her and whispered with Detective Steele. She didn't know why he over did it with the aftershave, maybe he thought it was sexy, not that he needed to turn that up a notch. Chief Rainier was an attractive middle-aged man, distinctive with his black hair salted with white and his dark eyes.

Wondering if they were whispering about Zac, Ivy tried to listen in on their conversation, but to no avail. Detective Pearl Steele was a petite woman with a voice to match. Ivy couldn't hear a thing, she hoped she didn't suffer from hearing loss like her grandmother, who always warned her she listened to her music too loud and one of these days it was going to make her go deaf.

Noticing Ivy's gaze, Detective Steele ran her fingers through her long, black hair before stiffening up like a cadet in bootcamp awaiting uniform inspection, her face becoming a blank slate. Chief Rainier winked at Ivy. She gave a half smile and faced forward once again to scan the pews for Zac.

Ivy didn't see Zac, but she quickly spotted Sammy. He sat with his family in the middle row in the first pew, dead center. *Butt kiss.* Mike's family was easy to pick out too, they were the row of red heads with freckles behind the Lopez family. "And Elsa, where is Elsa . . ." Ivy muttered. She pinpointed her light-blonde hair a couple of rows in front of her. She spotted Louie seated between two women, who she assumed to be his mother and grandmother. Tyrone sat with his mother and father in the pew behind Louie's family. Ivy was not surprised the youth group was all accounted for; she was there voluntarily after all, but there was still no sign of Zac.

"Wow, Grams, you weren't lying about Pastor Leeds having a good rapport," Ivy whispered to her grandmother, turning to watch more people shuffle into the small church.

Ivy was used to one or two faithfuls in the pews when she would make the occasional pit stop at church, but a church bursting at its seams seemed strangely odd. The Pleasant Mill Church was so humming it looked like they were giving away free tickets to Heaven—or at the very least cash.

Ivy knew what had really put the butts on the benches, the prats in the pews, and it had nothing to do with getting the inside scoop on Zachary Lewis. It was the same reason why she and her grandmother had gotten up early to fix their hair and makeup, and the same reason the church was packed with middle-aged women wearing low-cut sundresses that were sure to make the young pastor blush. There was no mistake—no doubt—they were all there to see the anything-but-average Pastor Uriah Leeds, and maybe save their souls in the process.

"We know why they are all really here," Ivy whispered to Grams. "Sins of the flesh."

Mary gave Ivy one of her infamous disapproving looks. "Mind your manners, Ivy Belle Teller, we're in church. But I will say, it helps not to have an old fuddy-duddy up there," Grams whispered as Pastor Leeds came to the pulpit.

Ivy had to admit to herself, Uriah's sermon was good. It kept her interest and had her genuinely hanging on his words. The anticipation of what delight would come out of his mouth next had nothing to do with that perfect voice of his and more to do with the quality of his words. He really was everything her grandmother had promised her.

Uriah finished up his sermon on goodwill and community by talking about not only nurturing themselves through positivity but the need to nurture their souls by helping others. *"And let us consider how to stir up one another to love."*

Ivy smiled as if he spoke directly to her. Mission accomplished; she loved. She was sure she 'loved with a love that was more than love'.

Ivy sat up in her pew when Pastor Leeds mentioned her name, along with the rest of the youth group, as his positivity pushers and thanked them in front of the entire congregation for their hard work cleaning up Pleasant Mills Road.

Ivy was already hooked. Pastor Leeds didn't have to entrap her like the living fence surrounding the town. Ivy knew she would be back to youth group next Saturday, and from now on, Sunday mornings would be spent listening to Pastor Uriah Leeds's electrifying voice as he preached to the Pine Rats of Pleasant Mills and the misunderstood Teller women.

Mary decided to take advantage of the church coffee hour since she'd made the sacrifice of getting out of bed early. Ivy followed her grandmother through the door to the meeting hall. It was a small extension that had been added to the original building to hold church events and the ritualistic coffee hour.

Everyone swarmed Pastor Leeds after church was dismissed, making the dessert lineup ripe for the picking. Ivy stacked a couple of desserts on her plate and went to sit down while her grandmother joyfully perused the venetian hour.

"Church isn't as bad as I thought it would be," Ivy said to herself, taking a big bite of a sticky bun.

"Hey there," Sammy said, sitting next to her.

"Hey Sammy," Ivy replied, wiping the sweet frosting off her face with the back of her hand. Sammy handed her a napkin.

"Thanks," she mumbled under her breath, wiping her hands on it. "They find Zac last night?"

"I overheard my dad talking to Devan. Looks like Zac's dad grabbed him. Zac's parents just split. It was pretty ugly. So there's nothing really to worry about. Mr. Lewis would never hurt Zac."

"Explains why no one is freaking out," Ivy said relieved, but she was still curious exactly what it was Police Chief Rainier and Detective Steele were whispering about so intently. She watched them move like hungry mosquitos spreading malaria, humming about and whispering to the parents that were at church last night.

Sammy's attention was not on Devan and Pearl, but on Pastor Leeds. "Isn't it gross how they all drool over him," Sammy said, flicking his finger toward the flock surrounding their shepherd. Ivy knew Sammy was not focused on the neglected housewives of New Jersey as they lined up to shake Pastor Leeds's hand. His eyes were on Elsa Tilton who just got in line to talk to Pastor Leeds.

Ivy laughed at Sammy; she couldn't help herself. He was so pouty. She could tell he was used to getting his way. "Boy Sammy, you look like someone just ran over your puppy. Let me guess, Elsa used to drool over you before Pastor Leeds showed up?"

Sammy smirked; it wasn't his good-natured grin she was fond of. "Something like that, but I don't have to worry. He's not gonna last," he said nonchalantly, stealing the blueberry muffin off her plate.

Ivy raised her eyebrows. "What do you mean *last*? There's no way he's getting fired. Everyone loves him. Well, besides you."

"Pastor Leeds is the new replacement for Pastor Steelman. Pastor Leeds has only been here for two months."

"I'm sure the new car smell will wear off soon," Ivy teased. *Or I hope*, she thought. *I don't mind used cars.*

"Aren't you going to ask me what happened to Pastor Steelman?"

"You're going to tell me anyways."

Sammy rolled his eyes. "Pastor Steelman died."

"Hate to sound heartless Sammy, but old people die."

He shook his head. "Pastor Steelman was old to us, but not *really* old. She was my dad's age . . . thirty-three. A heart attack did her in."

"Oh," Ivy said, scrunching up her napkin. "That's sad."

He leaned in. He was so close to her now that she could see the light dance off his blue eyes. "Yeah, and before she kicked the bucket, Pastor Somers died at forty-five—another heart attack."

"You seem to know a lot," Ivy said, her eyes narrowing as she resisted moving closer to him.

She didn't have to; he did, sliding his chair to hers so they touched. "My dad is the mayor. It's his business to know everything that goes on in this town."

"I'm seeing that. Must also get you a front-row-center pew," Ivy mumbled.

"Yeah," Sammy said, throwing his half-eaten muffin back on Ivy's plate and giving distance between them. "It's like the job is cursed."

"So uh, how old is Pastor Leeds?" Ivy asked, hoping he wasn't in his thirties, not that he looked it, but you never know.

"Dad said he's twenty-two, right out of seminary school. This is his first church."

She smiled; twenty-two was the perfect age. "Well, we don't have to worry about him dropping dead anytime soon," Ivy said, taking another stab at her sticky bun.

"I don't know," he said, his blue eyes going to the ceiling as he mulled it over. "He's been here for only a couple months, and he already looks different."

"What does that mean? *Looks different?*" Ivy asked, concerned for her new favorite person. She was sure Sammy was talking out of jealousy, but thought it was prudent to make sure nothing was really wrong with Pastor Uriah Leeds.

"Like tired or stressed or something." He shrugged. "His face just looks different." Sammy went for the rest of her sticky bun. Ivy restrained herself from slapping his hand. She was sure that would cause a scene. She wished he had manners like Louie. Louie would never have just helped himself to someone else's plate. Sammy was a spoiled brat; he wanted her sticky bun—he got it.

Ivy rested back in her chair. "I'm sure he's still adjusting to the job. It looks like Elsa and the rest of his fan club keep him pretty busy," she said rubbing it in.

"Yeah, I guess. Maybe that's it, or maybe there's a curse."

Ivy moved her plate of goodies away from Sammy. "You're really stuck on this curse thing. Maybe he's *just tired.* I'm sure that's all it is. He stays up pretty late doing something funny in his attic."

"Really?" Sammy asked, excited. "Did you see something?"

"Just a red light that starts at midnight, and there's this strange noise. It's been the same the past two nights." Sammy's eyes widened, putting so much importance on her words that it made her shrink away. "It only lasted for one minute, it's really not a big deal," she said, her voice trailing off. "I'm just saying, I'm not surprised if he looks tired; he must not be getting a lot of sleep. And after the scare with Zac last night, I'm sure he's exhausted. I personally can't wait to get out of here and go back to bed."

"Hmm," Sammy said as he thought, "I wonder."

Ivy's curiosity got the best of her. "What are you wondering?"

"I'm wondering if there's a connection to what you saw and what happened to those other pastors."

He was giving her a headache. "Why would there be a connection?"

"The house Pastor Leeds lives in is church property."

"Yeah . . . so?"

"And *so,* the stuff in the house isn't his, including the stuff in the attic. My dad went over there after Steelman passed. He said she had no family and her stuff, along with who knows who else's stuff, is still in there. My dad says the inside of the rectory looks like an antique shop meets a hurricane. He left everything in the house because he knew the new pastor was coming with nothing. He figured he'd let Pastor Leeds decide what he wanted to keep."

"Not following. You're proving my point Sammy—Pastor Leeds is tired because he has to rummage through someone else's junk in his free time. Sounds exhausting to me."

"What if something freaky is in the attic?" He leaned in again, closer than he had been before. She could smell his cologne. She liked it, it was nice, nothing like Chief Rainier's. "There could be something in the attic that got to Pastor Somers and Steelman and is now after Pastor Leeds."

"Like a haunted Christmas bulb?" Ivy mused, rolling her eyes at Sammy's overactive imagination.

"Come on, you aren't the least bit curious? Don't you want to know what Pastor Leeds was doing up at midnight—in that spooky house?"

Ivy shrugged. "Not really."

"Let me put it this way," Sammy said, reaching over Ivy's arm and taking her chocolate chip cookie. "I *know* you want to make sure Pastor Leeds is okay."

"I guess," Ivy said. "*I know* I wanted that chocolate chip cookie."

It was Sammy who rolled his eyes now. "That's it. I'm coming over tonight."

"Um Sammy, you're a boy. I'm not allowed to have a boy in my room, let alone have a boy stay over for a sleepover," Ivy said in a hushed whisper, as she scanned the dessert tables for her grandmother.

Sammy swallowed the cookie in two bites. "I'll be at your house at 11:30. Just open the door. Old Lady Mary will never know."

Ivy let out a huff of hot air as Sammy helped himself to her phone. He put his number in her contacts and texted himself. "Got your number. I'll text you. And you're not fooling anyone, you should wipe the drool off your face before Pastor Leeds sees it."

CHAPTER NINE
Breaking the Rules

Ivy pressed her face to the window of the front door, scanning the street for Sammy. He'd texted her over ten minutes ago that he was on his way. With every passing minute, she grew more anxious, pressing her face to the door until it resembled a pancake.

Ivy wasn't sure why she was so nervous, but she was. Perspiration dotted her hairline, and her mouth was dry. She chalked it up to fear—fear Sammy would wake up her grandmother, which she knew was silly. Her grandmother wasn't a light sleeper. As long as they were careful on the stairs to the attic, she would never know Sammy was there. But still she was nervous—very nervous. She didn't want to admit it had anything to do with having a boy in her room.

Ivy had doubted Sammy would actually come, but was ready in the event he did. She took a fresh shower and did her hair and makeup, with just enough attention to detail as not to look like she was trying. Making it look like you didn't care when you do, took a lot longer than she thought.

When her phone dinged, and she read: on my way, her heart jumped, along with the rest of her and she dropped her brush into the toilet bowl. It was a race to fish out her brush and finish her hair.

Ivy's heart jumped another beat when she saw Sammy coming up the sidewalk through the fogged glass. He looked handsome walking with his head bowed, his dark hair falling over his forehead. She slowly unlocked the door and went outside to make sure he wasn't going to do anything that would wake up her grandmother, like knock on the door. He was a stupid boy after all, and she couldn't take her chances.

"Hey," Sammy said, making his way onto the porch.

"Hi."

They looked at each other awkwardly. Sammy smiled and let out a nervous chuckle, shoving his hands in his windbreaker. "Um, are you gonna invite me in?"

"Oh how very vampire of you to ask."

He flexed his eyebrows playfully as if to say maybe he *was* a vampire. He approached the door. Ivy jumped in front of it like a warrior princess, her hands out ready to do battle. "First, a warning."

He bit back a laugh. "You Tellers are so aggressive," he teased.

Ivy put her index finger in Sammy's face, resisting shaking it like her grandmother did, but she needed to let him know she meant business. "Sammy, if you wake up my grandmother, I will kill you. And I will bury you in the backyard and turn your corpse into a veggie garden."

"You've put a lot of thought into killing me. I'm glad I'm on your mind," he said, his lips twisting into his sideways grin.

Ivy blushed. She was relieved it was an overcast night with no moon and no stars. There was no way Sammy noticed. "Not thinking of you," she said haughtily. "The opposite in fact."

"Got it," he whispered. "Wake up your grandmother and I'm dead."

"Glad we have an understanding," Ivy said, opening the front door with the same finesse as before.

Sammy followed her to the back staircase that led to the attic. In the tight space, Ivy turned around to whisper to him. She could smell his cologne; it was stronger than it had been at church, and she wondered if he had reapplied it for her—so that she would notice—so that she would tell him he smelled good.

Her heart was doing jumping jacks at the possibility. As unlikely as it was, being he had a big crush on the Barbie Elsa, she thought maybe, just maybe it *was* for her.

Her tongue stuck to the roof of her mouth as she spoke: "The stairs creak. Take off your sneakers and walk very slowly or you'll wake up Grams."

Sammy nodded, complying. He slipped off his Nikes and followed Ivy. They made it to her bedroom with only a few low ribbits.

"You can just sneak out of your house without your parents noticing?" Ivy asked, once they got to her bedroom and the door was snugly shut.

Sammy slipped his sneakers back on. "My parents think I'm at Mike's house. He covers for me all the time. We're practically neighbors, so the 'rents are cool with me just walking to his house."

"He covers for you all the time?" Ivy asked, only half surprised.

"A lot," he said with a wink.

"Ew,"she said. "Can someone say teenage pregnancy?"

Sammy laughed. "Get your mind out of the gutter." He jumped on her bed and crossed his hands under his head.

Ivy had to admit there was something about Sammy Lopez once you got past the annoyingness, arrogance, and narcissism. It had to be the blue eyes-dark hair combo, she was a sucker for light-blue eyes and dark-brown hair, put them together and she was in love, or at the very least in lust. If it weren't for Pastor Leeds taking up full-time residency in her heart, and Louie being a little too young, she would most likely be crushing on Sammy. He was definitely drool worthy in his own right.

"You have a thing for dead guys?" Sammy said, pointing at the posters of Kurt Cobain, Jimmy Hendricks, and Jim Morrison.

"The twenty-seven club," Ivy said.

"The what?" Sammy asked, confused, resting on his elbow.

"The twenty-seven club. They all died at twenty-seven. It's the curse of twenty-seven or something like that and they're all Rock icons," Ivy said, taking a seat on her bed.

Sammy smiled. "I thought you weren't big on curses," he said, sitting up and sliding next to her.

"Not all curses."

"I hear you," Sammy said distracted, peering out her small bedroom window from his spot on her bed. "Perfect view of Pastor Leeds's house."

"Yep," she said.

Sammy took off his windbreaker and tossed it on the foot of the bed. "Man, it's hot in here. Don't you have air conditioning?"

"Heat rises."

"Yeah, I can tell. I can feel my internal organs cooking." He wiped the sweat off his forehead with the back of his hand. "So, when does the red light go on?"

"I've only been here two nights, so I'm not guaranteeing anything, but both nights, the light went on at midnight."

"That's a strong enough pattern for me." He glanced at her alarm clock. "We have ten minutes."

"You think you can make it before your goose is cooked?" Ivy said. That sounded way funnier in her head. Out loud it sounded corny, and she wished she could take it back the moment it escaped her lips.

There was no way Sammy could ever like her. It was stupid to even entertain hope. She didn't have to be told Sammy was the popular kid at school, she knew it. His dad picked him up from church in a Mercedes SUV, and he was wearing all name-brand clothes. Not to mention he had the newest iPhone.

Ivy knew he was only there because her house was conveniently located across the street from his arch nemesis, Pastor Leeds. She was pretty sure Sammy was hoping to prove the young pastor was doing something *freaky* in the attic to get him booted out of church more than he cared about his welfare. Sammy wanted all eyes on him, or more specifically Elsa Tilton's, and the only way to do that was to take Uriah Leeds out of the picture.

"I'll make it Teller," he said, turning to look at her. He held her in his gaze, much as the red light had done the past two nights. "And if not, you already have a place picked out for me in your garden."

"True," she said with a large smile, her pulse hiccupping. She liked his nickname for her. Teller sounded cool. It made her feel special—like there was something between them.

He went back to watching the window, and she watched him. The summer had just started but he was tan, the kind of coppery brown you could only get from the sun. It made his eyes look extra light, that, and being in her dim lit room. The lamp on her nightstand didn't give off much illumination, but she didn't mind, she liked Sammy in this light.

"So, you and Mike tight?" she asked.

"Yeah, tight enough. He has a hot sister. We used to date."

"So, you're friends with Mike for his sister?"

"You can say it started off like that."

Ivy saw a pattern too. A pattern of Sammy using people to get what he wanted. "You're ridiculous."

Sammy laughed, breaking his concentration on the window. "I'm kidding. I just wanted to see your face. You make a lot of silly faces."

"I do not," she said, crossing her hands over her chest. "And about what part were you kidding?"

"Both. Mike's my best friend, and I never dated Tammy. After we're done here, I'm heading to his house."

Ivy noticed Sammy didn't say he was kidding about Mike having a hot sister, just that he never dated her. She wondered if Tammy was the reason he doused himself with designer cologne.

"How about you? You said you had siblings, but it's just you and Old Lady Mary."

"I have a hot sister too."

"Really?!" he asked, wide-eyed. He laughed at himself. "I'm teasing, Teller. I got my eyes on Elsa, as I'm sure you gathered."

The tips of her earlobes burned. "I have."

"I've been chasing her since last year."

"What happened last year?"

"She got boobs."

Ivy laughed out loud, covering her mouth with her hands before her grandmother could hear. "What? And before that she had no boobs?"

"Well, she kinda looked like a boy," Sammy said, trying to remember Elsa Tilton from a year ago.

"So much for thinking you're mature."

He smiled. "You thought I was mature? Thanks."

"I take it back."

They were interrupted by the red light beaming into the room. It came with all the intensity of the last two nights wrapping everything in Ivy's bedroom in red, including them.

"What the heck," Sammy said, getting up and going to the attic window. "You hear that?"

"Yeah, I think," Ivy said tugging on her earlobes. "I've got some eardrum damage from listening to my music too loud, but I can hear it. It's been the same noise the last two nights. It comes with the red light, and it all stops at 12:01."

"Sounds like a motor or generator," Sammy said, opening the window to hear better. He could make out a low, pulsating hum. It was distinctive and slow. He had heard it before, he was sure of it, but he couldn't remember from where.

"I guess it could be," Ivy mused.

"That it?" Sammy asked at the end of the minute. The light and the noise suddenly dying.

"That's it. Only one-minute worth."

The red light didn't seem so scary with Sammy there. If scared was even what she truly felt when she saw it. It stirred a mixture of emotions in her that she couldn't quite pinpoint.

"There has to be more. I'm gonna check it out."

Ivy grabbed Sammy's arm to stop him, surprised by her gut reaction to him wanting to get a closer look. "Check it out? It's the middle of the night. What do you think you're going to find?"

Sammy sighed in disappointment. "I guess you're right, it would be kinda hard to find anything now that the rumbling is over."

Ivy nodded. "Yes, it would."

Sammy walked back to the window, glancing at Pastor Leeds's house again before shutting it. He took a seat on the bed next to Ivy. "Fine, you win. Tomorrow night we're going over there."

She ignored him, thinking out loud. "Same time, three nights in a row, and only for a minute. Maybe something in the attic is on a timer."

"I want to make sure. It's my dad's town. If anything hocus-pocus is going on, I need to be in the know."

"Hocus-pocus?! You are most certainly not mature if you believe in magic and witches," Ivy said, thinking of the Sanderson sisters from the Disney movie *Hocus Pocus.*

With intensity burning in his sky-blue eyes, Sammy locked his gaze on Ivy. "Do you believe in God?"

"Yeah, I guess so . . . why?"

"So that means you believe in the Devil by default. You can't have good without evil."

"I guess," Ivy reasoned. Sammy's unblinking stare was beginning to make her feel a little uncomfortable. It was as if he was trying to penetrate her soul with those magical eyes of his. Besides, she didn't like to think about things like that when she had to sleep in the attic all by herself.

Sammy leaned in closer to her, he was so close now, she again smelled his cologne, the masculine, clean scent tingling her nose. "Well, with that belief comes all walks of the supernatural from both sides: angels, saints, miracles, and from hell: demons, ghosts, and witches." He eased up, giving space between them, and finger-combed his dark hair back. "Not that all witches are bad of course, but you get the point."

"Fine, we'll meet tomorrow," she sighed.

"I knew you were cool," he said, slipping into his grin. "We'll meet outside your house at eleven."

Her eyebrows furrowed; she was sure she was making one of her silly faces. "The red light doesn't turn on until twelve."

"We need time to find a good spot to hide in Pastor Leeds's yard," Sammy said as he thought, his face inclining to the cobwebs on the ceiling. "Do me a favor, in the morning try to scope out the yard."

"Okay."

"Cool." He got up, his eyes downcast, his face in shadows thanks to his dark hair falling into his eyes. "Well, I guess I should be getting to Mike's before it gets too late."

Ivy got to her feet, standing awkwardly close to him. She took a step backward to her door, blindly feeling for the doorknob. Finding it, she opened it slowly, stopping when the door let out a squeal. She turned around to better assess the situation, waiting for a couple of moments before she opened the door fully. Sammy already had his sneakers off and was ready to go.

Ivy walked with Sammy down the stairs, their descent met with very few croaking stair treads. She opened the front door for him. He stepped out into the moonless night, turning to face her. "Night Teller. This was fun. See you tomorrow." He quickly made his way down the porch steps, stopping to wave.

Ivy was half hidden behind the front door, giving a little wave of her own, before closing it. She leaned against the closed front door; her heart pounding in her chest like a bass drum as Sammy played on repeat in her head. She took a deep breath, hurrying back to her bedroom. She went to her window, pulling back the sheer curtain to watch Sammy make his way down the sidewalk. She watched him until he was just a speck on the horizon.

Ivy free fell into her bed. She could still smell Sammy's cologne. Her fingertips touched his jacket lying at the end of her bed. "Dummy," she said, her lips still curved into a smile as she smelled it, wanting more than a lingering scent. She got up and hung Sammy's jacket on her desk chair. She noticed it was heavy. She knew he'd left his phone in his pocket. She hesitated for only a second before reaching into his windbreaker and taking out his phone. "Password?" she asked herself. "Hmm . . . he's annoying, arrogant, and a narcissist. I bet his password is Sammy."

Ivy typed in Sammy, her smile widening until it hurt. "Yep, narcissist."

Sammy had Ivy listed in his phone as new girl. "Great, I'm not even worthy of my name."

Ivy saw that Sammy had texted Mike a couple of times before he'd made it to her house. She knew she shouldn't snoop but she did anyway. This was a once in a lifetime opportunity. How often did she have a boy in her room and how often would that boy be stupid enough to leave his phone behind? The temptation was too great, and she gave into it without putting up a fight.

Sammy: Go'n 2 new girl's house.

Mike: The fat girl from youth group?

Sammy: Yeah B over after that.

Ivy put Sammy's phone back in his jacket pocket as tears rolled down her cheeks. Ivy knew she was nothing to write home about. She was average height and average weight. Most would say she was carrying around a few extra pounds. But she always thought she had a pretty face. She rubbed her eyes, angry with herself for holding out hope. She knew it was too good to be true. Sammy didn't like her, and he wasn't her friend, he was just another stupid boy.

CHAPTER TEN
Visit from the Leeds Devil

There was a whistle in the still of Pastor Leeds's house. The sound traveled up the stairs in a howling melody as the whistler made his way to Uriah Leeds's bedroom. Uriah's bedroom door opened; a thin trail of light filtered into his room from the hall. It found its way onto the bed, highlighting Uriah's sleeping face where it took on an angelic reverence.

Like a moth to the flame, the whistler stepped out of the shadows and went to Uriah's bedside. He took a seat on the bed and watched the light dance around Uriah's flawless face. "My sweet, sweet Uriah, it's so good to have you home." The whistler's eyes flashed red, glowing like fire embers. They were alive in a way few things are.

"I'm always here for you," the whistler said, running his finger down the sleeping pastor's cheek. "Soon you will remember who you really are. You will remember where your faith really lies. Remember that your God was never there for you; it was always me. I answered your call for help. It was I who saved you, gave you a good life, not him. It was me who gave you your church. I gave you your followers."

The man tenderly brushed Uriah's dark hair away from his face before planting a kiss on his forehead. His lips moved to his ear, his voice coming out in a soothing lullaby. "I love you Uriah, and I always will. No matter how many times you curse the Devil, I am a part of you. I'm sending someone to help you, a guide. He will come to you soon. You will know him as your cousin Jesse when you see him. You have known him all your life, and you love him and trust him implicitly. Do as he says and trust him with your precious town." Another kiss found Uriah's forehead. "Now sleep well, until we can be reunited."

CHAPTER ELEVEN
Sammy Lopez, Landscaper Extraordinaire

Mary Teller walked to the front door still chewing her morning toast when she heard another strong knock on the front door. "I'm coming. I'm coming!" she yelled at the door, opening it frazzled to see Sammy Lopez.

"Hi," he said with a toothy smile. "Ivy around?"

"Sure is." Grams inclined her head into the house and yelled: "Ivy, that rich brat from youth group is here!"

"Well Old Lady Mary, you really say what's on your mind, don't you?" Sammy said, being a smart ass.

"I do," she said, slamming the door in his face.

Ivy knew why Sammy was knocking on her door this early in the morning; he wanted his phone. She took a deep breath, leaving her half-eaten breakfast to give it to him. It made no difference to her she was rumpled from sleep and didn't brush her hair yet. Her effort to look nice last night was stupid, he didn't deserve her consideration.

Ivy went outside, pulling Sammy's phone out of her pocket. "Your stupid phone has been blowing up all morning," she said, handing it to him. "I'll give you your jacket tonight, don't want Grams seeing it."

"Thanks," Sammy said, taking a seat on the porch bench. He wasted no time typing in his narcissistic password and scrolling through his missed messages.

"Shit, my dad texted like ten times!"

"I hope you don't mind, I texted him back. You know, to cover for you," Ivy said, glancing down. "Well not really for you. I didn't want it to get back to Grams you were here last night, in the event your dad sent out a search party."

"Thanks." His eyebrows arched in a funny face of his own. "Wait, you know my password?"

"I took a wild guess."

"Well, thanks. You saved my ass." Sammy put his phone in his jeans pocket. "I guess I need a new password now." Sammy looked away for a moment, she swore she could see the hint of a blush on his face. She wondered if he realized yet she read his messages and if he cared her feelings were hurt. "So anyway, did you get a good look at Pastor Leeds's place yet?"

Ivy's eyes moved into a half-lidded position. He didn't care about her. He only cared about one thing—getting rid of Pastor Leeds.

"Only what I can see from the porch . . . not like I can just go over there and snoop around." Ivy said, taking a seat in a rocking chair.

"Of course we can," Sammy insisted.

"Uh no, we can't."

He smiled at her, a smile of all teeth. "Sure we can. We're going to volunteer to cut his grass."

"Are you kidding me?"

"Not at all. Come on," Sammy said, jumping off the porch bench like he just downed a cup of sugar.

Ivy groaned, opening the front door, she couldn't believe she was going along with this. "Grams, we're doing youth group stuff. Gonna see if Pastor Leeds wants his grass cut," she shouted into the house.

"Tell the brat to do our yard!" Mary barked from the kitchen.

"You heard her," Ivy said, turning her face to find Sammy standing behind her. He no longer smelt of cologne, just stupid boy.

"Sure, I can do it, but first Pastor Leeds's lawn. Beauty before age, Old Lady Mary!" Sammy hollered so Mary could hear.

"Brat!" she snapped back.

"Way to get on Grams's good side," Ivy mumbled.

He wore his iconic grin. "She started it."

Together, Sammy and Ivy crossed the street to Pastor Leeds's house. Sammy knocked and then pressed the doorbell. Ivy stopped him from knocking again. "Give the man a minute."

Pastor Leeds opened the front door, a smile lighting up his face. Ivy let out a sigh, now she knew why she was going along with Sammy's idea. Pastor Leeds was wearing a white T-shirt and jeans. Ivy decided the white of his shirt proved it—he was on angel status, and she was in Heaven.

"Good morning, Sammy and Ivy. How can I help you this fine summer day?"

"Actually, we're here to help *you*," Sammy answered back quickly. "We're going to cut your grass."

"I was actually going to cut the grass today. No need for you two to spend your day doing it."

"I'm in the doghouse with my dad and Ivy needs to repent for giving her grandma hell. So you would be doing us a favor."

Ivy nudged Sammy hard.

"You really don't have to."

"We insist," Sammy said with a smile.

"Okay, thank you. If it will help you two out with your folks, my yard is all yours."

Pastor Leeds led them to the detached garage on the side of the house.

"How'd you sleep last night, Pastor Leeds?" Sammy asked as they waited for him to find the key to the garage on his key ring. "You look tired. You go to bed late?"

Ivy gave him an incredulous look, hoping he got her gist of toning it down a few hundred octaves.

"No, no, I'm an early bird. I went to bed before it was even dark out. I thought I slept well," he said with a yawn. "I don't know what's wrong with me, I'm just always tired."

Sammy shot Ivy a glance to say, "I told you something funny is going on with Pastor Leeds."

"I'm going to get my blood work done again. I think I may have Lyme disease. Apparently, it only takes one tick bite to get it and excessive tiredness is one of the main symptoms. So, make sure you check yourself when you're done with the grass."

"Will do," Sammy said. "You get some rest Pastor Leeds and let us take care of this."

"Okay. Thank you both. I appreciate this. I know the grass has been long for a couple of weeks now. I've just been exhausted, and I still have all the personal effects from the former pastor I need to go through. I'll get started on that while you two cut the grass."

Sammy lightly pushed Pastor Leeds out of his garage. "Good thinking Pastor Leeds. Leave this to us."

When Pastor Leeds was out of earshot, Sammy turned to Ivy. "We've only got a couple of hours to snoop. I've got work at noon."

"Work? I didn't know you have a job."

"Yeah, I'm a lifeguard at Poor Richard's Community Pool. It's easy and keeps my dad off my back. The pool is owned by a guy named Ben and his son, Cam. They're pretty chill employers. Probably the best summer job in town."

"Of course he's a lifeguard," Ivy muttered to herself.

"We'd better get a move on," Sammy said, pushing the lawn mower out of the garage.

"What am I looking for exactly?"

"Anything hocus-pocus. Anything that would make a rumble."

The tentacle-like branches of the large willow tree in Pastor Leeds's yard chattered in the wind, drawing Ivy's attention to the house. In the daylight, the house was creepy with its shuttered windows and darkened siding. It looked like it needed a full overhaul to ward off evil spirits, but really there was nothing blatantly abnormal about the house. The rectory was as quiet as a church mouse on Sunday—no sign of the red light or strange noise. Everything seemed normal enough to her. She wasn't sure what cutting Pastor Leeds's grass was going to accomplish besides a sunburn, but it was too late to back out now. They promised Pastor Leeds they cut his grass, and she didn't want to disappoint him.

Ivy went around with the weedwacker while Sammy pushed the lawn mower up and down the front yard leaving lines in the grass like a professional. She kept her eyes peeled for anything that could be causing the mysterious sound in the middle of the night but found nothing out of the ordinary.

Sammy tapped Ivy on the shoulder. "Here, take over for a bit with the lawn mower. Keep it going so Pastor Leeds thinks I'm outside."

"Why? Where are you going?" Ivy asked, raising her eyebrows.

"I'm going to the attic."

Now it was all making sense to her. Sammy had it all planned out from the moment they'd stepped foot in Pastor Leeds's yard—Ivy was the decoy. He was just using her again.

Sammy was already sprinting toward the front door of the rectory before Ivy could get a word out. He quickly opened it and slipped in, closing the door quietly behind him.

Sammy took a moment to look around. Pastor Leeds's house was dark and dingy. It looked like the home of an old spinster, not a young bachelor. There were crochet doilies covering every hard surface of the house. Sammy spotted one on the dining table, the coffee table, and on the radiator covers. There were even crochet doilies on the armrests of the plastic-covered couch.

When Sammy spotted the staircase, he ran to it. His pulse raced with every step closer to the attic. He tippy toed up the steps, taking his time as he climbed them, hoping his efforts would prevent the old floor from letting out a groan. He was glad he got practice in doing just that last night at Ivy's.

Sammy almost jumped out of his skin when he heard the steps creak from behind him. He turned around in a panic to see Ivy. "What are you doing?" he asked in a hushed whisper.

"Checking on you. So, this is the real reason you volunteered to cut Pastor Leeds's grass—you're an evil mastermind, Sammy Lopez."

"I'll take that as a compliment," he said, flashing her his sideways grin.

Ivy motioned for him to keep moving. They had just made it to the second story when they heard Pastor Leeds on the phone. "My name is

Uriah Leeds; I would like to make a follow up appointment. Yes, I know my blood work came back negative, but I'm feeling worse. I barely have the energy to get out of bed."

Sammy grabbed Ivy's arm as they ducked into a room just before Pastor Leeds walked by. Ivy's heart raced as she leaned against Sammy's chest, certain Pastor Leeds would be able to hear it.

"Any time is fine," Uriah said, oblivious to Sammy and Ivy.

Hearing Uriah on the stairs, Ivy exhaled in relief. Still pressed against Sammy, she slowly lifted her face to see him smirking. "You okay, Teller?"

"Fine," she grumbled shaking out her arms like he had fleas.

Sammy returned the favor and pressed himself against Ivy to stick his head out the door. "All-clear."

She pushed him off of her. "Good, now let's get out of here before we're caught."

Sammy ignored her. He was too busy looking around the room at the collection of odds and ends piled on top of each other. "Wow, would you look at all this stuff," Sammy said.

"Yep, your dad's right. I think a hurricane touched down here."

Sammy picked up a sweatshirt that was laying on top of a box.

"Hey, Ivy," he whispered. "Look at this." Sammy held up a Jersey Devils hoodie with a large red stain by the collar. "This is like the sweatshirt Zac was wearing at the church lock-in." Sammy ran his hand over the fruit punch stain. He put it up to his nose. He smelt a sweet, smoky scent. "I got a funny feeling this is Zac's."

"Why would Zac's hoodie be in Pastor Leeds's house?"

"I don't know," Sammy admitted, holding onto the sweatshirt.

"Have you talked to him?"

"No. I stopped by his mom's after church yesterday to check on him. He hasn't answered any of my texts, which is not like Zac."

"Well?" Ivy asked.

"Zac wasn't home. His mom looked pretty upset; she said he went to stay with his dad. I wasn't sure if he got his phone back, so I asked for his dad's number."

"And?"

"She said no and shut the door."

PLEASANT MILLS RECTORY: SPARE ROOM

"Is that typical behavior for her?"

"No, not at all. Mrs. Lewis is normally super nice. I guess she's just going through a lot. She made it seem like Zac's dad got full custody or something. I should try to stop over there again. I texted Megan a bunch a times about Zac, but she never responded. I always thought she liked me, but I guess not."

"Hey, Sammy, check this out," Ivy called to him in a low voice. She pointed to a painting on the wall. "This looks like your dad."

Sammy put down the sweatshirt and took a step closer to Ivy and the painting. "Wow, it really does."

"What's a painting of your dad doing in Pastor Leeds's junk room?"

Sammy chuckled nervously. "That's not my dad."

"Sure looks like him if you ask me," Ivy teased with a smirk. Sensing his agitation, she wanted to turn a knife in it. "There's your hocus-pocus, Sammy. Your dad has a Dorian Gray portrait."

Sammy scrutinized the painting. The man in the portrait had his father's dark eyes and dark hair and his chiseled jaw line, the same jawline he inherited from him, but there was a hint of something in the smile that wasn't his father.

Sammy took the canvas off the wall and turned it around. "See, told you. Japhet Dean Leeds, 1801, by J.R."

"Wow, that's old," Ivy said.

Sammy hung the painting back on the wall, taking a few steps back to look at it. "Yeah, it is. It's in really good condition for being that old."

"Yeah," Ivy agreed entranced by the portrait. She felt like Japhet Dean Leeds's dark eyes were staring at her.

He pulled on her shirt sleeve. "Teller, come on, we got this. We're almost to the attic."

Sammy stuck his head out the door. "We're good."

As soon as they stepped out of the room, they heard Pastor Leeds's voice. "You two looking for something?"

"Uh, Pastor Leeds," Sammy said, turning around. "Bathroom?"

"Oh, sure. Silly me, for not showing you. There's one right here," he said, pointing to the door across the hall, "and there's another bathroom on the first floor as soon as you come in. It's the first door to the left."

"Good to know," Sammy said with a toothy smile. "I'll take this one; Ivy, you take the downstairs."

"Sure," she said, giving him a scathing look. She knew he was going to try for the attic without her.

Uriah accompanied Ivy downstairs to make sure she could find the bathroom. Sammy went into the bathroom across the hall and turned the sink on to give credibility to his bathroom story. He inhaled. He smelled the same sweet smell from the Jersey Devils hoodie again. "Strange," he murmured, turning off the sink.

Sammy opened the door to the bathroom a crack, checking to make sure the coast was clear. He saw the stairs leading to the attic and went for it. His heart pounded as he took the narrow staircase to the third floor. With a big grin on his face, Sammy put his hand on the attic doorknob and turned.

"You've got to be kidding me! Urgh! Of course, the stupid door is locked!"

Sammy quickly made his way downstairs and joined Ivy and Uriah in the kitchen. Uriah handed Sammy a water bottle.

"Thanks. Well, Ivy and I better finish up," Sammy said, pulling on Ivy's arm.

"Thanks kids."

Ivy continued to smile at Pastor Leeds as Sammy pushed her out the front door, even though she wasn't thrilled he called her a kid. Sure, Uriah was older than them and too old for her. But high school girls her age liked older guys. Uriah was just out of reach, but in a couple years, age wouldn't be such a big deal. And who knows, maybe she could get her white doves and church bells.

Being back outside in the heat snapped her out of her reverie. It was significantly hotter out now, the sun fully overhead. Or, maybe it was because she was no longer in the presence of Uriah Leeds but Sammy Lopez.

"The attic door is locked," Sammy said, kicking the ground in frustration.

"You're kidding?"

Sammy exhaled loudly. "Wish I was. Biggest letdown of my life. I need to see what's in that attic. Don't worry I'll come up with something."

She was sure of that, he seemed to always get what he wanted.

Sammy's phone dinged, he pulled it out, his shoulders slouching. "I gotta go. Tell your grandmother I'll cut her grass tomorrow. I'm gonna be late to work." He slid his phone back into his pocket and raced down the sidewalk. He turned to yell at Ivy: "See you tonight!"

CHAPTER TWELVE
The Rumbling

Ivy made her way out to the porch to wait for Sammy. She sat on the bench, thinking the rocking chair would be too noisy. Her eyes naturally gravitated to Pastor Leeds's house. There was a moon tonight, it almost looked full, the smallest sliver missing. The sky was clear. There wasn't a cloud in sight, just lots of tiny, little stars that sparkled high above her like faerie dust. The moon and the stars were pretty, but somehow that translated differently on the ground. The moon cast Pastor Leeds's yard in shadows. The lanky branches of the willow tree reminded her of long fingers. Her mind went to zombies breaching soil, their fingernails tilling the land as they crawled out of their graves. She was scaring herself. She pulled out her phone to look at the time. It was past eleven, Sammy was late.

A mosquito bit her neck. She smacked herself, trying for a little payback when she was taken off guard. "Hey Teller."

Ivy held back a yelp, smothering her mouth with her hand.

Sammy grinned. "Sorry, didn't mean to scare you."

He walked up the steps, taking a seat next to her on the bench.

"You didn't scare me, you startled me. There's a difference."

"I stand corrected," he said, his smile shifting to the side. "I didn't mean to startle you."

"That's better," she said, her tone haughty. "Well, we already cased the outside of the house, I guess we should've pushed our meeting back." Ivy was wondering why Sammy needed her at all. He could creep around Pastor Leeds's bushes without her.

Sammy didn't say anything. The silence made her feel anxious. He was always talking.

"How was work?" she asked, nonchalantly.

"Good. My tan is awesome."

"Someone loves himself."

He smiled.

"My grandmother wants me to get a job."

"Yeah, sucks being our age, but nice to have the money."

"What do you mean, don't you already have it?"

"I think you're referring to my dad's money. His money is his money, not mine. If I want anything, I have to buy it myself, *build the man*," Sammy said in a deep voice meant to imitate his father. "I guess in a way my dad's right. He came from nothing, was left at the police station in a basket." Sammy chuckled. "Real story book stuff."

Ivy smiled awkwardly. "You mean given to a nice couple," she corrected, thinking somehow this story was familiar to her.

Sammy thought a moment. "No, pretty sure he was left at the police station. Point is, he bounced in and out of foster homes and made a fortune through hard work."

"Oh," Ivy said, a little more than surprised. She hoped her face didn't show it. She had assumed Jeffrey Lopez came from money. He had an air of self-privilege about him, the same look Sammy wore so well. "So . . . Lopez was . . ."

"My dad was fostered by a family for a few years until he went back into the system. He took their name as it was the only one he ever had. My dad speaks perfect Spanish, but he's actually French. He did one of those DNA tests they advertise everywhere. But, uh, that's how he met my mom. He helped her with her English after school."

"Oh," Ivy said again, not sure what she should say, but Sammy was looking at her like she should say something.

Sammy leaned back looking up at the blown-out porch light. "I wish my dad would have just had a normal childhood so he wouldn't act like everything I did was some stupid test of my manhood. I save up for everything I have. I want to get a car this year, so any hours Poor Richard's Community Pool throws at me, I take."

"Oh . . . I thought—"

"You thought my parents buy me everything? That I'm a rich spoiled brat that gets everything I ask for. Yeah, I get that a lot. I think that's why a lot of people are friends with me. They think my father's money means I'm rich." Sammy laughed to himself. "Obviously they don't know my father."

His laugh morphed into a sigh. "And I have to get a nice car."

"To keep up the appearance that you're a rich brat that gets everything he asks for. So, you can keep all your fake friends . . ."

"Something like that, I guess. It sucks 'cause I know my dad would buy my little sisters cars, but not me. I'm a man, got to pave my own way and all that bullshit."

"Daddy issues?" Ivy said in a teasing voice.

"I thought we were in a no-judgment zone?" Sammy said sarcastically.

"This is not youth group."

He laughed earnestly. "Oops, forgot."

"Youth group membership because of your dad too?"

"No. That's all my mom. She's big on church, *very* big. We never miss a Sunday service. She even makes my dad go. But I think he only goes because it looks good for his mayor gig."

"I see."

Sammy turned to look at Ivy. "It's not bad now that you've joined."

"We had one youth group Saturday together," Ivy said sharply.

"Yeah, like I said, since you've joined."

"I'm glad I can ease your mandatory suffering," she said with an eye roll.

He crossed his hands behind his head while he chuckled. "What can I say Teller, you're cool." That was twice he called her cool, but she wouldn't let his blarney throw her off her game. He was just saying that.

He nudged her knee with his. "So, what's your backstory? Why has Old Lady Mary put you in God's hands and stolen your Saturday and Sunday mornings from you?"

"She thinks I'm troubled."

"Well, you're not a musician, so I don't think she has to worry about you joining the twenty-seven club."

Ivy laughed. "Yeah, I don't think I'm troubled. I think my mother just never understood me and didn't want to deal with me, so she shipped me away."

"Oh, that stinks."

"Not really. I don't miss my old life. Feels like I can barely remember it."

"Where are you from?"

"Salem."

"You're from Salem, Massachusetts, and you don't believe in hocus-pocus?" Sammy asked, shocked.

"The witch trials were about persecuting people who were different, not about hunting down real-life witches. So no, I don't believe in hocus-pocus." She wasn't going to burst his bubble and tell him she was from Salem, New Jersey. She was a Jersey girl through and through.

"Fine, don't believe," he said, pointing across the street, "but I know some hocus-pocus is going on in that house."

Ivy pulled out her phone to look at the time again. "Well, you got ten minutes."

"We should move into Pastor Leeds's yard," Sammy said excitedly, hopping to his feet.

Ivy followed Sammy's lead and they crossed the road to Pastor Leeds's house. Sammy suddenly stopped, causing Ivy to bump into him. She stubbed her big toe against the heel of his sneaker. "What is it?" she hissed.

"I thought I saw something." Sammy went to the garage window and peered in before opening the window sash.

"Uh, do you think it's wise to do that?"

"Yeah."

"Hate to be a wet blanket, but I don't think so."

"It's fine Teller, relax."

"What exactly do you think you saw?"

"I thought I saw a face in the window."

"A face?!" Ivy nervously rubbed her hands together; she was ready to go back home.

"Yeah, I thought I saw my dad—nuts, right?"

"No, 'cause you know if he finds out you're not at Mike's, you're in big trouble. It's called paranoia Sammy Lopez."

"Maybe you're right. My mind must be playing tricks on me. There's no one in the garage, just the lawnmower and old tools. So we're good to go." He turned, facing her, his eyes running the length of her body. "And by the way, I like that you wore all black. Shows dedication."

Wearing black was more about looking thinner than going incognito, but she nodded like a team player.

Midnight struck and the bright red light from the attic painted the freshly cut grass red. The sound was coming from above them, from the attic.

"The sound is so familiar, don't you think?" Sammy said, his eyes fixated on the attic window.

Ivy anxiously rubbed her arms, moving her hands up and down them like she was cold. "Yeah, it is." She was glad this was only going to last a minute. Being closer to the source strengthened her feeling of dread.

"This is getting good," Sammy said, his eyes still glued upward. Ivy glanced at the grass and then to Sammy. They looked drenched in blood as if the red light became thicker coating everyone and everything in something more than light. She tugged on his sleeve to leave. She got a bad feeling that knotted up her stomach.

Ivy tried to shake it off by blinking, then blinking again, but each time Sammy was covered in crimson, the light becoming more concentrated as it turned to a deeper red.

As before, with the change of the minute hand, the light and the sound stopped. Sammy turned to Ivy and smiled mischievously. She didn't like that look. She didn't like being in Pastor Leeds's yard in the middle of the night. She wished she never told Sammy about the stupid midnight show.

"Maybe he has a generator in the attic," Ivy said, refusing to give Sammy an inch.

"For what? It's not like his electricity is out. Unless the good pastor wants to be off the grid," Sammy said with a wild smile.

She rolled her eyes. "You watch way too much TV. Maybe a generator is a less expensive way to meet his energy needs."

"No, what we got here is some bona fide, weird New Jersey hocus-pocus," he said, rubbing his chin in thought. "I've got to get in that attic."

"Not tonight, you're not."

He sighed. "No, not tonight unfortunately. I got to get to Mike's, but I'll walk you back to your house first."

"You don't have to. It's only across the street."

Sammy walked Ivy to her front door, walking so close to her his arm grazed hers. Ivy slipped inside, popping her head out. "Good night."

"I'll be here early to cut the grass."

"Okay," she said, pressing herself against the door as if it was the only thing stopping her from falling prostrate and smashing her face. She really hated how he made her feel: special one moment and like trash the next. When she felt special, as she did now, she felt like she couldn't stand on her own two feet and yet at the same time felt like she could fly. He intoxicated her.

Sammy lingered for a moment scuffing his sneakers against the worn wood of the porch floor as if he had something to get off his chest. "Well, um, see you tomorrow," he said quickly, turning to head back down the porch steps before Ivy could say anything else. She kept the door cracked and watched Sammy vanish into the night before closing the door.

CHAPTER THIRTEEN
Sammy's in Trouble

The next morning came and went. Sammy never showed up to cut the grass. Ivy had waited on the couch in the living room for him since breakfast. She kept her eyes on the bay window, hoping to catch a glimpse of him coming down the sidewalk.

"That grass is getting long," Grams said to Ivy, looking out the front window with her hands firmly planted on her hips.

"It's too hot now," Ivy groaned.

"I knew that good for nothing spoiled brat wouldn't show."

"I'll do it once the sun starts to go down, okay?"

"Fine," Grams said, irritated. She went into the kitchen to make them lunch.

Ivy pulled out her phone. No text from Sammy. It had been an hour since she'd last texted him: U on ur way? She didn't want to text him again.

Ivy had gotten up early to shower and blow dry her hair. She applied a little extra makeup than what was her usual, even putting on lip-gloss in anticipation of Sammy coming to cut the grass. When he didn't show her heart sank, and the longer she stared out the window, the more her chest burned. It was the same feeling she got when she ate Grams's southwest eggs smothered in diablo hot sauce. She knew it then—she liked him. Sammy had stolen her heart from Pastor Uriah Leeds. It now beat for him and him alone.

At dusk Ivy went outside to cut the grass. It was still hot and muggy out, but she knew if she didn't cut the grass today, she would never hear the end of it. Ivy had just started Grams's old lawn mower when she felt a tap on her shoulder. She jumped. She turned off the lawn mower and pulled out her ear buds.

"Hey," Sammy said. "Sorry I didn't show this morning."

Ivy shrugged it off. "No worries."

"I'll cut the grass," Sammy said, taking the lawn mower from her.

Sammy seemed different. She could tell he was off. He wasn't his usual smart-alecky self, and he wasn't wearing his usual grin, but she didn't want to pry. She left the lawnmower to him and went inside to get him a drink.

"So, the brat finally showed up," Grams said, moving the curtain away from the window to get a better look.

"Yeah, he just got here."

"I think I'll sit on the porch and make sure he does a good job. I want my yard to look as good as Pastor Leeds's. I don't want him to give our grass a quick-over."

Ivy groaned. "Grams, I don't think that's necessary."

Despite Ivy's objection, Mary made her way outside. Ivy had no choice but to follow. Together they sat on the porch and watched Sammy cut the grass, each rocking in a rocking chair.

"Not a bad looking kid," Grams said, taking a sip of her lemonade.

"Grams!"

"I think he likes you."

"I don't," Ivy said in a low voice.

"Then why is he cutting the grass, and why are you wearing makeup around the house?"

"Is it a crime to wear makeup? Besides, Sammy likes Elsa from youth group. He told me as much."

"Those things change."

"Well, not in this case. I'm not his type."

"He has a type at sixteen? Here I was thinking he still wet the bed," Mary laughed.

Ivy rolled her eyes. "Funny Grams, and yes, he has a type: tall, blonde, with big boobs. All three which I don't have."

"You've got something more."

It was Ivy that was laughing now. "Really, what's that?"

"Voodoo."

"Urgh, please Grams," Ivy said, giving her grandmother a stern look.

"It's true Ives, we have witches on my side."

"Great, more hocus-pocus, more of what I don't need," Ivy muttered to herself.

Mary took another sip of her lemonade. "It's true."

"Is that supposed to make me feel better about being an ugly duckling?"

"You're not an ugly duckling. Now that's just plain rubbish," Mary said authoritatively.

"Well, I'm not a swan, and Sammy Lopez, he likes swans. He's the mayor's son, so I guess he could be considered the town prince."

"You're giving that Sammy too much credit," Mary laughed, her laugh sounding like hiccups strung together. "You need to lay off the fairy tales. I think they're warping your teenage brain."

"You're right, maybe I should watch soap operas like you. That's sure to make me smarter."

Sammy walked up to the porch when he'd finished cutting the grass and the old lawn mower was put away. He had sweat dripping from his forehead and his shirt was drenched. It clung to every inch of him like a second skin. Grams handed him a glass of lemonade. "You smell, spoiled brat."

"Look at that, Old Lady Mary, we finally agree on something," he said, taking a seat on the bench. He took a sip of his lemonade, his eyes going to Ivy. "Your yard's a lot bigger than it looks."

Ivy smiled. "Thanks for doing it."

"Hmm, better late than never." Mary said, getting up to inspect her lawn.

Sammy leaned back, enjoying the breeze. "Your makeup looks nice."

"Um . . . thanks, had to run out earlier with Grams," she lied.

Mary smiled. She figured she better give her granddaughter some space. "Well, I better pull something out for dinner," Mary said, opening the front door. "Yard looks good, brat."

"Thanks."

Ivy breathed a little easier with Grams inside. She didn't like the idea of her grandmother having a front row ticket to her teenage angst.

"Old Lady Mary find you a job yet?" Sammy asked.

"No."

"We're looking for a lifeguard at the pool. It's not hard to get certified as long as you have a CPR license.

"I don't," Ivy said.

"Too bad. I think they have a class down at the hospital once a month. You should look into it; maybe you didn't miss this month's class. The pay is pretty good and, like I said, it's easy."

Ivy couldn't imagine working at a pool. That sounded more like Hell on Earth to her than a job, even if Sammy said it was easy money.

"Thanks Sammy, we'll look into it," Grams shouted from inside.

"Really Grams?!" Ivy yelled at her grandmother from the front porch.

"What? I was just admiring the grass from the window!"

Ivy waited until she heard Grams walk through the swinging door of the kitchen before she asked Sammy the question that had been waiting to spill out. "Where were you this morning?"

"Sorry about that. I got in trouble with my dad."

"Oh, for what?"

"Talking back. It was stupid. I know better. He took my phone."

"For how long?"

"What did he say," Sammy said, sardonically. "Until he feels I've learned to respect him. Which is bullshit because I bought that phone and pay the bill."

"Oh, I didn't know you bought that phone yourself."

"I told you, I buy everything," Sammy said, taking another sip of lemonade.

"I know, but I just figured . . . I know how expensive those phones are."

"Tell me about it. It took me forever to save up for it." Sammy exhaled loudly. "So, my dad took my phone, and I'm grounded today. My dad didn't believe me that I was coming over here to cut your grass, but my mom did. She convinced him to let me come over once the heat died down. So, don't be surprised if my dad calls your grandmother to make sure I cut the grass."

"I'll let her know."

"Thanks," Sammy said.

"What did you talk back to your dad about?"

His face turned bright red; it made her shudder. It brought her back to last night when she thought he looked like he was covered in blood.

"Stupid stuff. So, any action at Pastor Leeds's house?" Sammy asked, changing the subject.

"Nope."

"So, I did a thing."

Ivy lifted a skeptical eyebrow. She didn't like his grin, it made him look cruel. "A thing?"

"I asked Pastor Leeds if we could clean out his attic."

"You—what?!"

"Well, not specifically the attic—his house. Which just so happens to include his elusive attic. It just all fell into place, you know?"

She shook her head. "No, I don't know."

"When Pastor Leeds was complaining about all the stuff he had to go through, it gave me an idea. So, I got permission from my dad to call him this morning and asked if we could help him go through all the stuff in his house as a youth group thing and have a community yard sale to raise money for the church at the end of summer."

"Uh . . ."

"It's perfect, Teller. The community yard sale kills two birds with one stone. It'll get us into Pastor Leeds's attic and me back in my dad's good graces."

"And get you more time with Elsa," Ivy added.

"Yeah, I guess that too," Sammy said. "Better make that three birds!"

"Yeah, three birds with one stone. Yippie," Ivy mumbled, her cheeks warming with embarrassment. She knew Grams was wrong about Sammy liking her.

"Uh, so how exactly is cleaning out a bunch of junk going to help you out with your dad?"

"Community service has always been my penance for talking back."

"Really?"

"Yep, gotta make amends somehow," Sammy chuckled. "My dad's right; it will look great on my applications for college. All my talking back is my ticket into an Ivy League school."

Ivy smiled; she was glad he was back to his old self. "Yeah, I would say so."

"But anyways, Pastor Leeds is on board. Those who can are going to meet at his house for Saturday morning youth group. That gives us plenty of time to clean out the rectory before our big end-of-summer event."

"Sounds like you've got it all planned out," Ivy said, impressed.

"Nope, not all of it. I'm at the pool all day tomorrow. You should see if you can get Grams to drop you off so we can make a plan of attack for the attic. The other youth group members will be there Saturday, but we want to be the ones to get to the attic first."

"I think we're going shopping tomorrow," Ivy said, lying through her teeth. The pool all day—she didn't think she could survive, even if she wanted to go, which part of her did.

"Like I said, I'm there all day. We're short-staffed. So, whenever you get back from shopping, maybe?"

Ivy glanced at the Mercedes pulling into the driveway. It was Mayor Jeffrey Lopez.

"Hello Ivy," he said, getting out of his car. She had briefly met him the night Zac went missing, she hadn't realized then how much Sammy looked like his father, besides the eyes. Jeffrey was dark while Sammy was light.

"Hello Mr. Lopez."

"Hi Sammy."

"Dad," Sammy said drawn out, folding his arms over his chest, looking very much like a brat.

Mary came out to the porch. She was all sunshine and flowers as she talked to Sammy's father, batting eyelashes, and showing off her new smile that had been the cause of her not making it to youth group to pick up Ivy. She placed a warm hand on Sammy's shoulder. "Your son is such a good kid. I wish they were all like him."

Ivy was sure she made a face. It was like someone swapped out her grandmother. Maybe aliens *were* afoot in Pleasant Mills, flashing red lights into windows in the middle of the night and kidnaping mean old ladies.

"Glad to hear it," Jeffrey said, glancing at his son.

"He said he would cut my grass for the rest of the summer," Mary added.

Ivy smiled; there she was—Grams wasn't abducted by aliens.

Sammy shrugged when Mary's light touch became a hard squeeze. "Yep, the rest of the summer." The squeeze intensified. "The rest of my life."

"Good. Glad to see he's serving the community, especially our senior citizens."

"Who you callin' a senior citizen," Mary mumbled under her breath.

"Grass looks good Sammy." Jeffrey said, pretending he didn't hear Mary.

"Thanks Dad."

"And he did Pastor Leeds's yesterday," Ivy added, hoping that would help him out with his dad.

Jeffrey's eyes cut to Pastor Leeds's yard. "He did? I didn't know that."

"Trying to do good works Dad. I don't have to advertise them all, Mom wouldn't like that."

"Right you are." Jeffrey turned to Mary. "It was nice seeing you. I hope you and Ivy have a good night. I just came by to pick up Sammy. We want him home early tonight."

Sammy shot Ivy a look. It seemed to be more than a 'I told you I was punished' look, but she wasn't sure what it implied.

"See you Saturday at youth group, if you can't make it to the pool," he whispered as he got up.

Grams and Ivy sat on the porch and watched them pull out of the driveway. Sammy's smile was long gone as he sat in the front passenger seat with his arms still defiantly crossed over his chest, a thing Ivy knew wasn't going to win him any points with his father. He seemed like he was on his way to being grounded for life; his only outing doomed to be cutting their front yard.

"That Mayor Lopez is such a slimeball," Grams blurted out, watching the Mercedes go down the quiet street.

Ivy guessed Jeffrey Lopez did have a slimy look to him, if by slimy Grams meant that he could talk you into driving a brand-new convertible off the car lot when you came for an economy wagon to cart your kids around in.

Sammy had that same kind of sliminess to him. It was his face, Ivy decided. No one that pretty could be trusted. Sammy got it from his dad. Whether Sammy liked it or not he was a product of his father. The good, bad, and the very good looking. All but those eyes. His light-blue, dreamy eyes he got from his mother.

Ivy had witnessed Sammy's pull firsthand. It was hard to say no to him. He could probably talk the panties off a nun. But Ivy was okay with his charm; she liked his guts and confidence. It was becoming on him as it was on his dad. Sammy had the same sort of presence that his father had. He demanded attention just by standing there. She could see why Uriah Leeds coming into town ruffled his prize-winning feathers so much.

"Really, Grams, because you just acted like Mr. Lopez is the best thing since sliced bread."

"That was for Sammy's benefit."

"Sammy? You've called him by his name twice now. Does that mean you like him?" Ivy asked, surprised.

"He's growing on me, like a wart. What was he gabbing on about, something about making it to the pool?"

"Sammy wants me to stop by the community pool tomorrow to talk about the youth group yard sale he's organizing."

"You going?"

"I can't Grams."

"Why's that? Last time I checked you have no job, and you sleep till noon."

Ivy rocked herself back. "That's an exaggeration; I was up early today," she said, knowing she was only up early because Sammy said he was coming over.

"Don't dodge the question."

"I can't wear a bathing suit in front of him."

"You can wear a cover up. They're a lot cuter than the ones from my day. A lot of girls wear them now, even skinny minnies."

"I don't have a suit that fits."

"Well," Grams said, pulling her car keys out of her pants pocket. "Let's get you one."

"What about dinner?"

"The chicken needs time to defrost. It'll be ready by the time we get home."

CHAPTER FOURTEEN
Swimsuit Shopping

Ivy got into her grandmother's station wagon and rolled down her window. They were going to the mall to find her a swimsuit come Hell or high waters. Ivy was glad her grandmother was taking her. The truth was she really did want to see Sammy, and she didn't know if she could wait until Saturday.

The mall was about thirty minutes away and the whole time Ivy's thoughts were on Sammy. On that look he gave her right before he left.

"Grams, what do you know about Mayor Lopez?" Ivy asked, looking out the window to the dark woods, her hair whipping around her face.

"He's been Mayor forever. Everyone likes him. I guess I do too. I always vote for him. His wife is always very nice, and his kids are always polite, minus that Sammy."

"Grams, you are the most inconsistent person I've ever met. I thought you didn't like him?"

"I do. Kind of. Just sometimes he seems too perfect; rubs a seasoned woman like me wrong, depending on what side of the bed I wake up on."

"Looks can be deceiving," Ivy said, thinking of Sammy. He looked like a brat, even acted like one, but he worked hard for his fancy phone and clothing.

"What's Mr. Lopez's day job?" Ivy asked.

"He's a financial mind. Makes big bucks trading stocks and doing banking or something like that. The Lopez family live in a castle about two miles from the house."

"A castle? So he *is* a prince."

Mary parked the station wagon in a handicap parking spot, hanging her handicap tag off the rearview mirror. "Not a literal castle. There's no such thing as a happy ending in Pleasant Mills."

"Wow way to be a downer, Grams."

"I meant because things never end here. Now let's go find you a swimsuit."

"Grams, I look like a pregnant whale," Ivy said through the dressing room door of Macy's. She held her breath and puffed out her cheeks.

"Stop it. I'm sure you don't."

"I do! My belly is bigger than my boobs. I look horrible!"

Mary tossed a couple of swimsuits over the dressing room door. "Try on one of these suits with preformed cups. Give those puppies a little shape."

"Better," she said. "But now I have torpedo boobs."

"Better than whale blubber, Ives!"

"Thanks, Grams," she mumbled under her breath, putting her hands on her torpedo boobs and turning to view her side profile. The preformed cups were just what this teenager needed. Her padded chest stuck out more than her belly now. "This could work Grams, but I still need a cover up to wear over it."

After hours of trying on bathing suits, Ivy went with a solid black suit. She found a cute pair of boy shorts with a black and white hibiscus pattern to match. And to complete the ensemble, an off the shoulder crop top in black. Ivy thought she looked cute. "I could go to the pool in this," she said to herself, looking in the cloudy mirror in the dressing room.

CHAPTER FIFTEEN
Titan Tires

"**M**aybe you could've waited another millennium to get your tires changed if you didn't hit potholes like you just robbed a bank," Ivy said to her grandmother the next morning.

Ivy held onto her seat for dear life as her grandmother drove at warp speed down a long and winding pothole riddled driveway to Titan Tires.

On the way home from the mall, they'd gotten a flat tire. After a lot of effort on their part, Ivy and Mary were able to get a donut on and make it home but the donut wasn't going to cut it—they needed new tires.

Mary Teller thought tires should cost what they had cost the last time she'd taken the old station wagon in for a tire change. She was shocked at the price of four new tires and called around until she found the cheapest tires South Jersey had to offer. Titan Tires hit the mark and just so happened to have a morning appointment available.

As they pulled up to the small blue mechanic's garage, Ivy looked up at a large, weathered sign on the roof that displayed three winged-devils looming over a tire. "Probably would get more business if their logo wasn't so creepy," Ivy pointed out.

"Better for us," Grams said. "Now come. If we're going to get to the pool, we've got to make this snappy."

"The only snapping around here are your arthritic bones," Ivy said, slamming her door shut.

PLEASANT MILLS, NEW JERSEY: TITAN TIRES

Mary set her jaw and stared daggers at Ivy, but Ivy acted like she didn't notice and held the door open for her grandmother. They were pleasantly surprised by the interior of Titan Tires. The outside looked sketchy. It was the kind of place one would expect to find illegal activity at large with its piles of tires and scrap metal, but the inside looked like a respectable business. In the corner there was a fancy coffee machine and there was even a basket of treats set out for patrons to snack on while their cars got fixed.

A tall middle-aged man came into the waiting room from a back door. "Hello ladies."

Mary leaned on the counter. "Hello Daniel," Mary said, reading his name tag and batting her eyes at the attractive mechanic.

"Please, call me Danny," he said with a large grin. "What can I do for you today? Let me guess—tires?" he laughed.

"Hysterical," Ivy mumbled under her breath.

"Yes, I think I spoke to you on the phone earlier; Mary Teller."

"Oh yes! Mary, nice to meet you," Danny said, shaking her hand. "Got just the tires for you." He looked out the window at the white station wagon. "Should be done within thirty minutes."

"Great," Grams said.

"You ladies have a seat and help yourself to some snacks. Ivy, would you prefer a water or soda pop?"

"Water would be great."

Danny pulled a water bottle out of a refrigerator behind the counter and handed it to her. "Here, take a calendar and almanac too," he said, sliding it over the counter to her.

"Thanks."

Ivy sat down on one of the very stylish black chairs with chrome legs in the waiting area, trying to recall if her grandmother had said her name. She shrugged it off, figuring she'd mentioned her when they talked on the phone.

Ivy looked through the almanac as Mary helped herself to coffee and a bag of Grandma's Cookies.

"Yours don't taste like that," Ivy teased as Mary took a bite.

"Children are meant to be seen not heard," she hissed as she reached for another bag of cookies.

Ivy went back to the almanac. She looked for today's date:

Today will bring smiles and tears. When kind words save you money, smile. When cruel jokes make you sad, shed tears. But don't let tears drown out the light, for tomorrow the sun will shine bright.

"Great," Ivy said, closing the book on her twisted fortune.

Danny came through the back door, wiping his hands on a rag. Ivy looked at her cell phone. Exactly thirty minutes had passed. "Now that's service," she whispered to her grandmother.

"All done," Danny said with a smile. "Fixed the air conditioning for you too, Mary. I hope you don't mind."

"You did?!" Ivy asked excited, practically jumping to her feet.

"Sure did. You guys had a small hole in the hose, plugged it up. Should do the trick, but the station wagon really needs some good maintenance."

"I know," Mary said. "I've been putting it off."

"Yeah, for a millennium," Ivy scoffed.

Mary shot her granddaughter a nasty look.

"Well, you're in luck. We do more than tires here. If you ever need work done, just call. Number's on the calendar."

Mary was back to leaning on the counter, batting her eyes at Danny as he rang her up. "Do you give a senior discount, Danny?"

"Grams, you ate your discount in cookies," Ivy hissed.

Mary elbowed her granddaughter.

Mary smiled at Danny, showing off her new teeth.

"I don't think you're old enough to qualify for a senior discount, but I do give a discount to pretty ladies with great smiles."

Ivy thought she was going to barf as her grandmother laughed into her hand. *Smiles, when kind words save you money . . .* got that right," Ivy muttered.

"Oh my gosh, Grams, he's like half your age," Ivy said to her grandmother as they walked out the door.

"I do like a man that works with his hands."

"Me too Grams but come on! You know that was just a senior discount because you're old. Danny was only being nice because he wants to work on this hunk of junk," Ivy said, opening the passenger side door.

"Poppycock, that was a discount for being an attractive woman."

"That's so sexist. Way to bring women's rights back a generation."

Ivy looked at Danny through the clean windshield window. Apparently, he also gave Grams a freebee carwash.

"Well," Grams said with a smile as she turned on the air conditioner. "It looks like I may be seeing Danny for a tune-up in the near future."

"Ew, Grams. He meant the station wagon, not you."

For a middle-aged man, Danny was attractive; she would give Grams that much. He was in shape and had a nice face and all his hair. But the thought of her grandmother and Danny the tire guy swapping more than a business card made her feel nauseous.

"You never know," Mary said, looking at her smile in the rearview mirror.

"Either way, I'm staying home for that one."

CHAPTER SIXTEEN
Poor Richard's Community Pool

Mary was planning on dropping Ivy off at the pool and heading home to watch daytime television but decided to stay and enjoy the pool herself. Ivy wasn't thrilled about it, but her grandmother said she wanted to do some exercises for her bad knee, and she just so happened to have brought her swimsuit along. Ivy couldn't tell her to go home when she wanted to do something healthy for a change.

Ivy and Grams walked through the pool gate, looking up at the lifeguard tower to see Sammy. She blushed all shades of red, the little butterflies in her stomach swarming around like a hive of angry wasps. She knew it was the sting of unattainable love. He had his shirt off and his red swim shorts were on the shorter side, shorter yet thanks to them being stuck to the hot wooden seat. Ivy could see his tan line. "I'm starting to like the color red," she muttered to herself.

Sammy Lopez may have only been sixteen, but his body was mature for his age; not what you would expect from a church kid going into his junior year of high school. To Ivy, Sammy looked like a sun-kissed Spanish deity sitting on top of his lifeguard tower keeping a watchful eye over Poor Richard's Community Pool—his kingdom.

"Forget about all that hocus-pocus nonsense, who would've thought Pleasant Mills has their very own Spanish god," Ivy said, forgetting Grams was there.

Just like that Sammy went from being a prince to a god. She checked her face for drool, she couldn't believe she ever liked Pastor Leeds, Sammy seemed so high above him, and it had nothing to do with the lifeguard tower and everything with the sun wrapping him in an uncanny glow making him look every bit a god.

"What?" Grams said, wiggling her ear.

"Nothing Grams."

Sammy spotted Ivy and waved as she came through the gate. He flashed her a smile. It was different than his many grins, it was as if he was happy to see her. She could feel the pangs of lust in her stomach. The wasps were in a frenzy now. She hoped she wouldn't go into anaphylactic shock. But reasoned, that wouldn't be so bad, Sammy would have to give her mouth to mouth.

"Well, go over to him," Grams said, taking a seat on a lounge chair.

"Okay Grams."

Ivy took a deep breath, steadying her nerves, and walked toward the pool. The laughter of children playing in the water felt deafening, like everything around her was at maximum volume. She felt like everyone was looking at her—laughing at her. Her eyes darted around, making her dizzy. She felt like her footsteps shook the earth as she walked. She finally made it to Sammy, the background noise fading.

Sammy smiled down at her for a second before returning his eyes to the pool. "Glad you could make it. Perfect timing, I've got lunch in ten minutes."

Ivy was glad Sammy looked away. She could gaze at him now without him realizing she was staring. Ivy was engrossed with his face, the way his blue eyes matched the water, the way his dark hair twisted in waves around his tan face. Her eyes slowly worked their way down his firm chest and abs until they fixated on his hands that were resting between his legs. She checked her mouth again to make sure she wasn't drooling.

"How long is your lunch break?" Ivy asked.

"Forty-five minutes. So, we should be able to get some good planning done."

Mike came walking over to the tower. He was wearing a white T-shirt and lifeguard shorts. She guessed Mike was Sammy's lunch relief.

"Hey, Mike," Ivy said.

"Hey back," he said, his green cat eyes like slits. She got the distinct feeling Mike didn't like her, which was fine, she *didn't* like him.

"Well, I'm gonna go work on my tan until your break," Ivy said to Sammy, turning back in the direction of her grandmother.

"There should be a law against fat people wearing shorts," Ivy overheard Mike say to Sammy.

Her heart burned like the worst case of acid reflux in the history of the world when she heard Sammy laugh. She thought of her fortune in the Titan Tires almanac: *When cruel jokes make you sad, shed tears.* She didn't have to be told. They came. And they were plentiful, and they were hot, streaming down her face. She quickly made her way to where her grandmother was sunbathing, reading a tabloid magazine.

She pawed at her tears. "I want to leave now Grams!"

"We just got here," Mary said, taking off her oversized sunglasses to see her granddaughter's flushed complexion.

"I want to leave NOW, please Grams," Ivy pleaded as new tears made their way down her cheeks.

"What happened?" Grams asked, getting up as quickly as she could. Her bad knee was acting up again.

They made it to the car. As soon as the passenger side door closed, the floodgates opened, the waterworks becoming rapids interrupted with fits of hiccupping sobs.

Sammy came running up to the car with his perfect tan body, and knocked on Grams's window as they were about to pull out.

"Where you going?" Sammy asked.

"Family emergency," Grams said, putting her foot on the gas.

Sammy saw Ivy crying. "Shit, she must've heard Mike," he muttered, heat rushing up his neck to his face.

Sammy made his way back to the lifeguard tower, his hands like wrecking balls at his sides. "You're messed up Mike! Ivy heard you!"

"So what."

"*So what*?! She left crying."

"Trust me, she did her community service for the day by leaving."

Sammy wanted to rip Mike off the lifeguard tower and throw him in the pool. It wouldn't have been very Christian of him, but he was not feeling very compassionate toward thy neighbor at the moment.

"What's with you?!"

Mike's complexion pinkened to a few shades lighter than his red, curly hair. "Nothing's with me. You're the one who keeps dissing me to hang out with her."

"You're stupid," Sammy snickered, heading on his lunch break.

Sammy hung over his Italian hoagie, feeling sorry for himself. He had been hoping all morning that Ivy would finish her shopping and have a chance to stop by the community pool. He could have been eating with her, but instead he was eating alone.

He threw his hoagie down; he was too disgusted with himself to eat. He knew he should have stuck up for Ivy when Mike made fun of her. He didn't, he laughed, which was the same thing as making fun of her himself.

Sammy balled his fists, his self-pity turning to anger. He was such a chicken. He thought Ivy looked cute in her bathing suit. He liked her shorts. He liked that they were short. In fact, he would've liked them a little shorter. Sammy wished he would've told Ivy she looked good before Mike came to the lifeguard tower, but when it came to Ivy, his confidence failed him.

Jeffrey waited in his car for Sammy to get off work. "How was the pool?" he asked as Sammy opened the passenger side door.

He buckled up. "Good."

"How's your planning for the community yard sale going?"

"Good, got a lot done at lunch."

"Good," Jeffrey said, pulling out of the parking lot.

"Can I have my phone back?"

"No. I thought I made it clear at breakfast you weren't getting it back until Saturday."

Sammy let out a sigh. "I really need it Dad."

"You're sixteen. You don't really need anything."

"I need it to apologize to someone."

"Who?" Jeffrey asked, his eyes darting to his son before going back on the road.

"Ivy."

"For what?"

"I don't want to talk to you about it."

"Well, then you don't get your phone back," Jeffrey said matter-of-factly.

"Fine," Sammy said, leaning his head against the window.

Out of the corner of his eye, Jeffrey surveyed his son, noticing his flushed cheeks. He almost gave in, that was until Sammy got mouthy.

"I must have the worst dad in the entire town," Sammy mumbled under his breath, just loud enough for his father to hear.

"Sammy," Jeffrey said in a stern voice, trying to control his temper. "You just earned yourself another week without a phone."

"Makes no difference, we both know you were never giving it back."

"Now you're grounded till the weekend . . . So help me."

Sammy bit his tongue. He couldn't wait to get out of the car.

As soon as they pulled in the driveway, Sammy unbuckled as fast as he could and slammed the car door. He ran to the front door and darted up the stairs to his bedroom.

"What happened?" Lindsey Lopez asked her husband when she heard Sammy slam his bedroom door from the foyer.

"That kid just doesn't know when to quit. He's grounded till the weekend and no phone for two weeks."

Lindsey put her hand on her husband's shoulder to calm him. "Okay, he's grounded. I'm sure he understands, honey."

Jeffrey exhaled slowly. It took everything in him not to walk up the stairs and make sure Sammy knew to keep his mouth shut.

CHAPTER SEVENTEEN
The Spell Book

Sammy sneaked out of his house in the middle of the night and made his way to Ivy's. He was hoping Ivy would be watching her window at midnight and would see him outside. He wanted to apologize to her, or at least make sure they were still cool.

Sammy stood in front of Pastor Leeds's house and looked up at Ivy's window. Her light was off. He was sure she was listening to her music. He put his hands in his jean pockets. It was a cool night, the wind swept through the willow tree in the front yard, swaying its branches to and fro. It was dark. Most of the moon was tucked behind clouds. He sighed in disappointment, there was no way she would see him.

At midnight the red light radiated out over the street drawing Sammy's attention high above him to Pastor Leeds's attic window. He stood mesmerized by the red light and the rhythmic humming.

A tap on his shoulder, snapped him out of his trance. "Ivy," he said, a little startled, but relieved—happy. The red light vanished taking the sound with it, the minute spent.

"I forgot to give this to you the other night," Ivy said, shoving the windbreaker he'd left in her room into his hands.

"Thanks. Good news, I've got Saturday all planned out. Did it on my lunch break."

"That's good," Ivy said, walking back toward her house.

Sammy put on his jacket. "Hey, where are you going?"

"Home, just wanted to give you your windbreaker before Grams found it." Ivy popped her ear buds in and blasted her music.

Sammy smelled the same sweet, smoky scent he'd smelled earlier that week in Pastor Leeds's house. It brought him right back to the Jersey Devils sweatshirt that reminded him of Zac's. He inhaled the familiar smell. Then he heard a low-pitched tune being whistled, it was rhythmic and mesmerizing like the combination of the red light and strange, yet-familiar sound. It traveled through the rustling leaves of the old weeping willow tree like a voice carrying on its breath a sweet, smoky scent. The tune was both beautiful and sad. Sammy turned around to see where it was coming from. The tune seemed to spread over the yard in all directions, haunting the lawn with its melancholy song. Sammy scanned the darkness. The whistling stopped and was replaced with the roar of a car engine. He could just make out a bright-red Mustang up the street. It had its headlights off and was swerving on the road toward Ivy. She was oblivious to it as she bobbed her head to her music.

Sammy ran toward her. "Ivy watch out!"

Ivy stepped into the street only to find herself being yanked back by Sammy. He sent her crashing down on Pastor Leeds's front lawn just in time. Ivy saw the souped-up Mustang whizz by, just missing her and taking out Pastor Leeds's mailbox and recycling cans.

Sammy threw an empty water bottle at the car as it sped away. "Jerk-off!" Sammy, leaning over Ivy, offered her his hand. "You okay?"

Ivy turned off her music. Her heart was beating so fast she couldn't catch her breath. Her mind was racing to catch up with what had just happened. She could hear the screeching of the tires echoing in her ears and smell the burned rubber of the tires on the pavement.

Ivy took Sammy's hand, and he helped pull her to her feet.

"I didn't hurt you, did I?"

"No . . . you just saved my life."

Sammy looked down the dark street in the direction the Mustang went. "Yeah, I think so."

"Thanks," Ivy said.

"You're welcome. I couldn't get the jerk's license plate number, but that guy was definitely drunk."

Sammy picked up Pastor Leeds's recycling cans while Ivy stood in shock. "Looks like Pastor Leeds is gonna need a new mailbox."

Sammy picked up a package off the sidewalk. "Hey Teller, check this out." Ivy walked over to him, still shaken. Sammy went to open the package addressed to Pastor Steelman.

"What are you doing?" Ivy asked.

"I'm opening it."

"It's a federal offense to open someone else's mail."

"She's dead, not like she can open it."

"I guess you're right," Ivy said, rubbing her arms anxiously.

Sammy noticed Ivy was still trembling from the incident with the car. "Come on, let's go sit on your porch before another car comes flying by."

Sammy tucked the package under his arm and took Ivy's hand to walk her across the street. They walked hand in hand up the old porch steps of Mary Teller's house. The wasps in Ivy's stomach were back. They fluttered around letting her know how much she liked Sammy. Sammy let go of his grip on Ivy's hand as he took a seat on the two-seater bench on the porch. Ivy sat down next to him. She watched Sammy carefully pull the tab releasing the package. His face was illuminated by the moon which momentarily poked through the clouds.

"This is nuts."

"What is it?" Ivy asked, looking down at a large book with a dark leather binding. "And if you say a book, I'm going to hit you."

"This is hocus-pocus. I know it. A drunk driver almost mowed you over, knocks over Pastor Leeds's mailbox, all so we can find this—"

"What is this?" Her lips pursed to a straight line.

"A package meant for Pastor Steelman who's been dead just over two months."

"Sammy, what is it?!" Ivy asked, frustrated.

"It's a grimoire."

Her eyes went cockeye. "A what?"

He moved in closer to her, their legs now touching. The wasps started to swarm again. Sammy placed the old book on their laps and opened it. "It's a family spell book. You know, spells. As in witches, as in people who were persecuted because they were *different* according to you," he said, poking her side.

"I already told you there's no such thing as real-life witches. But uh, how do you know so much about this stuff?"

"My grandmother is a witch."

Ivy smothered a laugh with her hand. "Like, flying on a broom witch?"

He smiled. "She doesn't fly on a broom, but yeah, that kind of witch."

"Um, okay, sure whatever you say," she said, thinking he was lucky he was cute because he was clearly mentally unstable.

"Look," Sammy said, tapping on the inside cover of the worn leather book to read: Leeds Family.

"If it's a Leeds family spell book, why would someone mail it to Pastor Steelman?"

"I don't know, but that's a good question," Sammy said with excitement.

"Whose it from?" Ivy asked.

Sammy checked the package. "It just says Baker. No return address or anything else—just Baker." His attention was back on the spell book, thumbing through it. "It's so dark out here. Grams really needs to replace some of these bulbs. You've got your phone? Shine some light on the pages."

"It's in my room."

"Shall we?" he asked, his eyebrows resembling flying seagulls.

"Something tells me you're not going to take no for an answer."

He grinned, that sideways grin of his. She was powerless against it.

Sammy followed Ivy to her bedroom. She turned on her small desk lamp. He placed the spell book on her desk, and she noticed what looked to be three dragons carved into the leather binding. It made her think of the creepy logo from Titan Tires. He flipped through the pages. "This is awesome!"

"You think it's real?" Ivy asked.

"I do. Smell this book. It's really old."

"Yeah, it's musty." Ivy said, not sure if that proved it was old.

"I mean the first entry is from 1690! I think this thing is the real deal!"

Ivy had to admit to herself 1690 was old—really old.

"Check out some of these spells: *Revenge Spell, Chocolate, Protection Amulet, Beauty Spell, Cherry Pie, Sleep Spell.*" Sammy inclined his face to Ivy, his eyes catching the light from the lamp. "I guess it's a spell book and a cookbook. Both take ingredients . . . I just never put them in the same category, but it makes sense."

"You really think they work?" Ivy asked.

"Only one way to find out," he said with a devilish smile that made her think of the creepy portrait of Japhet Dean Leeds that looked like his father. "Let's try one."

Ivy pointed to the *Beauty Spell.*

"On whom?"

"On me."

"You're fine the way you are," he said dismissively, turning the page. "*The Laughter Spell*—This sounds like a good first spell to try out."

"*Laughter Spell?*" Really?"

His eyes went to her. "What?! We're new witches; we need to start out easy."

She chuckled. "We're witches now? —Wait you're right, I just laughed."

Sammy rolled his eyes, reading the spell out loud:

"Laugh your ways to happy times,
forget all of your past crimes,
as you mix a frog's tongue
with the hair of an old one.

Together in a bowl,
Swirl, mix, shake, and stir.

Add a pinch of green mold,
as together you take hold,
hand in hand,
as you say
let laughter come,
let laughter stay,
forever laughing on this day."

"Easy enough," Sammy said. "Only three ingredients."

"A frog's tongue?!" Ivy said, grossed out. "Where the heck are you going to get a frog's tongue at?"

"You get some of Grams's hair and let me worry about the frog's tongue. There're tons of frogs at my house. They hang out in my dad's Koi pond and sometimes a few get confused and hop into the pool and drown. Green mold is easy too, I can get that from the pond."

"Oh," Ivy said surprised and grossed out. "I guess we do have all the ingredients."

"We do!" Sammy said excited. "Come to my house tomorrow, and we'll try it."

"I don't know," Ivy said wearily, rubbing her arms nervously again.

"Come on."

"I don't think we should Sammy."

"How about twelve? My mom's a great cook. She would be thrilled if you came for lunch."

Ivy hesitated, "Sammy . . ."

"Remember, I don't have my phone, so just be there for noon." He took a pen out of the coffee mug on her desk and wrote his address on her calendar from Titan Tires that hung on the back of her bedroom door. "I'm going to tell my mother you're coming, so you have to come."

"Fine."

"Good," he said with a big grin. Sammy grabbed the spell book off Ivy's desk. "I should sneak on home before it gets too late."

Ivy walked Sammy to the front door. Sammy whispered as not to wake Grams up: "Almost forgot, bring that cute swimsuit you were wearing at the pool. We can go swimming after we're done spell casting."

Sammy couldn't bring himself to apologize to Ivy directly. He wanted to, but he just couldn't. He guessed he got that from his father. Sammy hoped his comment about Ivy's cute swimwear let her know he didn't share Mike's opinion.

Ivy's heart jumped, the swarm in her stomach alive with angst. "Okay."

CHAPTER EIGHTEEN
Lunch at Lopez Castle

Mary Teller agreed to drop Ivy off at Sammy's house for the afternoon so they could work on their youth group project. The Lopez house was set far back in the woods and wasn't visible from the street. As they pulled up to the front gate of the Lopez estate Ivy's mouth dropped. "You weren't kidding, Grams, this place is like a castle." The house had different elevations and rooflines and it was made from dark stone that made Ivy think of fairy tales.

Ivy took notice of the cameras as they drove through the ornate iron gates adorned with laurel leaves and the letter 'L' down the long, paved driveway. She wondered how Sammy was able to sneak out of *Fort Knox*.

Grams walked Ivy to the front door. Ivy knew her grandmother was not the polite kind of grandmother that baked cookies and knitted sweaters. Her grandmother was walking her up to the front door of the Lopez mansion because she was as nosey as they came and wanted to get a good look inside the house. She was just masking her nosiness with piety and manners. Church had taught Mary Teller a few things after all. She even wore a nice pantsuit—her Sunday best.

"Keeping up with the Jones's, Grams?" Ivy teased as she eyed her grandmother's very snazzy peach outfit.

"It is important for a seasoned woman to always look her best, my dear."

Ivy had to laugh at that. "Who you fooling, Grams?"

Ivy rang the doorbell. Mrs. Lopez answered the door. Ivy had only glanced at her at church before Sammy had distracted her with his ramblings of dead pastors and curses. Now that Ivy had a good look at Lindsey Lopez, she saw how beautiful she really was. Lindsey was tall and thin. Her figure reminded Ivy of a runway model. Her perfect body was completed with natural light-blonde hair and blue eyes. She had on pink high heels and a light sun dress that emphasized her impressive cleavage. *Father like son*, Ivy thought to herself, taking notice of the similarities between Mrs. Lopez and Elsa Tilton.

Lindsey greeted Ivy with a hug. "You must be Ivy!"

Ivy was surprised by Mrs. Lopez's thick Spanish accent. Sammy had told her the real Spanish roots had come from his mother and Lopez was just the last name his father had taken, but hearing Mrs. Lopez's accent thew her off. She looked less Spanish to her than Mr. Lopez.

"It's so nice to get the kids together to work on the community yard sale. Jeffrey is really happy with Sammy," Lindsey said to Mary at the door.

"Yep, sure is good to see the youngsters doing more. Sammy did a nice job on my grass. He's a great kid."

Lindsey's face lit up with mention of her son. "Mary, please stay for lunch. I made plenty."

"I couldn't intrude," Mary said, batting her eyes.

"Please, it's no trouble. I insist. I always make too much. I wanted to be a chef before I got married. I love to cook. Jeffrey and Sammy are never home, and my girls only eat macaroni and cheese."

"Well, if you insist," Grams said with a smile.

Lindsey beamed. "I do."

Ivy shot her grandmother an incredulous look before they followed Mrs. Lopez into the house. Ivy's eyes danced around at the splendor of the Lopez home, moving quickly over the marble floors, large paintings, and the impressive spiral staircase.

"Wow," Grams said when they entered the Lopez kitchen. "You really did go all out!" Mary's eyes were as large as golf balls as she took in the banquet provided by Mrs. Lopez. Grams had to take out her handkerchief and wipe the drool. "Grandmother like granddaughter," Ivy muttered to herself.

There were sandwiches, wraps, and salads. Not to mention hot pasta trays, dessert platters, and a fruit platter. It looked like Lindsey was having a large lunch party for her posh friends, not hosting a teenager and her grandmother.

"See, I told you I made too much."

Sammy made his way into the kitchen. Seeing Ivy, a huge smile spread across his face. "Glad you came!"

"You didn't give me much of a choice, if you remember," she whispered to him with a harsh nudge. "Your mother has a lunch spread like it's a wedding."

"Told you she's a good cook."

"I wasn't sure what you like, Ivy," Lindsey said, handing her a plate. "So, I made a little of everything. Let me know what you prefer and next time I will cater more to your taste."

"Thank you, Mrs. Lopez."

"Please Ivy, call me Lindsey."

Two little girls popped their heads into the kitchen.

"You can come in," Sammy said to his little sisters. They bashfully walked into the kitchen wearing matching light-pink bikinis with their blonde hair tied back in piggy tails.

"These are my twin sisters, Alba and Maria."

"Sissies, this is Ivy and Grams."

Ivy smiled at the two identical girls looking at her. "You two are so adorable."

They smiled. "Thank you, Ivy," they said at the same time.

"Stop being creepy," Sammy hissed. "When they talk at the same time like that, they freak me out."

"How on earth do they tell you two apart?" Ivy asked the twins.

"I was born two minutes before Maria," Alba said. "And I'm taller."

"Oh, I see," Ivy said, examining the girls standing side by side. She didn't see it, but she would have to take Alba's word for it."

"How old are you both?" Ivy asked.

"Six," said Alba.

"And a half," said Maria.

"Are you going to go swimming, Ivy?" They asked in unison.

Sammy groaned. "Being creepy."

"I think . . . maybe later," Ivy replied.

"First, you two need to eat," Lindsey said as she put two bowls of macaroni and cheese on the table. "They are so picky. They will only eat Kraft macaroni and cheese and only the one in the shape of shells. They wouldn't even give my homemade macaroni and cheese a try," Lindsey said with a pout.

"I love your homemade mac, Mom," Sammy said.

Lindsey kissed Sammy's forehead. "You're a good boy, I never had this problem with you. I hope your sisters outgrow this Kraft thing soon."

"Don't got to worry 'bout us, right Ives?" Grams said. "We eat everything."

Ivy flashed her grandmother a disbelieving look as if to say: Great Grams, tell the whole Lopez family I'm a hog.

"Ivy and I are gonna eat while we work," Sammy said as he made a plate of food to take outside. Sammy kissed his mother's cheek. "Thanks Mom, you're the best."

Ivy wanted everything, but she didn't want to come off like a Teller hog. She took two different sandwiches and some macaroni salad. She thought she should at least look like she was kind of health conscious and speared a couple of pineapple slices onto her plate along with some melon balls.

"You two have fun with your planning, us ladies will just be in here gossiping," Lindsey said with a smile. Lindsey took a seat next to Mary at the kitchen island. "It's so nice to see Sammy making friends."

Grams was already on her second egg salad wrap. "I thought he had lots of friends."

"He has a handful of boys he's friendly with from church." Lindsey chuckled. "But I was talking about meeting wholesome girls like Ivy."

"Oh," Mary said, understanding what Lindsey was getting at. "Well, you're not gonna find a better girl than my Ivy." Mary tried some of Lindsey's potato salad. "Lindsey, you really are a great cook!"

"Thank you. You're too kind."

"Do you cater?"

"No. I just cook for the family and coffee hour for church."

"Wow, that's all you?!"

Lindsey smiled in confirmation.

"I've got to tell you, if I knew about coffee hour, I would've started going to church years ago. I've got to get your recipe for those sticky buns."

"Your mom's very nice," Ivy said, taking a seat at an umbrella-covered patio table.

"My mom is awesome. The best mom ever."

Ivy enjoyed a fork full of macaroni salad. "Your sisters are cute."

"Cute and annoying, but usually just cute," he said with a smile.

Ivy saw a binder on the table. It was neatly labeled: Community Yard Sale Plans.

"How are the plans?"

Sammy took a bite of his sandwich. "They're done. Just an excuse to have you over."

Ivy's cheeks reddened.

"Not that I need an excuse, it's just that I'm groun— "

Ivy cut him off. "You don't have to explain yourself. You don't want people to think you're friends with the new fat girl. It's not good for your image; I get it."

"That's not it."

Ivy got up proudly. "This fat girl is getting another sandwich."

Ivy helped herself to an Italian sub wrap and some coleslaw. "What can I say, I love to eat," Ivy said to Lindsey when she came up behind her to see if she needed help with anything.

"I'm so glad," Lindsey said, hugging Ivy as if taking a second helping was accepting a proposal to marry her annoying, arrogant, narcissist son.

Ivy really liked Sammy's mom. He was right, she was awesome. She was warm and compassionate. Ivy going in for a second plate made her day. Lindsey hummed happily to herself as she piled more food on Ivy's plate before she was able to get to the door.

Ivy went back outside and sat down at the table. This time it was Sammy who got up to get more food. He wasn't hungry. He was just embarrassed.

"I almost forgot, Sammy," Lindsey said, opening the refrigerator. "I made fruit smoothies! I'll come outside and make them up fancy for you kids."

"Thanks, Mom."

Sammy sat across from Ivy as his mother poured them strawberry-banana smoothies. She hung orange slices off the side of the tall glasses and put a cute umbrella in them. She kissed Sammy's cheek and made her way back into the house to enjoy her gossip with Mary.

"My mom can't wait until my sisters are older. You should see the tea parties she throws for their stuffed animals."

Ivy smiled. "She really cares about you all; that's nice." She wished her mom had one drop of Lindsey Lopez in her.

"Yeah," he said, taking a sip of his fruit smoothie. "So, we're lucky. I got a frog out of the pool this morning."

Ivy rolled her eyes. "Great."

"So, after lunch, I figured we could try out the spell?"

"That's why I'm here."

Sammy and Ivy made their way behind the toolshed in his backyard. Sammy picked up a plastic bowl with a dead frog in it. "Crap," he said, attempting to shake ants off the frog. "This is my frog, get off!"

Ivy smiled as Sammy went about saving his frog from hundreds of tiny black ants.

"I'm gonna need your help for the next part," he said once he'd gotten rid of most of the ants.

"Next part?" Ivy asked, a little confused.

"Yeah, we need to cut the frog's tongue out."

"You didn't do it yet?"

"No, I was waiting for you." Sammy pulled out his Swiss Army knife.

"Cool," she said.

"From my dad. Great for when we go fishing."

Ivy was glad to hear Sammy say something positive about his father.

"You hold the frog, while I cut its tongue out," Sammy said.

Ivy couldn't look. Sammy opened the frog's mouth and rolled out its long tongue. She peeked. "Gross!"

"Come on Teller, it's not bad. It's just like in science class."

"One problem, we're not in science class. I wish I didn't eat so much," Ivy confessed. "I think I'm going to be sick."

"Don't be. It's over," Sammy said. "Let's get our green mold."

Sammy led Ivy to his father's Koi pond.

"Wow, it's beautiful."

"My father's pride and joy," Sammy said as he used a plastic spoon to scrape some green mold off the side of the pond.

Jeffrey Lopez's Koi pond was the pond of all ponds. It had cascading waterfalls and was just as big as the swimming pool. She looked at the large Koi dappled in bright orange as they swam close to the surface. They were so majestic they looked almost fake.

"You got some of Grams's hair?"

"I do," Ivy said, pulling a Ziplock bag out of her pocket. "Took it from her brush."

"Great. Let's go back behind the shed and give it a try."

Sammy went into his father's toolshed to get the spell book. "Had to hide this. My mom would freak if she saw the spell book. She's very superstitious."

Ivy felt nervous as Sammy turned the worn pages of the grimoire, not sure why. She didn't believe in magic and spells and witches. When he found the page with the *Laughter Spell* on it, he placed the open book on the ground. Sammy recited the spell as he added the ingredients to the bowl he held in the elbow of his arm.

> *"Laugh your ways to happy times,*
> *forget all of your past crimes,*
> *as you mix a frog's tongue*
> *with the hair of an old one."*

Sammy stirred the frog tongue and Mary Teller's hair in the bowl. He didn't have much cooking experience with his mother heading the kitchen, but he did his best to follow the instructions.

LEEDS FAMILY SPELL BOOK: THE LAUGHTER SPELL

"Swirl, mix, shake, and stir.
Add a pinch of green mold,
as together you take hold,
hand in hand,
as you say . . ."

Sammy added in the mold he scraped out of the Koi pond and set the bowl on the ground next to the spell book. He held his hands out toward Ivy.

"What are you doing?" Ivy asked, scrunching her eyebrows together.

He grinned. "The spell tells us to hold hands."

"Oh," she said, lacing her fingers with his. She swore she could hear the buzzing of the wasps in her stomach.

Together they recited the rest of the spell.

"Let laughter come,
let laughter stay,
forever laughing on this day."

Sammy and Ivy awkwardly looked at each other. "Did it work?" Sammy asked, still holding onto Ivy's hands.

"I'm not laughing."

"We better try it again," Sammy suggested.

"Hate to burst your bubble, but you know this is all fake. I mean, Sammy, please, let's look at the facts. It's a three-line stanza made up by a Dr. Seuss wannabe. If we read *Green Eggs and Ham* while holding hands were not going to magically make all the eggs in the world turn green."

Sammy gave her a frustrated look, his eyes veiled by his thick lashes. "This is a real spell in a real spell book. We're not just reading a poem out of some kid's book. We are reading out of a genuine grimoire."

Ivy shrugged.

"Come on, let's try again. And this time, try to have a little faith. Say it like you want it to work. There's power in belief."

"Okay, fine," she grumbled.

Ivy knew the whole thing was stupid, but it did get her invited to Sammy's house. In her heart, she hoped the spell would work. If it did, Sammy would invite her over again. And besides, she thought holding his hand is well worth feeling stupid.

Ivy took a deep breath in and tried to focus.

"One, two, three," Sammy counted.

> *"Let laughter come,*
> *let laughter stay,*
> *forever laughing on this day."*

Sammy was anxious, Ivy could read it on his face. He didn't blink and his jaw was set, making him look older than he was. He squeezed her hands. She savored the feeling of her hands in his. His sweaty palms made her sweat.

After a few moments Sammy relaxed a little, loosening his grip on her hands, their fingers still intertwined. "Did it work this time?"

"I don't think so," Ivy said sympathetically, but then a giggle popped out. She pulled her hands away from Sammy's to cover her mouth.

"What's so funny?" he asked. Then he felt it too. It was this uncontrollable need to laugh. It started in the pits of their stomachs, travelling to the backs of their throats. Soon their giggles became a howl. They got so loud that Lindsey and Mary could hear them from the kitchen.

"It worked!" Sammy said with a loud laugh.

"I see that," Ivy laughed. "But how do we stop it?"

"I don't know," he tittered, "but I don't know if I want it to stop."

Sammy's little sisters ran up to him. "Sammy, what's so funny?"

Sammy quickly knocked over the makeshift cauldron with his foot so his sisters couldn't see. He sent the frog's tongue along with Grams's hair flying into the dirt. As soon as the contents of the spell hit the ground the spell was broken, and their laughter stopped.

Ivy and Sammy looked at each other excitedly. "I guess that's how we stop it," Sammy said with a wide grin.

"That's easy enough," Ivy agreed. Sammy's smile was electric. And if she were being honest with herself, she felt just as excited as him. Pins and needles pricked her all over her body.

"Teller, we're onto something big; I can't wait to try another one! That was awesome!"

Ivy shrugged, trying to curb her enthusiasm. She was fairly sure the laughing was subliminal. They both wanted the spell to work for their own reasons, so they laughed. She knew the mind could be a powerful thing; Sammy was right about that. There was power in belief—a lot of power.

"Yeah, it would be cool, I guess," she said indifferently.

"Sammy, Sammy are you going to go swimming?" Alba and Maria asked, tugging on his arms.

"Yes, you two, now relax!" Sammy glanced to Ivy. "You bring your swimsuit?"

"It's in the car."

"Good thing Grams is still here. Get your bathing suit on, and I'll see you in the pool."

Sammy's sisters led him to the pool as Ivy walked back to the house.

"Can I have the keys, Grams? I left my bathing suit in the car."

"Sure," she said, handing her the keys.

"The bathroom is the first door on your right as you come in."

"Okay thanks, Lindsey," she said, feeling weird calling Sammy's mom by her first name.

Ivy went to the bathroom and put on her bathing suit. She did eat too much, her shorts felt tight. *What if the spell did work?* She thought. She wondered if the *Beauty Spell* would work too. She decided right then and there as she looked at her bloated reflection in the Lopez's downstairs bathroom mirror, she was going to snap a picture of the *Beauty Spell* on her phone the first chance she got. It was worth the try.

Ivy quickly made her way into the pool. She felt better once she was in the water and Sammy could only see her face.

Grams came to the pool, no doubt being nosy again as she looked over the backyard amenities. "Well kiddo, I'm heading home. I told Lindsey I'll pick you up before dinner."

"Can't she stay for dinner Grams? It's Tortellini Thursday," Sammy said.

"Yuck!" Shouted the twins. "We don't like tortellini; we only eat macaroni and cheese!"

"They know," Sammy said, trying to hush his sisters.

"Maybe another time. We don't want to be a nuisance," Grams said, like a responsible adult.

"It's no big deal; my father works late on Thursdays."

"Let's play it by ear. Ivy, text me and let me know when you're ready."

"Okay, thanks Grams."

"Wow, nice," Ivy said, looking around Sammy's room. Sammy didn't have his own floor, but his room was huge. He had a king-size bed with a big-screen TV. She popped her head in his bathroom. If she'd thought the downstairs bathroom was nice, she could live in Sammy's.

"Thanks," Sammy said, unwrapping the spell book he'd wrapped in his pool towel to get it up the stairs past his mother.

Ivy knew he had to hide the grimoire with his mom being superstitious and all, but she wondered if he had to hide everything from her. She gave his room another glance over and noticed it was empty besides his bed and dresser. "Your room looks like you just moved in. There's not one poster or knickknack."

"I'm not allowed to hang posters. My dad likes a clean house," Sammy said, kneeling by the side of his bed. "*Personality under the bed. . . one of his rules.*" From under his bed, he pulled out a large plastic tote on wheels. The tote held Sammy's personal things, some baseball cards and magazines. "I've been keeping the spell book in here."

"Kind of an obvious place to hide it, don't you think?"

"My mom respects my privacy. My dad, not so much." Sammy pushed the tote back under his bed as he thought. "Shoot, you're right; I really shouldn't keep it under my bed. I'm gonna have to come up with a better hiding place."

"Why not keep it in the toolshed?"

"No way. I just put it in there this morning after my dad left for work to get it close to the pool. He's always going in and out of there. Not to mention the number of cameras he has set up around the house. It's hard to get anything past him."

Ivy grinned. "I'm sure you'll figure it out."

He mirrored her. "I'm sure I will. So, you wanna try another spell?"

"Okay," Ivy said, taking a seat on his bed.

"Sammy, your father is on the phone for you," Lindsey called from downstairs.

"Be right back," he said, running down to get the phone.

Ivy quickly went through the spell book. She found the *Beauty Spell* and snapped a picture on her phone.

Sammy came back up to the room with flushed cheeks. "I'm sorry, Ivy . . . You've got to go home."

"Oh," she said, getting up.

"I wasn't supposed to have anyone over without asking my dad, and he's freaking out. I'm still grounded. My mom is super embarrassed . . . I'm sorry to ask, but can your grandmother pick you up?"

"It's fine. I'll text my grandmother right now."

"Thanks." Sammy pulled the tote back out from under his bed. He quickly put the grimoire in it before sliding it back out of sight.

"Are you in trouble now?"

"Yeah . . . big trouble," he said with a sigh.

"You still gonna make it to youth group?"

"Yeah, my dad wouldn't want people to know what a dictator he is. Besides he needs me there so he can say I ran this community event . . . it's election time soon." Sammy nibbled on his bottom lip. "Um Teller, can you not say anything to your grandmother?" Sammy asked in a low voice, his eyes darting to the floor. "I told my mom I would just tell you my dad was coming home early, and we're doing some family dinner thing with my aunt."

"Of course."

"Cool. Thanks."

"Sorry you got in trouble."

"I'm not. I had an awesome day, and so did my mom and sisters. Hopefully when I'm done being grounded you can come over again without an excuse."

She smiled. She would like that.

CHAPTER NINETEEN
Big Trouble

Jeffrey Lopez marched into his son's room as soon as he got home, opening the door without knocking. Sammy was sitting on his bed with his arms crossed over his chest scowling, his stance setting Jeffrey off right away.

"What don't you understand about being grounded?" Jeffrey asked, his voice slightly raised.

"I know Dad, but we were working on the church event. It was more punishment than fun today. It was. I promise. I can hardly stand that girl Ivy."

"Don't insult my intelligence, Sammy. Your sisters were just telling me what a fun time they had swimming with Ivy."

"They're six and a half, going to the doctor is fun for them."

"Don't get smart."

"Kinda hard when everyone in this house is so dumb," he mumbled, diverting his eyes down to his bed comforter.

Jeffrey couldn't help himself; he slapped Sammy's smart mouth.

"Knock it off. You're not the victim here. You're grounded because you have to learn to follow the rules."

"Yeah, your rules. All of your stupid rules. That's what they are—stupid!"

Jeffrey hit him again, this time harder. Sammy curled up protectively. "Don't Sammy. Don't make me." Sammy tucked his head into his chest and fought to hold back his tears as his dad hit him again. "When I say you're grounded, that means no one comes over without my permission. I don't care if you're working on a project for God himself, you approve it with me. Do I make myself clear?!"

"Yes," he said with a shaky voice.

"Look at me when I'm talking to you."

Sammy uncurled, locking eyes with his father, his voice laced with contempt. "Yes."

"At this rate, you'll never get your phone back."

Just like his father, Sammy couldn't help himself. He rolled his eyes.

Jeffrey took Sammy's phone out of his pocket. He hesitated only for a moment before he put the phone on the ground and stepped on it.

"Please Dad, no!" Sammy heard the screen crack. "Dad, no, that was so expensive!"

Jeffrey's voice was as sharp as a whip. "Next time you'll think twice before doing something you know you shouldn't." Jeffrey took his son's TV off the wall. "No TV, and you're staying in your room."

"I hope you weren't too hard on him," Lindsey said to her husband as he walked into their bedroom. "He did work on the event for Pastor Leeds."

He leaned Sammy's TV against the wall. "I know Lindsey; I just get so mad at him. He knew what he was doing when he invited Ivy over today." He exhaled slowly through his nose. "He has to stay in his room all weekend. I don't want to see him." Lindsey nodded. Jeffrey took a seat on the bed, regret washing over him. "I hit him again."

"Jeffrey, you didn't!"

He ran his fingers through his dark hair. "I'm sorry. I just . . . can you make sure he's okay?"

Lindsey rushed out of the room to check on Sammy.

"That kid," he said to himself. "If he'd only listen."

Jeffrey never laid a hand on his wife or his girls, but when it came to Sammy things were different. He took his anger out on him. Sammy just reminded him so much of himself.

"Maybe it's time I get help," Jeffrey muttered, running his hands over his knees. "I can't hit him like that . . . I can't."

But he did, and he did often. Sammy had a way of talking back without realizing he was doing it until it was too late. Sammy was naturally quick-witted, and words just rolled off his tongue. A trait the girls at school liked—his father not so much. And as much as Jeffrey tried to restrain himself, he was seldom able to. Sammy tried to do what his father asked, and Jeffrey tried to be a better father to Sammy, but somehow, they both fell short. And Sammy always got the worst of it.

Lindsey knocked on Sammy's door before she entered. He was sitting by his phone on the floor. "Are you okay?" she asked, sitting down next to him.

"He broke my phone."

"I'll get you a new one."

"It's okay; I can't have one anyway."

Lindsey wrapped her arms around her son. "I'm sorry, Sammy. I should have told your father you were having someone over. It's my fault."

"It's not your fault, Mom. I knew I should've asked, but I was afraid he'd say no, and I really wanted Ivy to come over."

Lindsey inclined her son's face to her. A bruise was already visible under his left eye. "I'm going to get an ice pack. I'll be right back."

Sammy's mom returned in no time with an ice pack. She held it up to his face. It felt good, relieving the sting. "Thanks, Mom."

"I had a nice day today, Sammy."

"Me too."

"Ivy and her grandmother are very nice."

"Yeah, Ivy is, and I'm warming up to Grams."

"Mary only had nice things to say about you."

Sammy smiled despite the hurt. "That's surprising for Old Lady Mary."

Lindsey hugged Sammy again. "You really are a good boy."

"Thanks Mom, at least you think so."

"Your father does too. He loves you very much, it's just that he loses his temper sometimes."

She squeezed him. "Your father said you have to stay in your room for the weekend."

"What about youth group? Can I still go?" Sammy asked in a panic. "Pastor Leeds is expecting me."

Lindsey released her hold on her son. "You can go, but after that, it's back to your room."

He nodded, agreeably. "I understand."

Lindsey kissed her son good night once he tucked into bed. On her way out she picked up his phone and threw it in his trash. She blew him a kiss from the doorway and shut off his light. "Get some rest. I love you," she said, closing the door behind her.

"How's Sammy?" Jeffrey asked his wife when she came back into their bedroom.

"Upset. You broke his phone. You know how long he saved to get that."

"I know. I'm sorry."

"It's not me you owe the apology to," Lindsey said, tears beading on her lashes. She sat on the bed and covered her face with her hands. "Oh Jeffrey, I don't care about the phone, we can buy him a new one. I care that you hit him again. You said you were getting help." She looked at her husband with teary eyes. "I can't let this go on anymore."

"I am. I'm getting help," he urged.

"You can't hit him like that. He already has a bruise on his face. You don't know your own strength. One day you're going to really hurt him." Lindsey got up to grab a tissue from the Kleenex box on the dresser. "What kind of mother am I to allow you to do that to my son?"

"Lindsey, I'm sorry." Jeffrey got off the bed and hugged her to him.

"I'm sorry. It won't happen again."

"I mean it. If you hit him once more, I'm leaving you. I can't do this any longer. I can't lie for you anymore, and I can't ask Sammy to lie for you either. I can't! You do it again and I'm taking Sammy and the girls, and we're gone. I don't care if we have to live on the streets, we will leave you!"

Lindsey buried her face in her husband's chest, weeping.

"It won't happen again; I promise. I'm going to get help."

CHAPTER TWENTY
The Attic

Sammy couldn't wait to get to Pastor Leeds's house Saturday morning. After spending all day Friday in his room, he felt like he was going stir crazy. And to make matters worse, his father was taking forever eating his breakfast. He waited as patiently as he could for him to finish. He reasoned he could have walked there faster, but his father insisted on driving him so they could talk. Sammy didn't want to talk about the bruise on his face; he wanted to get into Pastor Leeds's attic.

"I was hard on you the other day," Jeffrey said to his son, keeping his eyes on the road so he wouldn't have to see the yellowing bruise on his son's face.

"It's okay Dad, you were right. I know I should've asked permission for Ivy to come over."

Jeffrey drove slower.

"Dad, it's really okay. You were right. I deliberately went behind your back and I'm sorry." Sammy was hoping his omission of guilt would make his father put his foot on the gas, but it didn't, the car slowed to a crawl. "I learned my lesson."

Jeffrey was searching for the right words. "Sammy, it's not . . ."

"Dad, I was wrong. End of story. It's fine. I know better."

Jeffrey wanted to say sorry. His hands clammed up as he gripped the steering wheel. His car was almost at a stop now. Jeffrey took a deep breath in. "I'm sorry Sammy," he said quickly.

"Thank you for the apology, but it's not needed."

They finally pulled up to Pastor Leeds's house. "Thanks for the ride," Sammy said, hopping out of his dad's Mercedes before he had a chance to put the car in park. Sammy jogged over to the others waiting for him on the lawn.

"Great, Sammy's here, so we can get started," Pastor Leeds said, waving to Jeffrey as he pulled away. "Sammy is spearheading this project, so he'll hand out your assignments."

It had only been a day since Ivy saw Sammy, but it felt like weeks. The wasps swarmed around her stomach making her inhale sharply at the sight of him, the sting of love almost knocking her to her feet. She had stayed up till midnight last night hoping he'd sneak out of his house again. But he didn't. The red light and the rumbling came and went without Sammy.

"Where am I?" Elsa asked, twirling her blonde hair around her finger.

"You, Mike, and Louie are in the basement. Tammy and Tyrone are cleaning out the spare room, and Ivy and I are taking on the attic."

Tammy wrapped her arms around Tyrone's neck, becoming some weird sort of human necklace. "I like these assignments."

"Me too," Louie said, smiling at Elsa as he brushed his dark hair away from his light eyes. Mike stood indifferently. Ivy wished he would've been upset his best friend dissed him, but he didn't look like he cared. Elsa on the other hand, groaned, shooting daggers at Ivy with her eyes.

"Let's get everything out of the house and place it on the front lawn so we can go through it," Sammy said. "We need to determine if something is trash, donation, or if we can sell it at the yard sale. If we're selling it, it has to be priced fairly." Sammy held up sheets of brightly colored stickers for the youth group kids to see. "We've got little stickers here so you can mark the price. If you're unsure how to price something, ask Pastor Leeds. Once an item is marked with a price, put it in the garage. We've got some gloves in case things get gross and masks if you need them," Sammy said, passing them out. "Okay, let's get started!"

Elsa grabbed Mike's hand. "Come on, let's go." She shot Ivy another dirty look and flicked her hair off her shoulders.

"Hey! Wait for me," Louie said, pushing his hair off his forehead and hurrying after Elsa.

Pastor Leeds led Sammy and Ivy to the attic. Sammy could hardly contain himself as they walked up the old, wide plank steps that creaked and moaned under their weight. Pastor Leeds was out of breath before they made it to the third floor.

Ivy hated to admit Sammy was right, but Pastor Leeds looked horrible. Since last week, the color of his skin had changed to a sickly pallor and dark crescents had settled under his heavenly blue eyes. Ivy was really starting to worry about him.

Pastor Leeds pulled out his keys and unlocked the door to the attic. "You guys have one heck of a project in front of you; I don't think this attic has ever been cleaned out. I wish I was feeling better so I could be of more help."

"Did you find out why you feel so crappy?" Sammy asked.

"Yes, I think so. I came up negative for Lyme disease, but my doctor told me I'm severely anemic lacking iron and vitamin B12 in my blood. I'm on all sorts of pills and supplements for that now. It hasn't helped much, but I have my follow up appointment in a couple of days, so hopefully they can give me something more."

"I hope so," Sammy said, giving Ivy an I-told-you-so look.

Uriah pushed the attic door open and flipped on the light switch.

"Wow," Sammy said. The attic was filled from floor to ceiling with boxes. The boxes were stacked so high it blocked out the light overhead. "You ever come in here?" Sammy asked Pastor Leeds.

"I opened the door once when I first got here out of curiosity, and I shut it right away," he laughed.

"I see why," Ivy gasped.

"No, this is good," Sammy said. "I'm sure we'll find tons of great things for the yard sale and make some money for the church."

Uriah put his hand on Sammy's shoulder. "Great attitude. I'll leave you guys to it then."

"Thanks."

Uriah started down the stairs.

"Oh, Pastor Leeds?" Sammy called to him.

Uriah turned around. "Yes?"

"Why do you keep the attic door locked?"

Uriah looked at the keys in his hand, then back at Sammy standing in the attic doorway. "You know what, I have no idea. Seems silly." Uriah put the keys back in his pocket. "Really silly."

"Yeah," Sammy said. "Well, we better get a move on."

Uriah acknowledged Sammy's words with a nod. He held on to the banister and slowly made his way downstairs.

"What did you get us into, Sammy Lopez?" Ivy moaned once they were alone. "You can't tell me you actually believe the things that come out of your mouth."

"You're missing the big picture. How did the red light get through the window with all this stuff in the room?!"

"I don't know, how?"

"Hocus-pocus," he said, grabbing a box off the top of the stack. "Wow, this is heavy." Sammy put the box down on the ground.

Ivy teased, "Maybe you're just weak. I should probably go get Louie."

"Funny Teller," he said not amused. He opened the box to see folded antique garments. He pulled out a small white dress belonging to a child. "The boxes with clothes weigh a ton, leave those for me."

"Okay fine, but still, there's no way we're going to finish cleaning out the attic today."

"This is good."

Her face twisted up and she knew she looked silly. "How so?"

"If the light comes from the attic tonight, we know that whatever we are looking for is still up here. If not, we know that it's in one of the boxes we already carried down."

"Good thinking." She had to admit to herself, Sammy was smart, not that she was going to tell him that.

"Let's attack this by sections so we don't leave Pastor Leeds's house a mess. We should bring the boxes to the landing, then downstairs. And the boxes we don't have a chance to sort through we'll put 'em in the sunroom off the back of the house. That way we don't get the attic stuff mixed up with the rest of the junk."

"That's a good idea, but how do we know when we find what we're looking for?"

"I don't know," Sammy said, grabbing another box. "Hopefully the something *we're looking for* is obvious." Sammy gave Ivy a big grin. "Like your haunted Christmas bulb or my hocus-pocus."

Ivy rolled her eyes and picked up a dusty box.

Some of the boxes were really heavy. Sammy struggled to get the big ones down the stairs. His arm was still sore from where his father had hit him.

"How you guys making out?" Pastor Leeds asked, passing Sammy on the stairs.

"Good," Sammy said, "But we're not gonna finish today. I think we should start going through what we've brought down already, and Ivy and I will come back another day to finish cleaning out the rest."

"That sounds like a good plan," Pastor Leeds said, doing his best to help Sammy with a large box.

While Pastor Leeds was close to Sammy, he noticed his eye. "Is that a black eye, Sammy?"

"Almost. I was in the pool with my sisters the other day and Maria kicked me in the face while she was showing me she can do a handstand underwater. It was an accident, but man did it hurt."

Uriah chuckled. "Your sisters are quite the rascals."

"Yep, cute and annoying," Sammy said with a light laugh.

Ivy knew better; she knew where the bruise came from. But she had to give Sammy credit, he was quick to come up with a very believable story, especially considering the energy of the Lopez twins. Ivy had noticed the bruise when Sammy first got to Pastor Leeds's house but didn't want to bring it up. She knew that bruise was because of her.

"When is your dad picking you up?" Ivy asked Sammy as they headed back to the landing to grab the last of their boxes.

"Pastor Leeds said he'd call him when we're done for the day."

"Things okay with your dad?"

"Yeah, just grounded to my room for the weekend with no TV."

"That sucks."

"Nah, I already got a lot of reading done. I found the next spell I want to try."

"Which one?"

"*The Happy Spell.*"

She rolled her eyes. "*The Happy Spell,* you're kidding me? All the spells in that book and you choose that?!"

"What? I figure it's an innocent spell like the last one. We need to start off small. We don't want to hurt anyone or ourselves."

"I guess you're right. What are the ingredients?"

"Since I'm room-bound, I'm gonna need you to help with that," he said, pulling a piece of paper out of his back pocket. He handed her the ingredients list.

Ivy looked over it. "Honey, wax, a dead bee, a fingernail, a blade of grass . . . where am I gonna get all that?"

"It's not that hard of a list. Dead bee, may be an issue," Sammy admitted as he picked up the last of the day's boxes.

Ivy mumbled, "I'll try."

"By tonight?"

"Tonight?! You just said you're grounded Sammy."

"I am, but I'm sneaking out."

"You sure that's a good idea?" Ivy asked as they walked down the stairs.

"Yeah, I want to see if the red light is still in the attic. I'll be at your place at eleven."

"Okay."

They made their way outside. Ivy hurriedly put the list in her pocket when Mike walked toward them with a box from the basement.

"This project sucks Sammy," he complained. "I can't believe I'm going to say picking up trash is better than this."

"Well community service is supposed to be rewarding, not fun," he laughed. "Come on Mike, you got to spend the day with Louie and Elsa."

"Yeah, thanks for hooking me up," he said, looking at Ivy through slitted eyes.

"No problem. I knew you'd be happy with that."

"You always take one for the team Sammy."

Ivy shot Mike an evil glare. She wanted to punch him.

"Nah, Ivy's the best."

Ivy tried to conceal her smile as the wasps in her tummy fluttered.

"If you say so," Mike said nonchalantly, setting his box on the grass with the rest of the things from the basement.

He did say so. Sammy couldn't deny it anymore. He liked Ivy Teller.

CHAPTER TWENTY-ONE
Music of the Heart

Japhet Dean Leeds whistled as he made his way up to Uriah Leeds's bedroom. He dragged his hand on the handrail of the old staircase until he reached the second story of the rectory. He slowly turned the doorknob, not making a peep, and closed the door behind him. He walked over to the bed where Uriah slept. He climbed on top of his white sheets, making himself comfortable on his side next to the sleeping pastor. Since Uriah had come to stay at the rectory, he had come many nights to watch Uriah sleep, sneaking into his room undetected to say good night to his sleeping angel.

Japhet Dean silently stared at Uriah as he slept, not blinking as he watched Uriah's chest move up and down. He took rapture in listening to the sound of his lungs as they greedily took in air and expelled it. Japhet Dean laid his head on Uriah's chest and listened to the sound of his heart. His arrhythmia was music to his ears. A bittersweet sound he had missed for many years but always emulated when he whistled his haunting tune through the woods.

He ran his finger over Uriah's perfect lips. "You poor boy, so sick . . . so sick and the doctors can't help you, but I can." His voice grew deeper. "I alone can help you, for I alone know what it is you need to be well."

He rubbed his face against Uriah's. "I think you have suffered long enough. Tonight, I will give you a little reprieve. I think young Zachary will find peace in death, as you will find peace from his lost life. With each life I take, you will grow vital once more, and with each soul I reap, you will gain a memory of the real you. In no time you will be my Uriah again."

Japhet Dean put his lips to Uriah's ear and whispered: "I heard your prayers, but before I answer them, I need you to do something for me. Early tomorrow morning you will be called away from your church and summoned to Saint Anthony's on Bishop Baker's request. He will give you something special he has been holding onto for me for a long time. He will tell you it is an heirloom belonging to your church and that you should be the one to keep it. It's just a trinket really, a coin from my father. A coin I took out of his wooden casket before they laid him to rest. For a son is to inherit all that was his father's on earth."

Japhet Dean leaned in and softly kissed Uriah's lips. "Good night, Uriah, my beautiful son."

CHAPTER TWENTY-TWO
Uriah's Dream

In the middle of the night, Uriah woke up in a cold sweat. The sound of his heart echoed in his head as he inhaled and exhaled in fear. "It was only a dream," he said, in an attempt to comfort himself. Uriah got out of bed on shaky legs and went to the bathroom. He splashed cold water on his face. With trembling hands, he ran his fingers over his lips. "It had to be a dream . . . but that face . . . those lips. No—," Uriah said, turning away from the mirror. "It couldn't have been me . . . but it was so real—the emotion so real." Uriah glanced at himself in the mirror again, relieved at what he saw: the perfect cut of his chin, the perfect slope of his nose, his full lips and well-formed mouth. He kept his eyes on his reflection as he relived his nightmare.

BATSTO VILLAGE, NEW JERSEY: 1744

"Hello Uriah."

An eight-year-old Uriah Leeds stood up to see a well-dressed man. He wiped the dirt and blood from his face with his clammy hand. Uriah was surprised to see a man of his standing by the old sawmill. He had only ever seen Mr. Richards and his business associates dressed so clever. And they never came to the old mill.

The well-dressed man standing in front of the sawmill had on a black three-piece suit with tiny gray pinstripes. He wore a vibrant dandelion in place of a pocket square. Uriah took notice of the man's gold pocket watch that he now pulled from his vest pocket and glanced at. The gold shimmered in the hot afternoon sun, highlighting the man's young and attractive face. He looked to be from a family of note; his hands were clean and callous-free, like he hadn't done a day of hard work since his conception. The man tucked his timepiece away and traded it for a hand-rolled cigarette. Uriah stared on as the man lit his cigarette and took a long drag.

"I've been watching you, Uriah," the man said in a concise tone.

Uriah snorted the blood that now dripped from his nose.

"Uriah," the man continued, "I heard your plea for help, and I'm here to help you."

He wiped tears from his eyes. "You are?" Uriah asked, unsure of how a businessman could help him.

The man flicked the ash from his cigarette. The smoke smelled sweet and alluring. It didn't have the musty smell like the kind Uriah's grandmother smoked from a pipe.

"Uriah, I thought I heard you say you would do anything to save her."

"Miss Lilly?" he asked.

BATSTO VILLAGE: SAWMILL

"Yes Uriah, Miss Lilly. You said you would do anything to save Miss Lilly." The man took another puff of his cigarette and blew a smoke ring into the white sky as he waited for a reply.

"Yes sir, I did say that."

"My name is Japhet Dean."

"Yes, Mr. Japhet Dean."

"I like you Uriah; you can call me JD."

"Thank you, Mr. JD. But can you really help Miss Lilly?"

"Yes, I can."

"She is a good person, Mr. JD. She doesn't deserve to die because of me," Uriah said, holding back tears.

"What makes a person good, Uriah?"

A young Uriah didn't hesitate to answer. "Someone who is kind and does the Lord's work."

"What is the Lord's work?"

"Someone who *loves thy neighbor as thyself.* It's the second and greatest commandment to loving *the Lord thy God with all thy heart, and with all thy soul, and with all thy mind.* Miss Lilly always has been kind to me when no one else is."

"Why is that, Uriah?"

Uriah looked down at the ground, ashamed. "They think I'm irregular. Think I'm a cripple, Mr. JD, because I was born with what the doctors told mama is a cleft mouth, and my right leg is a little too short, so I walk with a limp."

"Are you a good person, Uriah?"

Uriah looked up to meet JD's warm brown eyes, "I am, Mr. JD."

"Prove it to me."

"I go to church, and I say a prayer every morning when I wake up and before I go to bed at night. I try to be well behaved for my mama."

"Tell me, why do those boys think it's your fault Miss Lilly is going to die?" JD pointed to a group of three boys barely visible down the dirt road. Uriah knew the boys well—the Hanson brothers. The brothers had just put a beating on Uriah, leaving him bruised and bleeding in front of the old sawmill.

"You see, Mr. JD, we were playing by the lake when my bum leg got stiff and I slid down the hill, knocking Miss Lilly into the water. It was an accident, really it was. I helped her up right away, but she got a cut that got infected. Now she's really sick. Medicine is not helping. We turned to prayer. Her father is the pastor here at Batsto church, I know God has to hear his prayers."

"God, Uriah?"

"Yes, our Lord and Savior. I have faith he will save her." Tears ran down his bruised cheeks.

"Uriah, why are you crying? If God is going to save Miss Lilly, you have nothing to spill tears over."

"It's just that I overheard my mama say she won't live through the night. Doctors say the infection is in her blood." Uriah sniffled. "But I have been praying so hard. I just know God has to save her."

"Uriah, if Miss Lilly is a good person as you claim, I'm sure your Lord will save her since her getting sick was just an accident."

Uriah nodded as he wiped his tears on the inside of his dirt-stained shirt. "Yes, Mr. JD, sir."

"But Uriah, I do wonder . . . why God would let a good person like Miss Lilly get sick in the first place, or a good boy like you be born with a cleft mouth and bum leg, as you put it."

Uriah's tears fell steadily. "We have to have faith Mr. JD, that's what mama says. God works in mysterious ways."

"That he does, Uriah." JD flashed Uriah a perfect smile revealing bright-white teeth. "I can save Miss Lilly and heal your ailments."

"You can?" Uriah asked through his tears. "Are you an angel?"

"Not quite." JD tossed his cigarette to the ground, stomping it out with the heel of his shiny black dress shoe. "But you have to do me a favor, Uriah."

"Yes, anything."

"That's a good boy. Go home now, and you will find under your pillow two small vials. One is for you, and one is for Miss Lilly. Tell the good pastor the Lord favors you and healed you and gave you the power to heal Miss Lilly." JD knelt, putting his hands on Uriah's shoulders. "One day, I will come back to ask you for a favor Uriah, if that's alright?"

"Oh yes Mr. JD, that is most certainly alright."

"Very good, Uriah." JD kissed his forehead. "Run home now and save Miss Lilly."

Uriah ran home as quick as he could, dragging his right leg behind him. He drank the elixir from the vial he found under his pillow. He felt his face and leg tingle. The tingling became a deep burning that radiated from within. It hurt only for a couple of seconds before the pain left as quickly as it had come. When Uriah looked into the looking glass, he was overwhelmed. His face was healed. The young boy staring back at him was flawless. Uriah smiled at the boy he now saw in the mirror, running his hand over his perfect lips. Uriah stretched out his bum leg, it was restored. JD had proven to be his guardian angel. JD had told him the truth—he was made whole.

Uriah wasted no time getting to Batsto church. He flew down the dirt street with his two good legs, leaving a cloud of dust in his wake. He flung open the doors to the church and ran to get Pastor Baker. The pastor saw Uriah's blessed face and didn't hesitate to give the elixir to his dying daughter.

Uriah was still shaking as he climbed back in bed, his fingertips cathartically tracing his lips. "It was just a dream, it has to be." He stared at the ceiling and focused on his breathing for a long time. After Uriah's nerves calmed down, he realized he felt better. He felt rested, despite being startled from his sleep. Uriah rubbed his eyes. "It's so strange. I feel better than I have in weeks. Thank you, Lord and Savior," he said, rolling onto his side and closing his eyes.

CHAPTER TWENTY-THREE
Cousin Jesse

Ivy waited by the front door for Sammy. He was right, they had to replace the blown out light bulbs on the porch. She was making herself cross-eyed staring into the night for a glimpse of him. Finally, seeing him coming up the porch steps, she opened the door.

"You got the ingredients?" he asked, excited.

"Hello, to you to."

He grinned his sideways grin. "Sorry, hi."

"And yes," she whispered, closing the door behind him.

They quietly made their way to the stairs, Sammy slipping off his sneakers. Once they were safely in Ivy's room, Sammy took the spell book out from under his jacket. "My dad is acting funny. I think this is safer with you."

"Funny?"

"Yeah, he apologized to me this morning. It was painful. That's why I was late getting to Pastor Leeds's house."

"Isn't that good?" Ivy asked, confused. "You know, that he

apologized, if he did something he shouldn't have?" Sammy hadn't told her the bruise under his eye was from his dad, but she was sure it was.

"Yeah, it is, but my dad is the definition of an alpha male. He doesn't apologize. It was just plain weird."

Sammy handed Ivy the spell book. "But I want you to make me a promise before I give the grimoire to you."

"Okay, what?" Ivy asked, placing her hands on the leather binding.

"I want you to promise me you will never do any spells without me."

"Okay," Ivy said plainly.

"Promise me, Teller. It could be dangerous. My abuela made me promise never to cast alone. You need to promise too."

Ivy had forgotten Sammy thought his grandmother was a real-life witch. "I promise," she said, sparing Sammy the-witches-aren't-real lecture.

"Good, me too," he said, releasing the spell book into her hands. "I can't wait to get back over to Pastor Leeds's place and go through the rest of the boxes."

Ivy nodded in agreement, but her body was sore; she could wait a few days, maybe weeks.

"You want to do the spell while we wait for midnight?" Sammy asked.

"Yeah sure. I'll be right back; forgot the wax in the bathroom."

Ivy slipped out of her room.

Sammy spotted Ivy's phone on top of a stack of magazines she had piled on her desk. He took a seat in the desk chair and stared at it. He couldn't resist picking it up. "I'm a narcissist," he chuckled, typing in his name as the guess to her password. "What do you know about that, it worked. I knew it! She does like me," he muttered to himself. "Take that, Pastor Leeds!"

Sammy swiped through Ivy's pictures. Seeing the snapshot of the *Beauty Spell*, he deleted it.

He heard a groan from the stairs and put Ivy's phone back where he found it.

"Got it," Ivy said as she came back into the room with Grams's mustache wax in her hands. Or what Grams liked to refer to as her whisker wax.

Sammy turned in the desk chair to face Ivy. "Hey Teller?"

"Uh, yeah?"

"You weren't planning on doing that *Beauty Spell*, were you?"

"What? No," she blushed, her heart jumping.

He locked eyes with her across the room. His blue eyes honing in on her. "Ivy, you *are* beautiful."

She rolled her eyes, her scoff sounding like a growl. "Oh save it."

"I mean it," he said. "I think so."

She rolled her shoulders, approaching her desk. "What's this, Sammy Lopez, you're straying away from your type now? I'm a far cry from Elsa."

"I don't like Elsa anymore. I like you."

Her face twisted like she just sucked on a lemon.

Sammy got up from Ivy's desk and stood in front of her, confidant after learning his name was her phone password. He took Grams's whisker wax from her and set it down on the desk.

"You're not fooling me; you're just like your dad. You like pencil-thin blondes."

"You know, my mom didn't always look like that. Actually, she's super self-conscious about her weight. She thinks she's too thin. My mom survived stomach cancer twice."

"Oh, I had no idea," Ivy said, embarrassed, her blush deepening to crimson.

"Yeah, the first time around I was super young and don't really remember it, but the second time I do. It was right after my sisters were born. She was really sick. Most of her stomach had to be removed. She could barely eat. The doctors said in time her stomach would stretch out, which it did. She can eat a little now before she's full, but she still has to take tons of nutritional supplements."

Ivy felt a little bad about judging Sammy's dad, and her red cheeks showed it. But that didn't change the fact Sammy had liked Elsa.

"My dad said my mom used to have killer curves. I guess I do have the same taste as my dad after all. I like your curves Ivy," he said with his sideways grin.

The butterflies turned wasps swarmed inside her stomach. She was hot. She was confused. She was in love. He leaned in, pressing his lips to hers. Ivy froze, not sure what to do, she had never been kissed before. Sammy put his hand on the side of her shock-stricken face and kissed her again, her lips parting for him.

"What's happening here?" Ivy asked in a whisper. Her face felt like it was on fire the moment Sammy pulled his cool, moist lips away from hers.

"I'm kissing you, silly."

"I'm getting that, but why?" She didn't want to question a good thing—a great thing—but the skeptic in her came pouring out of her yearning lips all the same.

"I told you; I like you, Ivy. I have for a while. I thought you were still drooling over Pastor Leeds, but since the password to your phone is my name . . . well, I think it's safe to say you like me too." He glanced down and tapped on the face of her phone.

"I don't know what's worse, that you are narcissistic enough to think my password was your name, or the fact that my password *is* your name."

Sammy smiled. "I like that my name is your password." He leaned in closer to kiss her again. Her face continued to grow hot, along with the rest of her body. *This is too good to be true,* Ivy thought to herself as she kissed him back. The wasps swarming around in her stomach felt like they were stinging her all at the same time, but the feeling she felt was not pain but a burning excitement. Sammy took her hand and sat down on her bed, pulling Ivy to sit next to him. His words smothered by his own need to kiss her again. "You're so hot."

She thought his father must have caused brain damage or maybe that he meant literally hot. The attic was hot as always and she was hot—very hot.

As if reading her mind, Sammy slid his hands under Ivy's T-shirt, going to take it off. She was very, very hot, scorching hot, sweating in fact, but she didn't know if she was ready for that. She knew Sammy must have loads of experience with all of the sneaking out of the house he did, but she didn't, and needed to put the brakes on.

Sensing her hesitation, he left her shirt on, taking off his own instead. That, she was more than okay with. It was like a first-row seat to the community pool in her own bedroom, now if only he had on those short red shorts, maybe she could learn to like the color red after all.

He leaned her back on her pillow, his experience showing, her hands going to his hair where the lingering scent of chlorine mixed with his cologne, intoxicated her. She never wanted this moment to end. She wanted to stay locked with Sammy Lopez, local Spanish god and hocus-pocus enthusiast forever—feel his firm body against hers, his soft lips, his silky hair weaved between her fingertips.

But as soon as she thought it. They heard a loud noise, making Sammy sit up. "I'm cursed," Ivy muttered to herself. She wanted to grab his arm and bring him down on top of her, but he was already at the attic window putting his shirt back on.

"It came from Pastor Leeds's house."

"It's probably nothing," Ivy said, hoping Sammy would forget about it, but she knew better, he must have been a cat in his last life.

He glanced at Ivy's alarm clock; it was 11:45 p.m. "That was loud. I think we should check on him."

There was no refusing Sammy. They were down the steps of the attic heading next door, before Ivy's mind could focus. Ivy didn't even try to talk him out of it, she was still giddy after being kissed for the first time and felt like she would follow him to the end of the Earth. That was until Sammy was about to march up to Pastor Leeds's front door and self-preservation kicked in. That, and she didn't want to lose her kissing partner.

Ivy grabbed his hand to stop him. "What if it's a robber? Maybe we shouldn't," Ivy urged.

"You're right. You wait for me in the bushes. I'm going in."

Ivy didn't see a good way to get Sammy to stop with his course of action and was unsure if she should just follow. But he insisted she wait for him, so she did.

Urgh, Ivy thought as she hid in the bushes. She'd left her phone on her desk.

Sammy tried the front door; it was locked. He made his way to the sunporch. It was another cloudy night, the moon smothered by rainclouds. The possibility that there was a burglar in the rectory had him rattled more than he cared to admit. The branches of the willow tree brushed against his shoulder as a hot summer breeze rustled the leaves, making him turn around. The tree looked eerily personified in the dark. Knots in the rough bark twisted to form eyes and a hollow mouth; the sweet smell of its sap bled into the night. Sammy shook it off. He didn't want to look like a chicken in front of Ivy, especially not now that they'd kissed. He tried the sunroom door, it was open. He slowly made his way in.

Sammy had only taken a few steps when he heard the familiar sound and saw a bright red light coming from the boxes they'd brought downstairs from the attic. It was so bright, it made him turn his head at first.

Realizing his good fortune, he rushed to the boxes, squinting his eyes as he dug through them looking for the source of the red light. Frantically, he moved aside the antique garments until he found it. He blinked to make sure what he was seeing was real. "It can't be," he muttered. He picked up the glowing mason jar and twirled it around. Inside the antique glassware was a human heart, flashing in the dark room in bursts like it was trying to spell out something in morse code. It beat against the side of the jar like it was alive. The noise that he had thought was a rumbling was not a rumbling at all. Now that the sound was not muffled by clothing, Sammy heard a clear rhythmic heartbeat coming from the jar. The noise was so loud it was almost deafening.

"Can I help you?" An unfamiliar voice said from behind him. Sammy quickly buried the jarred heart at the bottom of the box before turning around.

"Who are you?" The man asked.

"I'm sorry, I was across the street and heard a noise. I wanted to make sure Pastor Leeds was okay. Wait, who *are* you?!" Sammy asked, realizing he could be talking to a burglar.

"Name's Jesse Richards; I'm Uriah's cousin. Uriah has to run out of town tomorrow morning and asked me to come by. He said he had some kids from his youth group coming over and didn't want to reschedule. Something about them having it planned for weeks or was it months. What were their names," he said, tapping on his chin. "Sammy, Ivy, Louie . . . and a few more."

Sammy was relieved. Jesse was no burglar. "That's me, Sammy."

"Nice to meet you," Jesse said, extending his hand to Sammy for a handshake. "I think the noise you heard was me tripping over all these boxes when I came in through the sunporch. I wasn't expecting all this."

"That makes sense," Sammy said, shaking Jesse's hand.

"Thanks for coming to my rescue, but I'm all good here. It's pretty late; I think you should make your way home. You do have this mess waiting for you in the morning after all, "Jesse said, good-natured.

Sammy smiled sheepishly, showing all his teeth.

Jesse walked Sammy to the front door. "And Sammy, if you hear a loud noise in the middle of the night, don't check it out. Call the cops. You never know who you can trust."

"Thanks Mr. Richards, that's good advice. I guess I'll see you tomorrow morning at church."

"Nope, don't do church, but I'll be here when church lets out to supervise the youth group until Uriah gets back."

"Sounds good . . . um . . . Mr. Richards, can you do me a favor?" Sammy asked nervously.

"Yeah, sure—what's up?"

"Can you not mention that you saw me out this late. I'm grounded."

"Secret's safe with me," Jesse said with a big grin.

"Thanks." Sammy shook his hand again. "Nice meeting you. See you tomorrow."

"Who was that?!" Ivy asked in a hushed whisper, coming out of Pastor Leeds's bushes.

"Pastor Leeds's cousin, Jesse Richards."

"You sure?"

"Yeah, he knew the names of the youth group members."

"You better hope he doesn't tell your dad he saw you."

Sammy exhaled loudly. "I know, tell me about it. Let's get back to your room. You're not gonna believe what I saw."

"I saw it," Sammy said, taking a seat on her bed. "I saw the hocus-pocus that makes the red light and that strange noise."

"Well?! What is it?!" she asked with her hands on her hips.

"It's a jarred heart."

"'A jarred heart?'"

"Yes, that's what I'm trying to tell you," he said, using his hands to make the shape of a heart. "It was a human heart. It looked like it was just ripped out of someone's chest and stuffed in a jar. It was like it was still alive, beating in the jar. It was glowing red, but it wasn't a straight beam of light. The red light was flashing like it was trying to communicate with me. I know it sounds crazy, but it's true."

"A human heart? You're sure?" she asked leaving out the part about it being a human heart that was talking to him by flashing a red light. He was so lucky he was cute; he was more than mentally unstable—he was out of his mind.

"Yes. I'm sure. I wish this was some Disney movie where the huntsman gives the evil queen a pig's heart instead of Snow White's, but I'm telling you Teller, that heart was definitely human. I'm sure of it." Sammy said, his voice elevated with nervous excitement, like he'd just sucked on helium.

"Uh, you may want to lay off hanging out with your sisters. A Disney reference, really?"

Sammy sighed. "I know, they had it on yesterday. Just kinda fit the moment, you know?"

"No, I don't know. I hate to be the one that has to give you a reality check, but there is no way you saw a human heart."

"I did."

"I know you believe what you saw was a human heart, but think about it for a minute. It's probably just some Halloween prop."

He shook his head, his hair falling in his eyes. "I wish it were. It was real. Remember, I'm the one who saw it, not you."

"Okay, fine. Let's say for the moment the heart is real. If it's a human heart, that means it belongs to someone—a dead someone."

Sammy ran his hands through his hair, pushing it away from his eyes. "Yeah, they would be very dead."

"So, let's think about this rationally. It makes more sense that the heart you saw was just a heart that happened to look like a human heart. Like a pig's heart from your sisters' movie. I mean you can't just go around ripping hearts out of people's chests and putting them in jars; this is not Hollywood. There would be a body. The cops would've been called. I bet it's just some anatomy lab stuff that found its way into the attic along with all the other crap. Makes perfect sense to me."

"It's a human heart. I know it. I just know it."

"'I just know it' isn't good enough, Sammy."

"It has to be."

"Fine," Ivy said, her hands moving from her hips to cross over her chest. "If you're so sure it's a human heart, we should call the cops."

"No cops."

"You're stalling because you know it's not a human heart." Ivy said exasperated.

"It's human, but it's no normal human heart."

"I know it's fiber optic at midnight, but it's still a heart . . . and if you're so sure its human we should probably tell an adult."

"No. No adults either."

Ivy rolled her eyes. "You surprise me Sammy, I thought you'd be jumping at the chance to get Pastor Leeds in trouble. Him hoarding a human heart and all is definitely enough to get him booted out of town."

"Teller, this is serious. And I don't think Pastor Leeds knows about the heart. You want to hear something strange?"

She scoffed. "Stranger than a fresh human heart in a jar that seconds as a flare gun? I've got to hear this."

Ivy sat down next to Sammy.

"I don't think Uriah's cousin could see the light or hear the sound."

"I don't know how he couldn't. I heard and saw it from the bushes."

"Mr. Richards acted like everything was normal—Well, besides me being in his cousin's house in the middle of the night. He didn't say anything about it as if he couldn't see the light or hear the heart beating."

Ivy shrugged her shoulders. "Okay, what are you getting at?"

"Mr. Richards was oblivious to the jarred heart and so is Pastor Leeds, there's no way he could sleep through that. Trust me its loud."

"Sammy!"

"We're the only one's who can see and hear it."

Ivy leaned into her hand. "Oh my God Sammy Lopez, and why

would we be the only ones that can see and hear it?"

"Because we're witches. I think the heart is calling out to us. Like it wanted us to find it. The red light is some sort of supernatural SOS."

Ivy buried her face in a pillow. "There's no such thing as witches," she said muffled, preparing a lecture in her head.

"I'll prove it to you. First thing tomorrow, we'll grab the box with the jarred heart and bring it here. And when you see that I was right, I want a big apology kiss." Ivy lifted her face from the pillow to look at him. "And a little praise. Something like: *Oh Sammy, you're so smart, I never should have doubted you. Oh, and you're so brave, and so handsome,*" Sammy said, imitating Ivy's voice.

"I don't sound like that," she said, sitting up straight.

"You kinda do."

She nudged him. "Okay jerk, and if I'm right, and the heart is just a science experiment dud, you have to clean my room for a month."

"Deal. But do me a favor, if I'm late getting to Pastor Leeds's again, get in and grab the box. It's the first box as soon as you walk into the sunroom."

"Okay, I'll make sure I'm the first one in."

"Good."

Sammy lay down on Ivy's bed, pulling her down next to him. "Since I know I'm right about the heart, I think I'll collect my apology kiss before I go home."

Ivy rolled her eyes and smiled. The wasps were already swarming inside of her, making her hot and light-headed. "Fine. But this is nothing more than a sympathy kiss. Because I feel bad for you that you still believe in magic."

Sammy beamed. "Yep, witches, Santa Claus, and the Tooth Fairy. I think that calls for more than one kiss."

Ivy giggled, enjoying Sammy haggling his childish silliness for more kisses. "I agree."

Sammy's hand cupped the side of Ivy's face, his touch gentle, his blue eyes sparkling like stars in her dim room. "Where were we before I found a beating heart in our Pastor's house?"

CHAPTER TWENTY-FOUR
Morning to Remember

Ivy stretched as she stirred in her bed. She rolled over to see Sammy fast asleep next to her. She glanced at her alarm clock; it was almost 4:30 in the morning. Ivy shook Sammy in a panic. "Sammy, get up!"

"Hmm . . . what?"

"You fell asleep; it's already morning!"

"Shit!" He hopped out of Ivy's bed and glanced at her alarm clock. "My dad's going to be up soon!"

They raced down the stairs to the front door. "See you in a couple hours." Sammy planted a quick kiss on Ivy's lips and sprinted down the sidewalk at lightning speed as the sun rose.

By the time Ivy got up to her room, she could hardly see him out of her small attic window, he was just a blur on the horizon. Ivy crawled back into bed. Last night was the best night of her life. Sammy Lopez kissed her and even said she was hot. She was still debating if he meant that literally but was thinking optimistically and besides, he had said she was beautiful. There was no denying that.

Ivy grabbed the pillow Sammy had been laying on and hugged it to her face, smelling his cologne, making her feel like a part of him was still with her. She only let the pillow go to prevent asphyxiation, but death via Sammy's cologne didn't seem like the worst way to go.

Still clinging to the pillow, she rolled over, her eyes landing on the Leeds's family spell book on her desk.

She got up to grab it and returned to her bed. Sammy had left a bookmark in the grimoire where he had stopped reading. It was one of those giveaways from the bank his dad was affiliated with.

Ivy's fingertips skimmed over the *Beauty Spell*. "I said I wouldn't . . . he said I was beautiful." Ivy closed the book; not wanting to be tempted. "I *am* beautiful," she said with modest conviction, sliding the spell book onto her nightstand, and knocking over her glass of water. "Oh crap," she said, jumping to her feet. The book was soaked. She shook it out, trying to dry it as quickly as possible. Luckily the leather cover bore the brunt of the spill, she didn't think she ruined any pages.

A piece of paper fell out of the grimoire along with Sammy's bookmark. She picked them up. She went to shove them back in the spell book when her eyes focused on the worn paper. It was a drawing of a woman rendered in charcoal. Ivy brought the drawing up to her nose to get a better look. "That's . . . strange."

The woman in the drawing had the same small, round nose she had. Her full lips were identical to her own. The charcoal drawing gave Ivy an unsettled feeling in her stomach, that bordered on nausea. She turned it over to read: Midwife, 1735.

"It has to be a relative," Ivy said to herself, turning the drawing over again to look into the woman's dark eyes—dark eyes like hers. Ivy sat down on her bed still holding the fragile paper, her hands shaking. She didn't like this drawing, didn't like how it made her feel, didn't like that the woman resembled her, didn't like that it was stuffed in some old book Sammy swore was a real grimoire. She opened the top drawer to her nightstand and threw the drawing in. She laughed it off, "Sammy is really rubbing off on me. I'm almost believing in all this hocus-pocus."

Sammy quietly came in through the garage. He was tiptoeing to the staircase when he heard his father in the kitchen.

"You're up early," Jeffrey said, taking a sip of his coffee.

"Morning Dad," Sammy answered back as he quickened his pace to the staircase. His mind was racing as he tried to think of an excuse to tell his father for why he was out of his room when he was grounded.

Leaving his mug on the counter, Jeffrey strolled into the foyer. He noticed Sammy was wearing the same clothes he'd had on last night at dinner, and he smelled like mothballs.

"Sammy, where were you?"

"Garage, I had to get this thing for youth group after church."

Jeffrey looked at his watch, "At 4:30 in the morning?"

Sammy started up the staircase. "Yeah, I thought I should grab it when it was on my mind, so I didn't forget. I'm going back to bed for a few hours," Sammy said, hoping his dad was buying it; it sounded good to him.

"Did you sneak out of the house last night?

Sammy froze. "Can we talk about this in the morning Dad. I'm tired."

"Do you know how dangerous it is to sneak out of the house in the middle of the night?!" Jeffrey asked from the foot of the stairs, his tone sharpening. "I can't believe you would pull a stunt like this after what happened to Zachary Lewis!"

Sammy turned around to face his father. "What do you mean *after what happened to Zachary Lewis*? I thought Zac was with his father."

"No Sammy, he's not. He's still missing."

"What?" Sammy asked confused. "But I overheard you say he was with his dad . . . Why didn't you tell me?"

"Because, Sammy you're a child. I don't want you worrying about things kids shouldn't worry about. I wanted you to think he was with his dad so you could have a carefree summer."

Sammy stood dumbfounded, a mixture of emotion seizing him. He didn't know if he should cry or yell.

"I just don't get you. I put this security system in the house to keep you safe, and here you are sneaking out and you don't even have a phone."

"Well, whose fault is that?!" Sammy snapped, his anger getting the best of him. He recoiled, regretting what he said, wishing he could take it back. If he wasn't in trouble already, he was in big trouble now. He headed up the stairs.

That was it. Jeffrey lost it. "Sammy, get down here right now!"

"Dad, can we talk about it in the morning?" Sammy asked, now taking two steps at a time.

"That's just it Sammy, it *is* the morning!" Jeffrey started up the stairs after him. "We are talking about this now." Jeffrey grabbed his son's arm at the top of the stairs, yanking him back. Sammy lost his footing, wobbling. Jeffrey tried to catch him before he fell, but it was too late. Sammy tumbled down the long spiral staircase, landing on the foyer floor with a striking thud.

CHAPTER TWENTY-FIVE
Church Without the Lopez Family

That morning Sammy wasn't at church. In fact, the entire Lopez family wasn't there. Ivy could hear the members whispering among themselves as they waited for Pastor Leeds's stand-in to start. Apparently, Lindsey Lopez never missed a service, but today seemed to be the exception, which meant no coffee hour treats. With Pastor Leeds away on business and no promise of coffee hour, everyone was wondering why they'd gotten out of bed.

Every time the church doors opened, Ivy turned around hoping to see Sammy. When the service ended and Sammy was still a no show, she felt sick. She had a bad feeling in the pit of her stomach, and it wasn't because she'd skipped breakfast so she could have one of Lindsey's famous sticky buns.

"Sammy's still not here," Ivy whispered to her grandmother.

"Maybe they had an emergency."

"That's what I'm worried about."

The youth group still met at Pastor Leeds's house after church. But without Sammy there, the rest of the kids, not including Ivy, talked their parents into just going home. Ivy stayed; she had a box to grab.

"Hi, I'm Jesse," the tall, handsome man with the dirty-blond hair and warm hazel eyes said, shaking Ivy's hand.

"Ivy."

"Looks like you're going it alone this morning, Ivy."

"Yeah."

"What happened? I thought a group of kids was supposed to be meeting here this morning?"

"The team leader didn't come to church."

"Sammy?"

She nodded. "Yeah, him. But that's okay, I know what I'm supposed to do."

"What can I do to help?" Jesse asked with a warm smile.

"Nothing, I'm good," she said with a smile of her own, before walking into the house and making a beeline for the jarred heart. She grabbed the box and came outside with it.

"These boxes are all going to the trash," Ivy told Jesse as he walked alongside her. "My grandmother and I are going to drop them off later, so I'm going to take them to my house. I'm just across the way."

"Let me carry that for you," Jesse offered as he went to take the box.

Ivy pulled away. "I got it. This is my community service. Enjoy your Sunday Jesse."

Sammy was right, the boxes weighed a ton. Ivy wished she could've handed the box off to Jesse, but she didn't want to risk him seeing what was in the box in the small chance Sammy was right and there was actually a human heart buried at the bottom of it.

Ivy put the box down in her grandmother's living room, quickly rummaging through it looking for the jarred heart. She gasped. There it was—the heart. She spun the mason jar around to get a better look at it. The moist heart sloshed around in its own fluids and blood. It looked like a human heart, she'd give Sammy that much, but she was no expert when it came to anatomy. It did, however, look like something from a science lab, there was no light shining from it and it wasn't beating, it just sat there in the jar, dead and gross.

She buried it at the bottom of the box, smiling to herself. Human heart or pig heart, it's still a heart. She was going to let Sammy have this one and an apology kiss.

Ivy walked the box up to her bedroom and slid it under her bed for safe keeping before going back to Pastor Leeds's to grab another box.

Lindsey sat by her son's hospital bed, holding his hand. Jeffrey was just about to walk in when he heard Lindsey talking to Sammy. He decided to give them a moment and waited by the door.

"Sammy, I need you to tell me the truth," Lindsey said to him, squeezing his hand. "Did your father push you down the stairs?"

"What?! Mom, no! Don't be crazy, of course not!"

Tears beaded in the corner of her eyes. "You need to tell me the truth. Do not protect him. I will take you and your sisters, and we will leave him."

"Mom, it wasn't like that. I swear. I sneaked out of the house last night and tried to get home before anyone noticed. I was half asleep, I was up all night, I was walking up the stairs and I just missed the step and fell back. It was an accident. I'm lucky Dad was downstairs when I fell."

Lindsey hugged her son. "I love you so much."

"I know Mom. I love you too."

Jeffrey took a deep breath before he entered the room. He knew Sammy held all the power in his words. He could have ended his life as he knew it right then and there; taken his family away from him, but instead Sammy chose to protect him. Jeffrey hadn't meant for Sammy to fall down the stairs. It was an accident—that part was true. He didn't want to hurt his son; he never did. As Sammy had lain unconscious on the cold marble floor, Jeffrey thought he'd killed him—thought that he had ended his son's life, a son whom he loved more than anyone or anything. He had prayed for Sammy to be okay, for God to give him another chance. He was going to change. Jeffrey promised himself, God, and Sammy that he would never lay another hand on Sammy if Sammy could just pull through.

"Your sister's here, she's with the girls," Jeffrey said to Lindsey.

"I'll be back soon." Lindsey kissed her son's forehead before she left.

"How you feeling?" Jeffrey asked, taking a seat on the side of Sammy's bed.

"Kinda crappy, but not that bad."

He had several bruised ribs and had fractured his right tibia. He'd suffered a gash on the top of his head that had bled heavily and required staples.

"Sammy . . . I need to—"

Sammy cut his father off, "Dad, I know it was an accident. You don't have to."

"No, Sammy. I do have to. I almost killed you. You could've died. We're so lucky you didn't."

Tears rolled down Jeffrey's cheeks. The color drained from Sammy's face with every tear shed. He had never seen his father cry before. Seeing it filled him with uncertainty and fear. He wanted him to stop. Wanted his father to be some unmovable rock as he had always been.

"Sammy, I'm so sorry."

"Dad, it's okay. I'll be fine. Please stop."

"I know I don't always show it, but you mean so much to me. I love you." He hugged Sammy.

"I love you too," Sammy told his father, biting back his own tears. It was true, he did love his father. They butted heads, almost every day, but he loved his father and respected him.

"Can you forgive me?" Jeffrey asked, pressing Sammy to him like he used to when he was still a little boy.

"I forgive you. But Dad, you're squeezing too hard. Bruised ribs, remember?"

"Sorry," Jeffrey said, releasing his bear hug and wiping his tears on the back of his hand.

"Any word on Zac?" Sammy asked. He had been thinking of Zac all morning and couldn't wait to ask his father about him.

Jeffrey hung his head. "No nothing, but I'm hopeful. We're doing everything Devan says and he's confident Zac will be home very soon."

Sammy nodded, not wanting to press the issue. He didn't want to risk his father crying again. His father was a great liar, but he was off of his game. Sammy could tell he didn't believe a word he said.

"I can't wait to get out of here. When can I go home?" Sammy asked, changing the subject before *he* cried. If his father didn't believe Zac would be home soon, there was only one alternative.

"Hopefully tomorrow. They want to keep you overnight for observation because of the concussion."

"Urgh, this stinks! I'm fine."

"It's only a day, and on the way home I'll get you a new phone."

"Thanks Dad."

"And that car you want. You've got it."

"Dad, you don't have to."

"No Sammy, you deserve it. You're a good kid. You get straight A's and you do untold community service."

"Well, in all fairness, not all my community service is selfless," Sammy said with a large smile.

Jeffrey smiled back. "I figured as much when you volunteered to cut Old Lady Mary's yard."

Sammy laughed. His laughter hurt his sides.

"You must really like that girl?"

"I do, Dad."

"Ivy seems nice."

"She is—really nice."

It was well into the afternoon when Pastor Leeds got home. Ivy walked over to him as he got out of his car. She was happy to see him looking better. He had color to his face and his whole demeanor seemed healthier.

"You look so much better than yesterday," Ivy blurted out.

"It's a funny thing, I do feel a lot better. I guess it just took time for my medications to work. I feel relieved."

Ivy smiled.

"Just you today, Ivy?" he asked, closing his car door, and putting his keys into his pocket along with the silver coin Bishop Baker had given him.

"Yep, just me. Everyone ran for the hills when Sammy couldn't make it. It's strange, he couldn't wait to get over here yesterday."

"I just got back from visiting him," Pastor Leeds said.

Ivy furrowed her brows. "Visiting him?"

"Yes, his mother called me this morning. I got there as soon as I could."

"What are you talking about?"

"There was an accident last night."

Ivy's body tensed. "Accident?"

"Sammy is going to be okay, but he's in the hospital."

Ivy's heart was beating so fast she thought it was going to jump out of her chest. She put her hand on her heart just in case. "What type of accident?"

"He fell down the stairs."

Ivy burst into tears, surprising herself a little. Her feelings came from a place she was unfamiliar with, and she couldn't control them. Pastor Leeds hugged her. "Ivy, he will be fine, don't cry. He broke his leg, but you know Sammy, nothing will keep him down. He's in high spirits. The Lopez's asked if I would let you know that he's at Mainland Hospital. I think Sammy would like it if you visited."

Ivy wiped her tears on her sleeve. "Pastor Leeds, I know I'm leaving your house a mess; I promise I'll finish up tomorrow."

"No worries, Ivy. Thank you for all you did today," he called to her as she ran home.

Grams drove to the hospital right away. They met Lindsey in the hospital lobby. She hugged Grams and Ivy with tears in her eyes.

"Can I go see him?" Ivy asked.

"Yes of course. Sammy will be very happy to see you," Lindsey told her.

Ivy made her way to Sammy's room as quickly as she could. She detested hospitals. They always bothered her: the odd quietness, the smell, the way all the hallways looked the same. But she was crazy for Sammy and wanted to make sure he was alright.

Ivy knocked on Sammy's door before entering. He had the room to himself. Seeing her, his face lit up. "Hey, how are you feeling?" Ivy asked, sitting down in the chair next to Sammy's hospital bed.

"Okay," he said.

"You look horrible." Not that he did, it was just seeing him in the hospital bed, in a hospital robe with his leg in a cast, made her say it. It seemed unnatural for him to be there amongst the sick and dying, he was Sammy Lopez.

"Please, I read your phone. I know you think I look like a Spanish god."

Ivy blushed. "That wasn't for your eyes."

He grinned and leaned over, ignoring the pain in his side to kiss Ivy's cheek. The kiss made Ivy very happy. It meant that last night's kisses and the peck in the morning were all real. Part of her thought she'd made it all up. She quickly kissed him back.

"Pastor Leeds said you fell down the stairs."

"Yep, sure did. From now on, I'm always holding onto the banister."

"I was worried," Ivy said in a low voice, nibbling on her bottom lip.

She wanted to hold Sammy's hand, but she was nervous. She put her hand next to his on his bed. Relief pulsed through her when he took her hand in his.

"Don't be. I'm fine, and with a little prayer, I'll be good to go before school starts. Pastor Leeds already kicked things off earlier with a special mass for the family."

"That's good."

"Yeah, it settled my mother down. I think she thought we were all going to burn in Hell because we missed church."

"Did you ever find out where Pastor Leeds was today?" Ivy inquired.

"I didn't ask."

"Strange for a pastor to take a personal day on a Sunday."

"I didn't think about it Teller, but you're right, that is really strange. I guess whatever it was couldn't wait, maybe it was a doctor's appointment."

Ivy considered that. It also seemed strange a specialist would have Sunday hours, but seeing how much better Pastor Leeds was feeling, she thought that was likely. And besides, since when was she a conspiracy theorist? That was more of Sammy's thing.

Sammy sighed. "Sorry I missed church and—"

"Don't worry. I got it."

Sammy leaned over and kissed Ivy again, this time on the lips. "I knew you would. And what did you think?"

"You're right, it's a heart."

"I love told-you-so moments," he said, grinning that grin she loved.

"Still not convinced it's human, but I better give you your apology kiss just in case."

CHAPTER TWENTY-SIX
Weekend Job

It had been a long week and morning at Pastor Leeds's house. Ivy went home for a lunch break. She threw herself onto the couch as soon as she made it to the living room. She was exhausted from lugging heavy boxes.

"Lunch is ready," her grandmother yelled from the kitchen. Ivy didn't stir.

Grams walked into the living room and kicked Ivy's legs off the couch.

"Ouch, Grams, what'd you do that for?!"

"No shoes on the couch. I'm not raising a barn animal." Ivy massaged her sore shin. "I said your lunch is ready. Oh, and I've got some good news. I found you a job."

"You didn't," Ivy moaned. "Cleaning out Pastor Leeds's house is a full-time job. I'm depleted, body and soul," she said, bringing her hand to her forehead and pretending to faint.

"Don't be such a drama queen. When I was your age, I had two jobs."

"Yeah, and when you were my age, you already had hair on your chest," Ivy giggled.

Mary ignored her granddaughter's jab. "Make sure you thank Jesse for the reference."

"This was Jesse's doing, was it? He's not allowed over here anymore. I don't care if he's the only one in town that will play dominoes with you. No more Jesse."

"Ivy Belle, don't you want to know what the job is before you go writing off my dominoes buddy?"

"No, not really. A job means work, and I'm too tired to even care what it is."

"Babysitting."

Ivy sat up straight. "You're kidding me, Grams! You know me and kids don't mix."

"Not possible. Kids all mix when you put them in a blender."

"What planet are you from? Urgh! You're the only one less qualified to babysit than me."

"Oh Ivy, give it a rest. You're not babysitting a kid."

"Oh, good," Ivy said, falling back on the couch. "You had me worried."

"You're sitting for a teenager. I forget what Jesse said . . . fourteen, fifteen, sixteen—around your age."

"You're joking, right?"

"Nope."

"Jesse found me a job babysitting a teenager? What planet is he from?"

"She's blind."

"Okay . . ."

"Her parents are going out of town for the weekend, and she needs a sitter."

Ivy scrunched up her face. "For a teenager?"

"I did say she was blind?"

"Yeah, you did. Just trying to figure out how Jesse falls into this and why a teenager—blind or not blind—needs a babysitter."

"He's friends with the family, and she recently became blind."

"Wow, that sucks, but since Jesse's a friend, why can't he do it?"

"Can't. He's busy."

"So am I. Busy laying on the couch and waiting for Sammy to call me. I feel like I've hardly talked to him. His father keeps carting him off to doctor after doctor for a second and third opinion on his leg. They all said the same thing: He'll recover, and it won't affect his ability to play sports. But Mr. Lopez still insists on taking him to another doctor."

"Fine. You lay on the couch and wait for that brat to call. Maybe Elsa or Tammy will do it for six hundred dollars." Mary said, walking back to the kitchen.

Ivy choked, getting to her feet. "Six hundred?!"

"Yeppers. Two hundred a day, Friday through Sunday." Mary said from her seat at the kitchen table.

Ivy took a seat next to her grandmother. "Well, I guess I can do it. It's only one weekend away from Sammy. I'm sure I'll survive."

"That's what I thought. I already told Jesse you'd do it."

"Thanks, Grams, you always have my best interest at heart," Ivy said with a mouth full of peanut butter and jelly.

Mary turned down a dirt driveway lined in Norway Spruce trees. Their green branches hung low over the driveway, making Ivy feel like they were traveling through a cave of evergreens.

"Nice property," Grams said, surveying the mature landscape.

"Try creepy. If it weren't for the mailbox, you would never know there was a house all the way back here." Ivy smirked. "If we lived here, you'd have to let me drive. I would never make it to the mailbox."

Grams and Ivy glanced at each other and laughed. "That's a fact, my dear."

Ivy put her hands on her belly. "Why wasn't I born with a love of exercise?"

"Those who are honey, are crazier than a drunk Piney. It's perfectly normal to preserve your energy. It's what separates us from the animals." Grams pointed to her head. "Our brains."

They parked, looking up at an old farmhouse. "Nice house to go with a nice piece of property," Grams said, turning the station wagon off.

In front of them stood a monstrosity that rose up three stories. Its original pine siding had recently received a fresh coat of bright-white paint. The house still had windows made from handblown glass. Ivy found it unnerving how the antique windows distorted the reflection of the nearby trees like circus glass. Nothing was what it seemed. She shrugged off a bad feeling.

"Well, you better get going, Ives."

Ivy reluctantly got out of the car and grabbed her overnight bag from the back seat, keeping the six-hundred-dollar-pay-check in her mind. It wasn't helping, she looked to her grandmother with pleading eyes, hoping Elsa or Tammy were free this weekend.

"Well, get going."

"I don't know about this, Grams. I'm not exactly a people person. Maybe we should tell them I got sick."

"Too late for cold feet. What's your problem?"

"The house is kinda spooky."

"Ivy, it's an old house. You live in an old house."

"Yes, and because of that, I have black circles under my eyes from all the creaks, moans, and whatever other noises your house makes."

"Get your butt in there right now before my boot goes up it!"

Ivy growled. "Fine."

Mary unbuckled and got out of the station wagon to escort Ivy to the front door. She reasoned it was the polite thing to do anyway.

"This is not worth the money," Ivy mumbled under her breath.

Mary walked alongside her granddaughter up the brick walkway. Her grandmother nodded toward the front door that was painted bright red. Ivy shuddered, she really hated the color red.

Mary knocked on the front door for Ivy.

A woman with dark hair opened it, her eyes landing instinctively on Ivy. "You must be Ivy Teller."

PLEASANT MILLS, NEW JERSEY: LITTLETON PROPERTY

"Hi, Mrs. Littleton."

"Come in."

Ivy glanced back at her grandmother for reassurance. Mary gave her a kind smile and a wave goodbye.

Ivy followed Mrs. Littleton down a long hallway that had black and white photos hung closely together. There was so many, Ivy could barely see the striped wallpaper. She looked at the old photos as they made their way down the narrow hallway. They helped to distract her from the sound of their footsteps, which were eerily loud in the otherwise quiet house. The sound of her sneakers striking the hardwood floor made her anxious, her tension growing with each echoing step. "Nice house." Ivy fibbed, breaking up the sound of their heavy footfalls.

"Thank you. It's been in the family for generations. And thank you for clearing your weekend on such short notice."

"Uh, no problem."

"Rosa's grandfather usually watches her when we go out of town, but he's busy."

"No worries, Mrs. Littleton."

"I hope you girls have a fun time. Rosa has been very depressed since she went blind."

"Um, I'm sure we will."

Mrs. Littleton walked Ivy to the last door down the long stretch of hallway and knocked. "Rosa, Ivy's here." She gently pushed open her daughter's door. Ivy's eyes darted to a teenage girl with jet-black hair sitting at a desk. Ivy had never seen hair that dark and wondered if she dyed it that color. She wore it in two long braids that were thrown over her shoulders, making Ivy think of rope.

Rosa swiveled in her chair to face them. Dark tinted glasses obstructed most of her face.

Mrs. Littleton made her way to her daughter, kissing the top of her daughter's head. "Call us if you need us; we'll try to be back early Sunday."

"Okay Mom, have a good trip."

Mrs. Littleton handed Ivy money from her pocket. "Here you go, in case you girls decide to order out. Well, I'll leave you two to get acquainted."

"Hi," Ivy said, taking a step into the bedroom.

"Hi Ivy. Sorry you have to spend your weekend here."

"Um . . . it's okay. I wasn't doing anything."

"How old are you?"

"Uh . . . Sixteen," Ivy said, forgetting for a second.

"Me too!" Rosa said happily.

"You go to Pleasant Mills High School?" Ivy asked. She wasn't one to bring up school in the middle of the summer, but it would be nice to start school with some friends. She doubted she would be eating lunch with Elsa and Tammy.

"No. I'm homeschooled."

"Oh . . . " Ivy said, not sure what to say next.

"Do you have a lot of friends?"

Ivy took a seat on Rosa's bed. "Not really. I just moved here in the beginning of the summer.

"Me either, my only friend is Jesse."

"Jesse seems nice. He's my neighbor, well I guess sort of, I'm not sure how long he's planning to stay with Pastor Leeds. We talk sometimes, but I don't know if I'd call him a friend yet. But I guess I have a few from youth group."

Rosa ran her hand down the length of one of her braids. Ivy thought it made her look like she was petting herself. "I don't get out a lot. My family is more than a little overbearing. But, Jesse, he's friends with my grandfather so he comes over quite a bit. I know he's older than me, but I have the biggest crush on him." Rosa couldn't contain her smile. "He's the most handsome guy in the whole world, and he has such a dreamy voice."

Ivy could relate; she'd had a crush on Pastor Leeds who was older, handsome, and blessed with an angelic voice. "Jesse's cute, but I don't know about the dreamy voice bit."

"It's perfect. It's not too deep or soft and his laugh is the best. How it gets really high-pitched—I just love it."

"You sound like you *really* like him."

"I do. Jesse's the best. He drew me all these pictures."

Ivy got up to look at the framed drawings that hung on Rosa's bedroom walls. In small dark frames, drawings of different flowers were signed J.R. The signature looked familiar, but she couldn't remember from where. "Wow, he's a great artist. I had no idea."

"He is. He just drew me this one," Rosa pointed to a frame on her desk that housed a pencil drawing of a rose. "I know you probably think it's weird he still draws me pictures when I can't see, but that's why I like him. He doesn't treat me different because I'm blind now. Not like my parents, who think I need a babysitter at sixteen." Rosa blushed, her cheeks glowing a soft pink. "No offense, Ivy. I just meant they think I'm helpless."

Ivy took a seat back on Rosa's bed. "I knew what you meant. I'd be frustrated too. That's really cool of Jesse. Does he know you like him?"

Rosa's complexion deepened to a rosy red. "No, but I'm gonna tell him real soon. My grandfather said there's a new procedure that's guaranteed to give me back my vision. Once it's back, I know I'll have the confidence to tell Jesse the truth. No more just friends."

"That's great you're going to be able to see again."

"Yeah, my grandfather said it won't be long now."

Ivy anxiously pulled on Rosa's yellow quilted bedspread. She was curious about what had happened to Rosa. She didn't want to come off rude, but she had to know. "If you don't mind me asking, how did you lose your vision?"

"It was a freak thing. In the beginning of the summer, I woke up one morning and I just couldn't see. I opened my eyes and all I saw was black. I was so scared. I just screamed."

"Wow, that's crazy," Ivy said shocked. "I'm sorry . . ."

"It's okay. Funny thing is, I feel like I can already see a little better. Like sometimes I can see shadows. Maybe I'm not as bad off as the doctors say."

"Hopefully not."

"Yeah, I hope." Rosa exhaled loudly. "The only good thing is now I know how much Jesse cares about me. I can't wait to see again. It's been horrible."

"I'm glad he's been a good friend and that you're gonna get your vision back."

Rosa smiled. "It must be awesome to have Jesse as a neighbor. You're so lucky. I would do anything to have him live next door."

"Uh, yeah, he's pretty cool. He's been taking the trash out and just yesterday he came over to kill a really big spider."

"You think you could feel him out about me? See if he says anything, maybe hint that I like him?"

"Yeah, totally."

Ivy felt good talking with a girl that had self-esteem issues like herself. Rosa was so different than the uptight Elsa and clingy Tammy. She was genuinely a nice person.

Ivy noticed dandelions in a vase on Rosa's nightstand. She raised an eyebrow. "Are the dandelions from Jesse?"

"No from my uncle. He picks them for me this time of year. Every couple of days he brings me fresh ones. I know I can't see them, but at least I can smell them. It helps me to picture them in my head."

Ivy scooched over on the bed, hovering her nose over the dandelions. "They smell like weeds to me, but they're pretty."

Rosa laughed. "Maybe a little, but yellow is my favorite color."

"Me too."

Rosa beamed. "I think we're going to be good friends, Ivy."

CHAPTER TWENTY-SEVEN
Hard Talk

Jeffrey knocked on Sammy's door. "Come in," Sammy said. He was sitting in his bed reading, with his broken leg elevated on pillows like the doctor had directed him to do a couple hours a day. Jeffrey was glad to see his son was listening to the doctor's orders.

He took a seat on the side of his son's bed.

"What's up?" Sammy asked, putting his mandated summer reading for school down. He could tell something was on his dad's mind, there was something in the way he avoided his gaze.

Jeffrey kept his eyes on the floor and nervously rubbed the sides of his legs. "This is hard for me to say . . . "

Sammy sat up, rotating his broken leg so he could sit next to his father. "Dad, what's wrong?"

"They found Zachary Lewis."

"Found? . . . Dad, is he okay?" Sammy's voice hitched. He went to stand up. Jeffrey put his hand on his son's shoulder to stop him.

Jeffrey's eyes met Sammy's. "No Sammy, he's not . . . He's dead."

"What?!" Sammy whispered. He felt like his voice shook the room. His face turned beat red and hot, a nervous energy shaking his frame. "What happened?!"

"Sammy . . ."

"Dad, tell me. I need to know."

"He was murdered."

"Murdered?!" Sammy felt a whirlwind of emotions crushing him. He wanted to get up and do something, anything; but it was already too late, his friend was gone.

"Yes, he was murdered," Jeffrey said in a low voice, staring at the floor again. "A hiker found him in the woods not far away from church."

"I don't understand. Those woods were searched the night of the church lock-in."

"They were, Sammy. He wasn't there. Devan thinks that Zac was abducted and kept alive until recently."

Sammy's eyes burned with tears. "Dad, this can't be right. I thought Devan said not to worry."

"I'm sorry Sammy; I wish it weren't true. Devan broke the news to his mother this afternoon." Jeffrey empathetically glanced at Sammy. "Devan said he had everything under control. He asked everyone at the lock-in that night to keep Zac's abduction to ourselves. He thought if we made Zac's disappearance public it could force an abductor to act out of fear and hurt Zac." Jeffrey ran his hands through his hair. "We did what he said, and he was still killed. Keeping Zac's disappearance a secret felt wrong, but I guess I went along with it because I didn't want your mother to have to relive what happened to her little brother." Jeffrey exhaled slowly, shaking his head, his eyes still on the floor. "I know Devan is the Chief of Police, but I can't help but think he went about it the wrong way. We knew it wasn't Zac's father who'd grabbed him the next day. I kept thinking we should've scared the town, flipped it upside down, put pressure on the person who abducted Zac, maybe if we did, we would have found him alive."

"Dad, you can't put that on yourself. You're not the police force."

"I know, but now Zac's dead and there's no suspect. They've got nothing, Sammy. I should have used my influence to organize manhunts . . . done something to help bring Zac home."

Jeffrey put a hand on each of Sammy's shoulders and looked him dead in the eyes. Sammy flinched. His father had been so keen on avoiding eye contact, the sudden change startled him. "Sammy, that means the person who killed Zac is still out there. I know you're not sneaking out of the house anytime soon. But don't, okay? It's not safe. There's a lunatic in this town, and it could be anyone."

"I won't, Dad; I promise. I'll be careful."

Jeffrey patted Sammy on the back. He wanted to hug him like he had done in the hospital, but he refrained.

Sammy's face twisted, tears beading on his thick lashes.

"Are you okay?"

"No Dad, I'm not. I know Zac left the church that night to be cool, 'cause I did it first."

"Sammy, just as it's not my fault, it's not yours," Jeffrey said. "Zac should have been able to go outside and scare everyone and come back in like you did. This is a good town; things like this aren't supposed to happen."

Sammy looked at his father with glassy eyes, a few tears spilling over his lashes. "What are we going to do to make sure it doesn't happen again?"

"Good question. I'm not sure. First things first, we need to tell everyone the truth about Zac. No more secrets; no more brushing things under the rug. Keeping things quiet didn't help Zac. I'm going to give Devan a couple of hours before I call him. I'm sure talking to Mrs. Lewis wasn't easy for him. Zac was a great kid, and everyone liked him."

"Yeah Dad, he was. I'm gonna miss him."

Jeffrey gave his son's shoulder a squeeze and got up. "If you need to talk Sammy, just let me know."

"Okay, thanks Dad."

With his father gone, the tears freely fell. The guilt of what happened to Zac was eating him up. He felt responsible. If he had stayed in the church and followed the rules, Zac would still be alive. His father had asked him that night: When will you learn to listen? He buried his face in his pillow to stifle his sobs. He'd learned the hard way.

CHAPTER TWENTY-EIGHT
A Dandelion

Ivy settled into the bed in the spare bedroom across the hall from Rosa's room. She couldn't sleep. To her own disbelief, she missed her attic bedroom. Although at night it was spooky, she loved her room by daylight. She would often daydream that she was Rapunzel, stuck in the attic, hidden from the world by her wicked grandmother.

Ivy smiled to herself when she thought of Grams. Grams was as stubborn as a mule, but she wasn't wicked. She missed her grandmother. She was the peanut butter to her jelly.

Ivy's thoughts drifted to her mother. She closed her eyes. She couldn't see her mother's face. She really focused. She couldn't recall her mother's hair color. Was she a brunette like her, or have black hair like Rosa, or was she a red head like Mike and Tammy, or maybe blonde, like Elsa? In fact, she couldn't recall anything about her mother.

She couldn't recall anything about her mother or her sisters. She couldn't remember if she had a hot sister like she'd teased at Sammy or not. Or, if she even had more than one. There was nothing there, like they didn't exist.

Her eyes flew open in a panic. "What if I have amnesia from when Sammy knocked me to the ground? What if I have brain damage?" She muttered to herself. "Maybe I should tell Grams—no—she'll cart me off to every doctor and head shrink in South Jersey."

Ivy sat up in bed, hearing a shrieking noise like nails on a chalkboard. She pulled her blanket to her chest as if the down comforter was a shield that could protect her. She heard it again. Her eyes followed the sound to the window. It was just a tree branch scraping across a glass windowpane as a gust of wind blew by.

Ivy rested her head back on the pillow. "I officially hate old houses." She put her ear buds in and closed her eyes, she had done enough thinking for one night. She focused on the music until she finally fell asleep.

Japhet Dean Leeds made his way to the vase of dandelions in Rosa's room. He threw the wilted flowers in the trash can and replaced them with fresh ones he'd picked on the way to her house. He then plucked one of them out of the vase and put it in his suit pocket. He took one more dandelion and made his way to the room where Ivy slept. He knelt by the side of her bed and placed the dandelion in her open hand. After doing so, he turned to leave, whistling lowly as he made his way back to the woods.

Ivy woke up startled. "Rosa?" she whispered, placing her bare feet on the cold hardwood floor. She cautiously walked across the hall to Rosa's room. "Rosa? Was that you?" Ivy made her way to Rosa's bedside, her yellow bedspread kissed in golden moonlight. She noticed Rosa's glasses sitting on the nightstand next to a vase of fresh dandelions. "Rosa, are you awake?" Ivy shook her lightly. "Rosa, I think someone's in the house," she whispered. Ivy glanced toward Rosa's bedroom window as a tree branch scratched at it like a claw. "Rosa, please get up." Rosa stirred, slowly opening her eyes. Ivy let out a gut-wrenching scream when she saw Rosa's eyes were missing.

Ivy shot up in bed, screaming. Sweat dripped from her forehead, her chest moved up and down furiously as she panted for air. Rosa, hearing Ivy's scream, got out of bed as quickly as she could. She clung to the walls of her room until she made it to her door. She put her arms out in front of her to bridge the distance of the hall, then stumbled to Ivy's bed. "Ivy, are you okay?!"

Ivy looked at Rosa. Her glasses were off. Her eyes were where they should be. They were dark-brown and blank. Ivy exhaled in relief. "It was just a dream." She wiped the sweat from her hair line. "I'm sorry if I scared you."

Rosa hugged Ivy. She needed that. Her dream was so real. She felt unnerved to her core.

"What did you dream about?"

"Um . . . zombies," Ivy lied.

Rosa laughed. "Zombies?! They seem so fake to me. I want brains," she said playfully to ease Ivy's mind. "I'm scared of witches."

Ivy thought of Sammy and chuckled. "Yeah, well they're definitely not real. No such thing as hocus-pocus."

Rosa laughed. "Agreed, but how about I stay with you tonight. This old house can be a little spooky."

Ivy felt childish but relieved that Rosa offered to stay with her. "Uh, okay. Thanks Rosa."

Rosa climbed into bed next to Ivy and lay down. Ivy unclenched her fist to see a dandelion in her hand. She stared at the small bright, yellow flower. It made her feel tense, like it tugged on a memory she couldn't remember. Ivy put the dandelion on the nightstand and lay back down, keeping her eyes on the flower until she fell asleep.

CHAPTER TWENTY-NINE
A Sad Service

Pastor Leeds was holding a special service for Zachary Lewis the next night. The church was packed, more so than the typical Sunday full house and it was a Saturday. It was as if the whole town was there, stuffed into the small church. Ivy was glad Rosa's overprotective parents had cut their trip short and got home a day early so she could attend the service. She wanted to be there for Sammy, but as she looked over at all the crying faces wearing black, she felt like she had been swallowed up by a nightmare.

Ivy sat in her usual Sunday seat with Grams. She spotted Zac's cousin Megan. Her brown eyes were bloodshot as she dabbed a tissue to her face. She was with Zachary's mom. Ivy recognized her right away. Zac had looked like her. She was with a man whom she assumed to be Zac's father.

Pastor Leeds had prepared a beautiful sermon in honor of Zac. Thanks to his newfound health, he spoke with vigor and purpose as he talked about Zachary's life, not his death, concluding his sermon with hope. *"He will wipe away every tear from their eyes, and death shall be no more, neither shall there be mourning, nor crying, nor pain anymore, for the former things have passed away."*

Ivy had only met Zac the day he was abducted, but she knew they would've been good friends. She shed some tears as she thought about Zac's enthusiasm over Sammy. They had that in common; she guessed she was his cheerleader now too.

Mrs. Ball sang a song for Zac to close the service. Ivy enjoyed the singing. It seemed like a peaceful way to say goodbye to him. Ivy watched Mrs. Lois Ball intently as she sang, her thin hands shook as she stood in front of the congregation. Elsa had described Mrs. Ball as decrepit. Ivy reasoned that was not far off. The entire town knew she was sickly. There was nothing the doctors could do for her cancer. She had tried treatment after treatment, but nothing had worked. Now all she had was her God. She never missed a service. She was always the first to church and the last one to leave. She was as faithful as they came. Ivy shed another tear as Mrs. Ball finished her song and pulled out a handkerchief to dry her own tears.

Ivy followed her grandmother into the church extension for coffee and cake. Ivy listened to the louder-than-whispered voices all claiming to have thought Zac was with his father and asking how something like this could happen in Pleasant Mills. It seemed to be the thought on everyone's mind, and it eased Ivy's anxiety to know she wasn't the only one thinking it.

From across the way, she watched Sammy go over to Mrs. and Mr. Lewis and Megan after the sermon. She tried not to stare but she couldn't help herself. She knew Sammy was in pain; she wished she could do something. Grams grabbed her hand and led her to the coffee station. "Don't be a looky-loo."

Sammy approached Ivy after he was done talking to the Lewis family, moving slowly on his crutches. It was going to be a long while before he was able to sneak up the attic steps to her room.

Ivy pulled out a chair for him to sit on and leaned his crutches against the wall for him. She wanted to ask if he was okay, but she could tell he wasn't. Silently, she sat next to him, figuring he didn't need anyone else asking him silly questions.

Pastor Leeds came over to them. "How are you feeling, Sammy?"

"Crutches are a pain, but it's only for a couple more weeks," he said, relieved he didn't ask if he was okay.

"And how are you doing with the news of Zac?"

He slumped in his chair, holding back his tears. They were on the brink of spilling over and embarrassing him. "It's hard."

Uriah put a hand on his shoulder. "I'm here for you if you need someone to talk to. Please don't hesitate to come to me. You too Ivy," he offered, gently smiling at her. They nodded their heads. "I want to thank you both again for the great job you're doing at my house. Jesse said he never saw a house so clean."

Ivy looked around. "Where *is* Jesse?"

"He wasn't able to make it. He was already out on a hunting trip when we got word of poor Zac and couldn't make it back intime for tonight's service."

Ivy nodded. That made sense, that was why he couldn't babysit Rosa, not that she needed a sitter.

Uriah was called on from the other side of the room by a teary-eyed Megan. He patted Sammy's shoulder, before making his way to her, giving her a big hug.

"Looks like whatever was plaguing Pastor Leeds has passed. So much for a curse," Ivy teased, trying to cheer Sammy up.

He gave a faint smile. "I'll give you that one Teller, but something strange is still going on. Pastor Leeds is not like he was when he first got here. He definitely looks like he still needs some sleep."

"Well, he's not going to die from not sleeping."

"Actually, I think you can die from that," Sammy said, pulling out his phone and going to Google.

Ivy put her hand on his phone. "You know what I mean, it's not the heart attack curse—no hocus-pocus."

"What about the spell book?" he whispered to Ivy. "What about the glowing, beating heart?!" He didn't give her a chance to respond. "I'm gonna have my dad drop me off tomorrow at your place after my doctor's appointment. Luckily, I only have one tomorrow and it's early in the morning. I want to see it again and see if we can't make sense out of it."

It had been a week since Sammy found the heart. Between his doctor's appointments and his parents wanting him to stay home, he hadn't been able to get to Ivy's to see the jarred heart or her.

"Hi there," Elsa said, taking a seat on the other side of Sammy. Elsa had on a tight black dress cut well above the knee. It was hardly church appropriate in Ivy's eyes, but she couldn't deny that Elsa looked good. "How are you feeling?"

"Better."

"I'm so glad. I've been so worried about you."

"Thanks, Elsa."

"You want me to get you anything?" she asked, putting her hand on his arm.

"I'm good, thanks," Sammy said with a polite smile.

"Okay, well I'll be right back."

Elsa got up, pulling her dress down daintily, and walked over to the desserts and got into line with Mike, Tammy, Tyrone, and Louie. Elsa whispered in Tammy's ear as she hung on Tyrone's arm. Ivy could hear Tammy's annoying, high-pitched giggles from her seat. She tried not to look at them, but she did once or twice.

Sammy admitted defeat. "Well, I'm glad I was wrong about the curse. I actually like Pastor Leeds a lot."

"Me too," Ivy agreed.

Sammy laughed. "We know," he said, touching her lips. "You're drooling again."

"That was for you."

He smiled his classic sideways grin. "Good, 'cause I kinda want to make us official before we start school."

Ivy screwed up her brows. "Make what official?"

"You, as my girlfriend."

Ivy's heart fluttered. She could feel the wasps swarming around in rapture. She smiled wryly. "Am I being asked or told?"

Sammy blushed, looking down at the ground before meeting her eyes. "Ivy Teller, will you be my girlfriend . . . please?"

Ivy tapped her chin in thought. "Since you asked nicely, sure."

Sammy breathed easy. He leaned in and pressed a kiss to Ivy's cheek. "Good."

Elsa shot Ivy a dirty look from the dessert line. Ivy smiled back. She was glad the youth group kids saw Sammy kiss her publicly, even if it was only a peck on the cheek. Ivy knew and she was positive Elsa did too at this point, she'd waited too long. Sammy moved on, and no little black mourning dress was going to win him back—no matter how tight or short.

CHAPTER THIRTY
Witch

Ivy couldn't sleep. She couldn't get the sound of Mrs. Ball's voice out of her head. Her sad song resonated in her ears like she was still in church. No matter how loud she turned up her music, Mrs. Ball's voice bled through, haunting her. Ivy gave up. She shut off her tunes and let Mrs. Ball sing to her while she stared at the cobwebs high above her.

Her mind went back to church. Back to the crying faces and the black garments of grief. She thought of Zac. She wondered what had happened to him—what really happened to him. She knew the adults were keeping secrets. They had kept Zac's disappearance a secret at the request of the Pleasant Mills Police Department, but Ivy knew there was more to the story. She'd noticed Police Chief Rainier and Detective Steele moving in and out of the crowd at Zac's service like oily eels, asking questions in whispers. Ivy knew something bad had happened to Zac—something really bad. She could just feel it.

"Poor Zac," Ivy mutter to herself. "What happened to you?"

A bright red light flashed on the wall. She knew it came from under her bed, from the jarred heart, but it wasn't midnight yet. Ivy glanced at her alarm clock to make sure. She was right, it was only 11:50 p.m. She cautiously got out of bed. Pulling up her bed skirt, she removed the box from Pastor Leeds's house from under her bed where she kept the jarred heart and spell book. She picked up the mason jar with the heart, shaking it a bit.

"Was that you?" Ivy asked, remembering Sammy saying that he thought the heart was trying to communicate with him. Since she brought the jarred heart home, she had been sleeping downstairs on the couch. She was lying to herself again. Telling herself that the couch was closer than her bed and she was too tired from lugging boxes to climb the stairs. The truth was that the jarred heart was under her bed and for reasons not fully understood by her it made her very uncomfortable.

Ivy had made sure she swaddled the jar in the old clothes it was found with. Taking the extra precaution of turning her music up extra loud to make sure she wouldn't be woken up by a beating heart under her bed. It did the trick, she slept right through it, not hearing one little rumble from the attic on the living room couch.

After church she was on autopilot, climbing the steps to her attic room, the jarred heart far from her thoughts that were preoccupied with Zac, that was until she saw the red light.

Sammy had accused her of sleeping in the living room as a way to avoid admitting he was right about the heart being magic. This was partially true, but it had more to do with her wanting the whole thing to just go away, for it to be a figment of their imagination. Magic wasn't real. And she couldn't deal with it if it were. It was better to ignore the whole thing and hope it would just go away or be forgotten under her bed with stray socks. One of the good things about sleeping at Rosa's was she didn't have to worry about the jarred heart under her bed.

Ivy jostled the heart in the jar again, it flopped over in its own fluids.

"Ew, you're so gross." She tossed it back into the box, covering it with the old nightgowns. A bright light flashed again; her eyes darted back to her alarm clock: 11:55 p.m.

She dug out the jar, gripping it with both hands. "It *was* you . . . ?"

A quick burst of red light answered her.

"Okay," she muttered to herself, trying not to panic. "You're early. It's not midnight. I can't believe I'm going to ask this, but what do you want?"

It flashed again, a bright red beam illuminated her face before dying.

"Oh my God, Ivy Belle Teller, you're talking to a heart in a jar. Stop it, before Grams drives you to the insane asylum." She clutched the jar in her hands to stop them from shaking, her nails having a hard time gaining purchase on the slippery glass. "Okay Ives, this is probably just one of your strange dreams—just go with it."

She looked at the jar assertively as her own heart pulsated in her chest. "Okay jarred heart, so what is it—what do you want?"

It flashed yet again.

"Gonna have to do better than that." She shook the jar in frustration. "What do you want?!" she yelled.

Midnight hit and the heart became alive in her hands, beating in its glass prison. Ivy stared at it. She couldn't help herself. The red light drew her closer until her nose was pressed against the jar. She couldn't turn away.

When the room became dark again, she was panting. It took her eyes a moment to adjust to her dim room.

"Well," Ivy said in a whisper, "is that all you can do?"

It flashed.

Her eyes danced over the bright digital numbers of her alarm clock. 12:01 a.m. Apparently, it wasn't bound to the witching hour. "You're pathetic. I know lightning bugs with more umph."

The heart lit up again, flashing a steady stream of red light onto the bedroom wall. The shadow of a figure walked across the light. It was a human, a woman she thought. But it came and went so quickly she couldn't be sure. Ivy screamed and threw the heart at it. The jar shattered on the floor, the sound of the glass breaking reminding her of icicles falling from the gutters in the winter—beautiful and scary at the same time.

Ivy's eyes remained fixated on the wall as she strained to see. She wished she had more than her nightstand lamp on. She brushed her hair away from her face, not letting herself blink. Her chest rose and fell sharply, her heartbeat echoing in her ears.

The light was gone and with it the shadow. She pinched herself, hoping that if she was dreaming, the pinch would wake her up. "Is someone in here?" she asked, her voice timid. She listened intently, her eyes darting around the room before they fell on the heart that lay still on her bedroom floor.

"Oh crap, Sammy's gonna kill me."

Shaking, her kneecaps knocking together, Ivy got up and went downstairs to get a replacement jar to put the heart in.

"What's all the commotion about?" Mary asked through her closed bedroom door.

"Sorry Grams. I just killed the world's largest spider. There must be a nest in the house. I'm just grabbing a paper towel to clean the guts off my wall."

Mary huffed. "Well do it quietly, won't you!"

"Okay, sorry. Night Grams."

Ivy tiptoed into the kitchen and opened the pantry door. She dumped out what was left of the iced tea mix and ran the jar under water to clean it out before heading back up the stairs.

Ivy made it to her bedroom in record time. She turned on her desk lamp and approached the heart slowly. "Yuck," she muttered, picking it up with one of the old garments from Pastor Leeds's attic. With a shove, the heart was in its new home. She twisted on the lid hurriedly as if she thought it could grow legs and climb out of the jar.

She sighed in relief, leaning against her bed. She was grateful the heart didn't smell like the frogs from science class, she didn't think she would be able to handle that on top of everything else. She glanced down at the jar she still held, hoping Sammy wouldn't be able to tell she threw the heart against the wall.

Her grandmother, however, would notice the mess in her room. Knowing she wasn't going to get any sleep, she went over to the broken glass on the floor, picking each piece up carefully as not to cut herself and being mindful not to touch any of the icky fluids from the jar.

When she had a hand full of broken glass, she got up to throw it in her trash can, thinking it would've been smarter to move the trash can to her.

She stumbled to her knees, and closed her eyes, accidently squeezing the glass in her hand. A burst of pain bloomed on her palm, forcing her eyes open where they went to the writing on the floor. The fluid from the jar she had been avoiding had spelled out a message on her floor. Ivy's body quivered as she read: witch.

She scrambled to her feet, throwing the broken glass in the trash can and grabbing the tissue box off her nightstand. She threw a handful of them over the writing, wiping it up, not caring if her hands got dirty. She wadded up the soiled tissues and tossed them in the trash. Pressing a clean tissue to the cut on her palm, she gave herself a pep talk. "Ivy Belle Teller, you need to get a grip. You're sixteen years old. There is no such thing as magic, witches, or stupid hearts that glow. It's all in your head. You know that, so stop being childish." She closed her eyes, the pain in her palm a stinging ache. "Maybe I should see a grief counselor, Zac's death affected me more than I thought. That explains it—I'm just grieving for Zac."

CHAPTER THIRTY-ONE
Young Girls

"I'm not taking no for an answer," Jesse said to Ivy when she showed up at the rectory in the morning to continue cleaning out the house.

"Really, Jesse, I'm fine. It's just boxes."

"I get it, you're very particular about what goes up for sale and what gets trashed. I'm good at following orders; just tell me where you want me to put the boxes, and I'll make sure they get there. You're in charge."

"I can live with that," she said with a grin.

"So, where to with these boxes?" he asked, nodding his head at the stack nearest him.

"Living room, against the wall. Stack 'em high so Grams can't go snooping through them without causing a landslide.

"Yes Miss."

Ivy and Jesse both grabbed a box and walked across the street. Ivy's hand was still sore, forcing her to shift the box's weight in her hands. She was glad Jesse was so persistent about helping.

"You're a pretty awesome neighbor to have, Jesse."

He smiled. "I was going to say the same thing about you."

"Thanks for getting me that babysitting job. Rosa's cool."

"Yeah, she's a real sweetheart."

"She's pretty, don't you think?"

Jesse followed Ivy into the living room and put his box down on top of hers. A gray stone hanging from a hemp necklace fell out from his shirt. He quickly tucked it under the collar of his T-shirt before Ivy could notice. "Yeah, I guess."

"You know, I think she really likes you."

He chuckled, a blush breaking out on his neck, that looked a lot like hives. "Uh . . ."

Ivy lifted her eyebrows intuitively. "Would you go out with her?"

"Uh, she's a little young."

"Please, you look like the type of guy who likes young girls."

"Woah, thanks Ives," he said with a playful nudge. "So, I look like a dirt bag?"

She laughed, that didn't come out right. "I didn't say that."

They headed to the door. "Yeah, not directly, but makes a guy wonder how he comes off. Here I was thinking I was the cooler, older neighbor."

She put her hand on his forehead. He gave her a funny look. "Yes, I'm afraid you're suffering from delusions of grandeur."

Jesse laughed, and Ivy heard the high-pitched titter Rosa was so fond of. "Funny. Tell me my car's cool at least. Come on, a red Mustang has to earn me a few points."

Ivy giggled. "Your *car's cool at least*. Rosa thinks so."

He shook his head, a smile still playing on his lips. "I know what you're doing here, but I've known Rosa since she was in pigtails, so that's a pass."

"She's not in pigtails anymore."

"That's true, but every time I look at her, I see pigtails, and I draw the line at pigtails."

Ivy shook her head in disappointment as they crossed the street. "Well, hopefully you'll come around now that you know she likes you."

"I don't know, her grandfather would kill me if I even thought about

Rosa like that. He's more than a little protective of her."

"So I've heard."

Picking up another box off the sunroom floor, Jesse turned to Ivy and smiled, his hazel eyes catching the light from the sun. "Funny enough, I do like this younger girl."

"Oh really?" Ivy asked as they headed back across the street.

"Yeah, she's dating this bratty kid."

Ivy blushed, hiding her face behind her box.

"I'm just waiting for him to blow it, so I can swoop in and knock her off her feet."

Ivy beamed; she couldn't help herself. She liked the attention she got from Jesse. She wasn't used to being fussed over. Ivy had suspected Jesse had a crush on her. She had assumed him coming over to play dominoes with Grams was just a way for him to weasel his way into the house to see her. She smiled to herself again when she realized she'd been right about him all along.

"Sounds painful, Jesse. You should stick to playing dominoes with Grams and leave the knight in shining armor routine to the movies."

Jesse carefully stacked his box on top of the tower of boxes they were building in the living room. "Yeah, maybe you're right."

"Teller women always are. Let's go, we've got tons more boxes to move before Sammy comes over."

"You're the boss Ives, but hold up a second." He pulled a piece of paper out of his shirt pocket and handed it to her.

"What's this?" Ivy unfolded it. It was a drawing of a dandelion. It was drawn with so much detail, each little petal painstakingly rendered, so much so that Ivy found herself mesmerized by it. "Jesse, it's beautiful. You're truly talented."

His eyes diverted to the ground. "Thanks."

"Be right back, I want to put this in my bedroom."

Ivy went up to her room. She took a thumbtack out of her desk drawer and tacked the drawing next to her calendar from Titan Tires. She stood there for a moment to admire it. She felt a little guilty that Jesse liked her and not Rosa, but still, she smiled. Her eyes drifted to her calendar, where she read the poem for the day.

FOREST OF WHISPERS

Flowers are beautiful in the spring,
But a picture lasts longer than a seasonal fling.
In the heart of a girl, with locks of curls,
forever a vibrant flower in this world.

"Right you are calendar, a picture can last forever." Ivy glanced at the drawing from Jesse again before heading down the attic stairs. After Ivy left her room the words on her calendar began to change, rearranging the happy poem she had just read.

Flowers can wither in the spring,
But a picture lasts longer than a seasonal fling.
In the heart of a girl, with locks of curls,
Forever a dark power in this world.

CHAPTER THIRTY-TWO
Too Much of a Coincidence

Jeffrey Lopez dropped Sammy at Ivy's so he could help her go through the boxes from Pastor Leeds's house in preparation for the upcoming community yard sale.

"Let me see it," Sammy said to Ivy as soon as he got in the house. Ivy sat close to Sammy on the couch. She looked over her shoulder to make sure her grandmother was in the kitchen before she pulled the jarred heart out of her oversized purse.

Sammy examined it. "It looks different than the first time I saw it."

He moved the jar to the side and the heart flopped over.

Ivy shrugged it off, not wanting to hint that at the bare minimum the jar was different. "Maybe it's just because it's not lighting up."

"Yeah, maybe that's it." He continued to roll the jar in his hands. "When it was beating it looked so alive and now it looks like something my dad would grill up."

"Oh my God Sammy, you're going to make me puke!"

He chuckled. "Sorry. So, um, did it do the thing at midnight last night? Or did you fall asleep downstairs again?"

Ivy's heart jumped a beat, she really didn't want to think about last night—didn't want to validate it in any way. She hastily took the jar from Sammy and put it back in her purse.

"Affirmative. Red light accompanied by beating and nothing more."

He took her hand, feeling her Band-aid against his palm. "What happened?"

"Oh nothing," she said dismissively, "papercut."

"So, what's up with all this clothing?" Sammy asked, changing the conversation as Mary walked into the living room.

"Probably from the old orphanage," Grams answered.

"Orphanage?!" They asked in unison.

"The rectory used to be a state-owned orphanage."

"Really?!" Sammy asked, shocked. He had never heard that before.

"Yeppers," Grams said, pulling out a small, white nightgown from a box. "I had an outfit like this when I was little."

Sammy laughed. "Wow! How old are you, Grams?!"

Mary bopped Sammy in the head with a paper towel roll. "Mind your manners. It's impolite to ask a lady how old she is."

"Sorry," he said with a laugh.

"This house was the original rectory," before the township bought the property across the street."

Sammy's lips curled into a smile. "What?! You sure?" Sammy asked, giving Ivy an impish look.

"Yes."

"Were you alive then too?" he teased.

Ivy elbowed him.

"Watch it, brat!" Grams said, making her way back into the kitchen.

Not long after, Grams came back into the living room and threw a couple of packages of peanut butter cracker sandwiches on the coffee table, the kind you would find at a gas station, old and stale.

"Not a cook like your mom and not pretending to be. But you better get your strength up, I want all of these boxes out of my living room by today," she said, before she went back to cleaning.

"Wow, she must really like you, bringing you a snack and all."

"If this is what being on Grams's good side looks like, I don't want to see the bad side."

Ivy smiled to herself. She knew Grams had taken a liking to Sammy, even if she didn't want to admit it.

Sammy leaned into Ivy and whispered so only she could hear him, "You thinking what I'm thinking?"

"What's that?" Ivy asked, having no idea what Sammy was thinking. After we're done going through these boxes, I think we should clean Grams's house and look for clues."

"Clues?"

"Yeah clues?"

Her eyebrows furrowed. "Clues to what?"

"To what's going on in this town. We found a jarred heart at Pastor Leeds's, who knows what we'll find here."

"I don't see why we should find anything here."

"This house is really old. Old equates to creepy."

She couldn't deny that old houses were creepy, but she wasn't seeing a connection between Pastor Leeds's house and her grandmother's.

"The red light," he whispered. "It was shining into your window."

"Okay."

"Into this house."

"Okay."

"It was doing that for one of two reasons. It was focused on something in the house or you."

Ivy shivered, her arms wrapping around herself.

"I'm pretty sure the red light was trying to get your attention, Ivy," Sammy said, the sense of dread growing in her core. "But why not make sure. Besides the more stuff we find to sell at the yard sale, the more money for the church."

"Indeed," she said with mock enthusiasm.

I can't believe you talked me into this! Or that my grandmother agreed to it," Ivy mumbled as she walked down the basement steps.

"Wow, would you look at this, Teller, this is a hoard. I don't think your grandmother ever threw anything away."

Mary Teller's basement was dark and dank and had boxes upon boxes of junk stacked high. It reminded Ivy and Sammy of Pastor Leeds's attic.

Ivy gave Sammy a annoyed look, this was not how she planned on spending the afternoon with her boyfriend.

Sammy responded with a toothy smile. "Just remember, this is for charity."

"I'll try to keep that in mind," Ivy grumbled, standing in front of a stack of boxes as tall as her. "Grams said there's a mix of all sorts of stuff down here . . . said some of it was here when she bought the house."

"The good stuff is most likely toward the back," Sammy said cheerfully.

"Figures," Ivy muttered under her breath.

"I know I'm on crutches, but I think I can squeeze my way to the back and bring boxes toward the front."

"Sammy, I think it's safer if you just sit on the steps," Ivy said with authority. "If I return you in worse condition than you came, your mother will kill me. You can direct me just fine from the steps." Ivy assertively pointed to the steps for Sammy to take a seat.

"Okay Teller, take it easy."

After a long day in the basement, they'd found nothing hocus-pocus, but Sammy and Ivy did unearth lots of things to sell at the upcoming community yard sale.

Sammy was a little disappointed about not finding anything supernatural in Grams's basement, but the day wasn't a complete loss. He was alone with Ivy. He knew Grams's basement was a far cry from romantic, but he reasoned it was dark and they were away from prying eyes, and that was good enough for him.

Ivy sat next to Sammy on the steps, exhausted. He leaned in pressing a kiss to her lips. "It's nice to get some alone time with you."

"Yeah, but did you have to volunteer us to clean out this dirty basement?"

"Come on, you can't tell me you weren't curious to see if there was any hocus-pocus down here."

"Your need for everything to be shrouded in *hocus-pocus* is going to kill me, Sammy Lopez!"

"You can't tell me you didn't want to find stuff to sell for the yard sale."

"No, not really."

Sammy hugged Ivy to his chest. "You can't tell me you didn't want to spend time with me alone?" he asked with a big grin.

"One out of three isn't bad, but we could be spending time in my room."

"Not with Grams around. She's like a bloodhound . . . at least here she can't make it down these steep steps and we can have a little privacy." Sammy kissed her again.

"I can't believe you can kiss me right now. I stink from lifting all these boxes." Ivy got off the steps and stood in front of Sammy.

Sammy got up and pulled Ivy toward him, planting a kiss on her cheek. "You're right; you do smell," he said with a smile.

"Jerk!" Ivy pushed Sammy off of her.

Sammy lost his balance, thanks to his cast, and went falling back just missing the stairs. He hit the wall behind him hard. The wall had been put up in a hurry without the proper support and was merely a thin piece of drywall. The makeshift wall gave way the instant he hit it.

"Whoa!" Sammy yelled, falling through the wall and on to the ground, releasing a giant dust cloud into the air.

Ivy coughed and sneezed. "Sammy! I'm so sorry! Are you alright?!"

"Yeah," he said, sitting up. "Hand me my crutches, please." She did as he asked and helped him off the floor.

"I'm so sorry. I didn't think I pushed you that hard."

"You didn't. I'm just down a leg," Sammy said, a little embarrassed he'd fallen. Sammy focused his attention on the room he'd fallen into. "Ivy Teller, you found a secret room! Check this place out!" He pulled out his cell phone to use as a flashlight. "It looks like someone dry walled right over this place."

"Yippie another secret. Not as bad as the heart I have to keep under my bed for all of eternity but at least the heart doesn't smell." Ivy covered her nose and mouth with her T-shirt. The smell of mildew and stale air was stifling. She could taste the stagnant air on her tongue through her damp shirt. "Sammy, this room is gross. Let's go upstairs."

Sammy let out a few loud coughs as he walked over to a small desk and chair set up in the middle of the room. "Check this out . . . it's an old logbook from the church." Sammy was teeming with excitement as he opened the old church registry. "This has to date back from when this house was the rectory! It's great, it's like its own census. It has the names of the families who attended church, their addresses, and how many people lived in each household!"

Ivy rolled her eyes. "Yeah, exciting."

"Ivy, you're gonna want to see this!"

His tone had her somewhat interested. She walked up behind him with her nose pinched shut. "What?"

"Look what it says here under residing pastor," Sammy pointed. "Uriah Joseph Leeds."

"So," Ivy said.

"*So*?!" Sammy said dumbfounded. "Uriah Leeds is the name of our current pastor!"

Ivy pointed at the date in the book. "The book says 1843. Earth to Sammy; Pastor Leeds is twenty-two. It's just a coincidence they have the same name."

"With a name like Uriah?"

"Why not? It's a nice name."

"Maybe, but how do you explain this?" Sammy asked with a cocky smirk, pointing to an old daguerreotype photograph matted on the next page."

URIAH JOSEPH LEEDS: 1843

"Explain what? It's a picture. Please don't tell me you actually think that's a picture of *our* Pastor Leeds?!"

"Maybe," Sammy replied with tight lips.

"*Maybe*?! Now you think Pastor Leeds is some sort of immortal vampire?! Give me a break! He's in the sun all the time. And sure, this guy kinda looks like Pastor Leeds, but look at that haircut. Pastor Leeds would never rock that. This must just be a photograph of one of his great, great ancestors or something."

Ivy's mind went to the charcoal drawing she found in the spell book, how she shared an uncanny resemblance to the woman in the drawing—to the Midwife. Her head hurt, there was dust in her nose and in every fold and crevice of her body, and she smelled of sweat; she was done with the basement. She wanted to go upstairs. She didn't care if Grams was breathing down their necks or not.

Sammy exhaled loudly through his mouth. "That could be it," he admitted. "I don't think Pastor Leeds is a vampire. Vampires don't get sick. But I think you're in denial that something funny is going on in this town. I don't know why you're fighting the obvious."

Ivy rolled her eyes again. "And I think you're desperate to prove that anything weird has to be because of some supernatural activity! There is no such thing as vampires or witches. No such thing as hocus-pocus."

"Okay, then how else do we explain the jarred heart?" He tugged on her elbow. "Come on, it lights up!"

"Really, does it?" Ivy turned through the pages of the old church registry.

"Yes, I've seen it, and so have you. You can't deny that."

"I don't deny I saw something," Ivy said matter-of-factly. "But that doesn't mean what I saw was supernatural. Clearly what you think is a human heart is not a human heart, but something else entirely."

Ivy tapped on a page in the church log. "Here's more proof nothing supernatural is going on. Look at the amount of Leeds noted here." Ivy pointed to the book. "Yet another Uriah Leeds. And look at the amount of Tiltons, Somers, Steelmans, and Tellers. Look at all the Rainiers. There is even a Devan Rainier noted here; now that just has to be hocus-pocus," Ivy said sarcastically. "And look what we have here, a Handover Family. I knew

Mike was special, but I didn't know it was the hocus-pocus type of special. You must be really disappointed there's no one listed with the name Lopez."

Sammy held his tongue as he stared at Ivy point blank.

"Sammy, people in this town are the descendants of people who lived in this town before them. You're just trying too hard to make something from nothing."

"Teller, you can be a skeptic," Sammy said, his ego a little bruised. "But I'm taking this. It could be something."

"Fine," she said, frustrated. "Just keep it away from me and spray it with some Lysol, won't you."

"Will do, and then I'll spray you down," he laughed, wrapping his arm around her waist.

"Not funny, Sammy."

He planted a kiss on her neck. "I'm just teasing. Come on, let's finish up and get the heck out of this basement."

"You know we can talk about it if you want," Ivy said.

"Talk about what?" Sammy asked confused, raising an eyebrow.

"Why you are really going crazy with all this hocus-pocus stuff."

"What are you talking about? I've always been like this."

"Yes, but it's something more now. You're becoming one of those paranoid conspiracy theorists. You think the whole town is in on covering up some supernatural shit storm that got Zac killed. I mean you even pointed the finger at the Chief of Police!"

"Devan could have done more," Sammy said sternly.

Ivy frowned. "If you're going to go that far, what about your dad?"

His brows furrowed. "*What about my dad?*"

"I mean he's not exactly what he seems, and we did find that creepy portrait in Pastor Leeds's house that was a spitting image of him. If you're gonna start pointing fingers Sammy, you got to start at home."

Sammy's face turned bright red. "My dad would never hurt Zac, never."

"Of course he wouldn't Sammy, that's my point! Your dad would never hurt Zac, nor would Devan, or anyone else we know. Bad things just happen. I don't think obsessing over the weird in this town is gonna help you grieve. You know if you want, we can talk about Zac."

His eyes moved into a half-lidded position "I don't want to talk about Zac."

"Well, maybe you should; I know that's what's really bothering you."

"Ivy, I . . ."

"Sammy, I know you're looking for something crazy to be happening in Pleasant Mills to explain all the things we can't explain, like the pastors dying, Pastor Leeds getting sick, and now Zac's murder, but like I said sometimes bad things just happen and there's no boogeyman to blame."

"I know that Teller, but . . ."

"But what, Sammy?"

"I think there *is* a boogeyman."

"Sammy . . ." Ivy said, upset.

Sammy's eyes darted to the ground. "You just don't understand."

Ivy took Sammy's hand. "Help me to understand. I'm worried about you."

"My dad didn't think I could hear the truth about what happened to Zac—that I wasn't old enough—that I couldn't take it." His free hand balled into a fist at his side. "He was right. I hate that he's always right."

Ivy squeezed Sammy's hand.

"Devan and my dad have been best friends for years, he's like an uncle. Alba and Maria even call him that. He's their God father. Devan's always talking police business with my dad, getting his opinion or venting. Well, he was over last night, and I was eavesdropping. I heard some things I wish I hadn't. I even had a nightmare last night."

"What did you overhear?"

He shook his head, his hair falling into his eyes. "I don't want you to have nightmares too."

"Tell me. We'll share the nightmare."

Sammy slowly made his way back to the steps and sat down. Ivy sat next to him, taking his hand. "When they found Zac in the woods his heart had been cut out of his chest."

"Oh my God," Ivy said, nervous energy making her body tremble.

"There's more. His heart was cut out when he was still alive and it's missing."

"Oh Sammy," Ivy said, hugging him to her.

Sammy fought to hold back his tears. "I know I'm searching for something to explain all the craziness, but I have to. I need to figure this out so I can live with myself for egging Zac on to go outside that night." He inclined his face to hers, holding her in the frame of his dark lashes. "I need this to make myself okay with what happened to him. When I overheard my dad and Devan, I thought about the jarred heart and thought there had to be a connection. It's too much of a coincidence to be a coincidence. I need to get to the bottom of this for Zac."

Ivy hugged Sammy again, squeezed him, nothing could get him close enough. "You know I'll help you Sammy, but if what you said is true, we should give the jarred heart to the police. Just in case something like this happened before. We know the heart was in the attic before Zac went missing, but who knows maybe there's a cold case that's never been solved and the jarred heart could be the clue the police need to find his killer."

He broke free of her. "No cops. No adults."

"We could be withholding vital evidence to Zac's case."

He shook his head. "I don't know who I can trust."

"We went through this before, Devan thought he was doing what was best for Zac."

"I know," Sammy said, sniffing in, "but it's like my dad said, something just doesn't feel right about how he went about it."

"Fine then, give the jar to your dad."

"No."

Ivy clasped her hands together, to stop herself from shaking Sammy. "You don't trust your dad now?"

"I didn't say that."

She raised both her eyebrows.

"I trust my dad with my life, but he would just give it to Devan, then Devan would give it to some lab, then to who knows where. We need to stay in control. We have to be the ones who solve this."

Ivy shook her head.

"Besides, like I said we're probably the only ones that can hear and see the glowing heart, no one else will believe us. My dad definitely won't, he thinks witches and magic are only in the movies."

Ivy was relieved Sammy didn't say they were the only ones that could hear and see the glowing heart because they were witches. After seeing the word witch spelled out on her bedroom floor last night, it was getting harder for her to deny it. "I'm starting to like your dad more and more."

Sammy rolled his eyes. "I'm not sure where the jarred heart fits into all this yet, but I know it's important."

"That may be true, but I still don't like keeping this a secret, not after what you shared about Zac."

"Keep it for me?" Sammy asked earnestly, his light eyes glassy with tears.

"Don't ask me to do that."

He put his hand on Ivy's arm. "Please, do this for me. I want to be the one who solves this. I want to be the one who finds Zac's murderer."

Ivy nibbled on the bottom of her lip as she thought. "Okay, but I am only agreeing to this because . . ." She wanted to say because she loved him but was frightened. The wasps in her stomach swarmed around. She had never loved someone like she loved him. She would keep his promise, even if she knew it was wrong. "Because I don't want you telling the cops that you think the heart is magic. They'll cart you off to the loony bin, and I want you here with me."

CHAPTER THIRTY-THREE
Community Yard Sale

The summer was coming to an end and the day for the big community yard sale was upon the town of Pleasant Mills. The youth group had not only cleaned out the pastor's house, but they'd also provided assistance to every member of the town that needed help clearing away the clutter. Every house had something set out on the front lawn to sell. Sammy had wanted to impress his father with a town-wide turn out and he did. Jeffrey was indeed impressed and very proud of his son. Sammy's yard sale was a huge success.

The Lopezes set up a table in front of Pastor Leeds's house under the large weeping willow tree. This way no one had to walk down the very long driveway to the Lopez estate. Lindsey made cookies and cupcakes for a bake sale that the Lopez twins oversaw. They were happy as could be wearing matching flowered dresses and raising money for the church. Sammy was finally in a soft cast but was still having trouble getting around; he volunteered to stay with his sisters and help with the sweets station while his parents walked around and enjoyed the event.

Ivy decided to spend her time with Sammy and his sisters, while across the street Grams managed the table set up in her yard by the youth group kids. Grams was there to take people's money and to sell, sell, sell in the name of charity. The church needed a new roof, and Sammy hoped to make enough money to give the Lewis family a donation to help them in their time of need.

"I'll be," Grams said to a man in a light, cream-colored suit. "You look just like Mayor Lopez. If he didn't just walk by with his wife, I'd think you were him."

"Is that so?" The man in the cream suit asked Mary. "I was told that once before by a little boy I used to know."

"Not from around here?" Grams asked.

"Actually, I was born not too far from here at Leeds Point, but I move around the good state of New Jersey quite a bit, but I always find myself drawn home to the Pine Barrens. Just something about the sight and smell of the pine trees and the sugar sand."

"I can relate," Mary said, patting down the flyaway hairs the wind had just kicked up.

"This is quite a sale the community has going on here in Pleasant Mills."

"That's thanks to the youth group. Which, I may add, my granddaughter Ivy is a part of. She even cleaned out my basement with Sammy Lopez." Mary pointed across the street to where Sammy and Ivy were helping Alba and Maria count out change.

"It's great to see the kids involved."

"You have kids Mr. . . . . "

"Japhet Dean," he said, shaking Mary's hand.

"Heck of a name."

"I was named after my father. It's not what I would've chosen for myself."

"That's how it always goes Japhet Dean," Mary scoffed.

"Please, call me JD. And to answer your question, I do have children. Two sons, but I feel one can never have enough. I myself came from a large family—thirteen of us in total."

"Wow," Mary said. "I thought I came from a large litter—seven on my side."

He smiled. "Yes, large families are always the best, as long as you have a loving and caring household." He glanced over the trinkets set on the table in front of Grams. "I give my sons all the love I have, but still, they grow up and want to leave me."

"Ain't that the truth. My granddaughter is going to be a junior this year. Time just flies."

JD touched an origami frog on the table.

"Push the frog's butt down. It'll hop," Mary said.

JD did as Mary directed and watched the paper frog hop. "That's splendid," he said with a childlike smile.

"Ivy made that. She's into origami."

"I must have it." JD pulled out his wallet and handed Grams a dollar. "Nice talking with you."

"You too, JD."

"Hi Tyrone," Grams said as he came up to her table. JD smiled at Tyrone and then at Mary.

"Enjoy your day Mary, and your granddaughter," he said, putting the paper frog in his pants pocket.

Mary scratched her head. "Did I tell him my name was Mary?

"Wow," Sammy said. "Mr. Richards has no shame. I think he's selling that creepy painting that looks like my dad to a blind girl."

"You're telling me! He talked you into giving him ten dollars for that stained Jersey Devils Football hoodie."

Ivy turned around to see what Sammy was talking about. Jesse was manning a table on the other side of Pastor Leeds's yard. "Rosa!" Ivy called out to her, before walking over to her friend. "Hey glad you made it. Hi Mrs. Littleton."

"Hello Ivy. Just going to look around while you two girls chat," Mrs. Littleton said with a kind smile before perusing the long stretch of tables lined with secondhand things.

Sammy came up to them holding his little sisters' hands.

"Rosa this is Sammy and his sisters Alba and Maria."

"Hi Rosa, nice to meet you," Sammy said.

Rosa let the portrait she was holding rest against her leg as she adjusted her sunglasses and ID cane. "You too Sammy."

"You never told me your friend was blind," Sammy whispered to Ivy.

Ivy elbowed Sammy afraid Rosa heard him.

"Sammy!" Maria whined, pulling on the sleeve of his recently purchased Jersey Devils Football hoodie he had tied around his waist. "Someone wants to buy a cupcake. Come on we gotta go!"

"Duty calls. Nice to finally meet you, Rosa." Sammy leaned in and pressed a kissed to Ivy's cheek. "See you at the sweets table."

"Sammy sounds really cute," Rosa said.

Ivy beamed. "He is."

Jesse coughed.

Ivy glanced to him. "Oh please Jesse, you know you're cute too, right Rosa?"

Rosa's face turned bright red, under the cover of her large sunglasses.

Mrs. Littleton called Jesse over to get a price on an antique clock and Jesse was all too eager to help her.

"Did he say anything about me?" Rosa asked.

"Just the same old, that your grandfather would kill him."

Rosa huffed. "Anything else?"

The portrait fell over. Ivy bent to pick it up. "Just that you're a really good friend." Her eyes scanned over the old painting in her hands. "You know you don't have to buy that portrait because of Jesse."

"I know."

"Trust me when I say it's creepy."

"I don't know," Jesse said, coming up behind them. "I think the artist has a certain je ne sais quoi."

"I want it," Rosa said with a smile. "I trust Jesse's opinion."

Ivy shot him an incredulous glare.

"Thanks so much Jesse, for helping me pick it out," Rosa said breathlessly, her cheeks still flushed.

"No problem. It's good seeing you out of the house."

She beamed. "Maybe once my vision is a little better the three of us could hang out."

"Sounds good to me," Jesse said, giving Ivy a playful nudge.

"Yeah Rosa," Ivy said. "That would be fun."

Ivy strolled back over to Sammy, but she continually glanced at Jesse and Rosa. She watched Jesse pull something out of his shirt pocket. A drawing, she guessed. She wondered if he kept a stack of drawings in his pocket just in case a cute girl walked by. Her cheeks flushed with embarrassment at the thought of falling for his game. She felt more than a little bad for Rosa. She was blinded by him. She always thought the saying *love is blind* had a positive connotation, but now she wasn't so sure.

Tyrone walked over to where Rosa was standing across from Jesse. After a brief conversation, he picked up Rosa's painting for her. *That was nice of Tyrone,* Ivy thought, thinking it should've been Jesse who offered to carry the painting to the car for her.

CHAPTER THIRTY-FOUR
Highs and Lows

The next Sunday, Pastor Leeds addressed his congregation. It was another full house. All the pews were taken, and people stood in the back of the church and along the sides.

Uriah was happy to tell them about the success of last weekend's yard sale. They'd raised enough money to replace the roof on the church and to give a nice-sized check to the Lewis family. The church goers cheered for the youth group. Ivy was proud she'd been part of something positive. She had never been before. Ivy would never admit it out loud, but she loved Pleasant Mills and Sammy Lopez.

However, Pastor Leeds was not all smiles at church on Sunday. Despite looking healthier and seeming to be feeling better, the effects of Tyrone's disappearance showed on his saintly face in fine lines around his eyes. "Let us pray for Tyrone Jones."

Tyrone had gone missing during the big yard sale. After a week of combing over the woods, there were still no leads on his whereabouts. It was as if he'd vanished into thin air.

"Please stay vigilant and help the Jones family in any way you can. Do not hesitate to share any information about Tyrone with Chief Rainier and Detective Steele."

This time Pleasant Mills Police Department was taking a different approach to their missing person's case, chiefly because of Jeffrey Lopez and Pastor Uriah Leeds. Jeffrey was able to convince Devan that making Tyrone's disappearance public was in Tyrone's best interest. Devan agreed and he hoped this change in strategy would make parents and children alike more alert and would, in turn, help keep the children safe. Uriah agreed to use his pulpit as a platform to make sure everyone in town knew to be on alert. One child lost was a tragedy; the town could not bear another.

The youth group met after church, accompanied by adults, to hang up flyers with a detailed description of Tyrone. Their hopes were that someone would recognize Tyrone and contact the police.

"This is nuts," Sammy said to Ivy as they stapled Tyrone's picture to a utility pole.

"You think it's possible he just ran away?" Ivy asked. "Tammy said he has a pretty shitty home life."

"I know he has trouble with his dad, but I can't imagine Tyrone would just run away and put his mother through that. According to Mike, he hasn't called Tammy either. I think Tammy is just telling herself he ran away, so she doesn't go crazy. Hope is a powerful thing . . . I wish I had it." Sammy's eyes narrowed. "I've got a bad feeling, Teller. If Tyrone was just on the run, I'm sure he would have at least sent Louie a message. But Louie's a wreck. He's a big kid with a big heart. He's really having a hard time with Tyrone being MIA."

"I wish there were something else we could do to help," Ivy said, wondering if she should mention to Sammy they should give the police the jarred heart along with everything else they found. She kept that thought to herself. She didn't want to put the idea in Sammy's head that what happened to Zac could happen to Tyrone.

"My mom is making a whole bunch of food to bring over to the Jones's later."

"That's nice of her."

Sammy took Ivy's hand and crossed the street. Jeffrey was not far behind them, talking on the phone. "Yeah. My mother is really taking what happened to Zac hard. And now with Tyrone missing, she's manic. Her little brother was kidnapped when she was a kid."

"You're kidding?!" Ivy asked, shocked.

"No." Sammy took the stapler from Ivy and stapled a flyer to the tree on the street corner. "My mom's brother was taken right out of his bed in the middle of the night."

Ivy's eyes opened wide. "Holy crap."

"Worst part was my mom was sleeping in the same room and didn't hear anything. She blames herself."

"That's horrible."

"Yeah, that's why she freaks out about me sneaking out, and why our house is wired like a prison."

"I thought the security system was your dad's doing."

"Because you think of my dad as a prison warden?" He chuckled. "I think I gave you the wrong impression of him. He's not that bad."

Ivy shrugged her shoulders. "They ever find your uncle?"

"No. Never did. My mom never got closure."

"How old was he when he was abducted?"

"Young. Younger than Zac and Tyrone." Sammy reloaded the stapler as he talked. "I was named after him. Samuel Cameron Lopez. My mom's family had just moved here from Spain when my uncle was taken." Sammy took down a flyer for the community yard sale and put a *Have You Seen Tyrone Jones* flyer in its place. "My grandmother couldn't speak good English yet, nor my mom, really. It was hard for them to get good help. My dad's tried to find my mom's brother for her, or what happened to him at least, but the case went cold so many years ago, the private investigator couldn't find anything."

Sammy and Ivy looked both ways before crossing the intersection. "It's scary, there're a lot of sick people out there. I guess I forget sometimes because our town is so boring." He glanced to Ivy. "Well, that was until you got here."

Ivy smiled.

"Life in Pleasant Mills can give you a real sense of false security. Everyone seems happy all the time, but Zac was murdered and now Tyrone is missing. I'm telling you Teller, this town has a big problem, and it's nothing some flyers are gonna solve."

CHAPTER THIRTY-FIVE
Locker Room Talk

The rest of the summer flew by, and the school year was in full swing. For the first time in her life, Ivy was excited to go to school. She was ecstatic to start her junior year at a new school with a boyfriend. She was feeling good about herself. All the heavy lifting over the summer had helped her to lose an easy ten pounds. She wanted to lose a little bit more weight, but she was more than happy to go down two pants sizes and get some new tops. Her boobs stuck out over her belly, which was a new look for her, and she liked it.

She reveled in walking down the halls with Sammy Lopez. She wished the kids at her old school could see her now. Here she was dating the most popular guy at school. It looked like this ugly duckling transformed into a swan after all.

But the end of the summer didn't mark an exciting time for everyone. The police found Tyrone Jones. He wouldn't be going back to school; instead, his family was having a small service for him at Pleasant Mills Church. He was found in the woods not far from where Zachary Lewis had been found, and like Zac, his heart had been cut out and was missing.

It looked like Sammy was dead wrong about the curse of the heart attack. Pastor Leeds's health continued to improve, but there was undeniably something strange going on in the Pine Barrens. Louie Grindhouse, the school's shining star and key to an undefeated footfall season, went missing right before school started. By now rumors were circulating through town that there was a serial killer in Pleasant Mills.

Police Chief Rainier assured the town that the boys all being the age of thirteen was a coincidence. He promised they were doing everything they could to find Louie alive. And so was the youth group. It was another Saturday of stapling up missing flyers.

Mike came sauntering up to Ivy as she waited outside the church for Sammy and Pastor Leeds.

"Hey Ivy."

"Hi Mike."

"You have any extra staples? There aren't any more in the church."

"Yeah," she said, pulling a box of staples out of her pocket and handing them to him.

"So, I heard you and Sammy went all the way."

"What?" Ivy asked, confused.

"You know," Mike said, nudging her, "you guys made it to home base."

"Leave me alone." Ivy pushed past him and headed toward the church doors.

Mike followed. "Sammy was telling all the boys about it yesterday at school."

"Mike, can't you go bother someone else?!" Ivy hissed, walking quicker.

Mike took out his phone and pushed play. Ivy's eyes grew wide, turning to face Mike. She couldn't believe her ears, but she knew it was Sammy's voice.

"Crazy the things your boyfriend says behind your back," Mike said with a cruel grin. "Give me that," she said, snatching his phone and putting it to her ear to listen to it again. By the time Mike's recording was done, she was in tears.

He took his phone back. "And that's just a clip. Didn't know you were such a slut Ivy."

"Why are you doing this?" she asked, wiping her tears on her sleeve.

"What, telling you what your boyfriend's saying behind your back? Here I was, thinking I was being a good friend to you."

"Sorry we took so long," Sammy said as he and Pastor Leeds walked up to Ivy and Mike. Ivy walked away.

Sammy furrowed his eyebrows, glancing to Mike. "What's that about?"

"No clue," Mike said. He walked back over to Elsa and Mrs. Ball to hang up more flyers.

"Give me a minute," Sammy said to Pastor Leeds.

Uriah nodded. "Of course, take your time."

Sammy, happy to be cast free, jogged to catch up with Ivy. "Hey, what's wrong?"

"Nothing."

"Why are you crying," Sammy asked, grabbing her hand to stop her.

"I just thought you were different, Sammy."

Sammy's face twisted in confusion. "What are you talking about?"

Ivy turned to him and said sharply: "Fat girls are better in bed?"

"What?!"

"Yeah, Mike just played me a recording of all the colorful things you said about me yesterday in the locker room."

"That's just locker room talk."

"You told them I was easy! Excuse me, *fat girls are easy*!"

"They asked me if fat girls were easy."

"And you said yes! Now I know what you really think of me!" Ivy shouted, storming up the church steps.

"Ivy, I'm sorry."

Ivy pushed Sammy away. "Leave me alone."

"I just said those things, they didn't mean anything. All the guys say stuff like that."

"No, Sammy. Guys who respect their girlfriends don't say *stuff like that*. Last time I'm asking—leave me alone!" She gave him a hard shove.

"It's not safe to be alone; I'm staying with you." Ivy walked into the church. Sammy waited outside. He decided to give her some time to cool off before he tried to talk to her.

Soon after, Mary pulled into the church parking lot. She rolled down her window. "Sammy, if you're here, why am I here?"

"We had a fight."

"Dagnabbit, in the middle of my daytime television!"

Mary called Ivy on her phone. "I'm outside."

Ivy walked over to her grandmother's station wagon, her tears dried up, her face stoney. She got in without saying a word to Sammy or Pastor Leeds who had made his way over to them.

Sammy hopped in the back seat of the station wagon before Grams pulled out, giving Pastor Leeds a quick wave goodbye. As soon as they pulled into the driveway Ivy made a beeline for the front door. Sammy ran to catch up. "Hey, Ivy—"

Ivy cut him off. "If you didn't get it back at church, let me spell it out for you: We are no longer a couple. This is me breaking up with you. Now leave me alone!" Ivy walked inside, slamming the door behind her with a loud bang.

"Please talk to me!" he yelled through the door.

Grams walked past Sammy. She shrugged her shoulders and shut the door in his face.

Sammy waited outside Ivy's house for an hour, every minute growing more and more angry with Mike. He decided to walk to Mike's house. He knew he shouldn't with all the disappearances in the neighborhood, but he figured telling Mike off was worth being grounded over. Sammy marched over to Mike, who had just gotten out of his father's truck. "What's your problem, Mike?!" Sammy asked, pushing him hard.

Mike's dad closed the driver's door. "Is there a problem, boys?"

Sammy swung and punched Mike in the face, sending him down to the ground. "Stay away from Ivy and stay away from me. We're no longer friends!"

Mike's dad walked over to break up the one-sided fight. "Sammy, you need to go home, and I'm calling your dad."

Without saying a word, he walked home. He slammed the front door behind him and went straight to his room.

Lindsey came up the stairs. She knocked on Sammy's door before entering. "You're home early. Where's Ivy?"

He buried his face in his pillow.

Lindsey sat on the side of Sammy's bed, placing her hand on his back. "What happened, honey?"

"Ivy broke up with me," Sammy said, his voice muffled.

She rubbed her son's back. "Tell me what happened."

He tried to hold back his tears, but they'd already formed a lump in his throat. "I don't want to talk about it."

"Sammy, you can tell me."

"I was stupid! I was trying to fit in and sound cool but I'm just stupid."

"Come now, what did you say that was so stupid?"

"I can't even tell you mom," Sammy said through his watery eyes. "You'll think less of me. I shouldn't have said it. You raised me better than that."

Lindsey continued to rub her son's back tenderly. "We all make mistakes. Your father and I've had our share of fights, but we always work it out. I'm sure Ivy and you can do the same."

"I told everyone in the locker room we made it all the way. It was a lie." Sammy was crying now; he didn't have to hide from his mother. "I said really bad things, Mom. All the guys at school were talking this big game, and it was my turn to share. I couldn't just say we kissed a couple times. — I'm supposed to be the cool kid, so I just said a bunch of stupid things to impress them. Mike recorded everything and played it for Ivy."

Lindsey hugged Sammy as he lay face down in his pillow. "Oh, honey."

"I know, Mom. I messed things up. The worst part is, I love Ivy. I didn't mean to hurt her."

Sammy turned to face his mom. He was relieved to see his mother's eyes were kind and not judgmental. She hugged him, tears still falling.

"It'll be okay honey, but what you said must've really hurt Ivy. You have to give her some time to herself. But maybe it would help if you wrote her a letter to apologize or maybe a poem. I'm sure she'll come around when she sees how sorry you are."

"Okay Mom, I'll try that," he sniffled. "And to make matters worse, I went to Mike's house and punched him in the face for telling Ivy. Mr. Handover is calling Dad. I'm going to be in big trouble when he gets home. Mike's gonna have a black eye."

"I'll talk to your father first."

Sammy hugged his mother. He could always count on her. "You're the best, Mom."

Jeffrey knocked on his son's open door. "Hey, Sammy."

"Dad," Sammy said, not looking up from his notebook.

"Your mother told me what happened between you and Ivy and you and Mike."

"Uh huh," he said, waiting for his father to lose his temper.

"I'm sorry about Ivy. I know how much you like her."

His eyes darted to his father in surprise. "I'm writing her a poem." Sammy flashed his dad his notebook.

Jeffrey waved a dismissive hand. "You're better off buying her some flowers and chocolates and dropping them off after church tomorrow. Girls love those sorts of things."

Sammy looked down at his half-written poem that he had to admit wasn't very good and nodded.

Jeffrey took a seat on his son's bed. "And when it comes to Mike . . . well—I would have done the same thing."

"You would have?" Sammy asked, sitting up a little straighter. This was not going at all how he'd played it out in his head.

"Most likely. But that doesn't make it right. You can't go around punching your friends in the face."

"We aren't friends anymore."

"I hope you two can work things out. You've been friends since T-ball. After dinner you and I are going over to the Handover's and you're going to apologize to Mike. You don't have to be friends, but you do have to say you're sorry."

"I know. What Mike did was wrong, but I did say those things," Sammy said, closing his notebook.

"Exactly, Sammy. I hope you learned your lesson."

Sammy tried not to cry as his bottom lip trembled. "I did."

"Dinner will be ready in ten. Don't be late. Your mom made your favorite."

"I'm not grounded?" Sammy asked, surprised.

"No, Sammy. I think losing Ivy is punishment enough."

Jeffrey walked with Sammy to the Handovers after dinner. Jeffrey chatted with Big Mike as the two boys talked.

"Sorry I punched you, Mike," Sammy said, swallowing his pride.

Mike looked down at the ground ashamed, his freckles blending into his blush. "Sorry I recorded you and played it for Ivy . . . I deleted it."

"Thanks," Sammy said, also looking down at the ground.

"I'm sorry Sammy. I was jealous of all the time you've been spending with Ivy. Since you two started going out, you barely have time to hang out with me . . . but what I did was wrong," Mike acknowledged. "I know you better than anyone; I knew all the stuff you said was bullshit. I was just jealous. I know you'll never have feelings like that for me, but I thought we would always be best friends."

"We are Mike, you know that," Sammy said, glancing at Mike's red face. It was as brilliant as his hair. "It's just that, well . . . I really like Ivy. She's different than the other girls."

Mike slowly lifted his eyes to meet Sammy's. "She still mad at you?"

"Broke up with me."

"That's what I wanted her to do, but now I don't. I'm sorry," Mike said, his eyes watering. "I'll try to talk to her for you."

"Thanks, that may help." He raked his fingers through his hair. "I should never have said those things about her. Like you said, none of them were true. This is karma kicking me in my lying ass. I just hope she'll forgive me."

"Can *you* forgive me?" Mike asked. "I was a jerk. A real jerk."

Mike had regretted playing that audio clip for Ivy as soon as he'd pushed play. But then when Sammy punched him, he'd gotten it—the scope of what he'd done. He'd ruined Sammy's relationship with Ivy and his own friendship with Sammy. He hadn't imagined things going down that way, but they had, and now the damage was done. They both wore it on their faces.

"Yeah," Sammy said. "We're cool. Life would be boring without you, Mike."

Mike gave a faint smile.

"No hard feelings over the black eye?" Sammy asked, teasing.

Mike chuckled. "No, but I owe you one."

Sammy laughed. "If you're quick enough to land one."

"Hey, you want to check out this new video game I just got?" Mike asked.

"Yeah, sure."

CHAPTER THIRTY-SIX
Silent Treatment

The next day at church, Sammy got the silent treatment from Ivy. Mike tried to talk to her to smooth things over, but she wasn't having it. Ivy never liked Mike and she wasn't about to start to.

"I'm gay, Ivy," Mike told her as they stood in front of the church after service. Only Sammy and Tammy knew, telling Ivy his secret cost him more than she realized, but he had to try to make things right between Sammy and her.

"Um . . . . okay," Ivy said, wishing she could disappear, but her grandmother was conveniently taking her sweet time talking to Lindsey Lopez as she made up a plate of coffee hour desserts to take home. She was pretty sure Lindsey was in on the Mike ambush.

"So . . . I kinda have a crush on Sammy." Mike's face was beat red as perspiration beaded at his hairline and his palms. He hoped she would be able to string together the reason for his behavior without him spelling it out.

" . . . Okay."

He was in no such luck. "So, I did what I did out of jealousy, not that it makes it any better."

This was getting painful for Ivy. She'd known Mike had a crush on Sammy since day one. She didn't need him to tell her. He followed Sammy around like a lost puppy, or as Zac had called him—a shadow. Mike being mean was a defense mechanism. Ivy knew a thing or two about that. Mike was mean to girls so no girls would like him, and so no one would question why he never had a girlfriend.

Ivy locked eyes with Mike taking on her grandmother's no-nonsense attitude. "Mike, I appreciate you telling me all this, but when it comes down to it, Sammy still said all of those things. You were right, you were being a good friend, even if your motives were selfish. Maybe you and Sammy can get together now."

"Ivy, he likes you, not me," Mike said, desperate to patch things up between her and Sammy. Sammy said he forgave him, but Mike could still feel tension in the air. He had to help Sammy get back with Ivy; in his head it was the only way to save their friendship. But it didn't make any difference to Ivy that Mike had come out to her to explain his actions, and even less to hear from Mike how much Sammy liked her. Ivy was mad at Mike for the recording, but at the end of the day it was still Sammy who was in the wrong.

After church Jeffrey drove Sammy to Ivy's house. With a box of chocolates and flowers in his hands he knocked on the front door. Mary answered it.

"Is Ivy home; can I talk to her?" he asked urgently.

"She is, but she's not seeing visitors," Grams said. She took the box of chocolates from Sammy and opened them, popping one in her mouth. "Better go find yourself another easy girl." Grams slammed the door in Sammy's face. He stood there undeterred, the flowers still in his hands.

Glancing up, he saw Ivy's window was open. "Ivy, I'm sorry. Talk to me, please!" Ivy could hear Sammy from her bed. "Ivy, please. I got you flowers." She got out of bed and closed the window, his shoulders slouching with the bang of the window sash.

"Tough breakup?" Jesse asked, grabbing the mail out of the mailbox.

"You could say that."

"Chin up, Sammy; at least it's before Christmas."

"Not helping, Mr. Richards."

"Sorry," he said with a chuckle. He waved at Jeffrey waiting in his SUV before walking back toward the rectory.

Grams knocked on Ivy's bedroom door. "You want any of these chocolates? They're the good kind."

"No Grams, I don't."

"You gonna talk to him?"

"No."

"He looked sorry. He was all teary-eyed."

"Him, teary-eyed! Grams, I know you like his mom and her cooking and not going over for Tortellini Thursdays will most likely kill you, but what he said was wrong! Whose side are you on, anyways?!"

"Yours," Mary said, popping another chocolate in her mouth. "But I know how good you two are together. He's done wonders for your self-esteem."

Ivy punched her pillow. "Well not anymore! Hard to think highly of myself when my boyfriend is telling the world I'm fat and easy!"

Mary shrugged. "You sure you don't want any chocolates?"

"No Grams, you eat them."

Mary knocked on her granddaughter's bedroom door again. She leaned on the open door and tucked her flyaways behind her ears. "Sammy's been waiting on the porch for hours. Will you please go down and talk to him?" she asked out of breath.

Ivy scoffed.

"If you make him wait any longer, I'm gonna have to invite Sammy and Jeffrey in. I don't want Lindsey thinking I'm rude."

"Fine."

Mary started her descent downstairs as Ivy rolled out of bed. She pulled the box with the jarred heart out from under it. She put the Leeds's grimoire in with it and placed a magazine on top, hiding the hocus-pocus, before making her way down the old staircase.

The Teller door opened. Sammy's face lit up when he saw Ivy but was quickly extinguished by her tone. "Here," she said, pushing the box into Sammy's hands and crushing the flowers against his chest. "I believe these belong to you."

Sammy looked down to see the spell book, then to his father who was waiting in his SUV. He motioned for Sammy to start his apology.

"Ivy?"

"What do you want?"

"A chance to explain myself."

Ivy folded her arms over her chest, standing at the threshold, refusing to go out to the porch. "Go."

"I know everyone who meets me thinks I have things easy, that I come from a rich family, my dad's the mayor, I've got good looks, I'm getting a new car . . . but things aren't that easy. I want to fit in, and I said those things so the guys would think I'm cool. What I said was more about me being insecure with me, than me trying to hurt you. But in the process of trying to act like hot shit, I did hurt you. It was stupid of me. I was wrong and you were right. I disrespected you. It will never happen again. I promise."

Ivy knew she twisted her face into what Sammy thought was one of her funny faces. "Do you hear yourself? Are you really trying to spin this so you're the victim and I feel bad for you?! It's always about you, Sammy Lopez! I mean you have it all, and it's still not enough for you." Ivy scoffed. "You're right, you will never disrespect me again, because I will never let you be in a position to do it again. We're over!"

His blue eyes glassed over. "Ivy, please, I love you." He had never told her that before. He'd always felt silly saying it out loud, but it was the truth. "Please. I really do love you. I can't live without you."

"Sorry, Sammy. You can and you will."

He was getting desperate now; he was far from the cool kid. "Can we be friends at least?"

"I don't think so."

"Teller, please."

Sammy calling her by the nickname he'd given her made her heart ache. She was the victim here, not him. Ivy took a page from her grandmother and shut the door in Sammy's face, not validating the tears rolling down his cheeks.

CHAPTER THIRTY-SEVEN
Date with Jesse Richards

"Hey, I heard you and Sammy broke up," Jesse said, walking over to Ivy who was opening the mailbox.

Ivy flipped through the junk mail. "Uh huh."

"Sorry to hear that."

"I'm not; he's a jerk."

"Yeah, I always thought he was kind of a brat," Jesse said with a sly grin.

She let out a light laugh. She had to laugh, or she'd cry. "You sound like Grams."

"She must be wearing off on me."

Ivy smiled at Jesse before she hit him in the arm with the rolled-up mail. "Yes, please stop beating her at dominoes. If you don't, we'll have no money to buy food."

Jesse chuckled as he leaned on Mary Teller's mailbox. "Sorry, Ives. I promise to let her win the next game. And she's the one who insists on betting, you know?"

Ivy scoffed. "Oh, I know, so thank you in advance for throwing the next game."

Jesse smiled.

"So, how's Pastor Leeds doing?" Ivy asked, walking back toward her porch with Jesse by her side.

"He has so many doctors' appointments, I hardly see him, but he says he's better."

"That's good." Ivy reached for the doorknob.

"Hey, Ivy, I know this might be a little too soon . . . " he blushed, making himself look younger. "I know I'm a little older than you . . . but we've already established I'm the kind of guy who likes younger girls." She gave him an unsure smile. "But I, uh, would love to take you out to dinner."

Ivy's eyes danced over a flushed Jesse. "How old are you anyway?" She realized she'd never asked him before.

"Twenty-four."

"I'm sixteen; my Grams would kill me."

"Grams doesn't have to know."

Ivy grinned. She thought about how jealous Sammy would be if he saw her riding with Jesse.

"Okay, Jesse."

"How about tonight?" he asked with a big smile.

"Sure."

Jesse pulled into Mary Teller's driveway and got out to open the car door for Ivy.

"What'd you tell Grams?" Jesse asked as Ivy buckled up.

"The truth, well kinda. Told her you owe me dinner for losing a bet."

He smiled, a smile of all lips. "Clever."

She blushed, he looked very handsome when he smiled like that.

"Where do you want to go?" he asked, starting the Mustang's engine.

"I'm not sure," Ivy said nervously. She was starting to think going on a date with Jesse was stupid. She was still not over Sammy breaking her heart, and Jesse was her friend, not to mention her neighbor and Pastor Leeds's cousin. And he was Rosa's big crush. If Rosa found out, their friendship would be over.

"What do you like to eat?"

"Um . . . I'm not picky."

"How about we go to Oyster Creek?"

"Never been there."

"What—Really?! It's not far; it's right off the Mullica River at Leeds Point. I thought it was a hot spot for all you teenagers looking to spot the Jersey Devil."

Ivy scrunched her eyebrows. "The Jersey Devil?! Please, I'm not ten."

He grinned, his eyes glancing over her chest. "No, you're not."

"Jesse, I've got a confession," Ivy said on the car ride home after dinner.

"What's that?"

"I said yes to dinner to make Sammy jealous."

"I know," he said, keeping his eyes on the road.

"You knew?" she asked, shocked.

"Yeah," Jesse said with a big grin. "It was the only way I knew you would say yes. My one shot."

Ivy blushed, it spread over the bridge of her nose and down her neck. "I did have a nice time though."

"Good. So, maybe once you're over Sammy we could go out again?"

"I'd like that," she said, giving him a kiss on the cheek and hopping out of his car. "Thanks, Jesse."

Jesse made sure Ivy got into her house before he pulled into Uriah's driveway. He opened the front door quietly as not to wake Uriah and made his way up the stairs to the attic. He took a seat on the wooden stool in front of the window and waited for Ivy to undress for bed.

CHAPTER THIRTY-EIGHT
A Sleepless Night

Uriah knelt by the side of his bed to say his nightly prayer. He was tired but felt a restlessness deep inside him that could only be made better by praying. He'd spent all evening looking for the antique coin Bishop Baker had given him. He had been meaning to take it to Pleasant Mills Church to put it on display for the church members, but with everything that was going on he got sidetracked. He now feared the coin got sold in the church community yard sale. The bishop had told him the coin had belonged to the Leeds family, one of the most prominent families of South Jersey. He also told the young pastor the role the Leeds family played in settling the town of Pleasant Mills after they migrated there from Leeds Point. Uriah found the history of the coin particularly interesting as he shared the Leeds name and thought sharing the coin's history with the congregation would give the town something positive to focus on for a little while.

Uriah gave his dresser a quick sweep over again after praying. He distinctly remembered placing the coin, minted in 1735, on top of his dresser when he brought it home. He moved the dresser away from the wall in the hopes the coin had fallen behind it, but to no avail, the coin was lost.

Uriah's eyelids fluttered at a footfall outside his bedroom door. His eyes darted to his closed door to watch a shadow move across the threshold. "It's just Jesse," he told himself, before sliding the dresser back in place.

Uriah tucked himself in bed, closing his eyes to only repeat the Our Father prayer over and over again before drifting off to sleep. As he did, he heard a baby crying.

Pleasant Mills, New Jersey: 1758

Uriah picked up the crying baby from his bassinet. He smiled at the baby as tears rolled down his chubby cheeks. "Now, now, there's nothing to fuss over." Uriah soothed the infant, rocking him back and forth until the baby fell asleep in his arms. He kissed the sleeping child's forehead before putting him back into the bassinet. Watching the infant sleep, amazed by the tiny rises and falls of his chest, Uriah whispered to the baby: "I love you, my son. Sleep well."

"He is a darling baby. I could just eat him right up," Japhet Dean said.

Uriah looked up from his son to see his guardian angel. He recognized the gleam in his brown eyes and the curl of the corners of his lips. His face was as he remembered it as a boy, handsome and kind. "It's you!"

"It's me."

"You're real? I started to think you were just a figment of my imagination."

JD ran his hand over the sleeping baby's cheek. "I'm much more than what meets the eye."

Uriah excitedly spoke. "I ended up marrying Miss Lilly, the girl you helped me save. I became the pastor of Batsto Church. I took over for Lilly's father."

"I know Uriah, I have been watching you."

Humbly, he nodded. "Church attendance has never been so high and it's all thanks to you, my guardian angel. Thank you."

JD grinned. "You're most welcome, Uriah. But don't forget, my gifts come with a cost. I have come to ask you for the favor you owe me."

"Favor?" Uriah repeated.

"Don't you remember, Uriah? You said you would do me a favor when the time comes."

"Yes, I remember—anything you want Mr. JD."

"Good," JD said, looking down at the sleeping baby. "I want you to give me your son's heart."

"My son's heart?!" Uriah snatched up his son in a panic, his face writhing in fear. His elevated pulse made his body quake. "You're not an angel, are you . . . ?"

The corners of JD's mouth twisted downward, distorting his once gentle face. "No Uriah, I never was." JD took a step closer.

Uriah shielded his son from JD, twisting his body away from him. "What are you then?"

"A being you made a deal with."

The baby whimpered.

"I can't do what you ask of me. He's my first child."

JD took another step, Uriah in turn took a step back. "I know this. You will have more."

"What will I tell my wife?"

"That is for you to decide. You promised me, Uriah." JD waved his hand in front of Uriah's face. He saw his reflection in the mirror across the room. His angelic face was gone, and he was once again irregular. Uriah turned away from his reflection. "I can take away everything I gave you . . . and much more. Your church . . . your wife."

"Don't hurt Lilly!"

JD leaned in and whispered in Uriah's ear. "Bring the baby into the forest tomorrow at noon. Walk the red trail until you come to the tree that was split in half by lightning. Step over the fallen tree limb and walk deep into the woods until you come to a clearing. There, I will be waiting."

Uriah woke up in terror, his arms wrapping around himself. "My son—Lilly—so real . . . so, so real." He ran to the bathroom to wash his face. "So real." Uriah scrambled for his medication from his doctor, opening the medicine cabinet above the sink. Popping a handful of pills in his mouth, he swallowed, washing them down directly from the bathroom faucet.

Uriah crawled back into bed and closed his eyes tightly, trying to forget about his nightmare. He heard the floor creak and moan above him. He knew it was Jesse on his way to the attic. He had gone up there almost every night since the youth group cleaned it out, but tonight the groans of the old staircase unnerved Uriah all the more.

Uriah tried to distract himself by guessing what Jesse was doing in the attic, but he couldn't silence the nightmare that bounced around in his head. He couldn't wait for his medication to kick in and silence his mind for him. "It was just a nightmare. Block it out. It's all in your head. None of it's real. For the love of God Uriah, go to sleep."

"I'm not surprised to see you up here," JD said to Jesse who was sitting on a wooden seat pulled up to the attic window of the rectory. Jesse stared across the street, watching Ivy and Sammy make out in her bedroom.

"I want her."

"And when you're done with your work here, you will be free to pursue whatever and whomever you want, but not until your work for me is complete."

JD looked out the window at Ivy. "She does remind me of yesteryear, when girls had better shapes."

"Yeah," Jesse said, intently staring out the window.

"How are you doing procuring the next child? I already went through young Tyrone Jones."

"Good. Grabbing him tomorrow. He walks home alone from his grandmother's every Thursday."

"Perfect. And Uriah, how about him? Has he reached out to you yet?"

"He's in full denial." Jesse pulled the chair closer to the window as Sammy took Ivy's shirt off.

JD lit a cigarette. "Uriah will come around. He always does."

Jesse rolled his eyes. "That's what you say . . . "

"Maybe it's time for me to have a little talk with him. I just don't know why he fights it."

"You're a demon and he's a pastor."

"Speaking of that. You should go to church next Sunday."

"You know I don't do church, JD."

"It will help sell the story that you're Uriah's beloved cousin. Hard to believe a pastor's cousin would miss the insight and wisdom of a shepherd with Uriah's gifts."

"I hunt on Sundays."

"Jesse," JD said sternly.

"I'll try."

"Young Ivy Teller always goes."

"I said, I'll try. Unless that's an order?" Jesse asked, peeling his eyes away from Ivy's bra.

"No order, Jesse. Just a suggestion." JD pressed a kiss to Jesse's forehead. "Make sure you get what I put on my list."

Jesse directed his attention across the street again. "Yes father."

JD whistled as he left the attic, the melancholy tune filling the quiet house as he disappeared into the shadows.

CHAPTER THIRTY-NINE
Suprise in the Attic

In the morning Uriah woke up feeling better than he had in weeks. It was strange to him. He felt as if life was breathed back into him overnight. He stretched and went to the bathroom to brush his teeth. When he was done, he couldn't resist pulling up his top lip to look for evidence of a cleft. It had been a while since his nightmare, but he thought morning and night about the face he'd seen in his dream. "Nothing, just symmetrical lips . . . it was just a dream, Uriah . . . nothing to it." He sighed in relief that his nightmare was only a nightmare.

Uriah smiled at his picture-perfect reflection in the mirror. "Let's take advantage of feeling better." He went to go downstairs, but as he passed the staircase for the attic, he noticed the attic door was left open. "I wonder why Jesse comes up here?" Uriah asked himself as he walked up the narrow steps to the attic to close the door to save on the air conditioning bill. "Jesse, you in here? You want me to make you breakfast?" Uriah walked into the attic; Jesse wasn't there. He marveled at the spotlessness, mind the stool by the window. "Sammy and Ivy sure did a great job up here."

Uriah went to the window. His eyes lit up when he saw Ivy Teller across the street. He smiled and waved. He waited for her to wave back, but instead she took off her shirt and unsnapped her bra.

Uriah's face instantly turned bright red. He tried to quickly turn around before Ivy noticed him. He tripped over the stool and fell to the attic floor. He was grateful he fell. He prayed Ivy didn't see him. "Now I see why Jesse's been coming up to the attic," Uriah muttered. "I'm going to have to talk to him about this."

Uriah remained on his hands and knees on the floor while he waited for Ivy to move away from her window. While he waited, he noticed his hand had fallen on a loose floorboard. He lifted it up. "Hmm . . . this whole floorboard was never nailed down."

Uriah could see something glistening under the floor. He reached for it, pulling out a dusty glass jar. He sat on his knees as he wiped the jar on his shirt. He gasped when he saw a human fetus trapped behind the glass. His mind was instantaneously transported to a different time.

Pleasant Mills, New Jersey: 1758

"Do it!" Japhet Dean ordered Uriah as he sat on a tree stump in the middle of the woods. "Do it. You promised me."

Uriah dropped his knife. "I can't do it," Uriah sobbed, looking down at his sleeping baby boy. "I can't."

JD placed the knife back in Uriah's hand. "I want his heart; now give it to me."

"Please, I can't kill my own son." Uriah's hand trembled as he clutched his knife. His breathing became increasingly irregular and labored as he stared at the instrument of his son's demise.

JD grabbed Uriah's chin, forcing him to look at him. "Look at your life, Uriah Joseph Leeds. Look at your pretty face and your pretty wife. Your pretty house and your pretty church and all of your pretty followers. I gave you all of that! Did I not?!"

"You did," Uriah wept.

"And you promised me this heart. Now I want it!"

"Please, I can't." Uriah dropped the knife again. He sat on his knees crying into his hands as his son whimpered. "Take pity. Please take pity on me."

JD sat back down on the moss-covered tree stump.

"Oh, Uriah, how I do have a soft spot for you . . . there is another way."

"Anything! Please Mr. JD." Uriah looked up at Japhet Dean with his large blue, trusting eyes.

"I am all powerful, but yet I have my limits. You are the father of this village. The spiritual leader. Your job is to protect the innocent. You intercede for your God and to mine, do you not?"

"I do," he said in a shaky voice, picking up his crying son to soothe him.

"So, let's make a deal . . . I'll let your son live. And let you keep your pretty face and your pretty wife and all that I have given you. Grant me thirteen lives of your flock to save your little lamb today. Your son will live, and so will you Uriah, for a very long time."

"I will let you grow old and have many more children. But when your life is up, you agree to come back to this day. To this point in your life. You will be young and beautiful again not yet in your fifth lustrum of life. You will be in the prime of your manhood at a perky twenty-two. You will come back to your church where you will spread the good word of the Lord your God. Be Pleasant Mills' shepherd once again and, in doing so, grant me permission to claim thirteen of your faithful. And when it is all over, we will do it again. What do you say, Uriah Leeds, do we have a deal?"

Uriah's body quivered as his mind wheeled. "Thirteen?"

"Yes thirteen," JD said, looking to the heavens. "The number has a certain sentimental value to me as I was my mother's thirteenth child. The superstitious lot always consider the number unlucky, but for me, thirteen is, in fact, my lucky number. It does seem a fair price to save your first son, thirteen souls for his. Is he not worth it to you my sweet Uriah? Would you not do anything for your son?"

JAPHET DEAN LEEDS: 1758

Uriah glanced down at his son's face. "Yes. We have a deal," he replied through tears, cradling his infant son in his hands.

"It is done." JD hopped off the tree stump. He knelt and kissed Uriah's forehead tenderly.

"Now, that that whole mess is taken care of, what did you end up naming the little babe?"

"Joseph."

"That is a strong name. You take care of little Joseph. I will be watching you, Uriah . . . always and forever my son."

JD turned from Uriah, walking deeper into the Pine Barrens, all along whistling a low-pitched, haunting tune that hushed baby Joseph as his father held him close to his heart.

Uriah dropped the jarred fetus he held into his lap. "What's happening to me? What's going on?" His tears fell in provocation, and they fell hard. He had a sinking feeling in his heart that made his entire body ache. "Thirteen faithfuls . . . oh God, no—Zachary Lewis—Tyrone Jones . . . could it be?" He rested his head in his hands, his tears falling through his fingers. "Is it possible that my dreams aren't dreams? Could it be real . . . was that my life? Did I, a servant of God, make a deal with a devil?" A sob broke free. "Is Louie Grindhouse already dead?"

Uriah leaned against the wall, panting, letting his tears flow down his face unrestrained. He stayed like that for a long time until his breathing slowly returned to normal. Once he regained control of his faculties, he went back to the loose floorboard and looked for anything else that could help him make sense out of the images he'd seen in his head.

Uriah found an old brown leather journal hidden in the floorboards. He untied the leather strap and opened it to the first page. He recognized the handwriting as his own. "Property of Uriah Joseph Leeds," he read out loud, his shaky voice echoing in the empty attic. "I don't understand how this is possible." He hesitated for only a moment before he turned the page and began to read.

Journal,

Today my guardian angel paid me a visit. To him, I owe everything. All I have was given to me by him. My very face. My wife. My church. I watched my wife as she cared for our son and realized my very existence as I know it is thanks to Mr. JD. But the man I owe my life to, is not a messenger of God like I thought him to be as a naive child, looking to believe in something more. I know now that he is a messenger of the devil, perhaps his own son.

How could I have been so blind? I put my faith in the wrong man. I put my faith in the Devil. God save my soul and the soul of my son Joseph.

Uriah J. Leeds
5, June 1758.

Journal,

Today I willingly made a deal with the Devil to save my son. I know as a pastor, I should have refused. But as I looked upon my son's sleeping face, I knew I would do anything for him—even become a devil myself. There is no love like a father's love for his son. I would do it again. And I will for eternity, as that was my agreement. I will serve my community as best I can, knowing that thirteen children will be given up for me. Because of me. This is my greatest sin. This is my damnation.

Uriah J. Leeds
6, June 1758.

Journal,

Today my second son Peter died in his mother's womb. It is a loss my wife and I feel very deeply. My prayers do not comfort me.

Uriah J. Leeds
11, February 1759

Journal,

Death has claimed another Leeds. My wife has miscarried again. Forced to deliver yet another dead baby. We mourn Sarah Leeds.

Uriah J. Leeds
15, October 1759

Journal,

Mr. JD lied to me. He said that my family will live and continue to live, that I would have many more children, but that is not the case. My wife has had miscarriage after miscarriage, she cannot carry a child full-term. We have suffered the loss of twelve children; twelve children we have put to ground. With each loss, my wife has sacrificed a little bit of herself and has fallen further into despair. I look into her sad eyes and cannot ask her to try again.

As my wife, Joseph, and I gave Abbigail Leeds to God, I realized something most dreadful that had not crossed my mind. It was my wife's words that festered this horrific idea. Lilly wept in my arms that our daughter's death must be the devil at work.

I fear she is right. I fear that when I saved Joseph in the woods that day, I unknowingly created a feeding cycle for Mr. JD. I cannot imagine Lucifer Morningstar to be this malicious.

What have I done? Have I damned my own flesh and blood? Has he taken my children's souls? Did I unknowingly agree to this? Did I sacrifice my twelve children to save Joseph?

No woman should go through what my wife has endured in her attempt to make me happy. Lilly does not deserve this. She is an angel bound to Earth. I would be lost without her guidance and love. No man could ask for a better wife. Her beauty is only surpassed by her kind, understanding heart. I love her endlessly. She and Joseph are all I need to be happy. I will not give the Devil another one of my children.

Uriah J. Leeds
21, November 1768

Uriah looked at the preserved fetus in the jar, his trembling hands clutched around it. He read the tattered label that had long ago browned with age, the words almost lost to time. "Abigail Leeds—No, this can't be happening—this can't be real." In a fury, he went back to the lifted floorboard, feeling for anything else that may have been stowed away. His hand touched glass. One, after another, Uriah pulled out jarred fetuses. He looked them over in terror as he counted twelve. "I guess I couldn't part with them . . . " he said, looking over his dead children, his eyes swollen and red.

"It was me," he heard a voice say from the shadows of the attic. Japhet Dean stepped out of the darkness and walked toward Uriah.

"You?! You're real?!" Uriah said, scrambling back against the wall, putting as much distance between them as he could. "What are you?!"

"I thought I was your guardian angel, my dear Uriah?" JD asked, standing in front of him and looking down at his terrified face, the fear in Uriah's blue eyes casting them in darkness.

"No angel would ask a man to give up a child."

"Yes . . . because God doesn't let bad things happen to good people. Oh, how I forget," JD said sarcastically. "You can call me what you want, Uriah, but I have been there for you more than your God."

"It's true. It's all true. You're the Devil?!"

"Not quite. I'm what the locals referred to as the Leeds Devil, and my legend has coined the name Jersey Devil."

Uriah's heart thrashed about in his chest as he fixated upon the man from his nightmares and the demon of legend. The very legend he'd just talked about at the church lock-in the day Zachary Lewis disappeared. Uriah grabbed his head with both hands, feeling out of control. "This is not real!"

"It's very real Uriah. What you wrote in your journal centuries ago is true, all of it. And I *am* the Leeds Devil. I'm sorry if your Christian views pigeonhole me as something evil, for I am not. Part of me, yes—I can say it is so, just as it is for all of God's creatures. After all, we all have the potential to do evil things." JD crouched down next to Uriah. "Even you, Uriah Leeds, devoted man of God. Even you can do evil things when push comes to shove. Got to love free will."

"You stay away from me!" Uriah shouted.

JD turned his attention to the jars Uriah had lined up. "I saved them for you. In case you wanted to see them. Dead, yes—but preserved in magic for all of time as not to be forgotten." JD confusingly looked upon Uriah's frightened face, examining him. "This doesn't make you happy?" He asked earnestly. "I said I would let you keep everything I gave you forever, Uriah . . . I didn't lie about that."

Uriah pressed himself to the wall. "Get away from me!"

"Come now, can't you see I'm trying to help you?"

"You're not helping me!"

"I am, don't you see? You're starting to regain your memories. Memories of who you really are. Soon you will be your old self. Each soul I reap brings you back to me and fills my belly."

A muscle in Uriah's jaw jumped. "I don't want to be my old self. I don't want innocent children killed!" Uriah grabbed his head again, as if he could make it all go away by just squeezing. "This is not happening. This is not real. This is not real," he muttered to himself. "I just need my medicine, that's all, and this will all just go away."

"Come now, Uriah, this is not the first time we've done this. You're always so resistant in the beginning—always so frightened. All your medications do is delay the inevitable."

Uriah concentrated on his breathing while JD stood up and surveyed the attic. "I will say, Sammy and Ivy did a nice job up here. I can't remember when this place was so clean. Nice view of the budding girl across the street," he said, watching Ivy walk around in her underwear. "You really are quite the pervert, Uriah."

"I . . . I . . . I came up here to close the door."

"Uriah," JD whispered in his ear, kneeling next to him. "Get up off the floor. Eat your breakfast and ready your sermon. You've got church today and some bad news to break—another boy has gone missing."

Uriah couldn't speak. He felt like he couldn't breathe.

JD started down the steps, whistling a low-pitched, haunting melody. He stopped at the foot of the stairs, "Oh and Uriah, don't forget to shut the attic door."

CHAPTER FORTY
Ivy's Birthday

Sammy knocked on Ivy's front door. "Hey, Grams," he said when Mary opened the door.

"Sammy."

"Can you give this to Ivy for me?" He handed Grams a wrapped Kurt Cobain poster Ivy didn't have, along with a birthday card and a small box.

Sammy turned to leave. He knew better than to ask Grams to talk to Ivy. It had been almost a month since they'd broken up. She refused to talk to him at school or at her house. She went out of her way to avoid him. He'd known it was over when she quit youth group, but he couldn't let her go.

He loved her, even if she didn't believe him, and thought their love was worth fighting for. Yet, Sammy knew if Ivy wouldn't speak to him again, he had to face the music. He told himself he would try until her birthday, then after that, he would move on.

As Sammy walked down the porch steps of Ivy's house, he felt his heart break in two. "It's really over," he said to himself, opening his car door and looking up to the small attic window of Ivy's room. He hoped to catch a glimpse of her, but she had her curtains drawn shut. "Happy birthday, Ivy."

"Anything?" Jeffrey asked from the passenger seat.

Sammy shook his head and looked up to Ivy's window one last time before pulling out.

Grams knocked on Ivy's door. She was hovering by her window, peeking outside. She watched Sammy pull out of the driveway in his new black Hummer. That was sure to impress his fake friends, but it didn't impress her. Yet she had hoped he would stop by. Now that she'd quit youth group, she felt like all she'd seen of him was the back of his head during Sunday service or the top of it from her attic window.

"Sammy wanted you to have this," Mary said, handing her granddaughter the gifts Sammy had just dropped off. "I take it you're still not talking to him."

"No."

"Ives, I know I shouldn't put my two cents in here. . ."

Ivy put her gifts from Sammy on her bed. "Then don't, Grams."

"I've never seen a boy care so much. It's been nearly a month, and he's still trying."

Ivy shot her grandmother an incredulous look. "Well, that's because I'm easy, Grams."

Mary's lips flattened to a thin line. "Ivy . . ."

Ivy opened the poster; she liked it. It was Cobain smoking a cigarette in black and white. She thumbtacked it to an open spot on her wall.

Mary shook her head in frustration. "I'm going to go put dinner on," she said before heading back down the stairs.

"Okay, Grams."

Ivy opened the card.

Happy Birthday Ivy,

Roses are red,
violets are blue.
I messed up big,
but I'm still in love with you!

FOREST OF WHISPERS

Love,
Sammy

Ivy threw the card in the trash and opened the small box. Inside was a white-gold bracelet with a heart charm. She tried it on. The diamond in the heart sparkled as she held her wrist up to her face, the little facets catching the light from her desk lamp. She knew it was real. She also knew he'd blown his savings on it. She wished he hadn't, but part of her was elated he did. She was more conflicted than ever. She had never received jewelry from a boy, or any gift for that matter. She loved the bracelet. It reminded her of what had brought them together in the first place—the jarred heart, Sammy's hocus-pocus.

Ivy knew Grams was right: it had been almost a month of Sammy trying to get back in her good graces. He was relentless, and she liked it. She was glad Sammy stopped by today, but she wasn't surprised. Normally after school he and his father would come by and sit on the porch, waiting for her to come out, but she never did. Sometimes Ivy hoped Sammy would sneak out of his house like he used to and come to her window like a prince in a story book. But since their breakup, Louie was still missing, and everyone was losing hope of finding him alive. And to make matters worse, another boy had gone missing, a transplant to the community, a thirteen-year-old boy named Timothy Chen.

The town was spooked. They had themselves a bona fide kidnapper. Lindsey Lopez didn't let Sammy go anywhere unaccompanied, even though he wasn't thirteen and didn't fit the kidnapper's modus operandi. In fact, Jeffrey and Lindsey Lopez didn't let Sammy out of their sight. Ivy knew she had no chance of a fairy tale happily ever after.

Ivy missed Sammy, as a friend and as her boyfriend. She wanted to talk to him but felt like she couldn't because she'd made a declaration not to. Ivy was as stubborn as her grandmother, and she hated herself for it. She thought if she took him back, it would be admitting to all the things he'd said they'd done. And that would mean she was admitting to being a woman who didn't respect herself, because she was with a man that didn't respect her. Ivy wished she hadn't crucified Sammy. He was only sixteen after all. He had made a mistake and said he was sorry countless times. Forgiving Sammy would be the Christian thing to do. She just wished it wasn't so hard for her to forgive.

Ivy pulled the birthday card from Sammy out of the trash and put it on top of her nightstand. It featured a picture of a cat playing with balloons. Sammy had drawn smiley faces on all the balloons and added little hearts. "Oh, Sammy, why did you have to be so stupid."

CHAPTER FORTY-ONE
The Whisper Spell

"Home, Mom," Sammy yelled when he came in the front door. Lindsey kissed her husband and son hello. "Did you talk to Ivy?"

"No, it was Grams who answered the door."

"Sorry, honey," Lindsey said, giving her son a big hug.

"It's okay Mom. I'm gonna go to my room."

"Okay. I'm just finishing up dinner now."

Sammy lay down on his bed. He stared at the ceiling and thought of Ivy, thought of her dark eyes and dark hair, the way her mouth turned up when she laughed. He wished he could hear her laugh now.

He hopped to his feet with an idea. He quickly dug under his bed for the spell book. He hadn't looked at it since he and Ivy had broken up because they'd promised each other to never do a spell by themselves.

"Desperate times call for desperate measures," Sammy told himself, thumbing through the Leeds family spell book in his lap. He knew today was his last day to try to make amends with Ivy. After today he had to let her go, but he wasn't going to give up without a fight.

Sammy grinned and flicked a page in the spell book. "Perfect—the *Whisper Spell*. With this I can say happy birthday to her in person, well kind of. She'll have to listen to me; she'll have no choice." He hugged the book to his chest.

Sammy ran downstairs to collect the ingredients needed for his spell.

"What are you making?" his mother asked as Sammy rummaged through her spice drawer.

"Just trying my hand at a recipe I saw online."

The ingredients for the *Whisper Spell* were simple enough. More spices than anything else and, thanks to his mom, he had them all. He couldn't wait to do the spell tonight once his family fell asleep.

Sammy was in high spirits as he made his way to the garage. He grabbed his winter coat off the hook and bypassed the cameras to make his way to the toolshed in the backyard. Sammy thought of casting the *Laughing Spell* behind the toolshed with Ivy in the beginning of the summer and grew more excited. He couldn't wait to talk to her.

"Whisper low,
until it grows,
muffled cries of a voice that died.
Brought back to life by a loud cry.
Span time and space,
travel far to find a friend's lonely face.
With a pinch of basil, parsley,
hope and thyme,
words find Ivy Teller in her bedroom in the Pines.
Now whisper grow,

bring back my voice with a friendly hello."

"Ivy? Can you hear me?" Sammy whispered into the night. "Ivy?"

Sammy scoffed. "Stupid spell; what the heck is a pinch?! That's not even an exact measurement!" He dumped out the plastic bowl that was acting as his makeshift cauldron and started again, being very careful with the amount of the ingredients.

"Whisper low,
until it grows,
muffled cries of a voice that died.
Brought back to life by a loud cry.
Span time and space,
travel far to find a friend's lonely face.
With a pinch of basil, parsley,
hope and thyme,
words find Ivy Teller in her bedroom in the Pines.
Now whisper grow,
bring back my voice with a friendly hello."

Sammy prayed out loud before he spoke into the night. "Please let this work God . . . Ivy? You there?"

Sammy's dejection culminated in slouched shoulders as he waited for Ivy to speak back to him. "I can't believe my luck. The spell has to work, it just has to." He sighed. "Maybe it's just not powerful enough. Maybe . . . I need to be closer to Ivy. I'll just go there really quick and try it, and then head straight home."

Sammy put the spell book and the plastic bowl containing his spell on the ground behind the shed, securing them in their hiding space under a pile of freshly fallen oak leaves, before walking to Ivy's house.

It was a cold night. A light breeze rustled the golden leaves on the trees. The moon poked out from the clouds like a sad sun as Sammy stood outside Ivy's house. "Ivy?" He whispered. He waited for a couple minutes hoping she could hear him. "Ivy?!"

Nothing.

He scuffed the sidewalk in frustration. "Shoot, I must've messed up the spell. I can't do anything right." He slid his cold hands into his pockets, looking up at her window one last time before starting the walk home. He knew without the midnight show, Ivy had no reason to be waiting by her window.

"I blew it. It's over. I've got to let her go." Sammy hung his head low as he walked. "Some witch I am . . . I can't even do a simple spell."

Hearing the roar of a car engine, Sammy looked up. It was speeding down the road and passed him. The sound of breaks filled the quiet night, like a scream. It suddenly felt colder, the night darker. Sammy's heart jumped a beat. The car reversed until it was aligned with him on the sidewalk.

"Hey there," Jesse said, rolling his tinted window down.

Sammy sighed with relief. "Hi Mr. Richards."

"A little late to be out?"

"Um . . . yeah," he mumbled. "I'm heading home."

"I'll give you a ride."

"It's a close walk."

Sammy's head jerked toward the woods as a haunting whistle rattle the leaves of the trees next to the road. He had heard that strange song before, but he couldn't remember from where.

"I'll drop you off right before we get to your house, so your father doesn't see you. Come on, I'm not letting you walk in the dark with all the headlines lately."

Sammy's eyes searched the woods for the whistler before he got in. "Okay, thanks, I appreciate it."

Sammy had sneaked out of the house plenty of times but tonight felt different. He wasn't sure if he was just depressed over Ivy or if his parents' words of caution were finally sinking in, either way he was grateful for the ride. Sammy knew Mr. Richards was right; he shouldn't be out by himself. He knew he was being stupid going out in the middle of the night with all the kids that had gone missing in the neighborhood, but he was desperate to talk to Ivy.

"You and Ivy still not talking?" Jesse asked as they drove.

"No, and today's her birthday." He slouched in his seat. "I just wanted to say happy birthday."

"I understand, Sammy. You've got it bad. I can relate. That Ivy is a special girl. But you should listen to your dad. It's dangerous at night."

Sammy unzipped his coat and slid it off, he was sweating. Jesse had the heat on full blast. "I know. Please don't tell him. He'll freak out."

"I won't."

"Thanks, I owe you one."

"Do me a favor?" Jesse pointed to his glove compartment. "Hand me my wallet."

"Sure thing." Sammy opened the glove compartment. It was stuffed to the brim. He rifled through papers looking for Jesse's wallet.

Feeling a sharp prick on his neck, Sammy grabbed it. "What the heck?!" His hand closed around a small dart. He glanced to Jesse as darkness crept in from all directions.

"Good night, Sammy."

Before Sammy could say another word, he passed out.

CHAPTER FORTY-TWO
Trapped

Sammy woke up, jumping to his feet. He wobbled, shivering, his extremities covered in gooseflesh. He rubbed his hands up and down his arms trying to warm himself, wishing he had his coat. His surroundings spun around him in the dark like he was trapped on a merry-go-round. He took a deep breath in, smelling damp earth. It reminded him of how his backyard smelled after a heavy rainstorm.

"Easy, Sammy," Jesse said.

Sammy turned in the direction of Jesse's voice. "Where am I?! What did you do?!" He asked, grabbing his neck in remembrance. His eyes attempted to focus in the dark, but Jesse was hidden in shadows. Only a thin line of light filtered into the dark space cutting across his vision.

"You just got a taste of a tranquilizer dart. Comes in handy when I hunt. You'll be fine in a couple of hours; it just stuns you."

"Let me out of here," Sammy said, pulling on the iron bars that he now saw separated him from Jesse Richards. Sammy strained his eyes in the dark. He was surrounded by three dirt walls. He was in a prison cell scooped out of the Earth.

"Mr. Richards—Jesse, I don't know what you think you're doing, but this isn't funny—let me out of here!"

"Oh Sammy, I've got bad news for you. You're not going to be saying happy birthday to Ivy or anything to anyone. You're never leaving this place."

Sammy's heart pounded against his chest; his sides ached. It just dawned on him who Jesse was. "It's you! You're the one that kidnapped Zac, Tyrone, and Louie!" Sammy's breathing became labored, his legs felt unstable, like he could topple over at any minute. "No, no, no—let me out now, please! I won't tell anyone. I promise."

"Sammy, we both know you have a big mouth. I mean that's why you and Ives split in the first place, right? You can't keep that big mouth of yours shut," Jesse said, enjoying watching Sammy squirm.

"I won't say a word. I promise, I won't."

"I wish I could just let you go Sammy, but you're on the list."

"The list?" Sammy asked, confused as he ran his hands over the dirt walls of his cell looking for a way to escape.

"You're one of the thirteen."

"*One of the thirteen?* What are you talking about?"

"Now, Sammy, you're a smart boy . . . you already know what happened to Zachary, and Tyrone. They should be finding Louie Grindhouse's body soon."

"No!" Sammy shouted. "You're a liar!"

"Afraid so," Jesse said plainly. He moved closer to the bars keeping Sammy trapped. "Let me tell you, that big kid bawled his eyes out like a baby, he was so scared." Sammy shook his head. "Tell me, rich kid, are you scared?" Jesse asked with a cruel smile, his teeth flashing in the dark.

"This has to be some kind of mistake! I'm not thirteen."

"No, Sammy. No mistake. You caught the eye of the bossman himself, which normally may not have been such a bad thing, but it's a new cycle and he needs to claim thirteen souls."

"Boss? Cycle? Jesse—please! This isn't funny!" Sammy leaned against the iron bars to stop himself from falling over.

Jesse sighed. "Boy, oh boy, was your dad right. It's dangerous at night in the Pine Barrens, even for us Pineys. The Jersey Devil stalks the woods for anyone who comes close to his home. He prefers the taste of children and has an affinity for good little boys. Kind of like good ol' Saint Nick, except it's his skin that's red, and he has the wings of a bat and the horns and hooves of an ox. Well, and there's no toys. Sometimes, at night, if you listen carefully, you can hear him whistling his song. He's always there Sammy—watching. Watching us all."

Sammy knew all folktales came from real places; his grandmother had taught him that. He didn't doubt the legend of the Jersey Devil was true on the surface, but a real-life demon who had kids kidnaped for him so he could murder them seemed off—way off, even for his imagination.

"This can't be real," Sammy said, tears gushing out of his scared blue eyes.

"Can't it be, Sammy? Don't you believe in all that hocus-pocus?"

"I don't get it? Why the hearts? Why did he take Zac's and Tyrone's heart?"

"He needs them to keep his mortal form and blend in. Without them he would remain a beast. Something about the heart being at the center of humanity, or something like that. The hearts sustain him for a long time. Keep him young and handsome, but like I said there's a cycle."

"Sustain him? You're saying he eats them?"

Sammy could just make out Jesse's mop of dirty blond hair in the dark as he nodded. "Jesse, help me," Sammy pleaded. "Maybe we can work together to kill him."

"Kill him?!" Jesse chuckled, his laugh caring in the underground prison. "He can't be killed."

"Everyone can be killed."

Jesse shook his head. "Not him."

"How do you know?!"

"Because I'm one of his sons. He took me under his wing when I needed him. He helped me build an empire in Batsto Village. I was the King of Pleasant Mills."

"Wait . . . you're telling me you're Jesse Richards, the Jesse Richards of Batsto Village who lived hundreds of years ago?"

"One and the same. I had it all. I had my own town. Batsto served my every whim. I helped bring Batsto Village into a new era. Made a fortune in the process and cemented my legacy."

Sammy's eyebrows furrowed, as he tried to connect the dots. "I don't understand . . . if you're Jesse Richards of the Richards family, how are you here? How are you still alive?!"

"Alive is a relative term when in *weird* New Jersey. Come now, you can't tell me you haven't seen stranger things than people coming back from the dead?"

Sammy's eyes grew large like saucers.

"JD may only fixate on one child at a time, but he loves us in his own twisted way I suppose. He always keeps us close. You see he made a deal with each of us. Made us choose to live forever."

"Made you choose?"

"He acts like it's a choice when he propositions you with it. Like it's a great favor, but it's no choice, and you find yourself like me—living forever."

"And now you do his dirty work for him?"

"Sometimes . . . I have to play my part. After I help JD collect thirteen souls, I'm free to leave Pleasant Mills and live the rest of my years as I see fit. He gives me the power to do what I want when I want."

"But first you have to kidnap the thirteen kids he asked for?"

"I knew you were a smart kid, Sammy. So, here you are."

"Jesse please, my dad has a lot of money. He'll give you as much as you want, just let me go."

"Sorry kid, this is one problem money can't solve. It's too late for you, but it's not for me," Jesse said, putting his face up to the iron bars so Sammy could see the whites of his eyes. "I know you found the heart. Where is it?"

"*The heart*?" Sammy had wanted there to be a connection between the heart he found with Ivy, and what happen to his Zac but now that he knew that connection was the Jersey Devil, he wished Ivy was right and there was no such thing as hocus-pocus. He wished it was all just a bad dream and he was going to wake up soon.

"What are you talking about?" Sammy asked, playing dumb, thinking if Jesse wanted the jarred heart, it could be used as leverage to get himself out of there.

"You're in no position to play games. I know you have it because he told me you do. Now tell me where it is."

"Maybe if I *did* know where it was, I could tell you once you let me go."

"Not happening."

Sammy shrugged. "I have no idea what you're talking about."

Jesse opened the iron gates of Sammy's cell with a key he had on his key chain and pushed Sammy against the cold dirt wall. "You're going to tell me where it is, now!"

"I don't know." Jesse wanting the heart was a good enough reason to keep it away from him. If he wasn't going to let him out, he wasn't going to give him the jarred heart.

Jesse threw Sammy to the ground. "I forgot, you're used to getting roughed up. Maybe I'll just go ask Ivy. You know what, I should go wish her a happy birthday while I'm at it. She's still a virgin, right? All those tales you told in the locker room were just braggadocio. Tall tales of things you wish you could do, if you only had the balls to do it."

"Screw you!"

Jesse gave Sammy a swift kick to the stomach while he lay on the ground. "I watched the two of you play around through the attic window. Maybe it's high time she got with a real man, someone a little older and more experienced. I could give her a birthday gift she's sure to remember."

Sammy held his stomach in pain. "Leave her alone!"

"The heart, Sammy; where is it?!" Jesse kicked him again.

"You'll leave Ivy alone?" He asked, coughing up blood.

"I will."

"I buried it."

"Buried it?" Jesse asked.

"I had to. It kept glowing and thumping."

Jesse picked Sammy up by the collar of his shirt and looked him in the eyes. "It's alive again? Where, Sammy?! I need to get it before he can get to it."

Sammy coughed. "I don't understand. If he knew I had it, why didn't he just take it?"

"It's not his anymore, it's yours. He'd have to trade you for it. He can't just take it, but I can." Jesse shook him hard, talking through clenched teeth. "Where is it?! Once he kills you, it belongs to no one again and he can claim it! I need to get the heart now, before it's too late. Tell me or I'm going to Ivy's."

"It's in the woods. Behind my house. Marked with a stick in the ground."

Jesse released Sammy and gave him a large smile that distorted his face in the dark. "Now that's a good boy. Sit tight; this will all be over soon."

Jesse left and when he did, he sealed off the only light while a grating noise sounded overhead. Sammy's cell was pitch dark; he couldn't see an inch in front of his face. He sat against a dirt wall, his ribs sore. He tucked his arms inside his shirt for warmth. A light whimper cut through the silence. "Is someone down here?" Sammy called into the darkness.

"Yes," a voice said back.

"My name's Sammy; what's yours?"

"Timothy."

"Timothy Chen?" Sammy asked.

"Yes, that's me."

Sammy knew the name. Pastor Leeds had welcomed the Chen family to church a couple weeks ago, but Sammy hadn't had a chance to talk to Timothy before he'd gone missing.

"Is he really going to feed us to the Jersey Devil?" Timothy asked in a shaky voice.

Sammy also knew Jesse wasn't lying about the Jersey Devil or the horrible fate that would befall them if they weren't found, but Timothy was only thirteen. Sammy didn't want to scare him. He was already terrified; he couldn't imagine how Timothy must feel after being trapped in the dark for weeks.

"No. Jesse knows me and was just trying to scare me. Don't worry, my dad will find us. I know you're new in town, so you don't know my dad, but . . . he's kinda like a superhero. He'll save us. Don't be surprised if you hear helicopters overhead in a couple hours looking for us. My dad will tear this town apart looking for me."

"You promise?"

"Yes, my dad is Mayor Lopez. He'll find us. I promise. Just try to hang on, okay?"

"Okay, Sammy."

"Was a boy named Louie down here with you?"

"He was. They took him away when they brought you in. He was in the cage before mine."

"So, there're three cages then?" Sammy asked, thinking it did feel like he was locked in a cage like an animal.

"I think so," Timothy said, a sob breaking free.

"It's okay. My dad will find Louie too. You'll see."

"I'm hungry, Sammy."

"Jesse didn't give you anything to eat?"

"A water bottle every day . . . I think. And a pack of crackers sometimes."

Sammy nibbled on his lip. Jesse was keeping the boys weak, he reasoned that was to diminish their chances of escape. If he was going to get out of there, it was going to be now when he still had all of his strength.

Sammy got to his feet and tried the bars again. He pushed his body against them with all his might. They didn't budge. He went to the far side of the dirt cell to try to gain momentum before charging at the bars of his prison. He fell to the ground, dizzy.

Timothy's cries grew louder, as if he knew what Sammy was attempting and knew what little good it would do, because he had tried the same thing.

Sammy leaned against the bars to his cell and rubbed his shoulder. "Hey, don't worry. We'll be rescued soon. And my dad will get you a pizza all to yourself."

He whispered into his cell: "Ivy," hoping the spell he'd cast would finally work.

Ivy was in bed listening to music when she thought she heard Sammy call her name. "Ivy, can you hear me? Please, I need you!"

Ivy pulled out her earbuds. "Sammy?" She swore she heard a muffled cry. At that moment, a motorcycle sped down the street with a thunderous roar, and with that she shrugged off what she thought she'd heard and turned her music back on, blocking out Sammy's call for help.

"Ivy, I need your help. Ivy? Please, I'm scared."

"I don't want to die," Timothy whimpered in the dark.

"You're not going to die Timothy. My dad will find us, I promise. And I always keep my promises."

Sammy tucked his head into his shoulder to stifle his tears so Timothy couldn't hear. The air was thick, and it was hard for him to breathe. He still felt dizzy from the tranquilizer. Sammy knew Jesse let them see his face because it didn't matter if they did, because they were never getting out of there alive. "Ivy, please help me . . ."

CHAPTER FORTY-THREE
Bad News

Mary made it up the old attic staircase in record time, the steps croaking and groaning under her stubborn feet. She knocked on Ivy's bedroom door hard and opened it.

"Hey Grams," Ivy said, sitting up in bed and taking out her earbuds.

Mary took a couple of deep gulps in to catch her breath. "Didn't you hear me calling you?!"

"No. Sorry, what's up?"

"Have you heard from Sammy?"

"No, I blocked his number."

"Can you do me a favor and unblock him?"

"Why?" Ivy asked, confused, her brows furrowing.

Mary sat down on Ivy's bed and put a hand on her granddaughter's knee. "Sammy is missing."

"What?!" Ivy felt like time froze. Her heartbeat seemed to tick in her ears slowly, slower, slower. "What do you mean he's missing?"

"I just got off the phone with Lindsey. He wasn't in his bed this morning. She wanted to know if you've heard from him."

Ivy couldn't move; she was immobilized by fear. She knew what was coming next.

"Jeffrey thinks Sammy snuck out of the house last night to see you. They got him on camera leaving the house from the garage. Lindsey said it's not the first time he's snuck out; they were just hoping he came here." Mary squeezed her granddaughter's hand. "Did he, Ivy? I won't be mad. We all just want to make sure Sammy gets home safe."

"No Grams, Sammy didn't come here." Her tongue felt like jelly. "Are they sure he's missing?"

Mary nodded. "It's looking that way. Sammy's cell phone is in his bedroom, but Lindsey was hoping if he was in trouble, he might find a way to call you."

"Oh no, Grams." Ivy was crying, she didn't even realize she was until a tear drop hit her arm.

Her grandmother hugged her. "It's okay. They'll find him."

CHAPTER FORTY-FOUR
Alone

Sammy was trying to keep track of the days as they passed by, but he had no real way of knowing. Time seemed to pass differently in the dark of the underground. By the time Jesse brought Sammy his first water bottle and pack of peanut butter cracker sandwiches, Sammy felt like he had been kidnapped days ago. He felt weak and disoriented. He couldn't sleep, but he felt like he wasn't truly awake when he was up. He felt as if he were trapped between a living nightmare and a nightmare.

Sammy's only saving grace was Timothy. He was grateful not to be alone. Talking to Timothy kept him sane—gave him hope. He had to be strong for Timothy, so he was. He tried to be optimistic and confident his dad would cut through the darkness to save them at any minute, but it was always Jesse.

"Hey boys," Jesse said, throwing them a water bottle each and a pack of crackers.

"Can't you give us something more than crackers?" Sammy asked, reaching for his pack that landed on the other side of the bars.

Jesse stepped on Sammy's hand. "Don't complain or you'll get nothing." Jesse picked the crackers off the ground and threw them to Timothy. "Looks like you get two today. Well, just stopped by for a quick visit. Enjoy the empty stomach Sammy," Jesse scoffed before he left.

"Hey Sammy, maybe I can try to throw you the crackers and you can try to catch 'em through the bars," Timothy suggested to his best friend. That's what they had become, best friends—brothers. In the last week Sammy and Timothy had poured their hearts out to each other. Told each other everything, their biggest secrets and dreams.

"No, it's fine, you eat the crackers. If you toss them, I may miss, then no one will get to eat them."

"Shoot, I feel guilty."

"Stop Tim," Sammy said as his stomach growled. "It won't be long now. I'm sure my mom has tons of food waiting for us. I can't wait for you to try her sticky buns; they're world famous."

The next night Sammy woke up to Timothy screaming.

"Get off! Leave me alone! Sammy help!"

Sammy scrambled to his feet, light crossing his path. "Let him go, you piece of shit!" Sammy yelled. "Pick on someone your own size!"

Jesse smirked to himself. He pushed Timothy to the ground and locked him in before he went to meet Sammy's insults.

Sammy took a step back as Jesse stood in front of him. Only the cold iron bars separated them. "Let Timothy go, please. Take me instead; he's only a kid."

Jesse stared into Sammy's frightened eyes and respected him. All three of them knew where Timothy was going, and Sammy was still willing to take his place. "I like you, Sammy. I wish I could spare you, and Tim too, but it's just not gonna happen. Name calling is only gonna get me pissed." Jesse pulled two packs of crackers and two water bottles from his jacket pockets and tossed them through the bars. They landed by Sammy's feet.

"Might as well have Timothy's."

"Jesse, please don't hurt him. Please," Sammy begged as the tears streamed down his face.

Jesse took a deep breath in. "If you want to say goodbye, do it now," he said in a low voice. "You won't be seeing him again."

"No, please!"

Sammy listened to Jesse unlock Timothy's cell. He could hear Timothy struggle against the bigger, stronger man. Sammy grabbed the bars to his cell. "Jesse! Please don't do this! Please, Jesse, take me!"

"Sammy!" Timothy yelled through tears.

Sammy pressed his face against the bars trying to get a glimpse of his friend. "Timothy! It's gonna be okay!" Sammy couldn't bring himself to say goodbye. Him saying it would make it real. "Tim, I love you, man!"

Sammy heard Timothy's cries become muffled, and soon silence swept the underground prison. He heard Jesse's heavy footsteps on what he knew had to be stairs and heard a loud dragging noise before it went pitch dark again.

Sitting on the ground, Sammy wrapped his arms around himself. He cried into the darkness, "Dad, where are you?"

CHAPTER FORTY-FIVE
Body Found

"Hey Ivy, I'm going over to the Lopez house to give Lindsey a break with the girls," Mary said to her granddaughter as she ate a pack of peanut butter cracker sandwiches for breakfast. "They're doing a search in the woods again this morning and she wants to join. You want to come and help keep an eye on Alba and Maria?"

"Yeah, of course," Ivy said, taking a seat next to her grandmother at the kitchen table.

For the last week she had practically lived at the Lopez's. She and Grams went there right after school. She wasn't allowed to participate in the searches since she was a teen, but she did watch Alba and Maria for Lindsey, which was a big help.

The Lopez house looked like a crime scene. The place was crawling with cops and employed professionals Jeffrey hired. He spared no expense. They had dogs, hired hands, and volunteers. With every day Sammy wasn't found, more people would show up to help look for him. Thanks to Sammy's community service, the whole town knew Sammy Lopez and wanted to help.

Jeffrey, Devan, and Uriah had just returned from a search in the woods. It was cold out. They were getting worried the weather would play a factor in finding Sammy, Timothy, and Louie alive. It was a mild November, but temperatures were plummeting at night. Jeffrey and Lindsey were glad Sammy was wearing his winter coat. They saw that much in the video footage Jeffrey was able to pull off the surveillance cameras. They had given a detailed description of Sammy's gray plaid North Face coat to Devan along with a picture, praying it was enough to keep him warm.

"Anything?" Lindsey asked desperately, walking over to where her husband was hanging up his coat to give him a hug and a kiss.

Jeffrey shook his head. "No, but I've got another search starting in an hour. We're going to search a different section of the woods."

Chief Rainier got a call. He stepped away from the Lopez's to answer it.

"You sure?" he asked into the receiver. "On our way."

Devan pulled Jeffrey aside and spoke in a whisper. "I don't want to worry you Jeffrey . . ."

Jeffrey's pulse raced. "Tell me."

"That was Pearl. They just pulled a boy out of Batsto River. The coat fits the description of Sammy's coat." Jeffrey's heart beat so fast in his chest he thought he was having a heart attack, the pain staggering him. The only thing keeping him standing upright was Lindsey. He knew she was watching him. His mouth was dry, his tongue sticking to the roof of his mouth as he tried to articulate a sentence.

Devan put his hand on his arm. "We don't know it's him for sure. We've still got two other boys missing." He gave an encouraging squeeze. "I'm praying it's not Sammy . . . but we need to make an identification. Do you think you're up to that?"

With the color drained from his face, Jeffrey nodded.

"They found him?!" Lindsey asked, grabbing her husband's hand. "They found my son?!"

"We don't know, Lindsey," Jeffrey said, trying to calm his wife down.

"Where is he?!" she shouted.

Ivy could tell from Jeffrey's face it wasn't good news. She sunk unto a step, next to Alba and Maria, who went silent when their mother broke into sobs.

"Lindsey, I'll be back—stay here," Jeffrey said, pushing past his aching heart and remaining strong for his wife.

Grams hugged Lindsey.

"Uriah, make sure the next search party leaves on time if I'm not back by then," Jeffrey ordered through bloodshot eyes.

"Yes Jeffrey, of course," he said as he too comforted Lindsey.

Ivy took the twin's hands and led them to their room after they'd hugged their dad goodbye.

"Is Sammy okay?" They asked in unison.

"I'm sure he is," Ivy said hopefully.

"I love Sammy. He's the bestest big brother," Maria said.

Alba agreed, nodding. "Me too."

"Sammy knows," she said, trying not to cry.

Devan drove Jeffrey to the coroner's office. They rode in silence. Jeffrey was trying to prepare himself for the worst—that it was *his* son they'd found. He turned to prayer. He'd never been a religious man. He went to church for his wife, because it made her happy, and he thought it would give his children something to believe in. But he didn't believe in much. Jeffrey Lopez believed in hard work, and that was about it. He wished, like his wife and children, he believed in something bigger than himself. He wished he believed that if he prayed hard enough and had enough faith, God would help him.

When Sammy had fallen down the stairs, God had answered that prayer. Now he prayed God would answer the prayer he said in the confines of his mind. *Please God, don't let it be Sammy. Please God. I will do anything.*

Devan led Jeffrey down a long hallway. He stopped before he opened the door. "I need to prepare you. Pearl told me the body was badly mutilated and was in the river for who knows how long—"

"I understand, Devan."

Jeffrey's pulse quickened to a gallop as they entered the examiner's room. He held his breath and prayed as the coroner opened the body bag. Seeing the dark hair, Jeffrey covered his mouth with his hand and turned away. "I can't."

"It's okay," Devan said, putting a hand on Jeffrey's trembling shoulder.

"I can't do this," Jeffrey said in a low voice.

"I'll do it," Devan said, looking down at the boy in the body bag. It was hard to make out any definitive facial features, but the boy had brown hair and seemed to be about Sammy's height. He examined the coat. "Based off the description of Sammy's coat you gave me—"

Jeffrey's eyes diverted to the lifeless body. The air was sucked from his lungs, rocking him. "It's Sammy's. I recognize it," Jeffrey muttered in a barely audible voice.

Devan hugged him. "It's him, Jeffrey. I'm sorry."

Jeffrey's world felt like it had just come crashing down around him. He couldn't imagine a world where Sammy didn't exist. His perfect son, the son he was so hard on, but the son he loved more than anything in this world. He thought he couldn't exist in a world Sammy didn't exist in.

"I'm sorry for your loss, Mr. Lopez," the coroner said empathetically. "I'll call you when I get the DNA test results in, as it is hospital protocol."

Jeffrey nodded, barely keeping himself together.

"Come on Jeffrey, let me take you home," Devan said, putting his arm around his back.

Jeffrey looked at Devan, confused as he raked his trembling fingers through his hair. "I can't believe this is happening . . . Sammy was such a good kid."

The room began to spin under his feet, and his words came out sluggish to his ears. "Was it the same killer that murdered Zac and Tyrone? Is his heart missing?" Jeffrey asked the coroner as he zippered up the body bag.

"I still need to do a full autopsy to determine the time of death, but it appears the heart has been removed."

Jeffrey staggered out of the morgue. The sound of the door closing behind him echoed in his ears. He sat down on the ground before he fell over. "How am I going to tell Lindsey? . . . How?"

Devan crouched in front of him. "You have a strong wife, Jeffrey. You will both survive this for your girls. Let me drive you home; you should be with her." Devan took his best friend's arm and helped him to his feet.

Jeffrey walked into his house with Devan. Lindsey ran to him while Grams and Uriah remained seated at the kitchen table. She knew by the somber expression on his face. "No, Jeffrey! NO!"

Ivy could hear her cries from upstairs. She'd never heard such heartache as Lindsey Lopez's heart breaking upon the news of her son's death. Her cries shook Ivy. Her body trembled involuntarily.

"NO, JEFFREY!"

"I'm sorry, Lindsey. It's him. It's his winter coat," Jeffrey said in a shaky voice as he hugged his wife, her cries muffled by his chest. "Louie and Timothy are still missing. I'm going to continue the search for them. Sammy would want me to find the other boys. We're not going to stop looking until we find them."

"I want to see him. Take me to him!" Lindsey begged.

"Lindsey, you can't," Jeffrey pleaded, tears beading on his dark lashes.

"I want to see my son! Let me see my son!" she screamed, her cries ringing throughout the house.

"Lindsey, you don't want to see him like that."

"Take me to him Jeffrey. I want to see him." Lindsey slumped down to the floor. "I did this to him. I should never have named him after my brother. I did this to him! I cursed him!"

"No, Lindsey, this is not your fault. You were the best mother to Sammy, and he loved you." Jeffrey got down on his knees and hugged his wife, their tears falling together.

CHAPTER FORTY-SIX
Peanut Butter Cracker Sandwiches and Heartache

"I'm sorry about Sammy," Jesse said, hugging Ivy on her couch. Ivy tried to hold back her tears but was failing horribly. She felt guilty for Sammy's murder. If she had only talked to him on her birthday, he'd still be alive. Her stubbornness got him killed. There was a hole in her heart that would never close.

"Why did I have to fall in love with a stupid boy?"

Jesse brought her in closer, pressing his chest to hers. His body was heating up. He loosened his grip just enough so he could press a kiss to Ivy's lips. She did nothing. He kissed her again, sticking his hot tongue in her mouth.

Ivy pushed him off. "I can't Jesse, not now!" She ran to her room in tears.

Jesse got off the couch and went into the kitchen. "Grams, I'm taking some crackers, if that's okay?"

"Yes, please!" she shouted from the hall. "I bought so many when they were on sale. Had a double coupon. Now I'm worried they'll go stale before we eat them all."

"A couple of waters too?"

Grams popped her head in the kitchen. "Help yourself, Jesse."

"Well, Ivy's pretty upset; I'm gonna get going."

Grams walked Jesse to the front door. "Thanks for stopping by. I know it means a lot to Ivy."

"No problem," he said with a smile. "Just trying to be a good friend."

It was a still night. The wind died over the river before making its way to the forest. The moon shone bright in the sky, not a cloud in sight. Its autumnal haze festooned the headstones of Pleasant Mills Cemetery in an amber glow. Jesse slid open the top of his gravestone monument, a grating noise filling the quiet night before he descended the steps of his underground crypt. He walked over to where Sammy was leaning against the dirt wall of his cell.

"No hello?" Jesse asked. He took a pack of crackers out of his coat and dragged it against the iron bars of Sammy's cell. A clanking noise filled the crypt. "I guess you must be hungry." Jesse tossed the crackers through the bars.

Sammy quickly reached for the crackers and opened them. He tried to remember to chew, but he was so hungry. It had been two days since Jesse had come to terrorize him in the dark. Two days since he'd taken Timothy.

Jesse took the two water bottles from his coat pocket and threw them into the cell with the extra pack of crackers.

Sammy quickly grabbed the provisions before Jesse could take them back.

"Don't eat too quick now. You'll make yourself sick. I forgot I've only got one of you down here to feed now . . . guess you got lucky with double rations."

Sammy tried not to think about Timothy, but it was all he thought about since he was taken. Timothy haunted his every thought. Sammy knew he was next and there was nothing he could do about it. He didn't want to give up, but he thought he had already. Without Timothy, he had no one. He was all alone. He was trying to make amends with dying. He prayed to God to make him okay with it—prayed to accept God's plan for him and to accept this was supposed to happen.

Jesse was right, he was going to make himself sick. He tried to slow down. He held his breath while tears ran down his face. The thought that this could be his last meal bounced around in his head like a ping pong ball. Timothy had two packs of crackers before Jesse took him away. He looked at the second pack of crackers in his hand as the moonlight danced down into the underground. His hands were shaking. He wondered if this was it. If Jesse was there to take him to the Jersey Devil tonight.

"I found the spot you told me about in your backyard. Walked right past it on a search through the woods with your dad. I can't get to it now with all the good citizens of this town crawling about, but I'll grab it as soon as I can," Jesse said, letting out a loud sigh.

"Why is it so important anyway?" Sammy asked, opening the second pack of crackers, his spirit dampening. There was no point to holding on to the crackers for later.

"It's her heart."

Sammy wiped his tears with the inside of his elbow. "*Her?*"

"Deborah Smith Leeds."

"I don't know who that is," Sammy said, savoring the water in his mouth.

"Really, Sammy, and you call yourself a local. She's JD's mother. She's the one who cursed him."

"Uh JD?"

Jesse shook his head in frustration. "That's what he's called."

"I get it. JD's short for Jersey Devil."

"And Deborah was his mother. Legend has it that her husband was a good for nothing drunk that couldn't keep his hands off her. She was always barefoot and pregnant. She got pregnant again for the thirteenth time, this time with a boy. She cursed the baby. Gave him to the devil. When JD was born, the devil claimed him as his own. The very day he came into this world he killed his good for nothing father and they say some of his siblings. Not all of them of course, we still have members of the Leeds family all over South Jersey. But it's what he did to his own mother that's the interesting part. JD ripped out her heart and kept it. You see Sammy, Deborah started it all. It was her curse that created him. All of his power indirectly came from her. I think her heart is the source of his power."

"Think—you don't know?"

Jesse thought for a moment, his eyes scanning the darkness. "I don't know for sure, but I'm pretty sure. He always had it with him when he first took me under his wing. I was just a teenager, but I remember he would talk to it like it was alive. Like it could hear him." He shrugged. "It's all I have to go on. It was well known that JD's mother was a powerful witch. Whispers in the village gave her away."

"And you want her heart to kill him?" Sammy asked hopefully.

Jesse laughed. "Still on this killing-the-Jersey-Devil kick? No, I want his power."

"Uh, Jesse, I don't mean to punch holes in your power play, but if the heart is so important, why was it in the rectory attic with a bunch of junk?"

"I don't know. I can't remember."

"Convenient," Sammy mumbled.

"That's why I want the heart. When I die, I don't remember the former lives I've lived. They're lost. I have no idea what I did just eight years ago when my cycle started over. No clue. All I remember is my first life. My true life. I remember my father, my brother, my sisters, my wife, my sons, my daughters."

"Why only that one?" Sammy asked, finishing his last cracker.

Jesse exhaled loudly. "The memory of my first life was supposed to be a gift from JD for doing the favor he asked of me without question. I did what he asked, when he asked." Jesse stared off as he remembered. "I was always good at doing what I was told . . . Usually, he wipes his little helpers' minds clean. When they die, they're brought back with false memories, memories he gives them. It makes it easier for him to manipulate and control them that way. But with me, he let me keep the memory of my first life." Jesse sucked his teeth, muttering to himself. "It's not a gift. It's a curse. I will always remember what immortality has cost me." He ran his hands down the bars that separated them. "On top of that, I have a false sense of immortality. Sure, I get to live forever, but it's in cycles. I age. I live my life, die, and come back a teenager. Sixteen . . . that's how old I was when JD collected his favor from me. But I don't want to age. I want to stay young forever and keep my memories."

"Why stay young? Everyone else around you ages. You can almost live a normal life, minus kidnapping innocent kids and feeding them to a devil."

"Cute, Sammy, cute."

"It sounds to me like you don't want JD calling the shots and you don't want him manipulating you—so don't let him. Let me out of here, and I'll help you."

Jesse chuckled, his laugh laced with anxiety. "Oh Sammy, I like your fighting spirit, but you just don't get it kid. There's no escaping for you. He wants you, so he *will* have you. Wish I could change that, I do. You're not that bad, really. But once JD makes up his mind, he always gets what he wants."

Sammy sat up, feeling hopeful. "Forget him. We can both get what *we* want. Help me kill him and you can have the heart. No questions asked."

"My immortality is tied to him; he goes, I go. And I can't have that, Sammy. I don't want to die. I want to live forever and remember it all. I don't want to start at ground zero. I want to know who I was and where I'm going. I need that if I'm ever gonna have a real life."

Sammy exhaled audibly, his hope deflated. He rested his head back against the dirt wall. "I guess I can understand that."

"Good," Jesse said. "So you see why the heart's important. If I can just figure out how it works, maybe I can free myself from him."

Sammy crawled to the iron bars, he was too weak to get up, he didn't trust himself to stand on his feet. Jesse looked down at him, staring into his light blue eyes that seemed lighter in the dark space.

"I can help. I can. I'm a witch just like JD's mom. That's why I was able to find the heart in the first place. The heart can talk in its own supernatural kinda way. It called to me. I can help you figure out how it works."

Jesse shook his head. "Your fate's sealed, kid."

"I know you can't see the heart glow or hear it beat, but you know that I can. That has to be worth something to you. And I know that you think that the heart coming alive again is important even if you're not sure why. With my help we can figure it out."

Jesse rubbed his chin, nibbling on the inside of his cheek. "Tempting Sammy. JD always said when the heart came to life it meant his mother was up to something . . . Really tempting, but I know if I let you out of here, you'll run straight to your father and the police, and I can't have that. I can figure it out on my own."

"I promise not to go to the police. I'll just say I got lost in the woods. Think about it Jesse, what if the jarred heart makes you like him? He lives forever. Forever young. But he has to snack on kids to keep his human form. You said it yourself, that's why he eats people. He needs to. Having your own witch could come in handy if you go full blown demon. Think about it," Sammy pleaded.

"I was always human."

"So you don't think you'll have to kill like he does?"

"I hope not . . . but I will if I have to." Jesse sighed, leaning his shoulder against the iron bars. "My hands are already so dirty, Sammy. I don't think anything matters at this point."

"How did you get tangled up with the Jersey Devil in the first place?"

"He came to me when I was a child. Made me think he was my friend . . . I think that's how it usually works for him."

Jesse was silent as he thought about his past life.

"Let me guess," Sammy scoffed, taking a wild guess. "He offered you power. So, you can take Batsto Village away from your daddy and run it. What was it that you called yourself, *the King of Pleasant Mills*?"

Sammy's guess wasn't far off. It struck a chord, sparking Jesse's temper. He shook the bars of Sammy's cell. "Don't act like you know me, Sammy Lopez! You know nothing about me!"

Sammy backed up, scooting away. "I know what I need to know," Sammy shouted back. "You're the kind of man that helps kill kids. You're going to hell one day, Jesse. I just hope I'm around to see it."

Jesse glared down at Sammy. "You won't be. I can promise you that. We'll see how smug you are when JD is ripping out your heart you spoiled brat!"

Jesse made his way to the steps. "I hope you enjoyed your last meal," he called down to Sammy before closing the lid to his crypt and once again shrouding Sammy in darkness.

Sammy put his knees to his chest and wrapped his arms around his legs. He rocked himself, sobbing into his knees.

CHAPTER FORTY-SEVEN
Jesse's Lament

S ammy's words got under Jesse's skin. He walked to his Mustang angrily, his hands buried in his pockets. Jesse didn't want to be the henchman of the Jersey Devil, but that's what he was. He wished he'd known what JD was the first time he'd laid eyes on him.

As Jesse drove back to the rectory, his mind traveled back to the day he first met JD.

Batsto Forest, New Jersey: 1792

Jesse was out hunting with his father and brother when his father decided to make a little game out of it. William Richards always did that.

Pinned the boys against each other, tested his sons. Today he wanted to see which one of his sons would bring in more game.

A ten-year-old Jesse was by himself deep in the woods when he saw a man step out from behind a pitch pine. "You shouldn't be out here in the middle of the woods during buck season; I could've shot you!"

"That's good advice, Jesse."

Jesse nodded, thinking it was very good advice.

"You killed a lot today," the man said, gesturing to the dead squirrels that hung off Jesse's belt.

"It's a contest between me and my brother. See who gets the most."

"Oh, I see," the man said, lighting a hand-rolled cigarette, the sweet smoke scenting the air. "Tell you what, Jesse, I have a whole pile of little critters I caught today. Take them back with you, so you can win the contest." The man pointed behind the tree.

Jesse lifted up several rabbits. "I'll be! Where'd you get all these?" He carefully examined the dead buck that lay at the base of the tree. "There's not one bullet hole?!"

"I think something scared them to death. You know, they say something stalks these woods."

"That's just a bunch of flapping gums. Just stories," young Jesse scoffed.

"If you say so, Jesse, but please take the deer and the rabbits back with you, if you like. I couldn't possibly eat all of them."

"You sure?" Jesse asked, scratching his temple.

"Positive."

"I'll take them, thank you."

"You're welcome, Jesse."

"What's your name, hunter?"

The man leaned against the tree taking a long drag of his cigarette. "Call me JD."

"Thank you, JD."

Jesse sat in his car and let it idle in Uriah's driveway. He was riding down memory lane now as he remembered the day his fate became aligned with the Jersey Devil.

Batsto Village, New Jersey: 1796

Jesse sat in a rocking chair on the porch of his family home. He anxiously tapped his right foot on the ground and pushed off with the left. A gust of wind rustled the leaves in the nearby tulip poplar, bringing Jesse's attention to the north. He focused his eyes on the well-dressed man walking up the road to Richards Mansion. He kept his unblinking eyes on his familiar face all the way to his front porch.

"Hello, Jesse," JD said, walking up the steps to the porch.

"The hunter," a teenage Jesse muttered from his seat on the rocking chair, his rocking silenced.

"You remember me?" JD asked, inclining his head to the side.

"I do. I won that little contest against my brother because of you." Jesse kept his eyes on JD as he came closer. "You haven't aged a day since I was a child."

"Surely I have a little?"

"No, I don't think so," he said, studying him. "What brings you to Batsto Village?"

"I heard your father is ill."

"He is," Jesse said, slowly rocking again.

"What a shame he's leaving control of the town to your brother and not you."

BATSTO VILLAGE, NEW JERSEY
WHARTON MANSION, FORMALLY RICHARDS MANSION

Jesse jumped to his feet. "What?!"

"You didn't know?" JD asked, raising an eyebrow as he pulled out a cigarette and lit it. "I'm sure I heard that he was passing you over for your younger, smarter brother."

Jesse shook his head, his fist clenching at his side. "That can't be right."

"I thought the same thing when I heard the news whispered to me. I would have chosen you, Jesse. You have always caught my eye. But I will tell you this, you'd better check with your father to make sure it's just town gossip before his time is up."

Jesse marched into Richards Mansion and went to his father's sick bed.

Not long after, Jesse returned to the porch, distraught—his head bowed, his shoulders slouched.

"Well?" JD asked as he rocked in the chair Jesse had occupied moments earlier. "Did I hear right?"

Jesse's tone was low. "It's true . . . he thinks my little brother will do a better job running the town." He lifted his face to JD, his hazel eyes glassy.

"That's not fair! I work hard and everyone knows me. My brother locks himself in his room with his books and his numbers. I'm not saying my brother isn't valuable, but I should run this town." With flush cheeks he looked to the sky as if to ask God why.

"I could make it that way, if you would like? Make it so you're in charge of your father's assets."

Jesse locked eyes with JD. "You could do that?"

"I could, but you will have to do me a favor when the time comes."

"I can do that," Jesse promised.

"Good," JD said with a large smile. "You will find that your father has had a change of heart and will call on his lawyer to amend his will. I know you will do a good job running the town, Jesse. It's your destiny."

Jesse turned his car off and placed his hands on the steering wheel. Steady tears fell from his eyes onto his lap as he remembered the day JD came to collect his favor.

Batsto Village, New Jersey: 1798

Jesse lay in bed next to his young, beautiful wife. The town had just celebrated his wedding and Jesse had just consummated it. He closed his eyes, happy. Today was the best day of his life.

"She is beautiful, Jesse," JD whispered in Jesse's ear as he knelt by his bedside.

Jesse sat up startled. "What are you doing here?!"

"I'm here to ask you for that favor."

"On my wedding night?!" Jesse asked in a hushed whisper, trying to cover up.

"Yes." JD glanced over Jesse's sleeping wife. "Your wife . . . so beautiful, so young . . . she's still a child. I want her heart. Give it to me."

Jesse's eyes darted to his wife lying next to him, his pulse racing under his skin making him hot. "What?!"

"Cut her heart out, Jesse, and hand it to me."

Jesse was out of bed now and was frantically getting dressed. "I can't!"

"You can, Jesse. Take your hunting knife and carve out your pretty wife's heart and place it in my hand."

Jesse looked down at his wife in terror, his chest heaving.

"You will marry again, Jesse. Next time to a woman of even greater beauty."

Jesse grabbed his knife and hovered it over his sleeping wife's chest. "I can't do it."

"You can, Jesse. Or . . . I guess I could take back the town and give it to your brother."

"No. It's my town," he said in a confident voice, though his hands shook. Jesse plunged his knife into his wife's bare chest. Her eyes opened for a second before the light left them. Just long enough for her to see it was Jesse who'd killed her. He cut out her heart as tears trickled down his cheeks.

Jesse handed JD his dead wife's warm heart. "I knew you were a demon that day you came to the mansion. The one they call the Leeds Devil," Jesse said in a low voice as he sat in his wedding bed covered in his wife's blood. "I knew you would ask me to do something unspeakable one day . . . I just never thought it would be this." Jesse looked down at his trembling, bloodied hands and then at his wife's face. With his fingertips he closed her eyelids, so she no longer had to look at the monster she'd married.

"You did what I asked of you, Jesse, and for that, I thank you."

"I loved her, and I killed her. I'm going to Hell," he said, his tears turning to sobs at the thought of what he'd just done.

"Jesse . . . I can make it so you don't."

Jesse glanced at JD through his bloodshot eyes.

"If you want, I can make it so that after you live your life and die, you come back to this point. Come back to this very age and start all over. Would you like that?"

"You can do that?" he asked sniffling.

"I can, Jesse."

Jesse wiped his tears on his arm. "Yes. Yes, I'd like that. I don't want to go to Hell."

"Very well, Jesse. You did something for me and now I will do something for you. He pulled out a dandelion he had tucked into the pocket of his suit. "Take this dandelion and give it to Sarah Ennalls Haskins. She is a beautiful young girl, barely blossoming. Ask her father for her hand in marriage. He will say yes, and when she is of age, you will marry and be happy."

"Okay," he said, taking the dandelion into his unsteady hands.

"Jesse, enjoy your life. You don't have to fear the devil. I will watch over you from now on, my son."

The cold air cut through Jesse. He wiped his tears on his coat sleeve. "I don't want to go to Hell," he said in a low voice. Jesse slammed his fists on the steering wheel. "Dammit Jesse, you're living in Hell."

CHAPTER FORTY-EIGHT
Devil in the Dark

Japhet Dean walked down the stone steps of Jesse Richards's underground crypt, his footfalls silent. He went to the last cell and looked in on Sammy as he slept. He was hungry. He could have eaten his soul right then and there but instead he opened his cell and sat next to him in the dirt.

"What to do with you, Sammy," he said to the sleeping boy. "Your father has not called off the dogs with news of your death; in fact, he has doubled his efforts to find your killer. A very novel thing for him. It appears he does love you. I heard him praying to his God to save his perfect son, a son he never deserved, over and over until my ears hurt."

JD moved Sammy's hair away from his face. "And now your father cries privately in the bathroom to hide it from your mother. But I can still hear him." JD closed his eyes and leaned back against the cold dirt wall of Sammy's cell. "This moment, he whimpers into his pillow for his lost son."

JD opened his eyes and fixated on Sammy's face. "I will admit, your father intrigues me . . . perhaps just as much as you do, Sammy. It looks like

Zachary Lewis and Mary Teller were right; I do bear a striking resemblance to Jeffrey Lopez. This fascinates me, tantalizes my twisted brain. I've been watching him closely . . . studying him. It makes me wonder if I can have what he has—a wife, a family, a son like you, Sammy."

JD leaned in closer to Sammy. "A son that loves his father no matter what. I would like that more than anything. For all the good I think I'm doing in helping my sons achieve their wildest dreams, they both will grow to hate me. Every time it's the same. But, Sammy, I wonder if that would be the case with you. If I spared you and let you live, let you become one of my children . . . would you love me? Could you still love me when you know I'm responsible for your friends' deaths? Forgive me for my sins against you, as you forgave Jeffrey Lopez for his?"

JD ran his hand down Sammy's tear-stained cheek. "You and I, Sammy, we are a lot alike. My father was a hard man too. I understand that. Like you, I was the product of desire and power over the softer sex. You were made in sin, just like I was all those years ago. You're misunderstood . . . wanting to fit in. Pretending to be something you're not. I understand all these things, Sammy. You're too good for this world.

"You would no doubt taste delicious and help me keep this mortal form, all while breathing life into my Uriah, but I wonder if you would join me instead. Walk the world with me through the sands of time. Like I offered Uriah and Jesse all those years ago when they were misunderstood boys trying to fit in.

"I wonder if you would be my son." JD exhaled loudly. "It's been a long time since I took another son, but I could love you, Sammy. I know it. I feel it deep inside me." JD ran his hands over his chest. "I could love you more than your father and your mother. My love would be eternal and immortal. It would know no bounds."

JD sighed. "A mother's love is something I never knew, but . . . your mother's love does have its limits. She let your father abuse you for all those years . . . I mean, that was what it was, it was more than a little smack here and there. She knew it, and so did your father. Your mother lied for him, covered it up because she loves him more than you. But Sammy, with me, my love is absolute. I will do everything and anything for you if you accept me into your heart."

Tears trickled down JD's face. "I didn't ask for this, Sammy, but this is what I am." He looked down at his hands. "Would you consider joining me? Consider putting your faith in the son of the devil? Would you put your faith in the Jersey Devil himself?"

JD wiped his tears. "I think I'll give you a chance Sammy, a chance to let me into your heart. You're too special to eat. But in order to see how things will play out, I have to send you home, don't I? Fear not, I will be close. I will be watching . . . always watching. If you need my help, just ask." He bent down and kissed Sammy's cheek. "I love you, Sammy."

Sammy stirred to the sound of something heavy being dragged. He knew it was the door to his prison. "Is someone here?" Sammy asked into the darkness, scenting the air to a sweet, smokey scent. He sat straight up; the familiar smell was accompanied by a familiar low-pitched whistle. He recognized the haunting sound from the woods and the alluring smell of lavender and rose from the Jersey Devils Football hoodie he found in Pastor

Leeds's house. Tears dripped down Sammy's cheeks, cleansing his dirty face. Sammy whimpered. "Please, help me . . . Please."

Above ground Japhet Dean smiled as he shook the ash from his cigarette. "I'll help you, Sammy. All you had to do was ask."

CHAPTER FORTY-NINE
Confronting Jesse Richards

Ivy lay in her bed in tears. She couldn't sleep. Her music couldn't soothe her, she didn't even try listening to it. She hadn't been able to sleep a night through, since Grams told her Sammy had gone missing. All she thought about was Sammy and how he was abducted because she wouldn't talk to him. On top of that, she beat herself up over not going to the cops with the jarred heart when she had her chance. She wondered if she had, if Sammy would still be alive.

"If only I would have talked to him," she cried into her pillow. "It's my fault he sneaked out in the middle of the night."

"Ivy."

Hearing Sammy's voice, Ivy shot up in bed. "Sammy, is that you?!"

"Ivy, I need your help . . . I don't know if you can hear me."

She was out of bed, spinning around trying to figure out where his voice was coming from. "Sammy! I can hear you! Where are you?!"

"Ivy, help me." Sammy's voice danced around her room as if it bounced off the walls.

"Sammy," she yelled, tears streaming down her face. "Answer me! Where are you?!"

"I think they killed Tim. I'm next . . ."

"Sammy, where are you?!" she called again, this time at the top of her lungs. It was clear to her he couldn't hear her even though she could hear him.

"Jesse Richards is gonna feed me to the Jersey Devil. Please get my dad . . . this is no use . . . the stupid spell didn't work and now I'm gonna die."

Sammy's sobs washed over her room, growing into a nightmarish roar. "Goodbye Ivy. I love you."

Ivy's heart felt like it was going to jump out of her chest. "I love you too! Hold on, I'm getting your dad!"

Ivy raced down the stairs as fast as she could and threw open her grandmother's bedroom door. "Get up, Grams! Sammy's alive!"

Ivy pounded on the front door of the Lopez castle in the middle of the night in her pajamas.

Jeffrey came to the door.

"Mr. Lopez!"

Ivy was in tears.

"Ivy! What's wrong?! Is everything okay?" Jeffrey asked, looking to Mary for answers.

"This is going to sound crazy Mr. Lopez, but Sammy's not dead!"

Jeffrey raked his fingers through his hair. "Ivy. I know you're upset. We all are—"

"No! You don't understand," she said, hitting his chest with her fists. "That's what he wants! He wants you to think that body you found was Sammy's, but it's not! It's not him. He's alive. You've got to believe me!"

Jeffrey's heart pumped faster. He wanted to believe Ivy more than anything.

Jeffrey took Ivy's hands in his to try to calm her down and looked her square in the eyes. "Ivy, who has Sammy?"

"Jesse. Jesse took him."

"Uriah's cousin?" Jeffrey asked in disbelief.

"Please, you have to believe me! Sammy needs you! He told me to get you!"

Ivy was on the verge of hyperventilating. Grams hugged her to help quiet her. "Please. I know this sounds crazy. I know. But he's counting on you to save him. Please! Please save him! He doesn't have much time. He says he's next."

Lindsey made it down the stairs. "What happened?!"

"Jesse Richards has Sammy," Jeffrey said. He knew what Ivy said was crazy, but he'd take crazy if that meant there was a chance Sammy was still alive. He went to his gun cabinet, unlocked it, and took a gun. He grabbed his car keys and was out the door.

"Wait Jeffrey! We should call Devan!" Lindsey yelled after him.

Ivy tore herself away from her grandmother and ran after Jeffrey. "I'm coming with you," she said, wiping her tears on her pajama top. They got into Jeffrey's Mercedes and sped off down the street.

"Dagnabbit," Grams said. She pulled out her phone and called the police.

Jeffrey knocked on Pastor Leeds's front door. Uriah was upstairs in bed when he heard the pounding. He got up and quickly went to open it. "Hi, Jeffrey, Ivy," Pastor Leeds said. "Is everything alright?"

Before the pastor could get another word out of his mouth Jeffrey asked: "Where's your cousin?"

Jesse walked into view. Jeffrey pushed Uriah out of the way and pulled a gun on Jesse, backing him into a wall. "Where is he, you son of a bitch?! Where's my son?!"

"What are you talking about?" Jesse asked, confused.

Uriah looked to Ivy. "What's going on?!"

"I know you have Sammy!" Jeffrey pushed the gun into Jesse's temple. "Where is he?! I will blow your brains out right here so help me God!"

Devan came in behind Jeffrey. Ivy's nose twitched from his pungent

Old Spice after shave.

"Jeffrey, put the gun down. I know we're all upset here."

"Devan, he has Sammy!"

Jesse smirked at Jeffrey. That was it—confirmation he had Sammy.

"You sick fuck. You mutilated that boy so I would think it was Sammy. None of the other boys looked like that!" He pressed the gun harder into Jesse's head, his finger on the trigger.

"Why point the gun at me, Mayor Lopez?" Jesse said, tempting fate. "You should point it at yourself. You should be the number one suspect in Sammy's disappearance. Sammy told me how you threw him down the stairs and how you pushed him around all the time. Chief Rainier, I think we should bring Jeffrey Lopez in for questioning." Jeffrey slammed Jesse against the wall.

"Easy Jeffrey," Devan said in a calm voice. "Think this through. If you kill Jesse, we'll never find Sammy."

Jeffrey took a deep breath. He counted down from ten like his therapist told him to do when he was feeling out of control. *Ten, nine, eight, seven, six, five, four, three, two, one.* He handed his gun to Devan.

"Sorry, I've got to take you in Jeffrey," Devan said cuffing him. "You can't pull guns on people."

"What about him?!" Jeffrey asked, glaring at Jesse.

"I did nothing wrong."

"Good," Devan said. "Then you won't mind coming down to the station with me now for questioning?"

"Not at all, officer."

Jesse was sitting in the front seat of Devan's car with a smug look on his face when Lindsey pulled up with Grams and the girls.

Lindsey got out of her car and ran to Jeffrey as Devan escorted him to his police car. "Jeffrey, what's going on?!"

"Sammy's alive, Lindsey! Jesse has him! I know it!"

CHAPTER FIFTY
A Lot of Pills

Pastor Leeds stood dumbfounded in his front yard. He felt even more confused than the normal state of pandemonium he was living in. The only thing that made sense to him was the scripture. That he knew by heart. Everything else seemed foreign. The medications he was on were not helping his mind from unraveling. His vivid dreams had not stopped haunting him, and he was having an increasingly difficult time discerning what was real. He felt like he was losing it. He didn't know if he could trust what he was seeing. He felt like everything around him was spiraling out of control. He grabbed his head. "What's going on?" Pastor Leeds asked as Devan pulled out of his driveway with Jesse and Jeffrey.

"Jesse took Sammy," Ivy told him.

"What?! Why would he do that?" Uriah asked, terrified and confused.

"Think about it, Pastor Leeds," Ivy said. "The boys started to go missing right around the time Jesse showed up."

Uriah mulled over her words, his eyes growing large when he

realized she was right.

"How well do you know Jesse, Pastor Leeds?" Ivy asked.

"I . . . I don't know," he said, his head spinning. "I just know him. I think my whole life."

"Well, you better start remembering something," Grams said. "'Cause it looks like the cousin you *think* you knew your whole life is Pleasant Mills's very own serial killer."

Uriah tried to think about Jesse, tried to recall anything about him. "I don't know," he said, biting his bottom lip. "I really don't know anything about him."

Grams scratched the top of her head. "Well, that's just great!"

"Please, Pastor Leeds," Lindsey asked desperately. "Do you know where he has Sammy?"

"I'm sorry, Lindsey. I don't know. I wish I did." Lindsey wiped her tears with a tissue from her purse and nodded. He took her hand. "I will continue to pray for Sammy."

"Thank you, Pastor Leeds."

"Come on Lindsey," Grams said, motioning to the car. "We'd better get down to the police station before Jeffrey gets himself in anymore trouble." Mary turned to her granddaughter. "Let's get moving."

"I'm going to stay here with Pastor Leeds."

Mary pulled her granddaughter aside. "I don't know if that's a good idea." Grams glanced at Uriah, worried. "He looks like he's on the verge of a mental meltdown, and I don't want you near him when he goes off."

"Grams, that's exactly why someone should stay with him."

"I don't know Ives, that someone doesn't have to be you."

"I'm really worried about him, and besides the kidnapper is at the police station. I'll be fine. I got my phone on me."

"Fine, but if things get out of hand, call me."

"I will; I promise."

Grams grunted.

Mary and Lindsey got in her car and drove off leaving Uriah and Ivy in the front yard.

Ivy took Uriah's hand. "Come on, Pastor Leeds, let's get you inside; it's cold."

Uriah sat down at the kitchen table like a zombie. "I don't know what's happening to me, Ivy. I've been having some problems lately . . . seeing things that aren't real." He pointed to the kitchen counter.

Ivy saw a counter full of pill bottles. "You're on all these medications, Pastor Leeds? I thought you were just anemic."

"It started out like that, but I have bigger problems now . . . I think I'm losing my mind, and nothing is helping. I can't remember anything. My past—is a blur. The harder I think, the less I remember."

Ivy went over to the counter, reading the labels on the pill bottles. So many of the pills were brightly colored and so many of them were antipsychotics. She glanced back at Uriah sitting at the table, his pretty face sad and bewildered.

Ivy poured Pastor Leeds a glass of water and took a seat next to him.

"Thank you," he said after taking a sip. "I just don't know what's real and what's in my head anymore. I don't have any memories of Jesse until he got here this summer."

Ivy placed her hand on his to comfort him. "He's your cousin. You must have known him since you were a kid."

"It's so weird . . . I have no memory of my childhood. Not one. The first thing I remember is meeting Jeffrey Lopez at the rectory when he gave me the keys to this place and welcomed me to town."

Uriah rubbed his temples as if to spark a memory. "What's happening to me?" His blue eyes searched Ivy's for answers, but she had none for him.

All she had was questions. She thought about the gaps in her own memory. It was just like Uriah said, the more she tried to remember her past the less she could recall.

CHAPTER FIFTY-ONE
Lack of Evidence

Jeffrey and Devan talked in private as Jesse waited in a holding cell.

"Jeffrey, we have a problem," Devan said, leaning against the wall.

"What's that?"

"We have nothing on Jesse. Not one shred of evidence."

Jeffrey clenched his fist. "He has him Devan, I feel it!"

"Jeffrey, I can't count Jesse grinning at you as evidence. I need hard evidence to book him for a crime. I can hold him for forty-eight hours, but then I have to cut him loose."

Jeffrey felt like he was going to explode. He was pretty sure his blood was boiling in his veins. "That's bullshit, you can't let him walk out of here!"

"Jeffrey, I don't want you to get your hopes up. We are going off the word of a hysterical teenage girl who just lost her boyfriend."

"Sammy is alive," Jeffrey said sternly, staring point blank at Devan.

"I hope he is. But we—"

Jeffrey cut him off. "Where's the results from the DNA test? Why aren't they back yet?"

"I'm already on it. They had to run it again. I'll call first thing in the morning for an update."

"Something's going on here. They had to run the DNA test again—seems odd. Think about it. The boy found in the river was ripped to shreds. The only thing that wasn't was Sammy's coat. I can't believe I didn't see it before." Jeffrey raked his fingers through his hair letting his hands linger on the top of his head as he cooled down. "Jesse wanted me to think my son was dead in hopes that I'd call off the search for the other missing boys. We must be close to finding where he's keeping them."

Devan took out a cigarette and lit it. "That seems possible . . . sick, but possible."

"Devan, I am telling you, Sammy is out there, and Jesse knows where. We have to bring him home."

"Unless we find some concrete proof, shit, I'll take circumstantial evidence, I have to let Jesse go in forty-eight hours. I'm bound by the law, and I don't want you taking the law into your own hands. Jesse is cooperating. He gave us permission to search his house and so did Uriah. Hopefully Pearl can turn something up."

"If anyone can it's Pearl," Jeffrey said, still not happy there was a possibility Jesse would walk. He crossed his arms over his chest and leaned against the wall next to Devan.

"We're doing all we can. You know I want to bring Sammy home. Have a little faith in the system."

"Faith in the system," he scoffed. "The system failed three families already."

Devan put a hand on Jeffrey's shoulder. "You're lucky Jesse isn't pressing charges on you for pulling a gun on him. I think you should count your blessings. Go home and get some rest. Lindsey is waiting for you in the lobby. I'll call you if anything turns up. And in the event, I have to cut him loose, I'll keep a tail on him. If he's hiding the boys, he'll lead us right to them."

Jeffrey nodded, feeling a little better about that.

CHAPTER FIFTY-TWO
Lost and Found and Lost

"Hey kid, you okay?" A man asked as Sammy opened his eyes. Sammy looked around, confused, he was at a bus stop. "Help me! I'm one of the boys that was kidnapped! I need to—"

"Slow down. Slow down," the man said.

"Please help me. My name is Sammy Lopez. I was kidnapped."

The man glanced over Sammy; he didn't look good. He was gaunt with dark circles around his eyes, and his lips were dried and cracked. He shivered, like he suffered from convulsions.

"Here, Sammy, take my coat. I'll call the cops."

"Thank you," Sammy said, putting on the man's winter coat. "Please call my dad."

"Will do. My name's Gilbert Simon. Don't worry, I'll make sure you get back to your parents."

Gilbert pulled out his cell phone and called the local police station. "Hello there, this is Gil Simon. I'm at the bus stop at the bottom of Jimmie

Leeds Road with a kid named Sammy Lopez . . . Yes, that's right, Sammy Lopez. He said he was kidnapped."

Lindsey and Jeffrey ran into Sammy's hospital room with Alba and Maria in their arms. They hugged him, squeezing him as hard as they could. Sammy was overwhelmed. He couldn't hold back his tears. He'd thought he'd never see his family again. He closed his eyes for a moment and opened them, making sure this happy reunion with his family was real.

Sammy was disoriented. He still didn't understand how he'd come to be at the bus stop with Gilbert. He knew that a tranquilizer dart was used to knock him out again. He had the same woozy feeling he'd had before.

Lindsey Lopez kissed every inch of her son's face. "I love you. I love you," she said, fussing over him.

"I love you too, Mom," Sammy said, hugging her. His sisters shouted with glee, wrapping their small arms around him.

Sammy looked up at his father as he hugged his mother and sisters again. "I'm so sorry I sneaked out of the house again." His words were barely coherent through his crying. "I'm so sorry. I will never sneak out again. I'm so sorry."

Jeffrey took a seat on the side of his son's hospital bed. He wrapped his arms around Sammy, his wife, and the twins. He tried to hold back his own tears, but they came all the same. "It's okay Sammy, the important thing is you're alright."

"I'm sorry, Dad. You were right. I was stupid to be out at night by myself. I'm so sorry."

"It's okay, you're safe now. I'm not going to let anything happen to you."

Jeffrey couldn't get the image of the mutilated boy from the river out of his head. It had haunted his every thought since the coroner unzipped the body bag. Jeffrey felt blessed to be holding his son again, savoring this surreal moment with his family, yet his heart sank realizing another father was going to have to go through what he had when the DNA test came back.

"Sammy, I don't say it enough. I love you, and I'm proud of you. You're a better man than me and you're only a teenager. I'm sorry for everything I put you through. I promise to be a better dad."

"Dad, I love you."

Sammy glanced to his mother and his sisters. "Mom, Alba, and Maria, I love you all so much."

Jeffrey stayed at the hospital with Sammy while Lindsey took the girls home. The doctors wanted to keep Sammy overnight until the drugs from the tranquilizer were out of his system. They had him on an IV for dehydration but were hopeful he would be going home by tomorrow afternoon.

It wasn't long until Ivy showed up. She raced down the hallway, leaving Grams on the elevator, not paying notice of the sights and smells that normally bothered her about hospitals. She ran to his room, stopping dead in her tracks when she locked eyes with Sammy. He was sitting up in bed with his father sitting by his side.

"Hi Sammy."

It was the first words Ivy had said face-to-face to Sammy in over a month. Her words sounded perfect to him. When he was in the darkness of his cell, he would have done anything to hear her say his name.

Sammy gave Ivy the sideways grin she loved so much. "Hi Teller."

Her heart fluttered, sending the wasps in her tummy into a frenzy. She ran to Sammy, throwing her arms around him.

"I'll give you two a moment," Jeffrey said, excusing himself.

Mary made it to Sammy's room, winded. "Coffee, Mary?" Jeffrey asked.

"Sure," she said, following him out of the room.

Ivy hugged Sammy like her life depended on it. "I'm so glad you're okay. Why did you sneak out of your house?"

Sammy's heart raced, a flush of embarrassment painting his cheeks. "I had too; I wanted to say happy birthday to you."

That's what she and everyone else had thought, but she wanted to hear it from him. "You should have stayed home." She squeezed him tighter, forcing her head under his chin.

He breathed in the faint smell of mothballs in her hair. It wasn't the most sensual smell in the world, but it was her smell, and it made him miss her all the more. Her clinging to him the way she was now was like something out of a dream. It was as if they never broke up.

"I know. I just really wanted to say happy birthday. I cast the *Whisper Spell* from the grimoire we found. It was supposed to work like a walkie talkie, but it didn't work. I thought if I got closer to your house it would boost the spell's power."

Ivy buried her face in his chest. "You said no spells by ourselves."

"I know, but I'm glad I cast it. It worked after all. You got my message about Jesse Richards. My dad told me it was you who saved me." He squeezed her tighter. "Thank you."

"No, that was all your dad. He pulled a gun on Jesse like a real pistol-slinging cowboy."

Sammy chuckled. "That's my dad, but you're the one who got him."

Ivy kept her head close to Sammy's chest and listened to the sound of his heartbeat. It was the best bass guitar she'd ever heard.

"Ivy?"

"Yes," she said, looking up at him with watery eyes.

"Happy belated birthday."

"Oh, Sammy." She went back to hugging him.

"I'm so sorry for the stupid things I said." Sammy choked on his words, tears stinging the back of his throat. "I love you, Ivy."

"I love you too," she whimpered. She lifted her chin up, pressing a kiss to his lips. Sammy kissed her back softly, no longer able to stop his tears. They rolled down his cheeks as he sniffled. "Does this mean you forgive me?"

"Sammy, don't be stupid again! Of course I do." She cupped his face in her hands and kissed him passionately, pressing their lips together until it hurt. "I love you."

The old man in the bed next to Sammy's slowly moved the curtain dividing their space and watched as Ivy showered Sammy with kisses.

"Sammy, I love you so much. So much."

"I love you too," he said through kisses.

Sammy noticed Ivy was wearing the bracelet he had given to her for her birthday. "The bracelet," he said, flicking the heart charm.

"I haven't taken it off." She pressed another kiss to his lips.

They heard a cough.

"Is this a bad time?"

Sammy beamed. "Mike! Get over here!"

Sammy gave Mike a big hug. Mike could tell Sammy forgave him for breaking him and Ivy up. The tension between them was long gone. Mike was ecstatic to have his best friend back.

"Damn, I missed you, Mike."

Mike took a seat in a chair next to Sammy's bed. "I've been freaking out since you went missing. You have no idea."

"Glad to be back," Sammy smiled.

"Let me tell you, you've got a good girl. Ivy was relentless with trying to find you."

Sammy smiled at Ivy, taking her hand in his and squeezing it. "I know. Told you she was special."

"And Mike," Ivy said. "He's got your back."

"He always did."

"Well look who finally decided to show up," Grams said, walking into the room with Jeffrey.

"Hi, Grams."

"Let me tell you, brat, I don't think I've ever been so happy to see your ugly mug."

"Grams, does that mean you like me?"

"Nah, I tolerate you."

They all laughed, none louder than Sammy.

Ivy and Mike went home. Jeffrey stayed; he was spending the night. He wasn't going to let Sammy out of his sight.

Sammy rubbed the gooseflesh on his arms.

"Still cold?" Jeffrey asked.

"Yeah, a little. I feel like I've been cold for so long, I can't get warm." Jeffrey covered Sammy with the extra blanket folded at the foot of his bed. "Thanks, Dad."

"No problem." Jeffrey took a seat on the side of Sammy's bed. "Devan wants to stop by in a little bit. He has some questions he wants to ask you about Jesse. Are you feeling up to it?"

"Yeah."

"You sure? You don't have to if you're not ready to talk about it."

"I'm sure, Dad. I want to put Jesse behind bars."

Jeffrey patted his son's arm. "Okay."

Devan knocked on the open door.

"Speaking of the devil," Jeffrey said, getting up to shake Devan's hand.

Devan gave Sammy a warm hug, tousling his hair. "Glad to have you back, you really had us scared."

"Thanks, Devan."

Devan took a few steps back and stood at the foot of Sammy's bed. He took out a pen and a small notepad from his back pocket and talked in a low voice as not to wake the man sleeping in the bed next to Sammy's. "Sorry to have to do this now, but anything you can give me will help make a solid case against Jesse Richards."

"Sammy, who abducted you?"

"Jesse Richards."

"When?"

"November fifteenth. I was walking home from Ivy's house when he offered me a ride." Sammy glanced to his father. "I know I wasn't supposed to sneak out, but it was her birthday. And I wanted to try to talk to her."

Jeffrey put his hand on his son's arm. "It's okay, Sammy."

"Then what happened?" Devan asked.

Sammy rubbed his neck. "He pricked me with some kind of tranquilizer dart that put me to sleep. I think he uses them when he goes hunting."

Devan nodded, Jeffrey had already filled him in on the dart and his need to stay at the hospital over night because of it. "Were you wearing your winter coat when you were abducted?"

"Yes, I was."

"Can you describe it?"

"It's a gray plaid North Face with a hood."

"Where did he bring you?"

"I don't know."

"Can you try to describe it for me?"

Jeffrey squeezed his son's shoulder. "It's okay, tell him what you remember. Anything can help."

"I woke up in the dark. It was cold and damp. I think I was in an underground basement. The walls and floor were all made of dirt. And I was in a cell that had iron bars for a gate that he kept locked with a key."

"Was anyone with you in this underground basement?"

"Yes, Timothy Chen. He said that Louie was there too. Told me Jesse took Louie away the day he brought me down there. Timothy said that there were two other people helping Jesse."

Devan raised his eyebrows in shock. "He did?! Did he tell you who these people were? Did you ever see anyone besides Jesse?"

"No, I never saw anyone else and neither did Tim. He just heard them. He said he heard the voices of a second man and a woman, but he couldn't make out what they were talking about, just that they were talking to Jesse."

Devan dropped his pen. "A man and a woman?"

Jeffrey picked it up and handed it to him. He nodded his thank you.

"Yes, but we both only ever saw Jesse and I never heard anyone besides him, but I think I smelled someone smoking a cigarette and heard them whistling."

"This is good Sammy . . . How did you escape?"

"I don't think I did. I think they let me go."

Devan furrowed his eyebrows to a deep crease. "Let you go?"

Sammy shrugged his shoulders. "I remember feeling a prick on my neck when I was sleeping. I think I was put in a trunk. I remember the smell of pine needles. Like the smell of a Christmas tree. Kinda reminds me of your aftershave, but really strong. And I could smell gasoline. Like the smell when you miss the gas tank. That's it, and when I woke up, I was sitting on a bench at a bus stop and Gilbert helped me."

"We questioned Gilbert," Devan told Jeffrey. "That was his normal bus route to work. We don't think he was involved, and he saw nothing funny."

"Dad, Gil gave me his coat and stayed with me the whole time."

"I'll take care of him," Jeffrey said. "He won't need to take the bus to work anymore."

"Thanks, Dad."

Sammy locked eyes with Devan. "Did you find Louie and Timothy? Did they let them go too?"

Devan glanced at Jeffrey, his lips flattening out to a straight line.

Jeffrey sat on the side of his son's bed again. "Sammy, before you woke up at the bus stop, they pulled a boy from the river wearing your winter coat. We thought it was you, but the DNA test came back, and it was Louie. I'm sorry, he's dead."

"Louie's dead . . ."

Jeffrey hugged his son. "We're still looking for Timothy, and we won't stop until we find him and the three people responsible for this. I promise."

Sammy sniffled, holding his tears back with all of his will. He didn't want to cry in front of Devan.

"If you remember anything else, Sammy, let me know. I have Pearl and Weston on their way now to pick Jesse up."

"You let him go?!" Jeffrey asked furious, a flush coloring his cheeks.

"I could only hold him for forty-eight hours. He'd barely walked out the door when I got the call Sammy was found."

Devan's phone rang. "Excuse me," he said, taking a few steps away and turning his back to Jeffrey and Sammy. Sammy took the moment to wipe his tears.

"You got him?— What do you mean?! How is that possible?— Fix it Pearl."

"What's that about?" Jeffrey asked. He nodded toward the door sliding his notepad and pen back in his pocket.

Jeffrey understood.

Devan gave Sammy another hug and patted him on the shoulder. "Glad you're back kid. I'll check in on you at the house tomorrow."

Sammy was near bursting with tears, only able to nod.

Jeffrey followed Devan into the hall. "What's going on?"

"You're not going to believe this. Pearl and Weston lost him. They drove Jesse home from the station and parked outside the rectory. When they knocked on the door to arrest him, he was gone. Vanished. Pearl searched the house; he wasn't there, and Uriah said he wasn't aware he ever came home."

Jeffrey counted down from ten.

Devan's face was flushed with anger. "I'm sending Jesse's photo to all the districts. I will find him Jeffrey. I promise."

Jeffrey nodded.

"I've got to go. I'll call you as soon as we have him."

"He got away, didn't he?" Sammy said when his father entered the room.

Jeffrey took a seat in the chair next to Sammy's bed. "Devan will find him. We just have to sit tight."

Sammy spoke with down cast eyes. "Dad, why did they let me go?"

"I don't know, Sammy. I was thinking it was so I'd stop the searches. Which I'm not, not until we bring Tim home."

"Do you think they'll come back for me?"

"Hey, don't worry about that. Like I said, I'm not going to let anything happen to you. Think of me as your shadow. Where you go, I go."

"It's just that Jesse said he had been watching me."

"Who'd been watching you? What are you talking about?" Jeffrey looked into his son's scared eyes. He looked like a little boy; it filled Jeffrey with a burning rage that someone made his son feel so small. "Sammy, if you're holding back something, don't. Nothing is going to happen to you. I'm not leaving your side."

Sammy nodded.

"Sammy, you know you can tell me. Do you know who's working with Jesse."

"I know. Well, I know one of the two."

"Tell me."

"Dad, you're not gonna believe me if I do."

"Try me."

"Jesse told me he was kidnapping kids for the Jersey Devil."

Jeffrey looked at his son incredulously. He didn't mean to, but that wasn't what he was expecting to hear. Saying a local legend was behind the kidnappings was as crazy as saying aliens abducted him.

"See, I knew you wouldn't believe me." Sammy pulled the blanket up to his face and wiped his tears.

"I didn't say that. Maybe Jesse does think he's working for the Jersey Devil. He's obviously not right in the head. Don't worry about Jesse." Jeffrey hugged his son again. "Devan will find him and whoever's helping him."

CHAPTER FIFTY-THREE
Saying Goodbye

Louie Grindhouse's family decided to do a small, private service for Louie in light of the intense public scrutiny Pastor Leeds had been under, since Jesse was named a suspect in the Pleasant Mills murders. The town was in an uproar over Jesse Richards being the close live-in cousin of Pastor Leeds, and many members refused to go to church until the facts came out. More so that Jesse evaded the cops, seemingly disappearing. Fingers were being pointed at Uriah.

Mrs. Grindhouse couldn't handle anything else. She just wanted to bury her son while surrounded with those closest to her, and she adored Pastor Leeds and asked him to preside over her son's funeral all the same.

Sammy stood with his family in the cemetery as Pastor Leeds spoke. His words brought comfort as they all sought to understand the tragedy that befell poor Louie Grindhouse. Sammy felt inconsolable guilt like a knot in the pit of his stomach as he stood side by side his parents and looked over to see Louie's grandmother, Mrs. Grindhouse, and Trudy sobbing for Louie. It had been a long time since he'd seen Trudy. They had broken up the summer before last and she had started college in August. They would send the occasional text messages here and there, but it was different than seeing her in person, especially seeing her crying.

Sammy's guilt weighed him down. As the soft pitter-patter of rain fell on his shoulders, he closed his eyes, wondering why he was let go and Louie wasn't.

After the service Sammy remained in the cemetery to say goodbye to his friend. Tears streamed down his cheeks as he asked Louie to forgive him for surviving.

Sammy felt a hand on his shoulder. It was Trudy. "Sammy, you okay?" Trudy asked with teary eyes of her own.

"I should be the one asking you that," he said, turning to hug her. "I'm sorry about Louie."

"Thank you." She wiped her tears with her index finger. "He will be missed."

"He always thought you were the best sister. His first beer at ten."

"Oh my gosh, he told you that!" She chuckled. "It was only a sip."

He smiled. "Still, he thought you were the coolest."

Trudy ran her hand down his arm, her hand finding a home in his. "I'm glad you're okay, Sammy."

"Thanks, but it just doesn't seem fair to me. Why is Louie dead and I'm not?"

"You have nothing to feel guilty over, do you hear me?" He nodded. "Your family has been a godsend to us. I don't think my mom would have managed without your mom. When you went missing next it was like a bomb was dropped on this town. I'm glad you're still standing, Sammy."

He gave her the best smile he could muster. "Thank you. You know I'm here if you need me."

"I know," she said returning the smile.

While they stood in the rain a song mixed with the light shower. At first Sammy didn't notice it, but then his eyes darted to the dark woods behind the church. He swore he could hear a low-pitched harmony piggybacking on the sounds of the rain droplets as they hit the cold ground. Sammy squeezed Trudy's hand and led her out of the rain. He had a feeling they were being watched.

CHAPTER FIFTY-FOUR
Change of Heart

Sammy and Ivy lay in her bed talking. They had tiptoed to her room while Grams worked on putting together a new TV stand for the living room. She had been so engrossed in what she was doing, she never realized Sammy and Ivy went to the attic.

Ivy moved Sammy's hair away from his forehead. "How are you doing?"

"Louie's funeral was hard. I wish you could've been there."

She took his hand. "Me too."

"My mom has been awesome. I mean, I'm so grateful. She really is one of a kind. And Alba and Maria even let me pick the movie last night. First time in two years, but of course, I felt guilty and picked *Snow White*."

Ivy smiled. "Always a good big brother."

"My dad's been great. Really great. He took an extended leave from work. It's nice having him home. He set up a tent in the living room for the family. We're inside camping." Sammy chuckled. "I think he knows I don't want to be alone, and he didn't want to demasculinize me by putting me on the spot—which I'm very grateful for. I feel like my manhood is hanging on by a thread with all the crying I've been doing lately." Ivy squeezed his hand. "It's actually been a lot of fun camping out with my family in the living room."

"How about here?" Ivy asked, pointing to his heart.

"I'll feel better once we bring Tim home. I know he's out there waiting for us to find him. I promised he'd be alright."

"Maybe it's time we give the cops the jarred heart."

Sammy sighed. "Even if I want to, we can't. I tried telling my dad what Jesse said about the Jersey Devil, but he dismissed it right away. Everyone will just think I'm crazy. That I lost my mind because I almost died, and they'll lock me away and throw away the key. Then I'll never be able to help Tim. We just gotta keep the searches going. Besides, nothing they can pull off that jar can link them to JD. He's not human. Jesse said he only looks human. I just wish I would've asked him what JD looked like. He could be anybody."

"If you believe Jesse."

"I do. There was no point lying to me. He thought I was never making it out of that hole."

"But you did."

"Yeah," he said. "I did . . . which I'm not complaining about, but I just don't get it. Why was I let go and Zac, Tyrone, and Louie killed? I guess I'm just worried Jesse and JD aren't finished with me. Like I'm just waiting to die. It's a horrible feeling."

Ivy hugged Sammy. "Sammy you're not going to die."

"We all die, Teller."

"Well not you, not any time soon."

Sammy squeezed her, breathing in the smell of her berry shampoo and mothballs. "I hope not. I really hope not . . . but I think it's going to be a long time until I feel like the old me . . . if ever. My dad made me an appointment with a therapist . . . said he's the best in South Jersey. I'm gonna give that a shot. I hope he can help me straighten out all the things in my head and heart." He tenderly tucked a stray lock of hair behind her ear. "Just being around you makes me feel better. When I'm around you, nothing else matters but us. And that's how I want it. You're my therapy, Ivy

Teller.”

Sammy drew Ivy in closer to his chest, pressing a kiss to her lips. His kiss traveled down her neck, gracing her collar bone. Her hands found their way to his hair, twisting the dark tendrils between her fingers. Ivy guided his face back to hers, she needed to feel his soft lips on her lips, needed to feel the warmth of his breath on her face. Their eyes locked, their hearts beating together.

“The one thing I do have straight is that I love you, Ivy.” He pressed another kiss to her lips, letting his lips linger on hers, breathing her exhale. “So much.” He gazed into her brown eyes, admiring the shades of brown tones swirling in them. “I never thought I was going to get a chance to see you again, let alone kiss you again.”

“Sammy,” Ivy said breathlessly. “I want you to be my first.”

“We don’t have to.” Sammy placed his hand on hers to stop her from unbuttoning his pants.

“I want to.”

His pulse quickened, a flush painting his face rose-red. “You sure?” Ivy nodded, she couldn’t speak, she was all emotion and no words.

His voice came out as a whisper. “You’ll be my first too.”

Her eyebrows furrowed.

“I lied to sound cool.”

She smiled. He smiled back.

Jesse watched Ivy and Sammy from Pastor Leeds’s attic window. He slid his hand down his pants.

“I hope I’m not interrupting,” JD said, stepping out of the shadows.

“Actually, you are,” Jesse sneered, taking his hand out of his pants.

“Aw . . . I see, young love in the throes of passion for the first time.” JD lit a cigarette and sweet smoke filled the attic. “Do you remember your first time, Jesse?”

“I do . . . one of the few memories I do have.” Jesse kept his eyes across the street. "You?"

"I do . . . It didn't end well for her, but I must say, I enjoyed myself."

"Well, as long as you're happy that's all that matters," Jesse said sharply, turning to glare at JD.

"Now, now, Jesse. Why the tone? What's wrong?"

"What's wrong?!" Jessed said, standing up. "The whole town thinks I'm a kidnapper and a killer!" You tell me to grab Sammy when I can, and I do. Then you let him go! What gives?!"

JD leaned against the attic wall and shook the ash off his cigarette. "I had a change of heart. And in all fairness, you *are* a kidnapper." JD took a long drag of his cigarette.

"Great, a change of heart! Could you have found that ounce of human compassion before Sammy saw my face?!" Jesse shook his head, frustrated. "And how about a heads up?! Jeffrey Lopez almost blew my brains out!"

JD flicked his cigarette. "An oversight on my part."

Jesse clenched his teeth, a muscle jumping in his jaw. "Your unbelievable—an oversight."

JD glanced out the window to Ivy's room. "Do you think it's wise to be here in this attic when the town thinks you're a kidnapper and a killer?"

"You know I can't leave this stupid town until you have your thirteen souls. Remember, Mr. Compassionate, you made it that way! Trust me, as soon as you do, and Uriah goes wakey wakey, I'm leaving, and I'm never looking back!"

"Without Ivy?"

"I guess it's going to have to be that way now," he said, taking up his old seat in front of the attic window. "If she sees me, she'll run screaming. So, I doubt there's a chance she'll want to go on a road trip with Pleasant Mills's very own serial killer."

"Doubtful," JD said, taking another drag.

Jesse shook his head again. "It's different this time?" he asked, looking back at JD. "Isn't it?"

JD didn't answer.

"Whatever, don't tell me, but I think Uriah has finally snapped. He's on enough pills to knock out an elephant."

"Where is he now?" JD asked, putting his cigarette out on the windowsill.

"Locked himself in his room . . . talking to himself."

"Fear not Jesse, things will all be sorted out soon. Be patient and be a good boy."

"I thought I was always a good boy, father," Jesse said sarcastically.

JD put his hand on Jesse's shoulder. "Stay out of sight until you're needed. And remember Jesse, I love you." JD kissed Jesse's cheek and headed down the steps of the attic.

Sammy wore a large goofy grin as he buckled up. Jeffrey recognized the grin, it wasn't that long ago he was sixteen himself.

"Where are we going, Dad?" Sammy asked as they drove past the house.

"Got to get something."

He pulled into the Rite Aid Pharmacy parking lot, parking as close to the door as possible. "Be right back. Keep the doors locked."

Jeffrey quickly made his way down the personal care isle. He stood dumfounded at the choice of condoms they had. "Crap, what's the difference," he muttered. He decided to make this as painless on himself as possible and took one of each variety and put them in his hand cart. Jeffrey kept his eyes down as he made it to the check out. He didn't want to risk running into anyone he knew, which was hard when he was the mayor.

The clerk tried not to laugh as he rang up box after box of condoms. "Party?" The store clerk asked with a big smile.

Jeffrey rolled his eyes. "No party."

The clerk giggled into his chest. "I guess personal use then."

"What'd you say?"

The clerk rolled his shoulders. "I was just wondering what's it like having a twin. Do you like it?" he asked, to defer some of the awkwardness.

"A twin?" Jeffrey asked, confused. "Um . . . I wouldn't know—My twin daughters seem to like it, I guess."

The clerk gave Jeffrey a funny look. "That guy that checked out right before you, he wasn't your twin?"

Jeffrey looked toward the door. He'd been so focused on his mission of get in and out, he didn't look at anyone. "My twin?"

"Uh . . . yeah, that guy who looked just like you . . . spitting image."

"Are you sure?" Jeffrey asked.

"Um . . . pretty sure," he said.

"What did he buy?"

"Um . . . breath mints," the clerk said, unsure if he should tell Jeffrey what the man before him had bought if they weren't twins. He was hoping that wasn't something he could get written up for. He already had two strikes against him for calling out, one more mishap and he was out of a job.

Nervousness spread over Jeffrey, finding its way to his fingertips, where he tapped on the counter. "Not my twin." He paid his bill and rushed out of the store. He scanned the parking lot. Sammy was safe in the car. Besides his Mercedes, the parking lot was empty. The store was closing in fifteen minutes and the parking lot had already cleared out.

Jeffrey unlocked his car and got in. "Hey, Sammy?"

"Yeah, Dad?"

"Did you see anything funny out here when I was in the store?"

"Funny . . . uh . . . no, why?"

"You see anyone go in or out?"

"Sorry, was on my phone. I wasn't really paying attention. What's wrong?"

"Nothing," Jeffrey said, handing Sammy the Rite Aid bag.

"What's this?" he asked, looking into the bag.

"I was your age once, and I was too embarrassed to buy condoms." Jeffrey cleared his throat. "I got you one of everything. Let me know when and what you want more of. Just send a picture to my phone. No need to tell me anything else. I'll get it."

"Um . . . thanks, Dad," Sammy said awkwardly. "That obvious?"

"Yeah Sammy, your face must hurt."

Sammy felt his cheeks—they were a little sore.

"Just be safe about it. As you know, I got your mother pregnant when we were still in high school. It was hard on us both, but especially on your mother. I wouldn't take it back for the world; we had you and that was a good thing, but it was still very hard. You don't want that for Ivy."

"Okay Dad," he said, hoping the conversation would end. "Love these awkward conversations."

Jeffrey chuckled as he started the car. "Let's go home before we miss the movie and popcorn."

"*Snow White* again?" Sammy asked with a smile.

"I hope so," Jeffrey said with a half-grin, pulling out of the parking lot, the clerk's comment about his twin still weighing heavily on his mind.

CHAPTER FIFTY-FIVE
Jersey Devil at the Door

Japhet Dean Leeds stood in front of Mary Teller's front door. He knelt to pick up Ivy's spare key she'd left under the doormat. Inserting the key into the lock, he placed his hand on the doorknob, to only pull his hand away. His skin smoldered from the touch. He stretched his hand out and shook out the pain. "Silly me," he said. He reached into his pants pocket and pulled out the origami frog he'd bought from Grams at the community yard sale. JD carefully unfolded it. He placed the unfolded paper between his hand and the doorknob and turned it. He slowly walked up the stairs to the attic. The old floor was silent under his steps as he climbed to the small attic room where Ivy slept.

Slowly, JD opened Ivy's bedroom door. He walked to the four-poster bed centered in the middle of the room, entranced by the up and down motion of Ivy's chest, and the sound of her light breathing as she slept. Gently, he moved her hair away from her face. "What a pretty girl you are, Ivy Teller. You have cast a spell on the hearts of young Sammy, Jesse . . . and me. You perfect little witch, you."

JD picked up the birthday card from Sammy that Ivy had displayed on her nightstand. He smiled as he read it. When he was finished reading it, JD put the card in his pocket. He knelt pressing a kiss to Ivy's cheek. "Thank you, Ivy. Sleep tight, my dear." He pulled a dried dandelion from his suit pocket and placed it on her nightstand where Sammy's card had been. It was the same one Ivy had clenched in her fist the night she'd spent at Rosa Littleton's house. Before he took the stairs, he glanced back at Ivy, his eyes lingering on her face.

He left the Teller house as quietly as he'd come. He returned the spare key under the doormat and headed down the sidewalk, whistling a low-pitched, haunting tune into the cold night air.

CHAPTER FIFTY-SIX
A Different Side of Jeffrey Lopez

Jeffrey walked into his home and hung up his coat. He popped two breath mints in his mouth and walked into the kitchen to kiss his beautiful wife and greet his beautiful girls.

"You smell funny Daddy," Alba said.

"So do you." He kissed her cheek and then Maria's as they sat and colored at the kitchen table.

"Perceptive little tykes," he muttered to himself before he went to give Lindsey another kiss. She was preparing a salad for dinner at the kitchen island. He came up behind her, reaching his hand up her dress.

"Jeffrey!" she said in a hushed whisper, slapping his hand. "What's gotten into you?!"

He grinned.

"Not in front of the girls," Lindsey murmured, grinning back. She put her salad in the refrigerator and took her husband's hand. They made their way into the downstairs bathroom, where her husband showed her how much he loved her. Lindsey had no objections. She liked when her husband was spontaneous. The same-old all the time bored her.

"Where's Sammy?" Jeffrey asked, zipping up his pants.

"In his room."

"I'd better say hello while you finish dinner." He kissed his wife again as she fixed her hair in the mirror.

He went upstairs to Sammy's room, knocked on the door and let himself in.

"Hi, Sammy. How are you feeling?"

"Hey Dad, I feel better. Thanks," Sammy said, not looking up from his school textbook.

"That's good," he said with a large smile. "You remember anything?"

"No, nothing helpful."

Jeffrey pulled a silver coin out of his pocket and discretely left it on his son's dresser. "Well, I'll see you at dinner."

"Okay Dad."

He made his way back down the stairs. "Just stepping out Lindsey, be right back," Jeffrey shouted.

"Okay honey," she shouted back.

Putting on his jacket, he whistled to himself.

Lindsey stopped what she was doing at the sound. She had never heard her husband whistle before, let alone whistle a tune. She poked her head out of the kitchen and watched her husband leave. She shook off a funny feeling and went back to getting dinner ready.

Jeffrey walked past his backyard and entered the woods, whistling as he went. He walked deep into the forest passing closely rooted trees that shot up to the sky like torrents casting everything in shadows. He walked deeper still, only stopping when he reached a clearing. The clearing was surrounded by dead trees in different stages of decay. There were large holes in the trunks and the tree bark had long ago turned black. Now moss and lichen clung to the rot like a green plague. He reached his hand into a hole in a tree trunk and pulled out a rusty metal tin. He placed Ivy's birthday card from Sammy in the tin of trinkets and closed it. "Thank you, Ivy, that came in handy," he said, tucking the tin back into the hole in the tree. "Wouldn't have been able to get into the Lopez house without it." He smiled to himself, his fingertips brushing over his lips. "I really enjoyed playing Jeffrey Lopez. Maybe I should do that more often."

Jeffrey walked into his home and hung up his coat. "Can you believe I got a flat? And then I couldn't get the stupid lug nut off!" he said as he kissed Lindsey's cheek.

She pulled him in for a more intimate kiss.

"I'm glad you're happy to see me."

"Very happy," she said.

He kissed his girls hello.

"You smell pretty Daddy," Alba said.

"Thanks, honey," he said, patting her on the top of her head. "So do you. Where's Sammy?" he asked his wife.

"I imagine still in his room."

"I'm going to go say hi."

"Again?" Lindsey asked.

Jeffrey gave his wife a funny look. "For the first time," he said. He kissed her again and went up the stairs.

"Hey Sammy, how are you feeling?"

Sammy looked up from his schoolwork and smiled awkwardly. "Um . . . fine, Dad. Same as I was five minutes ago . . . still working on homework. Really, I'm fine."

"What's this?" Jeffrey asked, noticing the coin on Sammy's dresser.

Sammy got up to see what his father was talking about. "Huh . . . I have no idea."

Jeffrey picked it up. "It's an old French coin."

Sammy took it from his dad. "It says 1735. Wonder where it came from."

"Maybe the cleaning lady dropped it," Jeffrey said with a shrug.

"This has to be worth something, don't you think?"

"Maybe, it's really old. Not sure since it's not American currency.

Either way, put it away," Jeffrey told Sammy.

"Yes Dad," Sammy said, opening his wallet and putting it in the fold.

Jeffrey went back downstairs and kissed his wife again. "Time for a quickie?" He whispered in Lindsey's ear.

"Who are you and what have you done with my husband?" Lindsey asked, kissing him back. She shut off the oven and smiled at her husband. She wasted no time taking his hand and leading him to the bathroom.

"Good, he took the coin. Time to get to work," JD said pleased. "If only all my deals were this easy. Thank you, Sammy. You have something of mine, so I get to have something of yours. You accepted my coin and now I choose to take my mother's heart back."

JD walked to the spot behind the Lopez house where Sammy had buried the jarred heart from Pastor Leeds's attic.

"I wondered where Uriah hid you, Mother. I'm not surprised it was Sammy Lopez and Ivy Teller who found you. No doubt you had something to do with that. Up to your old tricks, I see . . . but it's no use, Mother. My children never fail me. That's right, Sammy told Jesse where he hid you. Spoke it within the very ground that answers to me. What it knows I know. No secret can be kept from Japhet Dean Leeds while in my woods."

JD whistled while he dug through the damp earth with his hands, his breath filling the cold air like a steam locomotive. He reached down into the ground and pulled out the jar. Wiping the dirt from the glass, his lips curved into a smile. "Hello, Mother, did you miss me?"

JD held the jar to his chest and hugged it. The sky opened up and rain fell, striking him on the temple. He could feel the texture of the rain and the weight of the invisible air. His smile widened consuming his face. "You belong to me, Mother. Now, let's go home."

JD whistled as the rain continued its onslaught, pouring down in sheets and smothering his tune. The wind picked up, swaying the trees in a lyrical dance. The chill in the air, the first taste of winter's bite, reminded him of the day he was born.

Leeds Point, New Jersey: 1735

The wind howled as the rain crashed against the windowpanes. Leeds Point had not seen a nor'easter like this in years. The newborn baby's cries were barely noticed amidst the storm that raged outside.

"A boy!" The Midwife declared, swaddling the baby. "Your first boy, Deborah. God has finally blessed you with a boy!"

The Midwife brought the baby to Deborah Smith Leeds so she could look upon him. Deborah glanced at the small, helpless baby in the Midwife's arms. "Another bad man in a bad world. Let the devil take him if he wants. I denounce it," she said, pushing the Midwife and the baby away.

"The baby is good. Born perfect in God's image. No ailments. He is healthy and strong," the Midwife said, smiling down at the baby. "Won't you hold him?"

"I will do more than hold it. Give it here," Deborah said as she sat up in bed.

The Midwife handed Deborah her son. The baby whimpered against her. Deborah placed a pillow over the baby, stifling his cries. "It was made in sin, and I need to send it back to Hell."

The Midwife pulled on her arm, to no avail. She ran out of the room to get Japhet Leeds. "Hurry, your wife means to hurt the baby!"

Deborah removed the pillow. "There, my son . . . sleep. You will go to Heaven now and not grow to be a monster like your father. Rest in peace."

The baby was cold and still in her lap, his countenance like marble. The silenced baby twitched. The infant's chest moved up and down. At first it was barely noticeable, but then the little chest filled with air, his chest and tummy rising as he breathed again. "What dark magic is this?!"

Japhet stormed into the room with the Midwife behind him.

"What have you done?!" Japhet yelled.

Deborah climbed out of bed, pressing herself against the wall in terror as her dead son reanimated. With every miraculous inhale, the perfect baby boy matured and changed before their eyes. The small, sharp tips of bony horns pierced through the baby's forehead. Veined wings sprouted from his back unfolding like a dark cloak. His skin turned as red as a ripe tomato and his back arched over his thick, strong arms. His toes and fingers fused to form cloven hooves as a forked tail sprouted from his back and whipped around the room.

"It's a devil!" Japhet shouted. He went to get his rifle. A direct shot pierced the back of the beast that now stood taller than his father. The shot had no effect. The creature lunged at Japhet Leeds, killing him at will and feasting on his warm body. The creature turned his attention to his mother who had smothered him.

The now looming demon jumped on top of his mother. His hands clamped her chest, tearing through flesh and bone to rip her heart out. Through cloudy eyes Deborah could see the creature standing in front of her with her still beating heart in his hand. "Just like your father," she said, spitting in his face with the last of her strength. "You're just like your father. You're no good. You should have never been born." The demon licked the spit off his face and kissed his mother's lips as she faded away.

CHAPTER FIFTY-SEVEN
Fine China

Uriah brushed his teeth and washed his face. He carefully unscrewed the tops to his medications, taking his pills out. He held the brightly colored pills in the palm of his hand for a moment before popping them in his mouth and swallowing. "Please work," he begged, staring into the bathroom mirror. "Please, please work. Make it all go away."

Uriah entered his bedroom and knelt by the side of his bed to pray. He laced his hands together and closed his eyes. "Please my Lord and Savior help this town and give me the strength to be their shepherd."

Uriah remained silent for a moment reflecting on the troubles of the town before crawling into bed. Not long after closing his eyes a memory from his past crept into his dreams.

Pleasant Mills, New Jersey: 1769

Uriah made his way home from church. He opened his front door to see JD sitting at his kitchen table. He had a cigarette burning in the ash tray and a human heart placed on his wife's fine china. It was the set the Richards family had given them for their wedding. They only used it on special occasions. JD pulled the plate to him and cut through the fresh muscle piece by piece. Chewing slowly, he savored the taste.

"Hello, Uriah," he said as he patted his lips with a linen napkin.

Uriah fixated on the heart. "What are you doing in my home?"

"You mean the home I gave you. I'm enjoying my dinner, Uriah; what does it look like?"

"Lilly!" Uriah yelled.

No one answered.

"You know, Uriah, I'm disappointed in you," he said, slamming his hand down on the table. "I thought I told you thirteen souls. You and your wife gave me only twelve. I needed one more. I know you and your wife decided to stop procreating, but I'm still hungry."

"Lilly?!" Uriah yelled again, running down the hall to the bedroom.

There Lilly was, lying on the bed drenched in blood, her heart ripped out of her chest.

"Lilly," he cried as he held her. "My dear angel. I have done this to you. I am so sorry."

Uriah came out of the bedroom with his rifle in his hand and pointed it at JD's back, where he still sat at the kitchen table.

"All those years ago, you said that Lilly was good . . . didn't deserve to die. I can honestly say you were right, Uriah. Taste never lies. I can always tell a good soul by the way the heart tastes. And Lilly, she was divine." He kissed his fingertips. "So decadent, so sweet, like a fine French dessert—light, and just melts on the tongue."

As tears ran down his face, blinding him, Uriah placed his finger on the trigger.

"Uriah, put the gun down," JD said plainly, turning around to meet his gaze.

"You lied," Uriah said through tears.

"I did not lie. I said that you will live, and your son will live. I said you can keep Lilly. Those were my exact words, and I plan on keeping my word. You can keep her."

Uriah's finger put pressure on the trigger.

"If you pull that trigger, Uriah, the bullet will go right through me and into the street where children are playing. Your child to be exact. If you kill him, that's different than me killing him. I suggest you put the rifle down."

Uriah collapsed on the floor, sobbing into his hands. "How could you do this to me?"

JD took the last bite of his dinner. "It's simple, Uriah. A deal is a deal. And I am a man of my word. You had no intention of giving me another child, so I took the contract into my own hands. We're settled now in this life. You will marry again. And have many children. I see this for you, if you want it."

"But Lilly . . ."

JD left his seat at the kitchen table and lifted Uriah's chin to him. "Yes, she was beautiful and good, Uriah, but she was always meant to die. God wanted her to die as a child. I gave her years he never would have given her. Can't you see that?" I made sure she didn't feel anything when I killed her. It may not look like a peaceful death, but it was. That I promise you." JD's hand shifted to Uriah's shoulder. "I really do love you, Uriah. You will always be special to me. Since infancy, you showed the grit to climb above your station. The want to believe in something so badly, only to be faced with constant disappointment . . . I wanted to help you. I hope that you see that. Now mourn your wife and bury her. Enjoy this life, Uriah. I will see you in the next."

Uriah awoke to a start, jumping out of bed. He ran down the stairs and outside to the garage not putting on shoes or a jacket. He grabbed a crowbar and raced to the attic. "You can keep her," Uriah repeated over and over to himself. He had a sickening feeling that ate away at him from the inside out—a feeling JD had kept his promise. He wasted no time pulling up the floorboards. He was crazed. He had to make sure nothing else was under the floor in the attic. Board by board he ripped up the attic floor in a frenzy. He stopped when he saw her. There she was, his Lilly. Like JD said, he could keep her. She was perfectly preserved like Snow White—dressed in blood and lying dead in a frozen sleep.

"Lilly," Uriah picked up his dead wife and hugged her, bringing her body close to his as tears fell on her lifeless face. She still felt warm as if she had just died—as if JD had just ripped out her heart.

"Lilly, my dear sweet Lilly, I'm so sorry. I love you. Please forgive me." He kissed her lips as his trembled. "What have I done? What have I done!? It's all real! JD—Jesse—me—Uriah Leeds . . . born 1736. I cursed my family and my town." He pressed his face to his wife's still cheek. "I love you, Lilly. Please forgive me . . . please . . . please, I beg you."

Uriah sobbed, covered in his dead wife's blood as he held her tightly. "Lilly, I will stop him. I promise you, I will stop him."

CHAPTER FIFTY-EIGHT
Anita Gomez and the Cleansing

Sammy walked through the front door with his dad to see his grandmother waiting for him with a big hug. Anita Gomez had made the long trip from Spain to see her grandson. She didn't get around much anymore. When her father died, she went back to her homeland to take care of her mother while her two daughters remained in the United States. She visited once a year, and the Lopez family took a flight to see Anita twice a year. That was about all Jeffrey could handle of his eccentric mother-in-law.

Anita had sensed something was wrong before her daughter told her Sammy went missing, and although she knew he was home and safe, she couldn't stay away any longer. When she arrived at Philadelphia International Airport, she was glad she'd made the trip.

"Abuela!" Sammy said, hugging her excitedly. "No one told me you were coming!"

"Me either," Jeffrey mumbled, not so excited.

"I'm so happy you're here, Abby," Sammy said, calling her by her pet name as she squeezed him.

"Samuel Cameron Lopez, you are dirty!" Anita said with a thick accent. "You need a bath!" She took his hand and led him to his room.

"Hi to you too," Jeffrey said under his breath. He went into the kitchen to kiss his wife and girls hello.

"Please tell me she's not staying long," Jeffrey whispered in his wife's ear so the twins couldn't hear.

"She didn't say."

"This counts as her annual visit, I hope?"

"Oh Jeffrey," Lindsey said, putting her hand on her husband's arm to settle him. "She's harmless."

"What's that smell?" he asked, sniffing in.

"Abby gave us a soul cleanse! She got us nice and clean in the bath," Alba shouted.

"You're next Daddy. Abby said you're always very dirty," Maria informed her dad as she tugged on his shirt sleeve.

He smiled through clenched teeth. "Great, can't wait."

Sammy made his way into his bathroom to see the bathwater was already drawn.

"Get in," Abby said, taking a seat on a small stool next to the tub.

Anita Gomez was a petite woman, not even standing five feet tall. Her heavily wrinkled skin drooped over her eyes and hung from her cheeks as if she were made of only skin and bones.

"What are you waiting for? Get in," Abby commanded, as if giving her teenage grandson a bath was a totally normal thing to do.

Sammy put his fingertips into the water. "Abuela, it's cold!"

"I will add hot water as we go. Now get in!"

"You never have it this cold. I'm gonna get hypothermia."

"You are late, Samuel Cameron. Now get in before the temperature drops more."

Sammy moaned. "Fine." He undressed, taking a deep breath before he sat down in the cold water.

Anita slid off her many silver rings and rolled up the sleeves of her black dress. She gripped the rosary hanging around her neck, saying a prayer before she began.

"You are filthy, Sammy. You reek of the Devil. What have you gotten yourself into?"

"Nothing, Abby."

"He touched you. I can see it." She pointed to his cheek.

Sammy looked at his grandmother as his teeth chattered, his fingers moving over his cheek "He? What are you talking about?""

Anita tossed different herbs and plant roots into Sammy's bathwater.

"Your sisters had also been touched on their cheeks and your mother was covered head to toe in his residue."

Anita started the hot water. Sammy let out a sigh of relief and moved as close to the faucet as he possibly could.

She gripped her rosaries again to pray and then took a washcloth to Sammy's cheek.

"Abby, that kinda hurts."

"Better than being touched by a demon."

Anita scrubbed his face until his cheeks were bright red.

Sammy looked at his grandmother. "Demon?"

"Yes. Your mother told me you'd been abducted but I knew it was not by a man, it was a demon. When we moved here from Spain all those years ago, I sensed him. Those with the gift always attract their kind. I was hoping you'd fly under the radar as you have not awoken your magic yet." Sammy's shoulders slouched. He knew he wasn't a powerful witch, that was the whole reason Jesse was able to kidnap him. He couldn't even perform an easy spell to talk to his girlfriend. He had grown up on stories about his uncle who was a magical prodigy, coming into his magic at a very young age. Sammy wondered if that was the reason his uncle, the uncle he was named for, went missing. He wondered if a demon, if JD, had sensed his gift and came for him.

Anita sniffed Sammy's head. "You reek of Hell." She applied shampoo to Sammy's hair, working it into his scalp with her small hands.

She leaned his head back, rinsing out the suds. Pressing her nose to the crown of her grandson's head, she sniffed. "Much better."

"Abby, I know the demon you're talking about. The one that's after me. I learned his name."

Anita looked at her grandson with serious eyes.

"JD. Around here he is known as the Jersey Devil, JD for short."

"JD," she repeated to herself, picking up a large scrub brush and scrubbing Sammy's back.

"I told my dad about JD, but he doesn't believe me."

"Your father is a non-believer; it's not his fault, Sammy. He could never see what was right under his nose."

"I must've got his attention when I did a spell. I think I'm getting stronger," Sammy said, looking for his grandmother's praise, but none came.

"It's dangerous to cast by yourself; you are not ready."

"I am, Abby. I thought you'd be proud. I did a safe one."

"Samuel Cameron, no spells are safe. They all have repercussions, even ones that seem innocent. Did I not teach you that?"

"You did," Sammy said, hanging his head low.

"But still, I am proud you cast it. You are growing up. It is time for your real lessons to start, maybe that will help stir the magic I know that's in you."

During the three times a year Anita saw the Lopez family, she spent most of her time with Sammy teaching him his craft. But she knew three times a year wasn't enough. Anita decided right then and there as she bathed her grandson; it was time to teach Sammy all she knew. She needed him to reach his full potential. She wasn't getting any younger.

"I'm going to stay, Sammy, and make sure you know all you need to know."

Sammy's face lit up. "Thanks Abby!"

"This spell you cast; you wrote it yourself?"

"No, I read it out of a grimoire."

Anita dropped her scrub brush. "A grimoire?" she asked, surprised.

"Yeah, I found one."

"Samuel Cameron, you know better!" she said in a raised voice. She picked the scrub brush off the floor and bopped him over the head with it.

Sammy rubbed his head. "Abby, it was fine."

Anita shook her head in frustration at her eager grandson, mumbling profanities in Spanish. "Whose was it?"

"Well . . . I'm not entirely sure." Sammy gave his grandmother a sheepish smile. "Sorry, Abby."

She responded with a scowl.

Anita put the scrub brush down and got a towel for her grandson. She dried his hair and then wrapped it around his shoulders. "How do you feel?"

"A lot better. I needed that. Nothing feels better than a clean soul." Sammy looked back at the tub water to see it had turned black. "Wow, Abby, you were right—I was dirty!"

Once Sammy was dressed, Anita took his hands in hers. "Sammy, promise me you will never read from that grimoire again or any grimoire that is not of our family."

"But Abby . . . "

"Sammy, it is time for me to pass our grimoire on to you."

A smile spread across his face. "You mean it?"

She nodded. "We will begin our first lesson after I bathe your father, but Samuel Cameron, you must promise me to only read from our book. Our family spells ensure that we do not bring ill will to our family. Reading a spell of unknown origin can bring pestilence on us all."

"I promise, Abby. I swear."

She pulled his neck down with her frail arms so she could kiss his forehead. "You are a good boy, Samuel Cameron."

Abby came downstairs with Sammy. "All clean," she said.

Lindsey hugged her son. "You look better."

"Abby was right, I really needed a bath."

"Good," she said, kissing her son's rosy cheeks.

"And great news, Abby's moving in!"

Jeffrey spit out his coffee. "You are?!"

"Sammy needs me," Anita told Jeffrey as she narrowed in on him with her cold blue eyes.

"What about the rest of the family, don't they need you?" He grumbled under his breath.

Anita tapped her son-in-law on the shoulder. "You're next, Jeffrey."

"Anita," he groaned.

"Now," she ordered. "I have the water drawn in your bathroom already."

Lindsey gave her husband a stern look.

"Fine," he said, following Anita to his room to find a drawn bath.

"Hop in, Jeffrey; be quick about it."

Jeffrey got down to his underwear.

"Underwear off," Anita barked as she tapped her foot. He gave Anita a scathing look, full of contempt. He really didn't like his mother-in-law. "Please, I'm not looking at you."

Jeffrey took his boxer briefs off and got into the cold water. "Anita, if you're going to live with us, we have to set some ground rules . . . like not bathing the family. I put up with this three times a year, but this can't be an all the time thing."

"Nonsense, you will feel better when I'm done. You are always so filthy. You hurt an old lady's hands with the amount of scrubbing necessary to get you clean."

He rolled his eyes.

Anita had never liked Jeffrey. When Lindsey brought him home, Anita told Lindsey to break up with him right away. She sensed a darkness in him. Anita wasn't sure how or why the darkness came to be in Jeffrey, but it was there, and she didn't want it around her daughter. But instead of breaking up with Jeffrey, Lindsey got pregnant. Jeffrey and Lindsey eloped shortly after, and there was not much she could do after that. Jeffrey was part of the family, whether she liked it or not. When Sammy was born, she'd thought maybe Jeffrey wasn't so bad. He had given her a beautiful grandson, inside and out.

"Jeffrey, you know you're always dirty," Anita said, scrubbing his back.

"I think you've told me that since the day you met me. *Lindsey, get away from him, he's dirty,*" Jeffrey said in a mocking tone.

"Well, I'm glad she didn't listen to me. You have proven to be good to my daughter and have given me three beautiful grandchildren."

"Thanks, Anita."

Jeffrey leaned back in the tub as Anita went to scrubbing his legs. "I'm glad you finally got help for that temper of yours."

"Lindsey, told you?"

"No, your water did." He looked down to see the water begin to change colors as Anita added more herbs.

"It's helped."

"Good," she said. "It will open doors for you."

He chuckled. "Practicing controlling my temper right now, in fact."

"Tell me, what do you know about this JD?"

"Sammy told you about that?"

"Of course."

Jeffrey pushed his hair off his forehead. "Anita listen, Sammy has been through a very traumatic event. Not to mention he lost his friends. He's looking for someone to blame. If he wants to blame the Devil, I'm fine with it, if that helps him cope. His therapist says it's normal for people who went through something like he did to cling to his faith. It's all part of the healing process. But we both know that the person who killed those boys and abducted Sammy is a real-life man. His name is Jesse Richards and Devan should hopefully have him and his accomplices behind bars soon."

"Have you learned nothing over the years?"

Jeffrey spoke sternly, "Sammy is hurting badly. I don't want you filling his head with all this witchcraft stuff." He locked eyes with Anita. "Do we have an understanding?"

"I know you think I'm a crackpot, Jeffrey, but JD has been in your home under your very nose. I can see it. Touched your son and your daughters. And your wife."

"Anita!"

"I heard you, Jeffrey. I will help Sammy in any way I can."

"Good, thank you."

She handed Jeffrey a towel. He went to get up. She put her hands on his shoulders to stop him, leaning in close to his face. "What are you looking at?"

"Your soul, Jeffrey Lopez."

"What do you see?"

"The same darkness I have seen in you since day one."

"Has it grown?"

"No."

"Good," he said. "Then we're done here."

CHAPTER FIFTY-NINE
Ivy Meets Abby

"Ivy this is my abuela. You can call her Abby for short," Sammy said. The small woman looked over her grandson's girlfriend for a couple minutes, circling her like she was prey.

"Sammy," Ivy whispered to him. "What the heck?!"

"You were touched, just like Sammy . . . touched by the demon," she said as she ran her thin finger along Ivy's cheek. Anita took Ivy's hand and led her upstairs. Ivy gave Sammy a look of concern. He nodded his head to reassure her, his smile slipping into his always charming sideways grin.

Sammy had warned her that his abuela would most likely give her a bath, but she didn't think he was being serious. But as she stood in front of Sammy's bathtub, she saw how serious he was. Anita turned the faucet on. Hot water spilled into the tub filling the room with steam. Ivy remained silent as Anita prepared her bathwater. She kept popping her head out into the bedroom hoping Sammy would come to her rescue.

"Come now Ivy, your bath is ready." Ivy walked closer to the tub uneasily, rubbing her arms, unsure what else to do with them. Anita closed the bathroom door, squashing Ivy's hope of being rescued, and sat down on the stool next to the tub.

"There is nothing to be afraid of; we are sisters."

"Sisters?" Ivy asked.

"Yes, we are both witches."

She laughed, her laugh laced with anxiety. "I'm not a witch."

"Of course you are. You are special. You are very powerful," she said, rolling up her sleeves after she'd taken her rings off.

Ivy smiled politely. She knew where Sammy got all the hocus-pocus mumbo jumbo from.

"Get in," Abby ordered.

Ivy glared at the old woman with a shocked face, she didn't care how silly she looked. "You're staying in here?!"

"Of course," she said.

Ivy nervously took off her clothing. She awkwardly tried to cover up as much of her body as she could with her hands, standing by the tub in her bra and underwear.

"Everything off. We want to make sure we get you clean."

"I'm feeling a little uncomfortable here . . ."

"Nonsense, child."

"Can you turn around, please?"

Abby rolled her eyes and turned around.

Ivy took off her undergarments and got into the water as fast as she could.

Anita Gomez turned around and began the spiritual cleansing ritual. She took her scrub brush and scrubbed away.

"My grandson has deflowered you recently."

Ivy's face turned bright red, and she remembered why she hated the color so much. "He told you?" Ivy asked, mortified.

"No, your body told me. I can tell by the color of the water as we wash away that sin."

"Oh," she said, embarrassed.

"The different colors mean different things. You don't know about your craft, do you?"

"No. I didn't even know I was a witch."

"You are. You have no mother to help you?"

"No, she sent me to live with my grandmother . . ." Again, Ivy couldn't recall one thing about her mother. She strained her mind and still nothing.

"Your grandmother is not a witch?"

"She never said she was. . . but I guess she did tease that we had witches in the family. I thought she was kidding."

"A lot of witches have turned on the craft in place of modern ways. But there is nothing more powerful than a witch born with natural ability. It was given to us by Mother Earth herself."

"Not from God?" Ivy asked.

"No, from Mother Earth. Gaia kissed some of God's children, making them special, but not all. It's like winning the lottery."

"Or being struck by lightning," Ivy mumbled.

"You do not want the gift; why, child?"

"I don't know. I guess I just don't," Ivy said as Abby scrubbed her back.

"Well, my child, whether you want it or not, you have it, and you have been touched by a demon. It is for the best you tap into your gift to protect yourself and my grandson."

"Abby is interesting," Ivy said to Sammy as they sat on his bed.

"She sure is," Sammy agreed, writing out a math equation for Ivy to solve. Sammy was set on helping Ivy study for her upcoming math test, but Ivy couldn't focus after the awkward bathing session she'd just had with his grandmother.

She pushed her damp hair out of her face. "You know she thinks she's a real-life, flesh-and-blood witch."

"Thinks? She is, Teller."

"Sammy, come on," Ivy groaned, shutting her textbook. "The reason the water turned colors was because she was adding in plants dried in food coloring, anyone could see that."

"You're still not a believer?"

"No . . . You don't actually think your grandmother is a witch?"

Sammy reopened Ivy's math book. "I know she is. I told you that's how I knew that book we found was a grimoire, I told you my grandmother's a witch."

"We didn't find the grimoire. You stole it out of Pastor Leeds's mailbox, and it was crazy then and it's crazy now! Actually, now it's more crazy or is it crazier?! Either way you know what I mean."

"And I'm a witch too."

Ivy leaned back on Sammy's bed, her head hitting his pillow. "I can't with you right now! Just because we read from an old dusty book that you think is a spell book doesn't make us witches."

Sammy reclined back, so they were face to face. "Abby said I was born with it. That's what makes me special. I haven't tapped into my magic yet, but it's there waiting for me to reach my full potential."

She moved a stray lock of hair out of his eyes. "Sammy, I know you're a narcissist, but come on, your ego can barely fit through the door."

He laughed. "It's true, Teller. And I knew you were a witch when I first met you."

Ivy sat up. "You what?"

Sammy stayed laying down. He tucked his hands under his head. "Yeah, I sensed it coming off of you. Abby calls it an aura. I just call it being witchy. I felt it as soon as you got out of your grandmother's station wagon."

"That's why you talked to me? Because you thought I was a witch?"

Sammy's smile moved into his sideways grin. "That, and I thought you were cute."

Ivy rolled her eyes, hitting him in the face with one of his pillows.

He tucked it under his head. "That's why I told you about the curse of the heart attack and the dead pastors. I thought you knew you were a witch, but I soon found out you had no clue."

Ivy gave Sammy a look of disbelief; she felt like her jaw hit the floor. Her mind went to the message spelled out in heart juice on her floor. As if Sammy read her mind, he sat up taking Ivy's hand. "It's like I said, it's the reason we could see and hear the jarred heart. My Abby agrees with me. She thinks the heart was calling out to us because we're witches. We're both special. We both have the craft in our blood, as Abby would say. Jesse basically confirmed I was right. He couldn't see or hear it. So that's two to one. I win."

"You told her? I thought we weren't telling adults?" Ivy asked, dumfounded.

Sammy laughed it off. "Abby doesn't count. She's a believer."

"Great," Ivy mumbled under her breath.

"She thinks the light show was definitely some supernatural SOS. That it wanted to be found. That it was reaching out to us. So, it looks like I was right again," he said proudly.

"I'm glad you found someone who buys into all of your delusions," she said with mock enthusiasm. "Your grandmother, who happens to be a real-life-witch, thinks that some magic heart that supposedly belongs to the Jersey Devil's mother was in our Pastor's attic calling out to only you and me. Well that settles it, it has to be true then."

"It is," Sammy said.

Ivy rolled her eyes, lacking the energy to argue.

"We're both witches and it's not so strange the heart was calling out to us at midnight. Midnight is the witching hour, or you can call it the Devil's hour. At midnight, the veil between Heaven and Hell is at its thinnest. Dark meets light, night becomes morning. The heart would be most powerful right around midnight."

"I knew that for some reason," Ivy muttered to herself. "And why did the jarred heart want to be found?" Ivy asked, thinking it sounded like the beginning of a bad joke.

"Maybe JD's mom is on our side. Maybe she wants to help us bring him down. Jesse did say he thinks the heart is the source of all his power. I didn't tell my grandmother about the jarred heart. She'd want to destroy it and I'm not sure if we should yet. It could still be a bargaining chip. Jesse wants it and so does JD, maybe we can use it to get Tim back."

Ivy was silent for a moment while she thought. "Yeah, that makes sense, I guess . . . but I just don't know, Sammy. The idea that Jesse is really hundreds of years old and is stuck in some warped time loop is too much for me to take in with my math test tomorrow. For right now can we just be two high schoolers alone in your bedroom?"

He flashed her his grin. "I can do that. So much for studying."

CHAPTER SIXTY
Taken

There was a knock on Sammy's bedroom door. He looked up from his book to see his father. "Dinner ready, Dad?"

"No, not yet." Jeffrey closed the bedroom door behind him.

Sammy could see the stress in his father's eyes where red webs shot across them. "Dad, what is it?"

"Devan's downstairs."

Sammy shot out of bed. "He found Timothy?!"

"No."

"Jesse then?"

"No not yet."

Sammy's eyebrows furrowed. "Then what?"

"When's the last time you talked to Mike?"

Sammy's heart jumped, his pulse spiking. His voice came out in a whisper. "Just a couple of hours ago. Why, Dad, what's going on?"

"Did he say he was going anywhere? Seeing anyone?"

Sammy shook his head slowly as he replayed his earlier conversation with Mike in his head. "No, nothing like that. We just talked about school. Dad, what's going on?"

Sammy knew what was coming next. He locked his jaw preparing for the worst. "Mike's missing. He was in his backyard, and then he wasn't."

Jeffrey hugged Sammy. Sammy pushed his father away, refusing to believe it. He pulled out his phone and checked for missed messages from Mike. When he found none, he called him. It went straight to voicemail.

"Devan wants to ask you a few questions, if that's okay?"

Sammy's eyes remained glued to his cell phone. "Uh . . . yeah."

Jeffrey opened Sammy's bedroom door and Devan entered.

"Hey, Sammy, how you doing?"

"Um, okay," he answered dazed, looking up to meet Devan's dark eyes.

"No pressure, but do you remember anything else? Anything at all. Like your father said, we're afraid Mike's been kidnapped."

Sammy tried to focus his brain for Mike. "No, Devan, nothing. Just the sound of cars. Muffled people talking. Somewhere public, maybe. I'm sorry. I want to help, but I just don't know."

"Don't worry, we'll find him."

"We can't trust what he says," Sammy said, glancing to his father. "Mike should never have been taken. How is it even possible?!" His attention was back on Devan, talking in a tone he never took with him before. "How is it possible you haven't found Jesse yet?! He's in town. He told me he can't leave!"

"Sammy," Jeffrey said in a stern voice.

"It's okay," Devan said. "You have every right to be frustrated, Sammy. I've made a lot of promises I haven't been able to keep. *How is it possible?* I've been asking myself that very question. I had just driven past the Handovers when I got the call from Big Mike. I don't know what's going on in this town, but I *will* get to the bottom of it."

Sammy nodded, his face hot and flushed.

"I better get going," Devan said. "If anything comes to you Sammy, let me know."

Jeffrey accompanied Devan downstairs. "You're not staying for dinner?"

"Can't tonight, I have somewhere I have to be, but I'll call you if anything turns up. And I promise, I will find Mike."

Sammy sat back down on his bed. He dialed Mike's number again. Tears stung the back of his throat, as he listened to Mike's voicemail greeting in dread, over and over. He glared at his phone for a few minutes before he called Ivy.

"Hey, Sammy."

"Mike's been taken."

"What?! How's that possible? Everyone and their mother is looking for Jesse."

"I just said the same thing to Devan."

"You okay?"

Sammy exhaled loudly into the phone. That was all anyone ever asked him these days. "No, I'm not. I don't know what to do. Devan asked me if I remembered anything, and I just don't. We need to do something, anything! Where could Jesse be hiding?!"

"Sammy, try to relax. We'll figure this out. Just relax," she said again, trying to do the same. "Mike will be fine."

Sammy heard his father calling him for dinner. "I've got to go. I'll call you after I'm done eating dinner."

Ivy called Rosa when she hung up with Sammy. She hadn't talked to her in a while. It seemed like life kept getting in the way. She had texted her to let her know Sammy was found, but that was it. She'd missed several calls from her and hoped Rosa would answer now.

"Hey, Ivy."

"Hi, Rosa, how are you?"

"Doing really good. My vision is getting a little bit better every day."

"Wow, really?! That's great."

"Yeah, it's like magic."

"I'm really happy for you." Ivy was getting anxious. She wanted to ask Rosa about Jesse, but she had to play it cool. Sammy had asked her where Jesse could be hiding, and Ivy's mind went to Rosa, to her family's large farmhouse set back in the woods.

"Yeah, I can see pretty good during the day but at night it's really blurry. But enough about me, how are you? How's Sammy?"

"Good. . . Sorry I haven't called you back. Things are crazy around here, but uh, Sammy, he's good too."

"That's great!"

"Yeah, it is. But that's not what I wanted to talk to you about." Ivy couldn't take the pleasantries anymore. Her mind felt like a bull in a china shop. "Rosa, have you seen Jesse or know where he may be?" She reasoned if anyone knew where Jesse was it would be his number one fan. Ivy didn't think Rosa or Mrs. Littleton would hide Jesse after what he'd done, but she thought maybe Rosa would know where he'd go if he was in trouble.

"No. I haven't seen him for a while. Why what's up?"

Ivy paused. *Does she not know about Jesse?* "You know, I think the cops want to talk to him."

"Really? Why?"

Ivy was silent for a moment, shocked Rosa didn't know the whole town was looking for Jesse. She knew her family was overprotective, but this was on another level. Ivy supposed ignorance was bliss. If Rosa knew the man she loved was a kidnapper and accomplice to murder, Ivy didn't think she would sound so chipper on the phone.

"Uh, not sure, but hey, can you do me a favor? If you see Jesse, can you call me?"

"Sure, I can do that. Is he in trouble?" Rosa asked, her voice anxious.

"Uh . . . no," Ivy lied. "I just want to talk to him."

"Will do."

"Well, gotta run," Ivy said, trying to sound upbeat for Rosa's sake. "Okay, talk to you soon."

Ivy hung up the phone, slumping against her headboard. "That was my only lead on Jesse, now what?"

"Who was that?" Rosa's grandfather asked, walking into her bedroom.

"My friend, Ivy, looking for Jesse. Don't worry, I didn't tell her anything."

"Good," Devan said, kissing the top of his granddaughter's head.

CHAPTER SIXTY-ONE
Uriah Leeds's Meeting

That Sunday, Pleasant Mills Church was almost empty. Only the Lopez family was there, Anita included, along with Grams and Ivy, the three Henry Sisters, and the ever-faithful Mrs. Ball. By now word had spread through the entire town that Uriah's cousin was wanted in the kidnappings of the missing boys and was a suspect in the murders of Zachary Lewis, Tyrone Jones, and Louie Grindhouse. Police Chief Rainier had cleared Uriah of any involvement, but still, church attendance was at an all-time low. Pleasant Mills was restless. Jesse had found a way to evade the police at every turn. And despite all of Jeffrey's efforts, Timothy Chen was yet to be found. To make a bad situation worse, Mike Handover had gone missing over two days ago and the police department had no leads.

After church, the line to shake Pastor Leeds's hand was so short, Ivy got in line. "Nice sermon, Pastor Leeds." Despite the turmoil, Uriah gave another award-worthy sermon that gave Ivy hope.

"Thank you, Ivy. I appreciate you coming." He shook Mary's hand, "And you, Mary, thank you. I was wondering if you would both join me at my house after coffee hour. I would like to show you something." Uriah looked at them wide-eyed while he waited for their reply as if he anticipated them saying no.

Grams shrugged. "Since you live just across the street, why not."

"Thank you, Mary and Ivy."

Uriah shook Mrs. Ball's hand. "You're looking well, Mrs. Ball."

"Yes, my new medications are finally working."

Still holding her hand in his, Uriah said: "I'm so glad. I have been praying for you, morning and night. I'm grateful God has answered them."

"They have been answered, thanks to you, Pastor Leeds. They wouldn't have been without you."

Uriah shook Lindsey's hand followed by Alba and Maria's. He shook Jeffrey's hand and whispered to him so Lindsey couldn't hear. "I was wondering if you and Sammy would join me at my house after church."

"Not the family?"

"No, this is a delicate matter," Uriah said, nibbling on his bottom lip anxiously. "I don't want to get Lindsey upset."

"Um . . . okay. I'll drop Lindsey and the girls off at home, and Sammy and I will head right over."

"Uriah, is everything okay?" Jeffrey asked as soon as Uriah opened his front door. They spotted Grams and Ivy sitting at the dining room table. Sammy kissed Ivy hello, surprised to see her there, but happy.

"No, Jeffrey. I think this town has a big problem."

Jeffrey and Sammy took a seat around the table. Jeffrey's eyes danced around the house. He hadn't been in the rectory since the youth group cleaned it out and was impressed with their decluttering efforts.

"The congregation will come back when Jesse is caught and we get the boys back," Jeffrey said.

Uriah picked at his cuticles. "Yes, I hope, but there's more . . . I . . . I . . . I think it's just easier to show you," he stammered in a shaky voice.

"Show us?" Jeffrey asked.

"Yes, in the attic."

Sammy and Ivy exchanged glances.

Jeffrey got up and tucked his chair in. "Okay then, show us."

Uriah led them up the stairs.

"It's always on the third floor," Grams mumbled under her breath.

Uriah stood in front of the door to the attic and turned to his friends on the stairway. "This is going to sound crazy, but please hear me out." He took a deep breath. "I thought I was going mad." He pulled pill bottles out of his sweater pockets. "I was on so many antipsychotics, but I stopped them all."

Mary raised an eyebrow. "Is that a good idea?"

He shoved the pills back in his pockets. "I'm not crazy, Mary; this town is haunted."

"Haunted?" Jeffrey asked.

"Yes. Haunted by the Jersey Devil."

Sammy squeezed Ivy's hand; she squeezed back.

Jeffrey groaned. "Not you too, Uriah."

Uriah pleaded, "Please just hear me out. I know this sounds crazy." He shook his head at himself." I will just show you." He opened the attic door. Jesse hid in the corner of the attic as the door swung open.

"You wanted to show us you ripped up your floor?" Grams asked confused, scanning over the scattered floor planks.

Uriah went to the blanket on the floor and pulled it aside. "She was my wife."

Everyone gasped, filling the room with a hiss.

Jeffrey looked at Uriah stunned, then to the beautiful woman that was hidden under the blanket, his eyes fixating on her blood-soaked chest. "Your wife? . . ." He knelt to see if she was okay. He noticed at once her heart was missing. "You killed her?!"

Uriah's eyes were downcast, his thick lashes dusting his cheeks where they were beaded with tears. "Lilly Baker Leeds was born in the spring of 1735 . . ." He looked up to meet the stares of his friends. "I am Uriah Joseph Leeds, born 1736. We married in the summer of 1757. The Leeds Devil, our Jersey Devil, killed her and preserved her as some demented token of his affection for me. He is real. I have seen him."

Ivy glanced at Sammy, her grip on his hand tightening. Her mind went to the logbook Sammy found in her basement—to the picture of Uriah Joseph Leeds that Sammy swore was their Pastor Leeds. Then her mind went to the picture she found in the grimoire, to the picture of the Midwife that looked so much like her.

Uriah's eyes fell on his dead wife where she lay on the floor amongst torn up floor planks. "The more time that goes by, the more I remember. His real name is Japhet Dean, but he goes by JD. I saw him months ago. I thought it was part of my psychosis . . . I didn't know he was real, but he is. I know that now." He wiped his clammy hands on his pants. "I didn't think he was real because . . ." He turned to Jeffrey. "Because he looks just like you, Jeffrey. I thought it was just my mind playing tricks on me. Twisting reality. Taking people I know and plugging them into my nightmares."

"Me?!" Jeffrey asked, shocked, his mind going to the Rite Aid cashier asking him about his twin.

Uriah nodded. "Your face was the one thing that kept making me second guess my gut feeling. I kept telling myself you couldn't be Japhet Dean from my dreams. I know you in the here and now. You're my friend and the mayor. It just made me more confused."

"Wait a minute!" Mary said. "I met that Japhet Dean at the church yard sale. Come to think of it, he told me to call him JD."

"You met him too?" Jeffrey asked, concerned. He pointed at himself. "You saw a man that looks like me?"

"Sure did. At first, I thought it was you, but you'd just walked by."

"The painting," Ivy whispered to Sammy. "Japhet Dean Leeds, remember?"

"And, Dad, there's a painting of a man that looked like you that we found in Pastor Leeds's junk room. It was a painting of Japhet Dean Leeds from the 1800s."

"That's him," Uriah said. "Japhet Dean Leeds is JD."

"A painting?" Jeffrey asked.

"Well, there was. It was sold at the yard sale, but Ivy and I both saw it. It was a painting by J.R."

"Jesse Richards!" Ivy shouted, thinking of the signed drawing hanging up in her room and all of the drawings plastered over Rosa's bedroom walls. She now knew why Jesse thought the artist had a certain je ne sais quoi, he was the artist.

Sammy smiled at Ivy impressed. He hadn't put that together, but now he couldn't believe he missed it. There was no denying it, Jesse was Jesse Richards of old.

"This is getting strange," Grams said.

"Too strange," Jeffrey admitted, raking his fingers through his hair.

"I never asked Jesse what JD looked like," Sammy said. "But with my dad's face he could blend in, and people would trust him."

"Yes, I think that's what's happening," Uriah said, as he covered his wife's corpse with the blanket, his hands trembling. Ivy helped him spread it. "JD is the one killing the children, and it's my fault. This whole thing is my fault."

"What are you talking about?" Jeffrey asked.

"I made a deal with him centuries ago—a deal to save my son. I gave him thirteen souls from my congregation for him to spare my Joseph." Uriah broke into a sob, his hands going to cover his face. "He's back and he seeks the thirteen children I promised him. Please tell me you believe me."

Sammy placed his hand on Uriah's arm. "I believe you."

"Thank you," Uriah sniffled, wiping his face on the inside of his elbow. "I was hoping you would, that's why I asked you here. You escaped from him, if anyone would believe me, I thought it would be you."

Ivy nodded. "Me too. I believe you, Pastor Leeds." Ivy surprised herself a little, she wasn't sure if she believed it or if she just believed in Pastor Leeds.

"I've lived a long time and I've seen some weird things. Nothing like this, but I guess I believe you too," Mary said. "It's easier to believe the devil did it than you murdering your wife and stuffing her under the floor boards."

"Am I the only one that hasn't lost my mind?!" Jeffrey asked, running his fingers through his hair repeatedly.

"I know it sounds crazy, Jeffrey, but I have no memories before I met you at the rectory. I have no memories of going to school or how I got to Pleasant Mills, just that I was here and I'm the pastor. It's part of the contract I signed with JD. I die and I come back to Pleasant Mills to be the pastor, and he gets thirteen souls every time I'm brought back from the dead." Uriah ran his hands nervously over his sweater, his fingers tracing the buttons. "I was fighting this too, not believing it. But with every child he murders, I get a piece of my old memory back. I started to remember things. I searched for my name. A Uriah Joseph Leeds died in a long-term nursing facility right before I showed up in Pleasant Mills. He was touch and go for several months. They even resuscitated him twice. I was told he had left strict instructions to be resuscitated at all costs and for life support never to be terminated, regardless of quality of life. He didn't want it to start again—*I* didn't want it to start again!"

Sammy whispered to Ivy, "That explains what happened to Pastor Steelman and Pastor Somers."

"What?" Ivy whispered back, confused.

"They did die of a curse, well kinda. They were just at the wrong place at the wrong time. JD needed to make room for Pastor Leeds to come back to his church. So that meant out with the old, in with the new."

Ivy thought out loud, "Wow, that's grim."

"I truly am Uriah Leeds, born in 1736. I have selfishly put a curse on this town to save the life of my son, and now we're all paying for it. I need your help to stop him. He has to be stopped. His cycle of bloodshed has to end. Please help me!" Tears streamed from his bloodshot eyes. Ivy knew now what angels looked like when they cried. It was wrong, and she wanted to make it stop.

Sammy was the first to speak up. "Of course we'll help. We need to stop him for Zac, Tyrone, and Louie." He took Ivy's hand again. "And we still need to find Timothy and Mike."

"Thank you, Sammy."

"Dad," Sammy said, turning to his father. "I know it's hard for you to believe, but it's true. It's like I told you, Jesse was collecting children for the Jersey Devil. This is all real and Tim and Mike need us now."

"Jesse only said that bit about the Jersey Devil to scare you," Jeffrey said, feeling like he was on repeat.

"No, Dad. He didn't!"

"Sammy . . ." Jeffrey said, putting his hands on his shoulders to try to calm him down.

"Dad, Uriah is really old! We found an old church logbook dating back to the 1800s, it has Uriah's name and picture in it. It proves that Uriah Leeds was in Pleasant Mills before. And Jesse is Jesse Richards from Batsto Village, his signature on the painting of JD we found proves it. We also found this spell book. It belongs to the Leeds family, probably JD's mother. Jesse said his mother was a witch and Ivy and I found a jarred heart in Pastor Leeds's attic that's hers. It's no coincidence that we found a jarred heart and my friends' hearts were torn out!" Sammy's eyes teared up. "I can prove it to you; it's all back at the house under my bed."

"It's true, Mr. Lopez," Ivy said.

Jeffrey glanced at everyone's faces and back to the blanket that covered Uriah's dead wife. He ran his fingers through his hair again. "You better show me everything you found, Sammy."

Everyone swiftly made their way down the steep attic steps. When the rectory grew quiet again, Jesse stepped out of the shadows. He pulled out his cell phone and spoke low into the receiver. "It's time."

CHAPTER SIXTY-TWO
Thirteen

Everyone gathered around Sammy's bed as he pulled the plastic bin out from under it.

"Why doesn't your room look like this?" Mary whispered to Ivy.

"Really, Grams?!"

Sammy pulled out the church logbook he'd found at Grams's house and turned to the picture of Uriah Joseph Leeds. Ivy pinched her nose, it still smelled. "And there is this," Sammy said, showing his father the Leeds family spell book." He pointed to the Leeds insignia on the cover—to the tree dragon-like creatures.

Jeffrey scratched his temple. "Let's say what you're saying is true, and we're working against some supernatural devil—"

"Jersey Devil!" They all said at the same time.

"Jersey Devil," Jeffrey corrected. "What do we do? How do we kill the bastard?"

"The jarred heart," Sammy said. "Jesse thinks it's his power source, but I don't think we should kill him until we get Tim and Mike back. If we do, we may never find them. I know Jesse and JD both want the heart, so I was thinking we should use it to barter for Tim's and Mike's safe return and double cross them or something. I just don't know how to get in touch with Jesse or JD, but maybe together we can figure it out." He glanced to Ivy for collaboration. She nodded.

"The jarred heart, the one you found in Uriah's attic?" Jeffrey asked, his eyes darting to the tote Sammy pulled out from under his bed, and not seeing anything that resembled a heart.

"Yeah, according to Jesse it was JD's mom who cursed him, and he draws his power from her heart, so we think."

"I don't recall anything about his mother's heart from my past," Uriah said. "But it's something to work with."

"Well," Grams said, "where's the heart now?"

"That's what I was thinking," Jeffrey mumbled.

"I buried it in the backyard."

Jeffrey raised an inquisitive eyebrow. "Why did you bury it?"

"Well, it's a special jarred heart, it comes to life at night."

"Okay," Jeffrey said, raking his fingers through his hair, "I've heard it all now."

"What are we waiting for?!" Grams said. "Let's get that heart and run JD out of our town!"

They made their way to the backyard trampling over a collage of brown and gold leaves and fallen branches. Sammy told his father where to dig. They stood waiting in the cold as the wind whipped around them while Jeffrey shoveled, their anticipation mounting with every scoopful of damp earth he threw over his shoulder.

"Sammy, how much deeper?" Jeffrey asked.

"I don't get it; it should be here. This is where I buried it." Sammy took the shovel from his father and dug deeper. "It has to be here still. Jesse said he couldn't get to it because of all the volunteers at the house."

"Is it possible Jesse *did* get it?" Ivy asked, putting her hand on Sammy's shoulder to stop him from digging.

"I . . . I don't know. I guess it's possible." He looked at everyone, concerned. "What are we going to do now?"

"Maybe we can get ahead of him. Find out who he's targeting, and I don't know set a trap," Jeffrey said. "Devan thought the killer was going after boys who were thirteen, but that's changed."

Sammy's face twisted in thought. "Maybe not. I think it's all about the number thirteen. JD was the thirteenth child of Deborah Smith Leeds. He's pretty bent on his mom not wanting him and giving him to the devil and what not. He's obviously targeting those who are thirteen. I guess it's just his warped sense of humor. Zac, Tyrone, and Louie were all thirteen. And Tim's thirteen too."

"Sammy, you're sixteen," Jeffrey said.

"And what about Mike," pointed out Mary.

"There has to be more to it than that. Jesse said I made the list. That means Mike and I weren't taken at random." Sammy thought out loud. "Mike's seventeen, but his birthday is January third. Take the one from January and the three from the day he was born, and you got yourself a thirteen!"

"Clever, Sammy," Uriah said.

"And I'm a thirteen too," Sammy said. "I was born on December thirteenth. —Actually, I'm a double thirteen."

Grams scratched her head.

Sammy had the answer to everyone's confusion. "December is the thirteenth month of the International Fixed Calendar."

"The what?" Ivy asked, baffled.

"You know, the International Fixed Calendar. We learned about it in school. It's a calendar where every month has the same number of days and instead of twelve months there're thirteen months. December being the thirteenth month, and I was born on the thirteenth of December—double thirteen."

"You're way too studious, and wow, that's creepy," Ivy said.

"Yeah, and my sisters were born on December thirteenth too!"

"Get out of town?!" Grams said.

"My mom had to deliver via a c-section, and she let me pick the date. I thought it'd be cool if we all had the same birthday."

"Good thing no girls have been taken," Ivy said with relief. Just then her body involuntarily trembled as if she was just shocked by lightning.

"Teller, you okay?" Sammy asked, his hand going for hers.

She looked back toward the Lopez home. "I just, I don't know. I feel scared." She felt how she felt the first time she saw the red light from Pastor Leeds's attic shining into her bedroom. She felt frightened and she felt helpless, and she didn't quite know why.

Jeffrey's pulse raced as he glanced from Ivy to Sammy. Sammy was thinking the same thing.

"Dad . . . Alba and Maria are six and a half. Six and a half plus six and a half is thirteen. They're double thirteens too."

Jeffrey mumbled to himself. "We're trying to get one step ahead of Jesse and JD but they're one step ahead of us, they have the heart." He looked back at the house. He had a bad feeling that twisted his insides. Without another word, Jeffrey ran back toward the house.

Jeffrey's heartbeat sounded in his ears, blocking out the sound of the wet leaves and fallen branches underfoot and the trickle of the rain that now fell from a white sky. He raced into the kitchen. No one was insight but the oven was on. "Lindsey!" Jeffrey yelled frantically.

Sammy came in through the front door behind his father and ran upstairs. "Dad, they're not here!" Jeffrey's pulse surged, his blood under his skin hot. He spun around in a panic, the floor spinning under his feet.

Anita staggered into the foyer, bracing herself against the wall for support.

Sammy ran to help her. "Abby!"

"Anita, where are Lindsey and the girls?!" Jeffrey asked desperately.

Anita opened her hand to show them a tranquilizer dart.

Sammy recognized it. His eyes widened. "He has them."

CHAPTER SIXTY-THREE
High Heels and Prayers

Lindsey woke up to find herself in the dark. She felt light-headed and weak. Her body shivered from the cold. Peering into the darkness, she tried to ascertain where she was. She could make out the silhouettes of her daughters next to her. She shook them lightly. "Alba . . . Maria, are you okay?" They were out cold.

"Hello?" Lindsey called into the darkness.

"Mrs. Lopez, is that you?" Mike asked.

"Michael, thank goodness you're okay."

"I don't think for much longer," he said, trying to stifle his tears.

"Michael, it's okay. Jeffrey will find us."

"You don't get it, Mrs. L., they're going to kill us. One by one, and I'm next."

Lindsey took a deep breath to calm her nerves. She would not fall to pieces.

Lindsey got up and pulled on the bars.

"Don't bother, Mrs. L., they won't budge."

Lindsey's high heels sunk in the mud giving her an idea. She took them off using the heel of her shoe to dig under the bars of her cell. It had rained so much the ground was soft. Water continued to drip in from the sides of the underground prison, making the ground muddy. The deeper she dug, the looser the soil became, thanks to the rainwater. She started digging with her hands. Soon it was deep enough for her girls to fit through. "A little deeper," she said to herself, "and I should be able to clear it."

Lindsey shook her daughters lightly to wake them up.

"Mommy, where are we? Maria asked.

"Come on girls, we have to go."

Lindsey had her daughters squeeze under the doors of their prison cell, then pressed her body under the iron bars and pulled herself through to the other side.

Lindsey handed Mike her high heels through the bars. "Start digging. I'll be back to help." Lindsey reached the crypt steps. She stretched her hands high above her to feel a stone lid. It was very heavy. Her first attempt to move the lid aside was fruitless. She pushed on it with all her might. She knew if she didn't budge it, her girls would be killed. The lid began to slide. "Come on," she said, "just a little more." Daylight poured into the darkness. Lindsey sat on the steps out of breath, her arms throbbing. She couldn't move the lid anymore, but she'd been able to move it aside just enough so the twins could escape.

"Alba, what do you see?" Lindsey asked her daughter once the twins climbed out.

"Church, Mommy. We're in the graveyard at church."

"Good girl. Do you remember where Mrs. Ball's house is? The big blue one right next to church?"

"Yes, I remember."

"Good. I want you to go to Mrs. Ball's house and tell her to call Daddy and Uncle Devan. Tell her Mommy is trapped, okay? You girls hold hands and run to Mrs. Ball's house. Talk only to Mrs. Ball."

"Okay, Mommy, we'll get help," they said together.

Lindsey rushed to Mike's cell to help him dig. The floor to Mike's prison was barely damp. His cell was uphill to Lindsey's cell and the water had pooled at the bottom of the sloping crypt. They merely scratched at the clay floor. "It's okay, Mike. The girls will be back soon with help. Stay strong."

"Okay," Mike said, trying to be brave.

Her hand clutched his where it held on to an iron bar. "I'm going back to my cell in case someone comes down here before the girls get back with help. If they do, hopefully, they won't realize Alba and Maria aren't here."

Mike nodded, seeing the sense in that.

Lindsey made her way back to her cell and prayed to God to watch over her daughters as she pushed the loose soil into the hole under the bars.

Alba and Maria ran to Mrs. Ball's house. They knocked on the front door and waited as they held hands. Mrs. Ball came to the door.

"Alba and Maria, what a pleasant surprise," she said, smiling down at them. "You girls are coated in mud, what did you get into?"

"Mrs. Ball, we need your help! Mommy is in the cemetery. She's trapped!" Alba shouted.

"Can you call Daddy?" Maria asked.

"And Uncle Devan too," Alba added.

"Come in, girls," she said. "I'll call right away."

The twins followed Mrs. Ball into the house. She closed the door quickly behind them and picked up her phone. "Devan, this is Mrs. Ball," she said into the receiver. "Alba and Maria are at my house and told me their mother is trapped in the cemetery."

"I'm on my way."

Devan made his way down the dark steps to where Lindsey and Mike were being kept.

"Devan!" Lindsey cried, happy to see him. "Thank goodness." She put her hand over her heart. "Are my girls alright?!"

"They're fine, Lindsey. I just got the call from Mrs. Ball. She's fixing them lunch."

"Thank you, God," she said, looking up and blowing a kiss to the heavens.

Devan kicked at the loose dirt Lindsey had tilled up with her high heels before he opened the door to Lindsey's cell. "I wouldn't be thanking him just yet."

Lindsey's eyes darted to the keys Devan held in his hand, then to the grin on his face. She took a step back, her heels sinking into the mud.

"I will say, you surprised me Linds. You really did. You're a lot stronger than we thought you were."

"Devan, what's going on? Where's Jeffrey?"

He approached her, backing Lindsey up against the dirt wall of her cell. With the back of his hand, he wiped mud from her cheek. "The way you let Jeffrey make all the decisions for you, I thought you would just lay down and cry in the dark."

"Devan?"

"I'm sorry about this, Lindsey, I truly am. But we need your little girls and now that you know about me . . . well, we have a little problem on our hands. I dragged you down here to keep the brats quiet, but they seem content with Mrs. Ball, thinking help is on the way for their mommy. With Mrs. Ball playing babysitter, I don't really have a use for you anymore. I can only think of one solution to solve my problem."

"Devan, please," she said, putting her hands on the dirt wall behind her, trying to make space between them. "We've been friends for years."

"I do like you," he said, pushing himself closer to her. She could taste his breath on her face. "No one makes a steak like you, but I've got a feeling once your kids' hearts get ripped out, you're not going to be so keen on keeping our friendship alive."

"Stay away from me!" she yelled.

"Leave her alone," Mike shouted at Devan from his cell.

"Lindsey, without a reason to keep you alive, I'm afraid you're just a liability. Boy, oh boy, do we have a problem on our hands." He kissed her neck. "Unless you and I can find a reason to keep you alive," he said as he ran his hand down her chest. Devan flipped Lindsey around, pushing the side of her face against the dirt wall. He pressed his body against hers, pinning her to the wall and reaching down to unbutton his pants.

Devan's phone rang. He hesitated for a moment before he looked at it.

He pressed a kiss to the side of Lindsey's face. "Looks like this is going to have to wait."

Devan grabbed Lindsey by the nape of the neck and pushed her out of her cell. He opened the doors to the cell next to Mike's with his free hand and threw her in. She landed on the ground in a heap.

"Lindsey, stay put." Devan said harshly.

"Wait, Devan! Wait! Please, Devan, don't hurt my girls! I'll do anything!"

CHAPTER SIXTY-FOUR
The Jersey Devil Takes a Servant

Lindsey's words rattled inside Devan's head. "*I'll do anything*," he muttered to himself.

Devan was once a lot like Lindsey. He would do anything to keep his family safe. He wondered if that's why he always liked her. She was a good wife and a good mother to her children. His heart had yearned for her since he'd come to town eight years ago with Jesse to wait on Uriah's miraculous rebirth.

Devan had secretly desired Lindsey Lopez since he'd first befriended her husband. Now that the Lopez family was about to be ripped apart, he didn't see why he couldn't finally get Lindsey all to himself.

Power had corrupted Devan Rainier over the years. He had once been a good cop. But gaining immortality and having a master that could make his wildest dreams come true, drove Devan to indulge in his darkest pleasures. As much as Devan desired Lindsey Lopez, there was something about her honest tears that made him feel guilty. It made him remember why he'd agreed to help JD all those years ago.

Elwood, New Jersey, 1843

Devan sat on a bench in the park watching his granddaughter play. It was a nice day. The sun was out, and the spring flowers were in bloom. It was a perfect way to spend a Sunday afternoon.

A handsome young man in a black suit sat down next to him. Devan tilted his head in the man's direction and smiled hello. The man returned the smile and pulled out a cigarette case. "Care for one?" he asked. Devan took a cigarette, and the stranger lit it for him.

"This is good," Devan said as he took a drag.

"Agreed, I prefer to wrap my own when I have the time," the man told him before lighting his own cigarette and blowing a smoke ring into the air. The stranger looked out at the screaming children as they played. "Which one's yours?"

Devan pointed to a dark-haired little girl in pigtails.

"Oh yes, little Rosa, she is a beauty."

Devan almost choked when he heard the man say his granddaughter's name.

"You some sort of pervert?" Devan asked, fixating on the stranger sitting next to him on the park bench.

"Hmm . . ." The stranger looked up to the sky and let out a light chuckle. "I think there are a few that would say my very existence is a perversion of humanity."

"I think you'd better get a move on, friend," Devan said, pulling back his blazer to reveal a pistol.

"That's just it, Devan—I want us to be friends."

"How do you know my name?" Devan asked, keeping his eyes on the man.

The stranger put out his cigarette on the bench, beaming. "I know so much about you. I've been looking for someone just like you, Devan

Rainier. You see, I know how much you love your family. Me too! I am a family man." The stranger grabbed his chest. "I love them so much, it hurts sometimes. They mean everything to me. But I, like any good father, worry. I'm looking for someone to watch over them . . . someone with your unique skill set."

"You know I'm a police officer?"

"Yes, Devan, I know that. I need someone like you to keep them safe."

"Listen mister—"

"Please, call me JD."

"JD. I think you need a shrink, not an officer of the law."

JD covered his mouth as he giggled. "A shrink! That's funny, Devan; I didn't know you were funny. I think you'll add a delicious flavor to my quirky little family."

"Look there," JD said, pointing at a man walking down the street. "See that man?"

"Pastor Leeds?"

"Yes. Pastor Leeds. He's my son."

"Pastor Leeds is your son?" Devan asked surprised, as there seemed to be no age difference between the two.

"Yes," JD said with a proud smile.

"I see why he turned to God."

"Again with the funny, Devan. I like it. I could just eat you up if I didn't need you."

Devan didn't look amused.

"I take it you know my son?"

"I do."

"So, you know he's not well?"

"I've heard he's fallen ill."

"It's true, but don't worry, he'll make a full recovery. My other son is hunting for his medicine now."

"See there," JD said, putting his hand on Devan's shoulder. "You see him. The tall man with the dirty-blond hair and the brooding look?"

Devan flicked his cigarette butt. "Yes."

"That's my other son, Jesse."

"Jesse Richards, I know him," Devan said.

"Good, he also needs you, Devan. You see, sometimes he can run into trouble when he helps me hunt for Uriah's medicine. He needs protection from the law. For you see, I love both my sons. I don't want Jesse in trouble."

Devan took another drag of his cigarette. "Why would Jesse be in trouble for getting medicine?"

"The medicine Uriah needs is of a sensitive nature." JD leaned back on the bench and watched Rosa play leapfrog with another little girl. "I'm sure you know about the children that have gone missing?"

Devan was already uncomfortable. With the mention of the missing children his pulse raced.

JD whispered in Devan's ear. "Between you and me, they gave up the ghost." Devan turned and glared at JD. "What? That's not funny?"

"No," Devan said plainly. "It's not funny."

"Okay, fine . . . I tried. I will leave the funny to you. I killed them and ate their hearts. My son Jesse helps me find the medicine, and I'm the one who administers it."

Devan reached for his gun.

"Stop that, Devan. We both know that can't hurt me."

The tension was broken between Devan and JD when a child kicked a ball their way. JD got up and tossed the ball to the smiling little boy before sitting back down on the bench next to Devan.

"Devan, do you see why I would like you to watch my family? Times are changing. It's not as easy to get away with what I once did. I need someone like you to make sure I do."

"What's in it for me?"

"For you—anything you want: money, power, women . . . immortality. How does living forever sound? You can watch over little Rosa and her little Rosas and so on and so on forever."

Devan put out his cigarette and locked eyes with JD. "I can tell you're the kind of man who's not used to being told no . . . but the answer is no. I have money, power, and women in this life. I don't need immortality. I appreciate the offer. I hope you find your guy."

JD stared at Devan, studying him, as a large smile bloomed on his face. "Oh, Devan, I've already found him. Your conviction, your character, your love for your family—that is exactly what I need. I need you, Devan, so very badly."

Devan took out his cigarettes and handed one to JD. JD leaned in and Devan lit it for him.

"We're even now," Devan said.

JD twitched. He got up from the bench and stomped out his cigarette with the toe of his dress shoe. Devan kept his eyes on JD as he slowly made his way to the playground. JD picked a dandelion out of the grass and went over to where the children played. Rosa ran up to him. He handed her the dandelion. JD looked back at Devan and smiled. His brown eyes flashed red prior to turning solid black. He patted Rosa on the head before she went back to playing with the other children. JD whistled as he walked away from the playground. The sound traveled to Devan like a shot through the heart.

That night Devan returned to the playground, under the cover of a cloudy night. "I thought you'd be here," he said, taking a seat next to JD on the bench they'd occupied earlier that day.

JD smiled. "I'm glad you came to your senses."

Devan locked eyes with JD. "Are you going to kill Rosa if I don't take your offer?"

"No, Devan."

Devan let out a loud sigh of relief.

JD pushed his face into Devan's. Their foreheads now touched. "I will do way worse than kill little Rosa. Death will be a kindness I will not give her or any member of your family," he said in a deep, demonic tone.

Devan didn't blink. "That's what I thought. And that's why I came to accept your offer. I want my family taken care of and I'll take care of yours."

"I need more, Devan," JD said, leaning back on the park bench.

"What more do you want? I told you, I'll do it."

"I need your loyalty." JD got up and reached his hand out for Devan to take it. "Come with me."

JD led Devan deep into the woods. With every step the darkness grew, the tree trunks springing from the ground like an obstacle course. That was until they came to a clearing.

"What is this place?" Devan asked, looking around at the dead trees that surrounded them.

"This is my home, Devan. Welcome. Few have been invited here."

JD sat down in the middle of his clearing on a patch of moss. "Come, Devan, sit next to me." Devan did as he was asked and sat down next to JD. "Devan, you will be a servant to my family for the rest of time. You will be charged with protecting my sons and me. Do you understand?"

"I understand," he said with a shaky voice.

"It's time for you to show me your loyalty. Give me your soul."

Devan's heart beat uncontrollably in his chest. He kept his mind on Rosa—on saving Rosa. "My soul?"

"Yes. The cost of your immortality is your soul. I can take souls easily, but to be given a soul is a different matter. To be given a soul is special. It will bind us. You will want to protect me and my sons because we are one, not because you feel I twisted your arm to ensure Rosa's health and safety. But be warned, I always have an insurance policy. For I will be your master and you will be my servant; do you understand?"

"I understand. How do I give you my soul?"

JD leaned into Devan until their noses touched. He stared into Devan's eyes. "They say you can see the human soul in the eyes, Devan . . . It's true. I can see your soul in your beautiful onyx eyes. Now give me your eyes."

Devan's pulse surged. "But how will I see?"

"Devan, trust me. I will make all things okay. Now take your eyes out and put them in my hand."

Devan's face contorted as his eyes remained on JD who was as still as a gargoyle and looked as fierce as one with his cruel smile and stony eyes. Devan knew it was too late to run, if he did, JD would kill him, but more importantly, he'd kill his granddaughter. With a trembling hand, he cupped his right eye, pressing his thumb into the corner of it. Pain shot through his face like a bolt of lightning as he pressed deeper and deeper, gripping his eye in his hand, and yanking. Devan bit back a moan and handed his eye to JD. His entire body trembled as blood trickled from his empty socket.

JD hungrily swallowed Devan's eye, savoring the taste. "Good, Devan. Now the next one."

With a tearing yank, he popped out his other eye. Blood streamed down his face dripping into his mouth making him choke. Blind, he felt for JD's hand.

JD took Devan's eye from him greedily and swallowed it.

"You are going to be a good servant." JD leaned into Devan, pressing a kiss to Devan's closed eyelids, his lips now crimson with blood. "Now my servant, open your eyes."

Devan opened his eyes. "I can see!" The pain that penetrated his skull was gone.

"Of course you can, Devan. I will watch over you and yours as you will watch over me and mine. Love them as I do."

"Yes, JD."

"Go now, Devan, and watch my boys."

Devan got up to leave.

"And, Devan," JD called after him. "Enjoy life; you don't have to fear the Devil."

Devan shook off his morality and walked toward Mrs. Ball's house. "If JD wants the hearts of the Lopez twins, then that's what he's going to get."

CHAPTER SIXTY-FIVE
The Midwife

Ivy felt unnerved knowing Lindsey and the twins were missing. She was worried. Her heart was so full of worry, she couldn't sleep. She worried about Sammy, worried about Uriah, but most of all, as selfish as it made her feel, she worried about herself.

Ivy was in a panic. Uriah coming clean about his past had gotten Ivy thinking about her own. Uriah had no memories of his life before showing up at the doorstep of the rectory a few months ago. She could relate, that's how she felt.

Ivy knew she'd come to live with her grandmother. She knew she didn't get along with her mother. But that was it, that was all she knew. She didn't remember anything else. She couldn't recall her sisters or if she even had sisters, she'd thought she did, but was drawing a complete blank. Ivy thought she remembered her old school, but now that she tried to recall just one face from her past, she couldn't. She didn't remember anyone; the girls who were cruel to her, the boys who made fun of her, not one of them. Her memories started the day she arrived at her grandmother's house in the beginning of the summer.

With shaky hands Ivy opened her nightstand drawer and fished out the black and white drawing of the Midwife. She examined it. She had a horrible feeling in her stomach that stung worse than her butterflies-turned-wasps. She had a gut-wrenching feeling the woman in the illustration was her, just as they now knew the picture from the logbook Sammy found was Pastor Leeds.

Ivy put the drawing back in the drawer and slammed it shut. Her eyes watered while she looked at the closed drawer in her nightstand. "Did I make a deal with the Jersey Devil too? Like Uriah and Jesse? —No!" She told herself. "I wouldn't have. I know it. There's no way!"

Ivy tried to fall asleep. She lay in bed staring at the ceiling of cobwebs for what seemed like hours. She couldn't get the drawing of the Midwife out of her head and her rock 'n' roll was not doing the trick to soothe her soul. She decided to call Sammy. She hoped he was still up. Maybe he'd have some good news.

"Hey, Ivy," he said into the phone picking it up on the first ring.

"Hi Sammy, any news on your mom and sisters."

He sighed. "Nothing yet. What are you up to?"

"I can't sleep. I'm scared."

"Don't be."

"I am."

"Want me to come over?"

"I do, but—"

"I'll be right over."

Ivy got out of bed to go downstairs. As she reached for the doorknob, she glanced at her Titan Tires calendar hanging on the back of her bedroom door. "Dreams do come true," she read off her calendar. "I really do like this calendar," she said to herself, opening her bedroom door and heading downstairs to wait for Sammy.

Ivy liked the positive anecdotes the calendar gave on special days. It was like having a horoscope and a calendar in one. And today she could use some positivity. Ivy smiled as Sammy's handsome face popped into her head. *Dreams do come true.*

Mary was already out of her bedroom, by the time Ivy made it down the stairs, having received the call from Jeffrey that they were heading over.

Ivy opened the door for Sammy before he got a chance to knock. She hugged him as soon as he stepped over the threshold, practically pushing Mr. Lopez out of the way.

"I feel bad. You and your dad didn't have to come over."

"It's okay, we couldn't sleep either. You alright?"

"No, Sammy."

He hugged her. "It's okay. We'll figure this all out."

Jeffrey joined Mary in the kitchen for coffee while Ivy continued to hug Sammy in the foyer. "Sammy, do you love me?"

"You know I do."

"No matter what?" she asked, looking into his beautiful blue globes thinking how much they reminded her of the ocean.

"Yes, of course."

Her eyes grew glassy. "Even if you found out that I did something really bad?"

"Ivy, you wouldn't do something really bad."

"What if I did? Would you forgive me?"

Holding her close, he gazed into her dark eyes like they held the secrets to the universe. "Yes, I would forgive you. You forgave me, remember?" he said with a squeeze.

She nodded, afraid if she spoke her tears would break through.

Sammy took Ivy's hand and led her to the couch. He sat down, bringing her close to him, her head resting on his firm chest. "Close your eyes. Try to get some rest."

Ivy felt safe in Sammy's arms, like nothing could touch her there, not her past, not the Jersey Devil. She soon drifted off to sleep.

Leeds Point, New Jersey, 1735

When the Leeds Devil had finished with his mother, he made his way to the Midwife, his mother's heart still in his hand. He stood directly in front of her and breathed his hot breath on her face.

"Please, Japhet Dean, don't kill me," she struggled to get out in a shaky voice as she cowered in the corner of the room.

The beast's glowing red eyes changed. They turned a soulful brown. "You gave me a name," the creature said, his voice wavering.

The Midwife couldn't believe her eyes. She watched as the beast became a man, his transformation working in reverse. His curled horns shrank until they were gone. His cloven feet separated forming perfect fingers and toes. His tail and wings folded into his back, disappearing with the crimson color of his skin. In front of her now stood a young man with dark hair and dark eyes. His fair skin and handsomely chiseled face were bespattered in the blood of his parents. It didn't take away from his ethereal appearance, only strengthened it. The Midwife had never seen someone so beautiful.

He ran his bloodied hand down the Midwife's cheek. "I will not kill you. You showed me kindness when I was born. You tried to make my mother love me. You said I was perfect. The likeness of God." He looked her over very closely, studying her young face. His nose grazed hers.

"You are different," he said, smelling her. He buried his face in her hair, rubbing his cheek along hers as he took in her pleasant aroma. "It was you, wasn't it? It was you who brought me back to life after my mother smothered me."

Tears beaded on the Midwife's lashes. "I only meant for you to be alive, not for you to turn into—"

"A devil," he said, finishing her sentence.

She nodded her head slowly.

"What are you, girl?" Japhet Dean asked.

"I'm a child of the woods. I put my faith in the land and the trees . . . a Wiccan by religion, a witch to others . . . it's a secret."

"Your secret is safe with me. How do you yield such power?"

"I don't know . . . I was born with it, same as your mother."

"Her magic was different," he said, looking back at his dead mother slumped on the floor. "Dark . . . and you brought me back with light magic."

"You died before I could help you. I fear the Devil has already claimed your soul, and I merely reanimated you."

He looked at his human arms and hands. "So you have, Ivy."

Ivy woke up screaming.

"Ivy, it's okay. It was only a nightmare. You're okay; I'm here," Sammy said, hugging her, trying to calm her down. Ivy's entire body trembled, she was panting, trying to catch her breath. "It's okay," he said in a low voice, tightening his squeeze on her.

Mary and Jeffrey rushed in from the kitchen. "What is it, Ives?!" Grams asked, leaning on the couch.

Ivy's eyes lifted from Sammy's chest to her grandmother, landing on Mr. Lopez's face. It was *his* face—the man in her dream. It was true Jeffrey Lopez had Japhet Dean Leeds's face. Her heart pushed against her chest, trying to escape. She could hear her blood pump through her veins.

"You alright?" Jeffrey asked.

"I . . . I . . . had a nightmare, that's all," she said, burying her face in Sammy's chest again, she couldn't stand to look at Mr. Lopez.

"You sure you're okay?" Sammy asked, concerned. "Tell me about it."

"It was silly. I was walking through the graveyard and killer rabbits from Mars were chasing after me."

Sammy laughed a light chuckle. "Teller, you need to lay off the TV."

"Sorry, I didn't mean to scream like that," she said, wiping her tears. "I'm really scared of killer rabbits."

"You're sure you're good, Ivy?" Jeffrey asked, concerned.

"Yeah, I'm sure." She couldn't bring herself to look at him again. She didn't know if she ever could.

Sammy whispered in Ivy's ear. "You know you can tell me what you really dreamed about."

Tears ran down her face onto his chest. Ivy wished she could tell Sammy she'd made the Jersey Devil, that she was the one that gave him his name, brought him back from the dead, but she couldn't. She was a witch. She did believe in hocus-pocus. "Dreams do come true," Ivy whispered to herself, thinking about the peculiar insight from her Titan Tires calendar. Dreams do come true—her dream was the truth.

"Sammy, just promise me you will *always* love me."

"I promise," he said, squeezing her. "Always and forever."

CHAPTER SIXTY-SIX
A Nice Poem

Jeffrey knocked on Mary Teller's front door. He was accompanied by Anita and Uriah and had breakfast.

"Food!" Sammy exclaimed, smelling breakfast. Ivy groaned. "Sorry, Teller, didn't mean to wake you up."

"You did." She gave him a quick peck on the cheek. "But it's okay."

"How'd you sleep?"

"Good."

"Good," he said, grabbing her hand and leading her into the kitchen. "I'm starving."

"I know it's not your mother's breakfast," Jeffrey said to Sammy, taking a sip of his coffee.

Sammy bit into an egg and cheese wrap with a sigh. "I know Dad, but thanks."

"I went back to the house . . . looked over the camera footage a million times. Someone had to have disabled it. There's nothing on any of the cameras," Jeffrey said to Sammy.

"And that's a lot of cameras," Mary whispered to Ivy, reaching for a breakfast wrap.

"I called Devan . . ."

"And?" Uriah asked.

"He won't be back in town until tonight."

"Convenient," Grams mumbled.

"Tell me about it. He had a family emergency. He said he'd call me as soon as he gets back. He sent Pearl to the house along with a handful of officers, of course they found nothing." Jeffrey shook his head. "This whole town has gone to Hell and that sicko has my wife and daughters."

Ivy kept her head down, not wanting to risk looking Mr. Lopez in the eyes. She screamed when she woke up from her dream, because she knew JD was bad, had killed her friends and that happened because of her. But in her dream, she felt other things for him, things that scared her more than killer rabbits.

"You find anything, Abby?" Sammy asked, helping himself to another breakfast wrap.

"I consulted the bones this morning, they have served me well in the past but today they show me nothing."

Sammy had helped Abby read bones before. He had thought it was funny that a few flinty chicken bones could tell the future, but he still believed in their magic. She had showed him the importance of reading them where they fell in respect to the cardinal directions and how they fell in relationship to each other. He remembered a lot could be learned from a bone reading; it was hard to believe a witch like his grandmother learned nothing. "Nothing at all Abuela?!" he asked.

"It's as if they are being masked by magic much stronger than my own." Anita's eyes narrowed in on Jeffrey. "We need to find them. I'm worried they don't have much time."

Sammy put his wrap down. He wasn't hungry anymore. He knew his grandmother was right.

Anita fixed her gaze on Ivy. She stared at her without so much as a blink.

Ivy pulled Sammy away from the table. "Why does your grandmother keep looking at me like that?" she whispered to him as they stood just outside the kitchen while the adults talked.

"It's nothing, Teller," he whispered back.

"Sammy, tell me."

"She thinks you have the magic to find them."

"Me?!" Ivy asked, shocked.

"Yeah. She said she feels your magic growing since she gave you that soul cleanse. Said you had a little bit of a witch block."

"Oh, she said that?"

"Yeah. Are you getting more powerful?"

She rolled her shoulders. "How would I know that, Sammy?"

"I don't know . . . I'm a poor excuse for a witch. I wish I were stronger. I'd do anything to find my mom and sisters. I can't let them get hurt, Ivy. You don't know what it's like down in that hole in the ground." He hung his head, his hair falling into his face casting his eyes in shadows. "It's so dark . . . my poor sisters must be so scared. I wish there was a way to find my family and Mike and Tim."

"We will, Sammy," Ivy said, hugging him.

Ivy felt a chill run through the air, which was silly she was inside, and her grandmother kept the house hot all year round. Yet, she couldn't stop herself from rubbing her arms, where gooseflesh covered them. "I'll be right back. I'm gonna grab a sweatshirt."

"I'll go with you."

"It's okay, Sammy. I'll be fine. I'm just going upstairs. Finish breakfast."

"Okay," he said with a smile. "I'll try not to be overbearing—try. But I make no promises, Teller."

Ivy went up the stairs to her room and grabbed the hoodie she'd left hanging on her desk chair. She still felt cold, but the hoodie was helping. Picking up her cell phone, she scrolled through her messages checking to see if she missed anything from Rosa. Nothing. Her eyes landed on the Titan Tires almanac on her desk.

"Let's see," Ivy said. She thought of Danny, the mechanic at the tire shop who had flirted with Grams. "Come on Danny, I could use a little more *dreams do come true* from my calendar . . . hmm, today's almanac tells me there will be rain. Really insightful," she mumbled to herself. "It's been raining for days."

Ivy scanned over the almanac. Most of the insight was weather predictions, from rain to shine to overcast to sunny. Ivy stopped when she read a short poem under the date of November fifteenth. The day of her birthday and the day Sammy went missing.

In a pleasant church,
you will find
those above,
and those left behind.

In the ground,
you will find
a little boy
who's on Ivy's mind.

Ivy's pulse raced as she read the poem over and over again. This was hocus-pocus. What were the chances her name was in the poem on her birthday?

"*A little boy who's on Ivy's mind* . . . Okay Ives, what is the poem telling you?" Ivy asked herself, dumbing down the poem to try to make sense of it like they did at school.

"*In a pleasant church* . . . That's easy . . . In Pleasant Mills Church . . . *In the ground, you will find a little boy who's on Ivy's mind.* Boy on my mind is Sammy . . . Sammy did think he was being kept in a basement, but what if he was at the church the whole time? *In the ground* . . . underground . . . underground with Jesse . . . with Jesse Richards of Batsto, who's buried in the cemetery at the church . . . under that huge monument with the top that looks like it could slide off!" Ivy tucked her hair behind her ears. "Oh my God! Jesse's not dead, so that means there's nobody buried in the ground under his monument! And if there's nobody under his monument, what is?!"

Ivy raced down the steps, the old treads croaking like the staircase was made of hundreds of frogs. "I know where they are!" Ivy shouted as she came barreling into the kitchen.

Jeffrey stood up. "Where, Ivy?!"

She locked eyes with him. Relief washed over her. They were not the soulful brown eyes from her dream.

Anita gave Ivy a proud smile.

"It's here, look," she said, showing them the almanac. "Look what it says!"

Sammy took the almanac and read the poem out loud.

"In a pleasant world
you will find
those above,
and those left behind.

On the ground,
you will find
a little bird
who's on your mind.

"Um . . . it's a nice poem," Sammy said, "Not sure how it's gonna help though."

Grams placed her hands on her hips awaiting an explanation.

"What?!" Ivy ripped the almanac from Sammy's hands and read it to herself. "No! It didn't say that a minute ago!" She tossed the almanac on the ground. "Forget the poem! Listen to me! They're at church in Jesse Richards's crypt. His monument has a top that can slide off. He's keeping them right there at the church!"

"Oh my God, I think you're right," Jeffrey said, his hands pushing back his hair. "Zac seemed to vanish into thin air. He was only missing for ten minutes before Megan got Uriah. And Devan was luckily right around the corner. We should have found Zac that night, but we never did because he was moved underground right under our noses."

"She is, Dad. That's it!" Sammy exclaimed. "When I was underground, I could hear cars all the time, and when Jesse came to feed me, I always heard this loud dragging noise. It was the top to his tomb as he pushed it open!" Sammy hugged Ivy. "You did it, Teller!"

"This is all connected to my church," Uriah said in a low voice. "It started there and it's going to end there."

"What are we waiting for," Sammy said, moving toward the front door. "Let's go!"

CHAPTER SIXTY-SEVEN
Worth It

Jeffrey stopped at his house and went over to the gun cabinet. He reached on top of the cabinet for the key and unlocked it. "I have no idea if bullets will work on a demon, but—"

Anita cut him off. "They won't. You have me for that."

"Good, but we don't know about the others on JD's bankroll." Jeffrey handed a gun to Uriah. "You know how to shoot?"

"Yes, I had a rifle."

"This is an automatic. Pull the safety back and push the trigger."

"Got it, easier than a rifle," Uriah said with a smile.

"Your dad has a lot of guns for someone with an anger problem," Ivy whispered to Sammy.

"He shoots to let off steam," he whispered back.

"I see," she said, a little surprised.

"I got a hell of an aim myself."

Mary watched as Jeffrey pulled out an arsenal. She couldn't believe she was going to be the voice of reason, but she figured someone had to. "I don't know if going to the church and shooting off a bunch of guns is a good idea, Jeffrey. You said it yourself, we don't know who JD has on his bankroll. We don't want Lindsey and the girls getting hurt."

"What do you suggest?" Jeffrey asked, closing the gun cabinet.

"Mrs. Ball lives right next to church and I stop by sometimes to chat. Why don't I stop by Mrs. Ball's place and see what's up? See if there are any vehicles at the church, get a feel for what we're up against before we go in guns blazing."

"Good idea Mary," Jeffrey admitted.

Uriah nodded. "It's set then."

"You guys wait to hear from me," Grams said, taking a gun from Jeffrey and slipping it into her purse.

Mary got into her station wagon and headed straight for Mrs. Ball's house. She drove down her driveway, parking in her usual spot. She got out of her car and made her way to the front porch, all the while looking toward the church. "Hmm," she said to herself when she spotted Devan's car parked behind it. "Jeffrey said he wouldn't be back until tonight . . ."

Mary knocked on the front door. "Maybe Mrs. Ball can shed some light on why his car's parked over at the church."

While Mary waited for Mrs. Ball to come to the door, she peeked into the windows.

Moving back her curtain, Mrs. Ball saw Mary Teller. Mary waved and flashed her a smile. She quickly opened the front door and stepped outside to talk to Mary on the porch. "Hi, Mary. What can I do for you?"

"Just here for my monthly stop and chat."

"It's not a good time."

Mary got a funny feeling. Mrs. Ball, who had been sickly for years and whose health was on a steady decline, looked surprisingly well for someone given a few months to live, considering Mary had just seen her at church a few days ago.

"You're looking well, Mrs. Ball. Not bad for an old broad with stage four liver cancer."

Mary heard Alba laugh.

"Is that Alba and Maria I hear?" she asked, trying to peek through the window. "You know, I overheard Ivy saying something about Jeffrey's been trying to reach his wife. I should come in and say hi to Lindsey. I don't want her to think I'm rude. You know her son is dating my granddaughter again."

"It's a private lunch, Mary," Mrs. Ball said, standing in front of her door like a guard dog.

"Just a quick hello, Mrs. Ball."

"It's best you don't. Lindsey is upset. She's going to leave Jeffrey and doesn't want her business around town. I'm giving her some guidance."

"Well, I know a thing or two about that. I'll help," Mary said, reaching for the doorknob.

Mrs. Ball stopped her. "No, Mary. I think it's time for you to go."

Mary knew a thing or two about a lot of things. She knew Mrs. Ball was playing for the wrong team. She had to make sure Lindsey and the girls were okay. And if she had to go through Mrs. Ball to do it, then she would. Mary went to reach for the gun. *Dagnabbit Mary*, she thought to herself. She'd left her purse in the station wagon.

"Now, Lois. You're being a real crab apple. It'll just be a quick hello."

Mrs. Ball pushed Mary. She fell down the three porch steps and landed on the sidewalk.

"You're strong for an old crow," Mary said, getting back to her feet and rubbing her sore knees.

"Grams! Grams!" The girls called from inside as they banged on the window. Mommy is trapped in the graveyard, help her!"

Mrs. Ball pulled a gun out of her purse. "Oh, Mary, you picked a bad day to come visiting."

"Lois, what the hell are you doing?!" Mrs. Ball's finger moved to the trigger. Mary lunged at her, tackling her to the ground. "Tellers don't go down without a fight!"

The bang of a gunshot filled the air.

Mrs. Ball picked herself up from the ground. "Stay down, Mary; I don't want to kill you."

"You shot me! You shot me in my good knee!" Mary put her hand over her oozing kneecap. "Whatever he offered you, it's not worth it. Help me save the girls and Lindsey!"

"I wasn't ready to die, Mary. God wouldn't cure my cancer, but JD did. It's worth it. I have to." Mrs. Ball went back inside without looking back.

"I never liked that woman," Mary mumbled under her breath, keeping pressure on her knee.

CHAPTER SIXTY-EIGHT
Anita Gomez's Spell

"Grams, what happened?!" Ivy asked, hopping out of Jeffrey's car, and rushing over to her grandmother.

"That old church lady shot me!"

"Mrs. Ball?" Uriah asked, shocked.

"Mary what happened?" Jeffrey urged.

"Mrs. Ball dragged Alba and Maria off to the church. The girls said Lindsey's trapped in the graveyard."

"Jesse's crypt," Sammy said, glancing at Ivy.

"Come on, Sammy," Jeffrey said to his son. "We have to save your mother and sisters."

They raced off to the church while Ivy took off her hoodie to wrap it around her grandmother's knee. "It's a good thing Mr. Lopez is impatient, Grams. You could've bled out."

"Nonsense, it's just a little hole."

"Will you be okay, Mary, if we leave you here?" Uriah asked. "I think Jeffrey and Sammy will need back up."

"I'm fine, Pastor Leeds, go."

Uriah said a quick prayer while Ivy called for help. "Please, my God, Lord and Savior, watch over Mary Teller, your faithful daughter, until help arrives."

"Thank you, now go!" Mary said, shooing them away from her.

"Let's go, Pastor Leeds," Ivy said and together they ran for the church.

"Careful, Ives, if Mrs. Ball is in on it, who knows who else is!" Grams shouted as rain began to fall, her voice getting lost in the drizzle.

Anita got out of Jeffrey's SUV and walked toward Mary, the rain already building momentum as a storm moved in. "Well, what are you waiting for, you old witch? Make sure that bastard doesn't get away!"

Anita purposefully made her way through the cemetery to the church.

Jeffrey and Sammy made it to Jesse Richards's monument. The rain was coming down in driving sheets now, making it hard for them to gain purchase on it. They dug their nails into the stone, sliding the lid off together.

"Lindsey," Jeffrey yelled. "Are you down there?"

"Jeffrey! Yes, Jeffrey! I'm here with Mike. Devan took the girls! He's going to kill them! Please, Jeffrey, save them!"

Sammy looked at his father. "Devan?" His mind went back to Ivy teasing him over the church logbook they found in her grandmother's basement. Ivy had pointed out the name Devan Rainier as just a mere coincidence. Ivy was wrong, it was hocus-pocus. The musty smell he'd remembered before he'd woken up at the bus stop, was Devan's aftershave. He'd never put the pieces together and now it may be too late. Sammy swallowed hard. "Oh no, Dad, Devan is—"

Jeffrey cut his son off. "Devan is dead. Once I get my hands on him, he's dead."

"Mr. Lopez, we're locked in! Devan has the key!" Mike shouted.

Devan came out of the church and walked toward the cemetery.

"Sammy, go save your sisters. I'll take care of Devan." Jeffrey handed Sammy a gun that Sammy tucked into his jacket, before he ran behind the church out of sight.

PLEASANT MILLS CEMETERY
JESSE RICHARDS'S CRYPT

Jeffrey didn't want Devan any closer to his wife and Mike. He knew they were sitting ducks, locked in a cage. He walked toward Devan. "Hey, Devan, you're back early, that's great! You should've called," Jeffrey hollered to him over the pouring rain. Without warning, Devan pulled out his gun and fired. Jeffrey fell to the ground.

Lindsey and Mike heard the sound of the gun going off.

"Jeffrey!" Lindsey screamed. "Oh God, no! Jeffrey are you okay?!"

Jeffrey grabbed his leg. "I'm okay, Lindsey." Jeffrey pulled out his own gun, stood up, steadied himself and pulled the trigger. It was Devan that fell to the ground this time. Jeffrey made his way over to him where he lay in the dirt parking lot of the church. Devan's hands attempted to cover the gushing bullet hole in his stomach, the blood already drenching his coat in a dark crimson tide. Jeffrey placed his foot on Devan's neck, pinning him where he lay. Taking the keys to unlock the underground cell out of Devan's pocket, he threw them to Uriah and Ivy who came running up to him. "Get Lindsey and Mike out of there."

Ivy caught the keys. They nodded and ran to Jesse Richards's crypt. As they ran, the rain pelted them. Ivy's sneakers sunk into the mud with every footstep she took, slowing her down. It felt like the ground had its own hands grabbing at her feet, trying to stop her from reaching Lindsey and Mike. The rain came down so hard and fast it was hard to see. The rainstorm had created its own haze, blurring the headstones into the sky that now turned a menacing gray. The wind picked up, shaking the trees around the cemetery like maniacal laughter.

They reached Jesse's crypt and walked down the slippery steps, holding onto the walls until they reached the cells.

"Thank goodness," Lindsey cried.

Ivy's hands shook. She couldn't get the key in the lock. Uriah helped her, and together they freed Lindsey and Mike.

Jeffrey turned his attention back to Devan. "You son of a bitch, you think you can touch my son, my wife, and my girls?!" Jeffrey put pressure on his neck with the heel of his boot.

"You're too late," Devan said, coughing up blood. "Their little hearts have already been cut out!"

Jeffrey pushed his wet hair off his forehead. "Well then, there's no point in keeping you alive." He aimed the gun at Devan's head and moved to pull the trigger.

"Wait, Jeffrey," Anita said, putting her hand on the gun. "He has been claimed by the demon. He will not die if you kill him today. I need to banish his soul to the underworld so he can never come back and hurt our family."

Devan's eyes grew wide.

"Jeffrey, hold him down," Anita ordered. "This is going to get intense."

"You can't do this!" Devan shouted, trying to get up. He was no match for Jeffery, he was already weak from the blood loss.

Anita crouched down as Jeffrey restrained Devan on the ground. She dragged her fingernail down Devan's forehead in a vertical line, drawing blood as her nail cut through his skin. Then she went over the cut with a horizontal line until he had a bleeding cross on his forehead. The rain unmercifully struck Devan's forehead, sending blood streaming down his face.

Jeffrey watched Anita with unsure eyes. "Don't fear, Jeffrey, we won't have to worry about him again."

Anita smiled at Devan, her wrinkly skin becoming taunt. He thrashed around as Jeffrey held him down. "I helped murder those boys. And I raped your wife. She cried for you to help her, but where were you?! Come on, kill me; you know you want to!"

Jeffrey took a deep breath counting down from ten. He struggled to control himself. He knew Devan was egging him on, but that didn't matter. He was right, he wanted to kill him.

Anita shook her head at her son-in-law and closed her eyes as she cast her spell.

"Take this soul, of this man,
from the demon who holds it in his hand.
Devan Rainier has abused his power,
and now it is his darkest hour."

Devan screamed, his arms and legs flailing. "Jeffrey, stop her! Please!"

Jeffrey's line of vision darted to Anita who kept her eyes closed while she focused on her hex, before holding Devan's scared eyes in his gaze. "See you in Hell, Devan."

"Lock his soul away.
Bind it for all of days.
Where no demon can go,
Deep in the blackest pits of hell's unknown.

Ferry his soul far,

Ferry his soul deep,
Take his soul to Hell's keep,
Where no demon can go,
Deep in the blackest pits of Hell's unknown."

The rain slowed to a pitter-patter, washing everything in an eerie calm. "It's over," Anita said, opening her eyes. Jeffrey looked down at Devan. He was dead and his eyes were missing.

CHAPTER SIXTY-NINE
The Jersey Devil in God's House

Sammy ran into the church. "Alba! Maria!"

"Help us, Sammy!" They cried together from where they were tied to the pulpit.

Sammy had gone to Pleasant Mills Church since he was a young boy. He had walked the church aisles hundreds of times, but today it was different. The outside sky had turned almost black as a storm of biblical proportions touched down. No light shown through the windows. The church was dim and still. There was a tangible feeling in the air; Sammy recognized it as dread.

He had just reached his sisters when he heard a loud bang. The front doors to the church flung opened and slammed shut in an instant. Sammy turned around to see a man that looked like a mirror's reflection of his father, but in place of his father's good-natured smile was something darker—an evil grin. Sammy knew the man that stood in front of him was no man, but Japhet Dean Leeds, the Jersey Devil. His heart skipped a beat when JD began to whistle a low-pitched, haunting tune. The familiar song caused the little hairs all over his body to shoot up, striking fear in the heart of him. He was sure JD could hear his heart as it thumped wildly in his chest, crying out for reprieve.

JD finished his little song with a large, toothy smile. He stared at Sammy for a few moments, taking him in, smelling the sweat as it dripped from his hair line. He tasted Sammy's fear as it danced in the air around him, delighting in the moment when Sammy first saw him. "Hello, Sammy."

"Daddy!" The girls cried.

"No, he's not our dad," Sammy said to his sisters. He took out his Swiss Army knife, putting it to the ropes that bound his sisters. He continually glanced back at JD, sawing the rope as quickly as he could. "Don't talk to him. He's not Dad."

JD plucked a cigarette from his cigarette case and lit it. The sweet smell filled the church, drifting over the pews like a ghostly haze. Sammy knew the smell. He'd first smelled it in Pastor Leeds's house, and then again by Pastor Leeds's garage. The smell took him back to the time he'd spent in the dark hole in the ground. There he'd felt like he was buried alive, the darkness acting as the crushing dirt, keeping him trapped, and the sweet smell letting him know he wasn't dead yet.

"It's true Sammy, I'm not your dad," JD said slowly, overpronouncing his words. "But . . . I could be . . . I want to be. I already love you like a son. Loving you will keep my heart full for such a very long time. Don't you see, Sammy? I have so much love to give."

"Stay away from us!" Sammy shouted in a panic as he finished cutting his sisters loose.

"Sammy, my son, you have caused me quite a bit of drama. I lost a good servant in Devan. But I will forgive you, if you ask. I can promise you absolution your God could never give you. All you have to do is take my hand."

JD put out his cigarette on a pew and stretched his hand out to Sammy.

Sammy picked up his little sisters, slinging one over each of his hips. "You're not my father, and you never will be," he said, locking eyes with JD.

JD withdrew his hand as a distorted smile bloomed across his face. Alba and Maria burst into tears. "Sammy, we wanna go home."

"Sammy Lopez, our fates are already intertwined, whether you like it or not. Who do you think saved you from Jesse's underground prison? . . . Ivy?" JD threw his head back and let out a loud, deep laugh that echoed throughout the small church. Alba and Maria covered their ears with their hands.

"No. That was me," JD said sharply. "Your spell was too weak, so I fueled it. You asked for help, and I helped you. I did that for you, my son. I had Devan drop you off at that bus stop so you could miraculously be returned home. You're welcome."

"You saved me from yourself, and you think that deserves a thank you? I was there because of you. Because I made your list! And you want thanks for sparing me?!" Sammy asked, his pulse racing. His worst fear was realized. He was let go, but JD wasn't finished with him.

"I do. Well, what do you say, Sammy?" JD cocked his head to the side as he looked Sammy over.

"Thank you for sparing me," Sammy said in an unsure voice.

JD glanced to Sammy's little sisters and licked his lips. "And what about them?" His voice became deep and sinister. He pointed at the twins. "What about them?!"

Alba and Maria cried louder. They buried their small faces in Sammy's chest, so they didn't have to look at JD. "What do I get if I spare them?" His eyes flashed a fiery red before they went black.

"I'm taking my sisters, and we are leaving," Sammy said, trying to be confident but his shaky voice gave him away.

"Thank me again, Sammy. Let me hear you say it again. Whisper it in my ear, my son."

Sammy slowly walked toward JD, still holding his little sisters in his arms. He stood before him now, his entire body trembling as he looked directly at JD's face—the face of his father. He slowly leaned in, bringing his lips to JD's ear. "Thank you for sparing my sisters."

JD closed his eyes and savored Sammy's hot breath as his words traveled down his ear canal. "I have a soft spot for you, Sammy," he whispered back to him. "I will let you take them, but know this, I will be watching you. And know that one day you will call me father."

JD stepped aside.

Sammy glanced back at JD as he made his way out of the church with his sisters. Japhet Dean Leeds stood at the threshold between the two large church doors with his arms stretched upwards to the sky, letting the rain hit his palms. The grin JD wore then, terrified Sammy. He could see his father in JD's face, and he could see himself.

Sammy heard the bang of a gun. The sound was deafening as the bullet shot through the rain. Before Sammy could turn around, Jeffrey tackled him and his sisters to the ground.

"Dad!" Sammy shouted, seeing the blood darkening his father's coat.

"I'm okay, it's just my arm."

Mrs. Ball walked over to where Jeffrey lay on the ground with his children. She aimed the gun at Jeffrey. "I won't miss this time."

Another gunshot echoed in the Pines. Pastor Uriah Leeds dropped the gun and fell to his knees as Mrs. Ball fell to the ground, dead.

Uriah looked at Jeffrey wide-eyed. "I just killed someone. I can't believe I killed Mrs. Ball. She never missed a Sunday service. She crocheted me a turkey potholder for Thanksgiving!"

"Mommy!" Alba and Maria yelled as they ran into Lindsey's arms. She hugged them fiercely.

Sammy helped his father to his feet. "It's okay, Uriah," Jeffrey said to him as he cried next to Mrs. Ball, his tears lost in the rain. "It's going to be alright. You saved me. Trust me, God understands."

"I hope so, Jeffrey. I've got a bad feeling this is just scratching the surface of my sins."

"I know I don't have the authority to forgive your sins. But today you helped save my family and Mike Handover. That has to count for something."

"I did, didn't I?" Uriah said, wiping away his tears.

"You did, but I also have a bad feeling. I think this is far from over. Jesse is still out there, and it's up to us to protect this town," he said, glancing to Sammy then back to Uriah.

They nodded.

Anita scanned the dark woods that stood like a fence behind Pleasant Mills Church for a sign of JD. "Far from over, Jeffrey." Her eyes settled on Sammy with worry in her heart. "Very far from over."

The sound of police sirens and ambulances rang in the air as they came flying down the driveway of Pleasant Mills Church. Ivy and Mike came running over with an EMT to help Mayor Lopez, but Lindsey wouldn't let him go. She hugged him and showered him with kisses. Then she grabbed Sammy and did the same. Mike and Ivy had to wait their turn to get their hands on Sammy. As soon as Lindsey let him go, Mike went in for a hug.

"So glad you're okay Mike."

"That makes two of us."

"My turn." Ivy grabbed Sammy's hand, pulling him in. She wrapped her arms around him and wasn't going to let go.

"How's Grams?"

"Grams will be fine. She's already complaining." Ivy pressed a kiss to Sammy's lips as the rain continued to pitter-patter. "I love you, Sammy Lopez."

Ivy's words traveled through the Pines and met Japhet Dean's ears. "I love you too, Sammy Lopez," JD said before he whistled into the rain. He walked deep into the woods as the rain picked up momentum again. The cold shower kept his low-pitched harmony close to the ground as it scattered through the haunted woods. "It's true, this is far from over. I'll be watching—always watching. These woods are my church. And you'd better pray to your God before you enter my house again. It's hungry work, Japhet Dean, meeting the sinful desires of this town," he said to himself with a devilish grin. "But someone has to do it, and who better than the Jersey Devil?"

To be continued . . .

Want more?

Read book two!
GET FOREST OF SECRETS NOW!

Thanks for reading!

If this book helped you escape, if only for a moment, please consider taking the time to leave a review or star rating on <u>Amazon</u> or whatever platform you use. It would warm the cockles of my little, black heart to hear from you.

Looking for something else to read? Don't forget to check out my other books on <u>Amazon</u>.

Follow me on social media (I'm on all platforms under <u>Holly Knightley</u>). Sign up for my <u>newsletter</u> for the latest news, glimpse into my wacky process, and occasional freebie. Stay spooky and happy reading!